WHOLE LIFE SENTENCE

Lynda La Plante was born in Liverpool. She trained for the stage at RADA and worked with the National Theatre and RSC before becoming a television actress. She then turned to writing and made her breakthrough with the phenomenally successful TV series *Widows*. She has written over thirty international novels, all of which have been bestsellers, and is the creator of the Anna Travis, Lorraine Page and *Trial and Retribution* series. Her original script for the much-acclaimed *Prime Suspect* won awards from BAFTA, Emmy, British Broadcasting and Royal Television Society, as well as the 1993 Edgar Allan Poe Award.

Lynda is one of only three screenwriters to have been made an honorary fellow of the British Film Institute and was awarded the BAFTA Dennis Potter Best Writer Award in 2000. In 2008, she was awarded a CBE in the Queen's Birthday Honours List for services to Literature, Drama and Charity.

✉ Join the Lynda La Plante Readers' Club at
www.bit.ly/LyndaLaPlanteClub
www.lyndalaplante.com
🖪 Facebook @LyndaLaPlanteCBE
🖸 Twitter @LaPlanteLynda

Lynda La Plante

WHOLE LIFE SENTENCE

ZAFFRE

First published in the UK in 2024
This paperback edition published in 2025 by
ZAFFRE
An imprint of Bonnier Books UK
5th Floor, HYLO, 103–105 Bunhill Row,
London, EC1Y 8LZ
Owned by Bonnier Books
Sveavägen 56, Stockholm, Sweden

This is a work of fiction. Names, places, events and
incidents are either the products of the author's
imagination or used fictitiously. Any resemblance to
actual persons, living or dead, or actual
events is purely coincidental.

A CIP catalogue record for this book is
available from the British Library.

ISBN: 978-1-80418-158-4

Also available as an ebook and an audiobook

1 3 5 7 9 10 8 6 4 2

Typeset by IDSUK (Data Connection) Ltd
Printed and bound in Great Britain by Clays Ltd, Elcograf S.p.A.

MIX
Paper | Supporting
responsible forestry
FSC® C018072

www.bonnierbooks.co.uk

Dedicated to Dame Helen Mirren.

*At the end of this book we meet the character of
Detective Chief Inspector Jane Tennison,
who nobody else could have portrayed as brilliantly.*

CHAPTER ONE

'On the charge of murder, how do you find the defendant, guilty or not guilty?'

Detective Inspector Jane Tennison leaned forward in her seat, her hands clenched tightly together. She could feel her heart beating furiously. This was it: the moment when she'd find out if Sebastian Martinez was going to get justice at last.

Jane had spent months of dedicated work preparing the case files for the trial at the Old Bailey. The pressure had been immense, checking and double-checking statements and forensic exhibits, as well as attending endless meetings with the Crown Prosecution Service and prosecution barristers. And it was not as if Jane had been able to focus exclusively on the trial. She had been the acting DCI at Bromley, running the CID in the absence of DCI Fiona Hutton, who was on maternity leave, having given birth to a beautiful baby girl. And on top of all her work commitments, Jane was studying for the DCI's promotion board interview, spending her off-duty hours memorising police regulations, criminal law and other related subjects. Jane had therefore requested the assistance of a detective inspector and was pleased when DI Polly Newbury, from the area drugs unit, agreed to take up the role, albeit on a temporary basis. Polly was an experienced detective in her early forties, with an approachable manner and a strong work ethic. Her presence allowed Jane to concentrate as much as possible on the Martinez case and be present at the trial every day, where she was subjected to hours of cross-examination in the witness box by the defence barrister.

During the three-week trial Jane had found the presence of Angelica Martinez, the mother of the murdered boy, very upsetting. She never missed a single day, sitting in the gallery, wearing her flamboyant embroidered Mexican shawls and often with her long hair coiled in braids with small flowers. She showed no emotion, her face impassive as she listened to the horrors that had befallen her beloved son. However, on the last day, when Patricia Larsson was brought up to hear the jury's verdict, Angelica was dressed all in black. Her face was white, making her resemble a ghost-figure from the traditional Mexican festival celebrating the dead.

The number one court had been filled with murmurs and quiet whispers, but had fallen silent when Larsson, who had pled not guilty, walked into the dock from the cells below. She maintained her arrogant demeanour, immaculate in a smart, dark blue suit with a white high-necked blouse. Larsson had a look of confidence as she calmly rested both hands on the edge of the witness box, watching the jury foreman preparing to deliver the verdict.

Jane looked up to the gallery and saw Angelica Martinez with a crucifix gripped tightly in her pale hands. For the first time Jane witnessed a frightening gaze of controlled hatred in her dark eyes.

'Guilty,' the foreman announced in a loud, assured voice. Larsson's confident expression crumpled, her legs buckled and the two female court officers in the dock had to assist her to stand up. Jane felt an instant surge of elation, followed by a wave of sadness as she saw Angelica fall to her knees, crying and kissing the cross, while giving thanks to God.

When the hubbub had subsided, the judge made clear that the harm caused by the death of Sebastian Martinez to his mother and family was immeasurable and the mandatory sentence he was imposing was life imprisonment. 'With a minimum term of fifteen years before you will be able to apply for parole,' he added.

Larsson gasped, then started screaming. 'No! It was an accident! It was all an accident!'

Angelica Martinez screamed too, a sound like the howl of a wounded animal. For her, a mere fifteen years could never be enough. She wanted Larsson to spend the rest of her life in prison.

In the local pub, where Polly Newbury had organised a celebration drink for Jane and her team, the atmosphere was less sombre. Amid the backslapping and congratulations, she took Jane to one side.

'Got a phone call this morning from the Yard. Your promotion board is ten a.m. Tuesday.'

'What, this coming Tuesday?' Jane asked anxiously.

'No, the following Tuesday.'

Jane sighed with relief. 'That's fantastic news. Though I have to admit I'm a bit worried as I haven't been able to do much studying for it lately.'

Polly put her hand on Jane's shoulder. 'Take next week off. I'll look after the office and make sure everything runs smoothly. But don't overdo the studying; take some downtime to relax as well. Now let's have a few drinks and enjoy the celebrations.'

'I can't have too much. I've got to drive home.'

Polly smiled. 'Don't worry about that. I'm good friends with the uniform night duty sergeant. He said he'd drop us both home.' She raised her hand to get the barman's attention. 'Two G and Ts, and make them large ones!'

Two hours later the patrol car pulled up outside Jane's house. Jane got out and was about to thank the duty sergeant for the lift and say goodnight to Polly when a 'suspects on premises' call came over the radio.

'That's not far away. I'll need to attend, I'm afraid,' he said.

'Don't worry,' Jane said as Polly got out. 'You can use my phone to call a cab.'

'I'll call my husband too, if that's all right,' Polly said. 'Being a police officer, he's always worried something's happened if I'm late home.' The cab company didn't have any cars available for at least half an hour, so Jane put the kettle on for coffee.

While they waited for it to boil, Polly admired the immaculate décor and furnishings. 'The place is so tidy, it hardly looks lived in,' she laughed.

Jane sighed. 'I've spent more time in the office than home this past year. The heavy workload plus all those hours preparing for the trial really consumed me. I haven't seen my parents for ages. My next-door neighbour's wife died and I couldn't go to her funeral because of work commitments. In all honesty, I feel exhausted. I don't know how I'd have coped without your assistance. If I get promoted to DCI . . .'

'No "ifs" about it – you'll pass with flying colours,' Polly said assertively.

'Fingers crossed. I'd love to stay on at Bromley until Fiona Hutton returns and have you as my DI.'

'Well, like a footballer, I'm only on loan, and as we both know, promotion generally results in a transfer.'

'Yeah, and knowing my luck I'll end up at some godforsaken station in the middle of nowhere.'

'Stop putting yourself down, Jane. You're a dedicated and intuitive detective. I've watched how you work and lead from the front. In all honesty, your talents are wasted at Bromley. You should apply for AMIT.'

'What's AMIT?'

'The new Area Major Incident Teams. Do you not read *The Job*?' Polly asked, referring to the free Metropolitan Police newspaper, which was published fortnightly and circulated to every station.

'I haven't had time lately.'

'The last edition had a big article about it,' Polly explained. 'To ease the pressure on divisions, the Yard is setting up pools of experienced detectives to investigate murders and other serious crimes at four stations, two north and two south of the river. A detective chief superintendent will be in overall charge of each pool, with DCIs leading the teams of experienced investigators.'

Jane sighed. 'I love the thrill of investigating murders, but even if I'm promoted, I doubt they'd even consider me for the role.'

'You're being negative again,' Polly chided.

'No, Polly, I'm being realistic, for two reasons. One, they'll say I don't have enough experience, and two, I'm a woman.'

'Then be the woman who broke the mould,' Polly said firmly. 'If you're posted to a divisional station on promotion, you won't have any murders to investigate as they'll all go to AMIT.'

'I'll think about it.'

'Well, don't think for long or you'll miss the boat and regret it.'

They could hear Polly's cab pulling up outside and stood up. 'Thanks for organising the celebration – and the encouraging words of advice,' Jane said.

Polly gave her a big hug. 'Never doubt yourself, Jane. With confidence you can achieve whatever you want in this job.'

After Polly had gone, Jane poured herself a glass of wine, got a pen and paper then sat down at the dining table. She started to make notes on the high-profile murder investigations she'd worked on, her leadership abilities and the reasons she would be an asset as a DCI on AMIT. She stopped, put her pen down and let out a big sigh, knowing it would all be a waste of time if she failed the promotion board. Then she heard Polly's voice in her head chastising her for being negative. Jane picked up the pen and continued writing.

On Saturday morning she received a circular from a local estate agent regarding their interest in properties in her location. Jane wasted no time ringing them to request a valuation of her house and a visit was arranged for late afternoon. As Polly had commented, the house was in immaculate condition and there was very little she needed to do, apart from run the hoover over some of the carpets. She went out and bought two bunches of flowers, a few essential groceries and some room spray to freshen up the place.

She was just walking back up her path when her neighbour Gerry returned from walking his whippet-terrier cross. She immediately went over and apologised for not being able to attend his wife Violet's funeral because of the trial. Gerry gave her a warm smile. 'That's all right. In all honesty Vi's passing was in some ways a blessing. She's in a better place now, anyway.'

'If there is anything at all that I can do, Gerry, please let me know,' Jane said, and handed him one of the bunches of flowers.

'That's very nice of you. I'll get Hazel to put them in a nice vase. We are still waiting for the headstone to be delivered – they really take their time doing the engraving.'

Jane nodded sympathetically. As he turned to head through his garden gate, he paused and looked back.

'I'm getting a decorator in to paint the house, inside and out. There's a lot of renovation that needs doing, and some work to the roof as well. I would have asked your Eddie, but Hazel's brother has got his own company and offered me a good price for the work.'

Jane nodded. 'That's good. Well, I'll no doubt see you around.'

'Yes, and I will introduce you to Hazel. She is a wonderful cook – does the best roast lamb I've ever tasted.'

Jane assumed Hazel was one of Vi's carers and was pleased Gerry was being looked after by someone.

She placed the other bunch of flowers in a vase in the drawing room, then put clean sheets on her bed and a new cover on the duvet, as Eddie had spilt tea on the old one. The house finally felt ready for inspection and when the doorbell rang Jane presumed it was the estate agent, although it was only two o'clock. When she opened the front door, a pleasant-looking elderly woman was standing on the doorstep.

Jane opened the door wider to let her in. 'I wasn't expecting you until later.'

'I just thought I should introduce myself, as Gerry said he had spoken to you. I'm Hazel Douglas. I looked after Gerry's wife until her passing.'

'Pleasure to meet you, do come in,' Jane said.

'No, dear, another time. I just felt that it would be neighbourly of me to come and say hello as I'm living next door. I'd best be off now, Gerry's waiting.'

Jane watched Hazel walk down the path towards Gerry, who was standing on the pavement smiling. As they approached his house, he put his arm around her, then kissed her on the cheek.

'My God, he didn't waste much time,' Jane said to herself, and then immediately felt guilty. The truth was that he was looking happier than she had ever seen him. He obviously had no intentions of selling now, as he had previously hinted. Jane remembered Eddie saying that it was so run-down he reckoned he could buy it at a low price.

She felt depressed when she thought about Eddie, but she was certain splitting up had been for the best and was determined to put all that in the past.

When the estate agent turned up, the valuation of her house was a lot more than she had paid for it. She didn't lose any time and put it on the market immediately. The 'For Sale' sign hadn't even gone up before she received an offer just shy of the asking price. The agency had three other potential buyers lined up to view, and so Jane arranged for the estate agents to have a set of keys for when she was at work. It began to feel as if she really was moving on.

On the following Monday, with the trial over, it was back to business as usual at the station, with Jane trying to catch up with all the cases that had been overseen by Polly. But there was another celebration in the pub after work, as Stanley had been given a commendation for his work on a drug bust. He was in high spirits as he approached Jane.

'I'd say your promotion is in the bag,' he said. 'So, it's onwards and upwards . . .'

Jane smiled. 'Thanks. Actually, I wanted to run something by you. Polly suggested I apply for AMIT if I pass the board.'

Stanley shook his head, chuckling.

'I think she's pulling your leg, Jane. Either that, or she's jealous and setting you up for a fall.'

'No, she's not. Polly was very complimentary about my work and thinks I'd make a good SIO.'

'Dream on, Jane. Like me, Polly knows it will never happen, not in a month of Sundays. My advice would be don't even bother applying.'

Jane was shocked by his attitude and especially his remarks about Polly.

'Well, thanks for your support, Stanley!'

'Look, I didn't mean any offence. But believe me, as good a detective as you are, you'll never be selected for AMIT.'

'Well, you might be wrong.'

He took Jane to one side. 'Do you know how it's all set up?'

'Yes, a DCS runs each AMIT with DCIs heading up the teams and—'

Stanley interrupted. 'That's not what I meant. When I say "set up", I mean it's a set-up as to who gets selected. The commander picks the DCSs, who in turn pick the DCIs and so on. It's the old-pals act, and senior female officers won't get a look-in.'

'That's discrimination!' Jane protested.

'It's a fact of police life, and there's not a lot you, Polly or any female officer in the Met can do about it,' he said, walking off and joining Detective Sergeant Bill Burrows at the bar while Jane was left feeling utterly dejected.

'What was all that about with Tennison?' Bill asked Stanley.

'Her promotion interview at the Yard tomorrow.'

'She is a damn good detective and deserves the next rank.'

'If she gets it, she wants to apply for AMIT.'

'Not a hope in hell . . . unless she grows a dick,' Bill laughed, gulping the dregs from his pint then banging it down on the bar for a refill.

It was 9 p.m. when Jane got home. She was still in a bad mood and threw her keys down onto the hall table before noticing there was a message on her new tape-recording answerphone. She rewound the tape and pressed play, recognising the estate agent's voice. She hadn't expected things to happen so quickly, as she listened to the agent telling her about the two offers on her house. One was from a young couple who wanted a quick cash sale and were offering three thousand pounds more than the asking price, if some of the furniture and electrical goods were included.

Jane decided she would call the estate agents and accept the offer first thing in the morning, even though she'd be giving herself no time to look for a new house or flat. But with Stanley's depressing words still ringing in her ears, she felt it was just the jolt she needed.

CHAPTER TWO

Jane was uncharacteristically nervous on the morning of her promotion interview. She didn't want to risk driving to Scotland Yard in case heavy traffic or an accident made her late, so she decided to get the train. And she had made sure she looked the part, wearing a dark navy fitted suit, white priest-collared shirt, dark stockings, and black polished high-heeled shoes. Her sister Pam had been unable to fit her in for an appointment at her salon, so she had gone to a local hairdresser, and her hair was now collar-length and looked sleek and conditioned. She had applied minimal make-up and removed the varnish from her nails.

Arriving at Victoria with time to kill, Jane went for a coffee in the Broadway, opposite the Yard, where she did some last-minute revision from crib sheets she'd prepared before entering the building. Having cleared security, she was told to go to the eighth floor and report to Inspector Monroe, the commander's staff officer.

Jane knocked on the inspector's door, entered and introduced herself. He told her to take a seat in the waiting room opposite and she would be called when the board were ready. The waiting room was sparsely furnished with just a few easy chairs and a table with copies of *The Job*. Jane picked up a copy with a front-page story headlined 'Area Major Incident Pools to Combat Murder and Serious Crime Across London'. She'd literally just finished it when the inspector came in and said 'You're on,' and wished her good luck.

Sitting behind a large desk were three men, two wearing dark suits and one in uniform. From the uniform officer's epaulettes, Jane knew he was a chief superintendent.

'Please sit down.' The man in the middle gestured, with a pleasant smile, to a chair placed in front of them.

'I am Commander Trayner. On my left is Chief Superintendent Bridges and to my right is Detective Chief Superintendent Kernan.' Bridges gave her a polite nod, whereas Kernan just stared at Jane with his dark, hooded eyes, his sour expression making her feel uncomfortable. He had a prominent nose and thick dark hair combed back from a high forehead.

Jane saw they each had a folder in front of them, which she knew would contain copies of her police file, application for promotion and her CV. The only person who hadn't opened his folder was Kernan.

Jane nervously licked her lips as the commander took the lead.

'Try and relax, DI Tennison. This is an interview, not an interrogation. We have spent some time reading through your police file this morning and I have to say I'm quite impressed. DCI Hutton has written a glowing report about your successfully leading a murder investigation, which led to a conviction.'

Bridges, the uniform chief, nodded in agreement.

'Thank you, sir,' Jane said. 'It wasn't an easy investigation, and I couldn't have done it without the great team of officers I had working alongside me.' Jane watched Kernan open his file, hurriedly flick through it, and remove a few pages.

The commander was about to continue when Kernan raised his hand. 'If I may, sir, I'd like to pick up on Tennison's remark about teamwork.'

'Carry on,' the commander replied.

Kernan held up the papers. 'This is a report by your DCI when you were attached to the Flying Squad. He states that one of your failings is an inability to be a "team player". Why do you think he said that?'

Jane knew she had to stand up for herself. 'I think you'll find his report also said I was a skilled investigator, with the ability to "think outside the box", and—'

'You haven't answered my question.'

'You didn't let me finish, sir. I admit in some of my previous post-ings I was not always a team player and I didn't share my thoughts during a major investigation. However, I have learned from my mistakes. Results at Bromley have shown that. I always encourage and listen to the thoughts of my fellow detectives now, so as a team we can get the best results.'

'Why did you keep your thoughts to yourself before Bromley?' Trayner asked.

'Because I often felt undervalued and patronised by my male colleagues. I'd put forward what I believed to be a constructive idea or line of enquiry, which would be totally ignored. I found myself in a position where I felt it best to keep my opinions to myself, then let the evidence I uncovered speak for itself.'

'Sounds to me like you can't take criticism,' Kernan suggested with an unpleasant smile.

'Not at all, sir,' Jane countered. 'As long as it's constructive.'

Kernan was about to ask another question, but Bridges, feeling things were getting a bit heated, changed the subject.

'What do you do in your downtime?'

'Due to my recent heavy workload I've not had a lot of time to relax, but I do like running and generally try to keep fit. At present I'm selling my house and looking for somewhere else to live, so that's taking up a lot of my spare time.'

Bridges smiled. 'I know from experience moving house can be stressful.'

Trayner continued: 'If promoted to DCI, you would be trans-ferred to another station. Is there anywhere in particular you'd like to work?'

At first Jane hesitated, then realised this was a 'now or never' moment. 'Yes, sir. I'd like to be posted to AMIT. I believe my inves-tigative skills, experience and leadership qualities show I would be a capable SIO on an AMIT team.'

Kernan almost snorted. 'Do you know what AMIT is and its role?'

Jane was now pleased she'd read *The Job* article before the interview. 'Area Major Investigation Teams. It was conceived by Commander Trayner to bring together experienced detectives to investigate murder and other major crimes across the Met.' She rattled off the rank structure and stations the teams would be working from, then looked at Trayner. 'If I may say so, sir, I think it should result in more thorough and successful major investigations. Not to mention reducing the workload of divisional CID officers.'

He nodded. 'Thank you, DI Tennison. We will obviously discuss your request for an AMIT posting after the interview.'

Kernan gave her a sour look. 'There are many DCIs across the Met with far more investigative experience than you. What makes you think you're so special?'

Jane thought it was more of a derogatory remark than a question. 'I don't consider myself "special", sir, but I am hard-working and dedicated. I am currently the acting DCI at Bromley and have had to perform my role of DI as well while Fiona Hutton is on maternity leave. Her report acknowledges that I was more than capable of running the CID office, leading major investigations, and managing the budget in her absence.'

Kernan leaned forward. 'And if *you* get pregnant, then someone will have to babysit your cases, which is not a good position to be in on a murder investigation.'

Jane smiled, concealing her growing anger. 'I've no desire to start a family at present. I know the responsibilities that go with being an SIO on AMIT will be challenging, but I love a challenge. As you said, sir, there are many more experienced DCIs in the Met, but part of being a good detective is to learn from the skills of your colleagues and respect the expertise they offer . . . no matter their rank.'

Trayner nodded. 'I remember as a young PC how much my first reporting sergeant taught me. He and others like him undoubtedly helped me rise through the ranks.'

Kernan sat in silence for the remaining fifteen minutes of the interview. Jane was asked questions about the law, police policies and dealing with officers who had broken the disciplinary code. She answered all the questions confidently and maintained eye contact throughout.

Finally Trayner concluded the interview. 'I don't think there's anything else we need to ask DI Tennison.' He looked at his colleagues. Bridges shook his head and Kernan gave a dismissive wave of his hand. 'Thank you for coming today. As I'm sure you appreciate, there are currently only fifteen vacancies for the rank of DCI. You will be notified of our decision after all the applicants have been interviewed. Whatever the outcome, I wish you well for the future, DI Tennison.'

After Jane had left the room, DCS Kernan slapped the file in front of him closed.

'Well, my vote is no.'

'Is that for promotion, AMIT or both?' Trayner asked.

'Both. There's no way she could run a team of tough, experienced AMIT officers – they'd eat her for breakfast.'

'That's not the impression I got,' Bridges said. 'I thought she stood up for herself well . . . especially in answering your rather derogatory questions.'

'What would you know, Bridges?' Kernan sneered. 'You've never been a detective.'

'No, but I know a competent and dedicated officer when I see one. In my humble opinion as a uniform officer, Tennison has the attributes and ability to be an excellent DCI . . . and SIO on AMIT.'

'Well, I hold the casting vote, but I'll make my final decision later,' Trayner said.

Kernan huffed and shook his head. 'There's no vacancy for her. My fellow DCSs at the other three AMIT bases have already selected their DCIs, who have been approved by Commander Trayner.'

Trayner opened a file on the desk. 'That's true, but you have only selected two DCIs, John Shefford and Brian Hickock . . . so you're one short at present.'

'DI Paul McGregor is my preferred choice. He's next on the interview list and will make a great DCI. He's also more astute and experienced than Tennison.'

Trayner frowned. 'I chaired one of the four misconduct hearings he's appeared on.'

'All of which were "not proven"', Kernan countered.

'That's not correct. He was reprimanded by me for neglect of duty and fined two weeks' pay,' Trayner said.

'He was going through a bad divorce at the time. I know McGregor can be a bit heavy-handed at times, but he's a great thief-taker. Besides, three of the complaints were made by career criminals.'

Trayner was dubious. 'Well, his future will be decided after the interview . . . if he passes.'

'Then let's get on with it,' Kernan said, flipping open McGregor's file.

* * *

After her interview Jane went to the ladies' to freshen up, then back to the waiting room to get her raincoat and briefcase. There was a man in his late thirties reading the *Sun*. He smelt of alcohol and was dressed rather scruffily for a formal interview.

'How'd your interview go, sweetheart?' he asked in a broad Glasgow accent.

'Hard to say,' Jane replied.

'I'm the last up, so we should get the results in the next couple of days.'

'Well, good luck,' Jane said.

'Shouldn't need it, darling. Mick Kernan wants me as a DCI on his Southampton Row team, so the interview should be a walk in the park. If you want to hang about, we could go for a drink after my interview,' McGregor added with a wink.

Jane couldn't think of anything she'd like less. 'Can I give you a word of advice?'

He shrugged. 'If you must.'

'Never count your chickens before they are hatched.' She picked up her belongings and walked towards the door. 'And brown shoes don't go with that tatty blue suit.'

For the next couple of days Jane hardly had time to think about the interview. Having accepted an above-market offer for the house and agreed a good price on the furniture, fixtures and fittings, she spent all her spare hours at home, packing up boxes with personal items she wanted to keep.

Jane decided to put the boxes into storage rather than ask her parents to have them until she had found a new place to live. She was waiting for the storage company to collect everything when her phone rang.

'Good morning, DI Tennison. Sorry to disturb you on a day off.'

She instantly recognised Commander Trayner's cheery voice, but the way he addressed her as DI felt ominous. 'I didn't pass, did I?'

'On the contrary, you passed with flying colours. You will be confirmed as a DCI on taking up your new post at AMIT in two weeks' time.'

Jane was ecstatic. 'Thank you so much for selecting me, sir. Can I ask which AMIT station I'll be working at?'

Trayner hesitated. 'There was only one vacancy left, which is at Southampton Row under the leadership of DCS Kernan.'

Her heart sank at the thought of working with Kernan, but she wasn't going to show it.

'I look forward to the challenge,' she said.

He laughed softly. 'I don't doubt that. However, you must be aware you will face opposition from some detectives on the team. I know how tough it can be for a female officer in the Met. My wife

Sally is a uniform chief inspector at Romford. She fought long and hard to get promoted. Like Sally, you have a lot of grit and determination . . . In fact, you've broken the mould as the first female DCI to be selected for AMIT, so you can be very proud of your achievements.'

'Thank you for your advice and support,' Jane replied.

After finishing the call Jane went and sat on the stairs, taking a few deep breaths before she let out a yell and punched the air with joy. By mid-afternoon all her boxes had been collected, and she had packed a suitcase to go and stay with her parents. But first, she decided to go to Bromley, announce her promotion, and extend her leave, knowing that her paperwork was up to date, and things were running smoothly under Polly and Stanley.

As soon as she got to the station, Jane went into the squad room and announced to everyone that she had been selected for DCI and was being posted to Southampton Row AMIT. Everyone clapped and cheered.

'That's a good excuse for an office celebration, ma'am,' Stanley said loudly out of respect for her new rank.

'The drinks and food are on me,' she shouted, which led to another loud cheer.

Jane handed Stanley a hundred pounds in cash. 'Can I leave you to organise it?'

Polly gave Jane a big hug. 'I'm so pleased for you. What you've done is a big step forward for every woman in the police force.'

Jane was sure her praise was genuine. 'Thanks, Polly. The thing is, I need to extend my leave, with so much to organise with the house and then finding somewhere to live. But I don't want to burden you and Stanley.'

'Don't be silly,' Polly said. 'He drives me mad at times, but he always pulls his weight. Together we can run things until Fiona Hutton comes back.'

'Why don't you ask to take my place?' Jane asked.

'I'm discussing it with my husband. I love the drug squad, but the working hours, coupled with his cabbing, means we hardly see each other. Working here allows for a much better home life.'

About half an hour later Stanley popped his head round the door and said everything was good to go. He opened the door for her. There was a loud cheer from the room full of detectives and senior uniform officers, and suddenly Jane felt quite emotional. She was surprised to see Fiona Hutton in attendance, clapping away enthusiastically. Polly had quickly organised a large 'Good Luck' banner, which was hung across the wipe board, and somehow a large bunch of roses and bottle of Moët champagne for Jane had appeared.

Jane spent as much time as she could chatting with everyone in the room until she found a moment to slip out unnoticed. She went to her office to collect her box of personal belongings and put the champagne and flowers in it as well. She headed down to the car park, where Stanley was leaning against her car, holding a bottle of beer.

'You off, then?'

'Yes, I left some things on your desk. I used to be fanatical about ballet and collected autographs, photographs and books. I know your daughters love ballet and thought they might like them. I was never really any good at it – the teacher said I had two left feet.'

'There you go, being negative,' he joked. 'Thanks, the girls will love it. Good luck, DCI Tennison. I'll really miss not seeing your ugly mug in the office.'

'Forever the charmer,' she smiled, kissing him on the cheek. 'I'll miss you as well.'

She put the cardboard box in the boot and Stanley opened the driver's door.

'Onwards and upwards, Jane. Take care of yourself and keep in touch.'

'Will do,' she replied as he closed the door.

Stanley waved as he watched her drive out of the yard. He'd wanted to say more about the chauvinism she'd be up against at AMIT, knowing that despite her bravado, she was insecure on the inside, allowing her emotions, or any form of criticism, to eat away at her, but figured she already knew what she was letting herself in for.

Feeling a little depressed, he headed back into the station and walked along the corridor, listening to the laughter drifting down the stairs from the ongoing party in the boardroom. He went to the office he'd shared with Jane. On his desk there was a cardboard box full of the items for his daughters. He picked up a copy of *The Life of Nijinsky*, flicking it open to a picture of *Swan Lake*, which reminded him of watching his eldest daughter performing at her ballet school. Now his younger daughter was taking classes, and the thought of her following in her sister's footsteps and performing the same role made him happy. He had a wife he loved, and retirement would allow him to have plenty of time with her and the kids and be a better father and husband. Too many times he had risked his life for the job, but no longer would his wife or family fear he might not come home. He put the book gently back into the box.

'Thank you, Tennison,' he said.

CHAPTER THREE

It felt strange waking up in her old bedroom at her parents' flat. Jane lay awake, mentally listing what she needed to do before she joined AMIT. The first priority was to start hunting for somewhere to rent near Southampton Row police station. She had already decided not to buy, and was keeping the money from the house sale in a high-interest deposit account.

Jane got up and spent the morning contacting letting agents and arranging viewing appointments.

By late afternoon she had turned down three flats and had arranged more appointments for the following day. She felt exhausted and wished she hadn't agreed to have dinner with her sister Pam, but she had left it too late to cancel. But it was probably good to get it over and done with, as her sister would be interrogating her about the sale of her house, as well as the end of her relationship with Eddie. She was doubtful Pam would be interested in her promotion or where she was going to be stationed, but she knew that as soon as she mentioned looking for a flat, her sister would be eager for her husband to help with any decorating or DIY jobs.

Jane arrived promptly at 7.30 p.m., parking her car behind her brother-in-law Tony's van. As she got out of her car a Range Rover pulled up at the kerb and Tony got out from the passenger side.

'Thanks for the ride, Pete. See you next Wednesday,' he called as the Range Rover drove off just as Pam opened the front door.

'About time!' she snapped.

'I'm not late, am I?' Jane said, taken aback.

'Not you, Tony . . . He was supposed to be here to take the boys to the cinema. In the end one of their friends' mothers picked them up.'

Pam pushed Jane into the hall as she continued to tell Tony off, not that he seemed in any way apologetic. He was carrying a sports bag with squash rackets sticking out as he followed them both down the hall.

'I had a shower, then Pete offered me a lift, but he had to take a long phone call, so I had to wait for him. Just gimme a minute to stash my gear and get out of my tracksuit.'

Pam grimaced and ushered Jane into their kitchen, where the breakfast table was set for dinner with an open bottle of red wine.

'Did you notice anything about him?'

'What?'

'He's lost fifteen pounds . . . joined this gym and plays squash three times a week. Sit down and pour yourself a drink.'

Pam checked the casserole in the oven and came to sit at the table as Jane poured a glass of wine for them both.

'So, Mum told me you've moved back with them and that you've sold your house? I couldn't believe it, Jane; I mean, you'd only just got it all perfect.'

'I was offered a really good price and the couple wanted most of the furniture on top of that. The rest is in storage,' Jane told her.

'Oh, well, I would have bought a few things if you'd offered. Did they buy all the curtains?'

'Yes, and all the kitchen appliances. I've decided to look for a rented place until I know where I'll be working.'

'So, you and that builder aren't together anymore?'

'No.'

'I bet that hurt him, after all the work he did. I mean, he was very clever. Dad said he could turn his hand to anything, electrics, plumbing . . . I have to say your house looked lovely.'

'Actually, he dumped me.'

'No, you're kidding me? You know Mum did say she doubted it would work out. He was younger than you, wasn't he – Eddie?

You've had quite a time of it, what with going through that ectopic pregnancy . . . I suppose in the end it was for the best.'

Jane was relieved when Tony walked in. She noticed he did look much fitter.

'Can I do anything?' he asked.

'Yes, toss the salad. We're not having a starter – it's lamb casserole, followed by ice cream with fresh fruit.'

'You look good, Tony,' Jane said, smiling.

'I've been playing squash at this club for eight months now. Feel better than I've felt for years.'

Jane nodded. 'I used to play for my college team.'

'We'll have to have a game sometime. They've also got yoga and fitness classes and a good weights room, with a nice little coffee bar. I've been trying to get Pam to join.'

'It'd be hard to find the time with making the kids' dinner, and now they're getting very stroppy about homework. I got them looked after this evening so we could all have a quiet time. They're constantly getting bigger and, my God, their feet! No sooner have you got them a new pair of trainers and they've grown out of them.'

'How is the salon doing?' Jane asked.

'Not bad, but I get tired being on my feet all day. And that's quite enough exercise for me, never mind running around playing squash.'

Tony brought the salad bowl to the table, then fetched bowls and serving spoons. The kitchen was quite compact, and he crashed around, banging drawers shut and opening cupboards, before he sat down as Pam served the salad.

'Business good for you too, Tony?' Jane asked.

'Not bad. I've made a good contact at the gym, actually. The bloke who drove me home. Him and his partner have got a contractors' company, but he's having a bit of a tough time right now – personal, not business.'

'Like what?' Pam asked.

'I'm not exactly sure, but that was one of the reasons I was late. He had this phone call and was pretty cut up about it. I'm not that friendly with him outside business and the club, but he implied that something was going on with his wife, and from what he said I think his business partner is mixed up in it.'

'What, she's knocking off his partner?' Pam said.

'For Chrissakes, Pam, I don't know! Like I just said, we're not really friends. But he has put some work my way and he seems a decent bloke – even though he always beats me at squash!'

He turned to Jane, raising an eyebrow.

'You should join the club if you're back in town – I can get you a membership deal. They've got a lot of women members and nice changing rooms with a sauna and hot tub.'

Pam rolled her eyes as she collected the salad bowls. But Jane was relieved to have Tony there, as it stopped Pam interrogating her about selling her house. Pam took the casserole out of the oven and started to serve it at the counter. Tony poured himself another glass of wine and offered the bottle to Jane, who shook her head. 'Thanks, but I'm driving.'

'I used to have a couple of pints every night with the lads, wherever I was working. But nowadays I stick to wine – I think that's why I've lost so much weight. I still want to lose another half stone, though.'

As she served up the fresh fruit and ice cream, Pam told Jane to put a date for the following week in her diary, as they were arranging a small get-together for their parents' ruby anniversary. 'We're getting caterers in – would you mind chipping in for the food and champagne?'

'Of course, just let me know how much. I could give you a cheque now if you like?'

As Tony cleared the table, Pam brought out her guest list. 'And perhaps we could get them something red – like candlesticks or a nice bowl?'

Jane nodded enthusiastically and handed over a cheque for eighty pounds, certain that it was more than her share, but by this time she was eager to leave.

Tony saw Jane to the door and handed her a card for the gym, telling her to mention his name to get a good price, while Pam loomed behind him, repeating the date for the anniversary party. 'And if you want your hair cut, call me at the salon.'

CHAPTER FOUR

A week later Jane had found a very suitable rental. It was in a refurbished Victorian house a short drive from Southampton Row in Buckingham Palace Road: two bedrooms, one a large double with a bathroom ensuite, and a small box room. Off the small hallway was another room that Jane felt would be perfect for an office. The furnishings were in a rather bland G-Plan style with grey fitted carpets throughout. But the kitchen had new appliances and there was residents' parking in front of the house.

And the blandness of the décor was actually quite soothing. The flat had a clean, fresh smell, and the atmosphere was very peaceful. Jane felt that due to the original property being Victorian, the thick walls meant she would hear little or no noise from the other tenants.

With only a few days before she was to join AMIT, she called Pam at her salon to have her hair cut and add some highlights, in preparation for her first day at work and also for their parents' anniversary party. She was in a confident mood, more so than she had been for a long time.

A clothes-shopping trip also buoyed her spirits as she bought herself two new suits from Next, three white blouses, two pairs of low-heeled shoes and one pair of very expensive high stiletto heels.

Arriving at Pam's salon, she was introduced to a very camp stylist who said she should really go for a change, suggesting an Eton crop, enhanced with tasteful highlights. Jane was dubious at first, but eventually agreed.

It was certainly a big difference to have such a short cut, but she had to admit that it was very stylish. It had taken over two hours, and the new sophisticated look gave her a slender neck and accentuated her cheekbones. By the time she had returned to her flat her newfound confidence had gone up another notch.

Arriving at her parents' for the ruby wedding anniversary party, Jane carried a bunch of roses and a large congratulations card. Her father greeted her with open arms.

'You look wonderful!' he said, smiling, and ushering her into the drawing room.

Mrs Tennison was less convinced by the new hairstyle, but Pam had already told her that she should not say a word, as Pam had encouraged her stylist to do it. Jane dutifully mingled with the guests, mostly her parents' friends and neighbours, and praised the lovely cake on display with its red icing and wedding bells. A young waiter was serving canapés while her father doled out the champagne, and everyone appeared to be enjoying the party. Then Pam, who was wearing a bright floral dress, clapped her hands and asked for silence while her father spoke a few words of welcome. He then asked everyone to raise their glass to his beloved wife and thanked the guests for joining them and for their generosity with all the beautiful gifts they had received.

Jane went and sat beside an elderly neighbour who was balancing her plate of scampi and rice on her knee. She asked Jane numerous times if she was still living with her parents and whether she was the police officer, as she knew one of the girls had a salon. Jane eventually escaped to the kitchen, where Tony was opening another bottle of champagne. He turned to indicate a man sitting on one of the kitchen stools.

'Jane, this is Peter Rawlins, my friend from the gym. He's been helping cart over all the decorations and equipment for the party, and he's offered to run a few of the oldies back home afterwards.'

'Nice to meet you,' Jane said, smiling.

When he stood up to shake her hand, he was at least six feet tall, and had a warm, friendly face.

'I'm returning the favour. Tony helped a lot with moving stuff from my office. Do you have a glass, or can I give you a refill?'

Jane accepted a fresh one from Tony before he headed into the throng of guests.

'You must be Tony's squash partner?'

'Yes, and I have to say his squash has really improved since we've been playing. You must be the Met officer he's so proud of.'

'It's nice to know he's proud of my career,' Jane smiled. 'The rest of my family don't really talk about it that much.'

'I have to say that you don't look like any police officer I've ever met. Do you play squash?'

'I used to, a long time ago. Tony was telling me about all the facilities at the club.'

'Yes, they're excellent. I've been a member for years and it's been quite a life-saver for me in many ways. Meeting Tony has been great, and I've been able to offer him a lot of work. He's an excellent carpenter and can really turn his hand to anything.'

'Are you in the building trade?'

'Yes, I'm a contractor, property investments mostly.'

Tony returned with an empty bottle and put it into the crate with the others, removing an unopened one from the fridge.

'I think your services are required, Peter – an elderly couple by the front door. If you could do the honours and take them back home to Putney?'

'Sure, do you need me to come back afterwards?'

'No, thanks, and thanks for helping me out. I can stack everything that needs clearing in my van.'

'My pleasure.'

Peter turned to Jane.

'Nice to meet you, Jane. Perhaps I'll see you at the club.'

Tony popped open the champagne as Pam came in.

'Go easy on the champagne, love, some of them are getting very sozzled. I need that dustpan and brush, Jane.'

Jane gestured to it on one of the counters.

'That old dear with rice and scampi has managed to drop cake crumbs all over the sofa. Did you see what we bought for Mum and Dad?'

'No, I didn't, actually.'

'It's a ruby red cut glass bowl – it's out on the side table. How did you get on with Peter?'

'He seemed very nice.'

'He's quite a catch, actually. He's got a lovely house over in Fulham, a successful business and he drives a Range Rover . . .'

To Jane's relief, before Pam could finish Tony reappeared and asked for her to go and see if the teapot needed refilling.

Jane remained in the kitchen sipping her champagne. She reckoned it was going to be quite a long evening.

The young waiter left at 9.30 p.m. By this time Pam had begun stacking all the dishes as Mrs Tennison collected trays of dirty glasses. Tony was scraping leftover food into bin liners. Jane insisted that her parents stop doing any more clearing up, assuring them that she, Pam and Tony would finish everything between them.

As Jane was getting the vacuum out to hoover the drawing room carpet, she overheard Pam arguing with Tony in the kitchen. 'What was all that about Peter being a good catch?' Tony said.

'Well, he is,' Pam retorted. 'And I think he'd be good for her. He's the right age, unlike that last builder she was living with. Actually, I thought Peter was quite taken with her.'

'Peter's not just a builder, he has a big company. Besides that, he has a lot of personal issues that he's having to deal with, so I doubt he's even interested in a relationship right now.'

Jane picked up the vacuum, shaking her head, and headed towards the drawing room. It was almost midnight by the time everything was tidied up. The crates had been stacked by the front door for Tony to take out to his van. The rubbish bags were piled up to take down to the bins and the dishwasher was on its third cycle.

Pam was checking over everything after making sure their parents had gone to bed. Jane was placing her roses into a vase after finding them in the bathroom washbasin, along with a couple of other guests' floral gifts. She felt exhausted and was eager to get back to her flat.

'Well, I think that went well,' Pam said. 'Everyone seemed to have a really good time.'

'Yes, you did a great job, Pam. And thank you again for the new hairstyle. I reckon I owe you and Tony a slap-up dinner. I'll be in touch with some dates.'

'Oh, that'll be nice. You must have us round to your new flat.'

'I just need to settle in first. I'm still getting stuff out of storage.'

'Well, if you need any work done, you know who to contact. Tony can turn his hand to anything.'

Jane smiled and edged out of the door after grabbing two of the bin bags, glad that at least Pam had not asked any questions about her new job. She was probably completely unaware that she had been promoted.

After putting the bags in a wheelie bin, Jane hurried to her car and drove off.

It was a relief to get home to her new flat, and she was especially grateful for the big double bed with fresh Egyptian cotton sheets and matching pillowslips. She quickly fell into a deep sleep.

The following morning, she decided that it would be a good idea to do a big supermarket shop and fill up her freezer with ready meals. It was just after 11 a.m. when she left Tesco, carrying two loaded food bags and several bottles of wine. She opened the boot of her car and was stacking everything inside when she heard a voice calling her name. Turning around, she saw Peter Rawlins unloading groceries into the boot of his Range Rover. She shut the boot and walked over to him.

'Morning, I was just stocking up my freezer with ready meals as I start work at a new station tomorrow. It's always a bit nerve-racking . . .'

Peter smiled. 'I have a young son and he changes his mind about which cereal he likes daily, so I've got to have a big selection. And he's addicted to fish fingers and chips.'

'How old is he?'

'Almost five. I have him one day and night a week, but hopefully there will be weekends as well soon.'

There was an awkward pause as Jane took in the fact that his son wasn't living with him and Peter obviously didn't want to elaborate. He closed the boot of his Range Rover, then turned to Jane as he took out his wallet.

'Let me give you my business card. If you ever want me to show you around the club, just give me a call.'

'Thank you.' Jane took the card as he opened his car door.

'Nice to see you again.'

Back at the flat, she chose a new suit and a blouse for the next day, hanging them up in her bedroom. After taking a long, leisurely bath, she washed and blow-dried her hair.

Jane sat up in bed reading, making a mental note that she would need a new bedside lamp. She then thought about buying a new TV set, which reminded her about Eddie and the huge TV set he had insisted on installing in their bedroom. But she refused to allow herself to get emotional about him no longer being in her life. Perhaps if she bought a smaller, portable, TV set it wouldn't dominate the bedroom.

'Well, I'm ready,' she said out loud to herself. She straightened out the pristine cotton sheet and folded over a section, patting it flat with her hand.

CHAPTER FIVE

A large modern building loomed into sight. 'I guess this must be it,' Jane said to herself.

Southampton Row police station was known as the 'pink palace' by local residents, because it didn't align with the architectural character of the area. The four-storey L-shaped building was clad in tan-coloured bricks, with bands of windows, arranged in stepped sections, facing onto Buckingham Palace Road. Both uniform and divisional plain clothes officers worked at the station alongside the AMIT staff who could call upon their assistance when required.

Jane pulled up by the rear entrance in Ebury Square. The electric blue doors were tall and wide, with a smaller door next to them and a wall-mounted intercom with a camera and number entry buttons on it. Jane got out of her car and pressed the intercom. A female officer in the control room asked Jane to identify herself and show her warrant card to the camera.

'Can you tell me where the AMIT officers park, please?'

'Yes, ma'am, right round the back. Follow the horseshoe route on the left side of the building. There's allocated spaces for the AMIT senior officers. I'll get them to send someone down to show you to your office.'

Jane thanked her and waited for the gates to open. Just inside were some uniform cars and vans with a large sign stating, 'Police Patrol Vehicles Only'. She drove slowly round the tight bend into a tarmacked area with an 'AMIT Vehicles Only' sign on the wall. There were several unmarked vehicles, which she assumed were either privately owned by officers or CID cars. Amongst them she noticed a parking bay and a metal sign on the wall with 'DCS Kernan' written on it and two further signs with 'DCI Shefford' and 'DCI Hickock' on them. The bays next to them were occupied, so Jane got out of her car to see if she could find her bay. She heard a female voice call out.

'Excuse me, are you DCI Tennison?'

Jane turned and saw a slightly overweight uniform officer approaching. She looked to be in her mid-twenties and had a round, pretty face. The buttons on her white, ill-fitting shirt were slightly gaping between her breasts.

'Good morning, ma'am. I'm WPC Maureen Havers, your personal assistant,' she said, holding up her warrant card, which was attached to a lanyard. 'This is your new warrant card, which has to be worn at all times within the station grounds.' She handed it to Jane, who put it on over her head.

'Thank you, Maureen. I can't seem to find my parking bay . . .'

She pointed. 'It's over there in the far corner, ma'am.'

Jane could see a laminated sheet of paper taped to the wall with 'DCI Tennison' written on it in marker pen. She also noticed a row of large pallet bins near the bay.

'Are there no other spaces available?'

'I was told it's only temporary, and I've ordered a name plate.'

Jane shook her head in disbelief.

It was hard work, even in her Mini, navigating into the space and avoiding the nearby bins. There was just enough room between the wall and car door for Jane to squeeze out. The smell from the bins was almost overpowering.

Maureen took Jane to a door near where the police vehicles were parked and pressed some numbers on the electric entry keypad.

'The door code is 1066, the year of the Battle of Hastings.'

'Is there one for the yard gates?'

'Yes, it's the Battle of Waterloo, but I can't remember the year.'

'That would be 1815.'

'That's it. I don't drive and only use the police front entrance – that's 1066 as well.'

'It's quite an impressive building.'

'It's not been open long. Gerald Road and Rochester Row stations have closed, so everyone's been moved here.'

They entered a long corridor with shiny grey epoxy flooring and Maureen led the way to the lift.

'Would it be quicker to walk up?'

'Not really. Your office is on the fourth floor. The AMIT team offices and Intel offices are on the third.'

'What about DCS Kernan's office?'

'He's on the second floor, next to the uniform chief superintendent's office.'

As the lift passed the third floor, Jane winced at the strong smell of fried food.

'Unfortunately, the canteen is on the floor below us,' Maureen said.

They stopped at the last floor and Maureen stepped aside for Jane to enter.

'I've ordered your door name plate,' she said.

Jane stood still in disbelief. A large wooden desk and a faded leather swivel chair were placed in front of five grey free-standing room partitions. Along the wall by the desk were two scratched and dented filing cabinets, and a large, skewed corkboard with coloured drawing pins scattered over it. Several fragments of torn paper were still attached to some of the pins.

'There isn't even a window in here!' Jane said as she straightened the corkboard.

'It's behind the partition, ma'am.'

Jane pulled one side of the partition forward so she could look behind it. There was a large area filled with stacks of chairs and old tables, one of which had several boxes on it that were blocking out the sunlight. Jane picked up a dirty coffee percolator from on top of a chair and put it on her desk. Replacing the partition, she noticed the carpet was old and heavily stained.

'I thought this was meant to be a new building, with modern equipment and fittings.'

'Some of it is, but to save money they brought a lot of the old furniture and fittings over from the stations they closed. I remember this carpet being in the PCs' writing room at Gerald Road.'

Jane was trying hard to control herself. She put her briefcase on the desk and took a deep breath.

'This office is like a furniture warehouse. I need to speak with DCS Kernan about something more suitable. Did you say he was on the second floor?'

Maureen nodded. 'He said he wants to see you at ten o'clock. I put it in your desk diary. I'm going to type a list of all the senior officers' direct lines and all the AMIT offices as well.'

'When you've finished, do a photocopy for yourself.'

'It might not be today, ma'am. The printer was playing up earlier and they're waiting for someone to repair it. Come to think of it, I'll type two copies.'

'How long have you been on AMIT, Maureen?'

'Er . . . a week or so.'

Having read *The Job* article about the AMIT structure, Jane knew that an experienced detective sergeant would normally be a DCI's assistant, a position commonly known in the Met as a 'bag carrier'. Not wanting to upset Maureen, Jane spoke softly.

'Did you have to sit an interview to be my assistant?'

'Sort of, but it wasn't a formal thing.'

Jane was becoming impatient, but remained calm. 'So how exactly did you get the job?'

'I was in the canteen having breakfast on my own when DCS Kernan approached me. He asked if I'd like to do some work experience on AMIT. I told him I didn't think my inspector would approve, but he said not to worry as he'd speak with my chief superintendent.'

Jane didn't have the heart to tell Maureen she'd been used by Kernan. Clearly, he didn't want to give Jane an experienced DS, and thought Maureen would be a hindrance rather than a help due to her lack of CID experience. But the last thing Jane wanted to do was hurt Maureen's feelings and ask for a replacement. She knew from her own experiences how much rejection could hurt.

'I'm pleased to have a female officer assisting me, Maureen. But obviously, you've a lot to learn, so if there's anything you're unsure of, always ask me first.'

'Yes, ma'am.'

Jane lifted the percolator from her desk. 'Could you get this cleaned up and fetch some cups from the canteen? We'll also need some ground coffee, milk and sugar. And see if you can find a decent desk and chair.'

'That was the best one I could find behind the partition, ma'am.'

'I meant for you! Where is the ladies'?'

'It's on the first floor, and there's a female locker room in the basement. There's only a gents' toilet on this floor, but it's got something wrong with the ballcock. I'll nip to the corner shop down the road for the coffee and other stuff.'

'Before you go, have you got any marker pens?'

'Yes, ma'am, in a variety of colours.' Maureen went to the filing cabinet, removed a box of marker pens, and handed them to Jane. She then put on her civilian coat over her uniform, picked up her handbag and left.

Jane shook her head, smiling ruefully. She checked her watch and saw she still had an hour before her meeting with DCS Kernan. She realised the allocation of her parking bay, tatty office and having Maureen posted as her assistant were all attempts to make her feel unwelcome from the start, and complaining would therefore only play into his hands. She unbuttoned her jacket and hung it on the back of her chair.

Rolling up her sleeves, Jane headed down the corridor and opened the door into the cleaning equipment storage room. There were buckets and mops stacked beneath shelves with containers of bleach and floor cleaning products. She picked up a pair of Marigold gloves from the edge of a bucket, then reached up to a shelf for a bottle of bleach and disinfectant. She then searched around until she found a worn wooden-handled toilet brush.

The gents' toilet was at the furthest end of the corridor, past the lifts. There was a white plastic 'Out of Order' notice hanging on the door handle. Jane went in and shut the door behind her, locking it firmly. Fifteen minutes later, having given it a good clean up, she came out and removed the 'Out of Order' notice.

Returning to her office, she wrote 'LADIES' with a black marker pen on the other side of the notice, then compiled a list of things she wanted for the office.

Maureen returned, looking flushed, having jogged to and from the corner shop. 'I got a pack of digestive biscuits as well.'

'Put a chitty in and I'll sign it off.'

'Sorry, but what's a chitty?'

'An invoice for the money you just spent. And don't forget to attach the sales receipt.'

'Oh, I didn't keep the receipt.'

Jane didn't know whether to laugh or cry. She removed some pound coins from her purse and held them out to Maureen, who politely declined. Jane hooked the 'LADIES' notice on her index finger and held it up.

'Hang this on the gents' toilet door, please. The ballcock was jammed, but I got it working again. If there's any more problems, contact the building manager and ask for a plumber to fix it. On that topic, I've made a list of things we need.'

'It's almost ten, ma'am. Would you like me to show you where DCS Kernan's office is?'

Jane shook her head and grabbed her jacket. 'I'll find it. You get cracking on that list. I'll speak to the buildings manager about the toilet seat and getting rid of the partition and all that furniture. There's more stuff I want, but we can sort that out when I get back.' Jane moved to the door, then stopped, and turned around. 'I nearly forgot, call technical support and tell them I need a HOLMES computer as a matter of urgency.'

'A what computer?' Maureen asked, grabbing a pen to write it down.

'A Home Office Large Major Enquiry computer. It's used to store details of murder and major incident investigations.'

Jane hurried out, leaving Maureen looking quizzically at the list.

Jane took the lift, and when the doors opened on the third floor, she heard a roar of laughter echo down the corridor. A uniform officer carrying a tray of teas and coffee got in.

'Sounds like someone's having a good time,' Jane remarked.

'AMIT incident room,' the uniform explained. 'Probably on the piss already, being detectives.'

Jane knew some uniform officers were not fond of the CID but said nothing.

Jane exited the lift on the next floor down, walked down the corridor, tapped on Kernan's office door and went in.

Frowning, Kernan half rose from behind the large modern desk and gestured for Jane to take a seat.

'First, let me apologise for the location of your office,' he said. 'Unfortunately, it's a temporary necessity as we have a full house and three teams working on very pressing investigations.'

'You only have two other DCIs, so may I respectfully ask who the SIO is on the third investigation?' Jane asked.

'DCI Shefford, he's running two teams.'

'If it's of any help, I'm happy to take over from Shefford on one of the cases.'

'I don't think that will be necessary. He was allocated the second case the week before your arrival. John excels under pressure, so I'm sure he can cope. Besides, it's not unusual for an experienced SIO to be running several cases at the same time.'

'So what do I do in the meantime?' Jane asked, trying to keep the exasperation she felt out of her voice.

'I'd like you to investigate a case that's been on the shelf for a few years.' He opened his desk drawer, removed a file, and put it on his desk.

'I take it you mean a cold case, sir.'

He nodded. 'A college student went missing five years ago. The lead detective and his team were very thorough in their enquiries ... but eventually the investigation stalled. He recently retired, but this file contains his detailed report.' He slid the file across his desk towards Jane, then pointed to four large boxes by the door.

'All the witness statements, interviews, photographs, and items retained as potential evidence are in those boxes. I'll have an officer deliver them to your office.'

'Was the disappearance treated as a potential murder or ... ?'

Kernan's phone rang. He raised his hand before answering.

'DCS Kernan. Morning, Brian, what can I do for you ... ?'

He listened for a few moments. 'That's terrible news, so sorry to hear that. As he's a friend in need, I'll approve it ... Give him my condolences, but I need you back on the case in Huddersfield asap. Pop in and give me an update before you go back.'

While Kernan was on the phone, Jane opened the file. The top sheet was a report from June 1986 concerning a seventeen-year-old girl called Brittany Hall, who had been reported missing by her parents. Jane knew from previous missing persons cases that when a child's body is found it gives some form of closure to the family, but when there is no body, the sense of loss is intensified.

Kernan dropped the handset back into the cradle and swivelled around to face Jane.

'I forgot what you were asking me when the phone rang.'

'Was the initial investigation treated as a potential murder or kidnap?'

'DCI Tennison, I don't have time to go through it, chapter and verse. I suggest you take the file and read it and the other documents thoroughly. If any potential lines of enquiry were missed, then investigate them.'

'And if there aren't any?'

'Your previous endeavours show a knack for finding missing persons . . . be it dead or alive. If you aspire to lead a major investigation, this is an opportunity to show your abilities.'

'If I do identify further lines of enquiry, will I be given some AMIT officers and a DS to assist me?'

'I'll make that decision when and if I feel it's necessary. For now, WPC Havers will assist you.'

'Maureen has no detective or major investigation experience.'

'I've heard she's a quick learner, and I can think of no one better to show her the ropes.'

Jane could tell from his thin-lipped smile he was deliberately burdening her with a thankless task. So much for leading an AMIT investigation, she thought bitterly.

'Could I just ask something, sir?'

He sighed and nodded.

'I just wondered how the cases are allocated to AMIT DCIs?'

'Depends who is on duty and available when a major incident occurs, day or night. The list is updated weekly and displayed on the incident room duty board.'

He stood up and extended his hand, clearly eager to be rid of her.

Jane shook hands and left, hardly able to keep her face from showing her disappointment and her resentment at the way he had described her handling of missing persons cases as 'previous endeavours'. She walked briskly up the stairwell, banging open the double doors to the third-floor corridor. Heading to the canteen for a bottle of water, she heard another hoot of laughter as she passed the incident room.

Leaving the canteen, Jane got in the lift to go to the basement and speak with the buildings manager. It stopped on the second floor and when the doors opened, she noticed a young man holding two large boxes in his arms, steadying them with his chin.

'Are you going up?' he asked, obviously unaware of who she was.

'Down, I'm afraid. I take it those boxes are for me?' Jane remarked, seeing 'Misper Brittany Hall' written on one of them.

He got into the lift. 'Yes, ma'am. There's a few more, I'm afraid.'

'What was all the hilarity in the incident room?' she asked

'I don't really know, ma'am. Something to do with a WPC asking the DS about a toilet seat.'

Jane sighed. She put the Brittany Hall file on the top of the boxes the DC was carrying and asked him to put it on her desk, then pressed the button for the fourth floor for him.

The dark and damp basement was a bit of a maze, and the sound of rattling heating pipes created an eerie atmosphere. Looking for the building manager's office, Jane had to step over puddles of water dotting the concrete floor. Eventually she found it, knocked and entered. To her annoyance, the fixtures and fittings were much better than the ones in her office. A man in a dark blue overall was pouring a cup of coffee from a cafetière.

'Are you the buildings manager?' Jane asked.

'I'm his assistant, Bill. Jim's at B&Q getting some bits and bobs.'

Jane introduced herself and told him she'd like a new toilet seat, roll holder and towel rail fitted in the men's toilet on the fourth floor and a 'LADIES' sign fixed to the door.

He looked dubious. 'I'll need Jim's permission for all that.'

'Then please ask him as soon as he gets back. I'd like it done as soon as possible. Also, half of my office on the fourth floor is being used as a furniture storeroom.'

He grinned. 'I know, me and Jim had to carry it all up the bloody stairs as the lift was knackered.'

'I want the furniture and partition removed – today, preferably!'

Jane noticed an open toolbox on a shelf next to her. She removed a hammer, two screwdrivers and some pliers.

'I'll return these later.'

Returning to her office, Jane saw the Brittany Hall boxes on her desk, along with some files, leaving her no space to work. Maureen was not in sight, but pinned to the noticeboard was a list of all the offices and the various contact numbers for the senior AMIT detectives and incident room officers and civilian staff. Jane looked over it briefly before removing her jacket and rolling up her shirtsleeves. She looked closely at the partitions to see how they were held together, then picked up the pliers from her desk.

'This should do it,' she said to herself, and set about undoing the bolts that held each partition together. Having removed them, she hit the bracket joints with the hammer to separate the partitions. It was hard work dragging them and the chairs out to the landing, but very satisfying to see the larger office space open up, especially when she removed the boxes blocking the window.

Jane was almost finished when Maureen appeared, carrying two shopping bags. She looked stunned as she gazed around the room.

Maureen held up the shopping bags. 'I remembered to keep the receipt this time.'

Jane smiled. 'Any luck with getting a fridge?'

'Yes, it should be delivered later today or first thing in the morning.'

'You haven't gone and bought one, have you?' Jane worried that an expensive invoice might be rejected by Kernan without prior permission.

Maureen smiled mischievously.

'A few months ago, I was involved in a raid on a second-hand shop that was full of nicked gear. Amongst the property seized was a small fridge, which I've managed to get for us—'

'That's handling stolen goods, Maureen!' she interrupted.

'It's OK,' Maureen assured her. 'I spoke with the property store manager. He said no owner has been found for it so it would just be going to the property dump. Unfortunately he didn't have any toilet seats.'

Jane nodded. 'Did you speak to someone in the incident room about the toilet seat?'

'DS Otley. But he wasn't very helpful.' Maureen's face fell. 'Actually, he told me to "piss off" and the other detectives he was with just laughed.'

Jane sighed. 'Just ignore them, Maureen. I'll sort out the toilet seat. Right, let's raid the cleaners' cupboard and get this office ship-shape before we do anything else.'

It took over an hour to get rid of the cobwebs, hoover the carpet and scrub the stained areas. They discovered an air vent by the window was blocked with dust and bits of paper, and Jane had to stand on the small table to clean it. Maureen brought one of the chairs back from the landing for her to sit at the end of Jane's desk. Until they could find a suitable cupboard, Maureen put the toilet rolls and air sprays in some empty filing cabinet drawers.

By five o'clock, they were covered in dust and their hands felt grimy, and Maureen was relieved when Jane said they'd done enough for one day and it was time to head off home.

'Thank you, Maureen, you've been a real trouper. I'll be in early to start looking at the cold case I . . . sorry, I meant *we*, have been asked to review.'

After Maureen had left, Jane dusted herself off, ran her hands through her hair and made ready to go. It had been a long and frustrating day, but she was determined to show them she could take whatever Kernan or any of his team threw at her and prove she deserved to be on the AMIT team.

Picking up her briefcase, Jane glanced at the Brittany Hall file lying on her desk. She knew Kernan thought he was giving her an unsolvable cold case, to waste her time and keep her out of sight, but that only made her more determined to find out what had happened to her. Despite her fatigue, she felt a surge of adrenaline.

Nothing was going to stop her; the fight was on.

CHAPTER SIX

Jane was at the station by 7 a.m. so she could start reading through the Brittany Hall investigation files. The partitions were still propped up outside her office, along with the stacked chairs. She had been there for over an hour when the nauseating smell of fried food started to permeate the room. She got up and walked down to the canteen.

She got there just as the blinds were being rolled up over the counter. A woman wearing an overall with a white hairnet was spraying down the empty counter as Jane approached.

'It's not open yet, love.'

'I'm DCI Jane Tennison. I'm not here for breakfast, but to find out whether your extractor fans above the cookers are working properly.'

The woman turned towards the large array of hoods above the various gas rings and ovens.

'I know we had someone in a while back to look at them, so they should be working.'

'I don't think they are. My office is on the floor above and the smell of cooking fat is very strong. It's a health hazard and I'd like something done about it.'

The woman nodded. 'I'll speak with the canteen manager.'

Jane thanked her and went back to her office. Bill, the building manager's assistant, along with another man, was moving the furniture from the corridor. 'We'll store this lot in the basement,' he told her, making her wonder why they hadn't done that in the first place.

As she sorted through the files and put the statements in chronological order, the pungent smell of fried food got noticeably worse, presumably because the canteen was now serving breakfast.

By the time Maureen arrived just after 9 a.m., Jane had already pinned up photographs and a timeline on her noticeboard and had placed the files in order in the filing cabinets.

Maureen stopped in front of the noticeboard.

'Good heavens, you must have come in early.'

Jane smiled. 'I did . . . but before we get cracking, I'd like you to give me vignettes of the DCIs you've listed.'

'I'm sorry, ma'am, but I'm not sure what you mean.'

'A brief outline of who's who, Maureen, because as yet I have not been introduced to any of them. It would help to have a heads-up as to what I can expect.'

'Oh, I see . . . Well, I haven't been here that long, and to be honest I've not actually worked alongside any of them on any specific case. I've really been a sort of gofer between them, until you arrived.'

Jan nodded. 'OK, but who would you say is the top dog? Apart from Kernan.'

'That would be DCI John Shefford, he's very much the number one man. He's good friends with DCS Kernan, who seems to think a lot of him. He's a big guy with a big personality – he even played rugby for England a few times in his prime.'

'Why is he the number one here?'

'He's cracked some heavy-duty cases and he's a hard worker who expects his team to follow suit, and God forbid if anyone steps out of line. His team are hand-picked by him and when he says jump, they are all like big kids.'

'Is he married?'

'Yes, with two kids, but he's got quite an eye for the ladies. After one awful murder investigation he threw a big party for his team – I wasn't actually here then, but I was told there were strippers. He's always buying rounds at the pub so, as you can imagine, he's well liked.'

Jane nodded and then tapped the list. 'What about the DS who upset you, Bill Otley?'

Maureen sighed and bit her lip.

'He's not a very likeable man. He's Shefford's ears, hangs out with him and runs after him, like a dog. Actually, he looks like a whippet, he's that thin.'

'Is he married?'

'He lost his wife to cancer a few years ago. Again, I wasn't around then, but one of the clerical staff told me that he had a major drinking problem as a result and that Shefford saved his skin when it got out of control. I did come across him one night asleep under his desk, obviously too drunk to go home. I've always steered well away from him. It was stupid of me to ask him about the toilet seat.'

'Don't blame yourself, Maureen. When you say he's Shefford's ears, do you mean he snitches on colleagues?'

'Yes, I know he was responsible for getting one officer sacked but I don't know what it was about, just that you can't trust him.'

'Right . . . What about DCI Hickock?'

'He's a lot more friendly. I think he was from Australia originally. He's worked on some heavy-duty cases – in fact, he's away right now in Huddersfield on a big fraud investigation. Like Shefford, he has a good team around him and is well liked.'

'And is he married?' Jane asked, realising it was Brian Hickock Kernan had been speaking to on the phone.

Maureen looked embarrassed. 'No, he plays the field. He's quite good-looking.'

They spent the next half hour going through the backgrounds of the other officers until Jane felt she had enough knowledge under her belt. She now wanted to get working on her cold case and turned to the board, gesturing to the photographs she had pinned up.

'OK, the missing girl is a seventeen-year-old student called Brittany Hall. Five years ago, she disappeared from her college. She was last seen on Friday the thirteenth of June 1986, but wasn't reported missing to the local police until Monday the sixteenth by her parents.

'Three boys were the last people to see her on the Friday evening at a pub, and all three claimed that she was intoxicated and behaving stupidly. They left her there, but then one of them returned to check up on her and said he saw her getting into a red vehicle with two older men. It was initially determined she was probably a runaway. She'd been at the college for just three weeks, and had complained to her mother about being bullied and feeling out of place.'

Maureen smiled wryly. 'I know how she must have felt.'

'There was no CCTV footage and no other witnesses. I've been through all the statements and the reports made by the investigating officers, and was struck by just one line from the lead detective who said . . .'

Jane crossed to her desk and opened her notebook.

'OK, he said that after extensive enquiries they had no leads, but he felt the three boys were lying, based on the fact that their accounts of what happened that evening were almost identical. However, there was no actual evidence to confirm his suspicions.'

'If they all saw the same thing, then wouldn't you expect their statements to be identical?' a puzzled Maureen asked.

'Similar . . . yes. But identical . . . no,' Jane said. 'Everyone remembers things differently. Some people will notice certain details which will be overlooked by others. People standing in different locations will see and hear different things. I've read the boys' statements and think they colluded together to hide the truth. Why or what for, we don't know, but I'm determined to find out.'

Jane looked through one of the files, then removed a document and handed it to Maureen.

'These are the personal details the boys gave when they made their statements. I want you to check if they still live at the same addresses because I'll need to interview them.' She frowned. 'Your notebook, Maureen, you'll need it as I have a lot for you to start working on this morning.'

Maureen took her notebook out of her handbag. She had to search for a pencil, flushing as Jane pointed to a jar on the desk. Jane put two more documents down on her desk.

'This is the head of the college and the ex-detective who handled the original enquiry. I think first up will be organising a visit to Brittany's parents, so we'll need to start filling in the desk diary. Keep the appointments well spaced and start in the mornings, allowing time for the journeys. Right, I will leave it to you while I go and get some breakfast. When I get back, we can go through the evidence boxes.'

'Yes, ma'am,' Maureen said in a shaky voice, as if her new boss scared the pants off her.

Jane walked into the busy canteen, filled out her order slip, handed it over the counter and joined the queue for her food. No one acknowledged her presence, other than the odd glance in her direction. She heard the man in front of her joking with the serving lady she'd spoken to earlier.

'How about a few more chips and an extra sausage for your favourite detective?'

'You know I always give you a bit on the side?' She winked.

'Cheers, Hilda.' Turning with his tray, he cast a disdainful glance in Jane's direction. She didn't know him, but then remembered Maureen's description of DS Otley as being like a whippet. The slender, thin-faced man was clearly him.

Jane placed her food on the tray and asked Hilda if she had spoken to the canteen manager about the extractor fans.

'Yes, and she spoke to the building manager.'

Jane nodded. 'Thank you, Hilda.'

She carried her tray to a small corner table and sat with her back to the room to avoid making eye contact with anyone. She ate her scrambled eggs and toast quickly, drank her cup of coffee and was back in her office ten minutes later.

'How are we doing, Maureen?' she asked.

'Well, I haven't had much luck tracing new addresses and contact numbers, but I have found a new address for Sandra Hall,
Brittany's mother. It seems she got divorced and moved to a flat in
a high-rise block in Hammersmith. She was quite eager to speak
to you, so I made an appointment for between midday and one
p.m., if that's OK?'

Jane checked her watch and picked up her briefcase.

'Right, I'll head off there now, though I can't say I'm looking
forward to it. Talking about her daughter's disappearance is going
to be hard for her.'

Maureen nodded. 'The three boys have all moved and are working in various jobs . . . I hope to have more information later today.
The ex-detective was not at home, but his wife said he would be
there late afternoon.'

'Good, keep at it. What about the headmaster at the college?'

'I've not got as far as that yet. But it's a private college for senior
students "cramming" for exams.'

'OK, I'll call you later.'

Maureen picked up a thin file and handed it to Jane.

'There's photographs and statements along with the address
and contact number for Mrs Hall. By the way, I heard that DCI
Hickock is back from Huddersfield – something about a personal
situation.'

Jane nodded. 'See you later, Maureen – and good work.'

Jane went to their newly appointed ladies', washed her hands and
checked her appearance before taking the lift to the car park. Her
attempts to tidy up her hair were immediately undone by the gusts
of wind funnelling across the parking area.

She drove straight to Hammersmith, delighted that Maureen
had copied the relevant pages from the *A to Z* and highlighted
a direct route. Passing the Odeon cinema complex, she took a
turning towards the Thames and drove by some new builds with
balconies overlooking the river. The older high-rise block was

at the end of the narrow road, with parking bays running along one side.

Sandra Hall's flat was number 34 on the second floor.

Jane rang the bell and waited. It was only a moment before Sandra Hall opened the door and stood back as Jane held up her ID and was ushered into a small, neatly furnished sitting room. Above the fake coal fire, the mantelpiece was crammed with framed photographs of the missing girl, from a toddler to a teenager. More framed photographs were on the walls and also lined up on top of a small bureau. Jane could almost feel Mrs Hall's sense of loss.

'Thank you for seeing me, Mrs Hall.'

'I was so taken aback to get the call and to hear that the case is being reviewed. The young girl I spoke to explained that there was no good news, but further enquiries were being made. Even now it still gives me terrible anxiety . . . Every time the phone rings my heart jumps, but there's never any good news. Over the years my hope turned to despair, fearing Brittany will never be found alive and well.' She started to cry.

Jane put her hand on her shoulder. 'I don't know if Brittany is dead or alive, but I will do everything I can to find out what happened to her.'

'Thank you so much, that means a lot to me . . . and Brittany. Would you like a cup of tea?'

'I'm fine, thank you. Now I know you've probably been asked these questions a thousand times, but it would help to go over everything again from the beginning, if that's OK?'

Mrs Hall nodded. 'I understand. Please ask me anything you need to know.'

'Thank you, Mrs Hall. Firstly, please could you describe what your daughter Brittany was like? I know she was only at the college for a short time . . . What was she like before she went there?'

'She was very shy, and I would say she was quite naïve. When she was younger, she suffered from anxiety because she had a bad stammer which affected her speech. We had a speech tutor who helped her, and she was also diagnosed with a form of dyspraxia.'

'What's that?'

'I think that's the right word. She didn't have good balance and was forever bumping into things. We had her eyes tested but there was nothing wrong with them, she just didn't have good physical coordination. But she made up for that by being very academic. Her father was an accountant and we always said she had inherited her gift for maths from him. She was also quite artistic, but she avoided sports because of her dyspraxia. I think her problems started at grammar school because she felt left out of that side of things. We had a meeting with the headmaster, and he encouraged us to enrol her in the MEC, that's Master Education Council. It's privately run, and concentrates on teenagers who are mostly young high-achievers academically but who have other special needs. It gets them through GCSEs and then A-levels for university.'

'So MEC is a private college?'

'Yes, and very expensive. They offer one-to-one tutoring and really encourage their students to do well in life. They have boarders and day pupils.'

'What were the dormitories like?'

'Very well maintained with pleasant single rooms and some staff living there, along with medical staff if required. Many of the students are from abroad, in fact most of the students using the dormitory facility were foreign.'

Jane knew she had to ask the next question carefully.

'It must have been a big decision to change Brittany's school and have her living away from home.'

Jane knew she had hit a raw nerve, as Mrs Hall immediately tensed.

'My husband felt that we had been overprotective of her. I probably had been, I admit that, but he was adamant that this would be a good opportunity for Brittany to gain more confidence as she had never been away from home. Anyway, as it turned out, it was a decision we regretted and eventually, because of what happened, my husband and I separated and then got divorced.'

'Do you know where your husband lives now? I'll need to speak to him.'

'No. We haven't spoken in years. I did hear he had moved abroad, but I don't know where.'

Jane could see Mrs Hall was getting upset, so changed the subject from her husband. 'How did Brittany get on when she first started at the college?'

Mrs Hall removed a tissue from her cardigan pocket.

'She amazed me, because she seemed to really like being independent . . . well, independent up to a point. She called me a lot, but seemed to have adjusted to living away from home.'

'When did you find out that she was unhappy there?'

Mrs Hall sighed, twisting the tissue in her fingers.

'About three weeks after she started boarding at the college, she rang me in tears and said that it had all started again.'

'What had?'

'The bullying, being mimicked because of her stammer. And when she became anxious, it would affect her balance. So, I told her to just come home.'

'Did she say who was bullying her?'

'No, and regrettably I didn't ask. I just wanted her to come home.'

'Can you remember the exact date of that phone call?'

'It was a few days before the thirteenth, when she was last seen. I said if she wanted to pack her bags and leave, I would come and collect her. She didn't want me to and agreed to call me on the Friday and let me know how she was feeling about the situation.'

'How did your husband react to this?'

'He said I shouldn't encourage her to leave the college and to give her space to make her own decisions. He was certain it would all blow over and she'd change her mind.'

'But, you didn't receive a call from her on the Friday . . .'

'That's right, and we didn't hear from her over the weekend either. My husband told me not to call the college, but to just leave it. He was certain Brittany had calmed down and decided to stay. On the Monday morning I called the college and asked them not to bother her, but I was just checking if she was all right. Later that day I received a call from the headmaster, who said they were concerned as no one had seen Brittany since Friday evening. I immediately reported her missing. I wasn't aware at the time, but the headmaster had also reported her missing.'

Mrs Hall remained dry-eyed as she shook her head.

'At first they just assumed she'd run away. But when they found her clothes and all her possessions still in her room, the police's attitude changed. That's when they organised a massive search. It was in the news, on television and the newspapers.'

'Mrs Hall, in the files there was a note to suggest that your daughter had in fact run away on a previous occasion, is that correct?'

Mrs Hall frowned.

'That was long before she went to college . . . She was being bullied at her grammar school by a group of girls, who also took her calculator. She was upset and went to a friend of mine.'

'I don't wish to appear rude, but why did Brittany go to your friend's house?'

'Her father had only just bought the calculator for her. Brittany was scared of the girls and told him she'd lost it. He was annoyed with her and said she'd have to do extra house chores as a punishment. At the time she didn't have the courage to say she was being bullied and ran off to my friend's, who persuaded Brittany to tell us the truth. That was the start of us worrying about her staying at that school.'

'OK, thank you,' Jane said soothingly, picking up on Mrs Hall's increased agitation.

'The people you should be speaking to are those three boys. They're all filthy liars . . . They said they were in a pub with my Brittany, and she was drunk. She never drank, in fact she hated the taste of alcohol. Mr Morgan, he was the detective who led the investigation, he told me they were the last people to see Brittany and he thought they were lying about her getting in a sports car . . . but he couldn't prove it.'

Jane nodded. 'He's retired now, but I will be speaking with him. Did Brittany ever speak to you about the boys?'

'No. To be honest, Brittany wasn't interested in boys . . . She spent all her time studying hard so she could get into a good university.' She closed her eyes for a moment. 'If my husband had let me go to the college and bring her home that night, none of this would ever have happened . . . She'd have been at home with me, safe in my arms.'

Jane was ready to draw the interview to a close. Even though she now had more of a personal insight into Brittany's life before she went missing, there had been nothing new gained from the meeting that was not already recorded in the files.

She thanked Mrs Hall for her time and stood to leave.

'I've got some photographs of Brittany if you want them.'

Jane knew there were already plenty in one of the files, but not wishing to offend Mrs Hall, accepted her offer, waiting until she brought an envelope to put them in. She put it in her briefcase and Mrs Hall accompanied her to the door.

'You know we went to that college day after day, trying to question those boys but we were not allowed to. My husband said we were achieving nothing. So I kept going on my own. One afternoon I was heading down through the arches outside the college entrance when this girl approached me. She suddenly appeared from behind one of the pillars and seemed very nervous. She told me she'd seen the boys huddled together behind the groundsman's shed, talking. She knew they'd been spoken to by the police, so crept up on them to listen. She heard one of them saying, "This is bad, real bad, John, what if they find her?" Then another voice said to shut up and stick to the story, before they all walked off.'

Jane's eyes lit up. 'Do you know the girl's name?'

'No, she only said she was frightened of them and ran off.'

'Did you tell Inspector Morgan about it?'

'Not directly. I phoned the station and one of his detectives came to see me, but I can't remember his name now. I gave him a description of the girl.'

Jane was now eager to leave because she had just been told something that was not in any of the files. It could be that Mrs Hall was exaggerating, or just desperate, but she had a gut feeling that it might produce a lead.

CHAPTER SEVEN

Jane used a call box to contact Maureen, who proceeded to tell her about the further work she'd done to trace the three boys. 'I've found out where they're now living. One of them works on an oil rig, though, which could make interviewing him tricky. But he does come home to stay with his mother occasionally.' Jane told her it was already mid-afternoon, and the information could wait until she was back in the office, as she was keen to interview Francis Hardcastle, the head of the college.

'I spoke briefly with him earlier. He said he's happy to speak to you, but I didn't make a confirmed appointment time . . .'

'I'm going directly there, so don't bother making an appointment,' Jane said. 'You've worked hard today, so head off home if you want and I'll see you first thing in the morning.'

MEC college was located near Ascot and looked impressive at first glance. At one time it had been a sprawling Victorian manor house with manicured lawns. Now there was a modern structure attached to one side, with signs directing visitors towards the glass double doors leading to the reception area.

Jane drove slowly down the S-shaped lane, passing the new building, which appeared to be quite empty, then continuing on to the main house.

She parked in the visitors' bay, and made her way to the main entrance. Jane rang the bell that had a small notice printed above it saying 'House Master'.

While she waited, a small coach full of students drove in and headed towards the new extension.

Eventually the front door was opened by a young woman wearing a black gown over a business suit. She smiled as Jane held up her ID and asked to speak to Mr Hardcastle.

'Do you have an appointment?'

'No, I'm afraid not . . . but it is rather important.'

'Do come in, then. I am Francesca Gordon, the student liaison officer. I'll just go and see if Mr Hardcastle is still in his office. It's choir practice in the Hall today, so he might have to leave for that. I'm sorry, I didn't catch your name?'

'Detective Chief Inspector Jane Tennison.'

Jane sat on one of a row of polished hard-backed chairs in the oak-panelled hallway. Miss Gordon returned after a few minutes, and ushered Jane along the hall to an open door. Miss Gordon gave it a light tap, then gestured for Jane to go ahead of her.

'Detective Chief Inspector Jane Tennison for you, Mr Hardcastle.'

The room was panelled like the entrance hall and dominated by huge floor-to-ceiling bookcases. An ancient-looking desk was stacked with manuscripts and files.

Francis Hardcastle was a tall, middle-aged man with gaunt features and a prominent hooked nose. He held out his hand and Jane shook it.

'Inspector, please do sit down. May I order you a cup of tea, or perhaps a sherry, as it's getting to be about that time?'

'No thank you, Mr Hardcastle. I will get straight to the reason I'm here as I am aware that you have choir practice. I should have made an appointment, but I was in the area and thought I'd chance it – so thank you for agreeing to speak to me.'

Hardcastle moved round to sit behind his desk. Jane noticed that his suit was rather worn and the sleeves of his jacket were too short. He gave her a quizzical look as she rested her briefcase on her knee.

'I am reinvestigating the case of the disappearance of Brittany Hall, a student at this college five years ago.'

Hardcastle made a short intake of breath, hesitating for a moment.

'Yes, at the time I gave the police every possible assistance . . . but if there's anything more I can do, of course I'd be happy to.'

'Thank you. Firstly, I apologise if you are going to be repeating information that you have already provided. I was also wondering if there are any photographs of Brittany's class, or perhaps a college photograph showing all the students in the same year?'

'Yes, we will have them in the archive files.'

'Were you not asked for these when she went missing?'

'I can't recall, to be honest, but I will check with my secretary. It will probably take until tomorrow morning, when she is here. I have to say that Brittany's disappearance really was a very emotional and unsettling period for everyone at the college. I felt terrible that we did not discover she was missing until after the weekend. We do have a number of students that return to their families at the weekend, but we keep a log. It was a serious misjudgement that her room was not checked, and it was not until the Monday that the alarm was raised.'

Jane opened her briefcase and removed a file, placing it on his desk. Mr Hardcastle looked at his watch and Jane gave him a small smile.

'I will try to keep this as brief as possible . . . or if necessary, I can return at a more suitable time.'

In the end, Jane remained with Mr Hardcastle for forty-five minutes. He was very cordial and patient, but when he was asked about the three male students who were the last people to see Brittany, he become less informative. He told her that the three boys were academically bright, one gaining a place at Oxford, another gaining high A level results and the third being a very athletic student and captain of their cricket team.

'You know, these were young adults, and whether or not I approve of them drinking is irrelevant. They returned to college that Friday evening and were not in any way inebriated. I know they said they hardly knew Brittany and found it all very distressing.'

'Brittany was very shy and reserved. Don't you think it was odd that she would go to the pub?'

He shrugged. 'As I say, what the students do in their own time is not really my business.'

'Can you tell me anything else about the boys? Did they have any learning difficulties or mental health issues? Is that why they left school?'

'Absolutely not. Many of the UK students come to MEC having failed previous exams, and yes, some of them suffer from anxiety issues or even, in a very small number of cases, eating disorders. But that was not the case with these students.'

He looked pointedly at his watch, and Jane decided to conclude the interview. 'I'd just like to make a note of Brittany's tutors, and the school matron in case Brittany had any medical issues.'

It was now after 5 p.m. and Mr Hardcastle was already late for choir practice, so Jane agreed to join Miss Gordon for a tour of the college. She left his office and waited in the hall, flipping through the pages in her notebook to make sure she had recorded everything.

Miss Gordon came in via the main front door with a map of the college grounds and, for the next half hour, Jane followed her through well-appointed classrooms, an impressive science lab, the manicured grounds with its lush cricket pitch, the canteen and the main student dormitory with its small but well-designed rooms.

'I'm afraid if you want to talk to any of the current students about Brittany, most of them wouldn't have been here at the same time,' Miss Gordon said. 'The majority of students are usually enrolled for three to four years, so the turnover is substantial term by term.'

Miss Gordon walked with her to her car, and Jane noticed the coach she'd seen earlier driving into the lane with many students wearing sports kit on board.

'Oh yes,' Miss Gordon explained. 'A big rugby match this afternoon.'

'How many students are there here?' Jane asked.

'Oh, I would say about a hundred.'

'It's all very impressive and obviously must cost a lot to run.'

'It does, but we have numerous benefactors. In fact, that extension was funded by a very wealthy Chinese family. I think they are so grateful of their children's success . . . We have a very high success rate for Oxford and Cambridge places each year.'

'Thank you for the tour, Miss Gordon. Would you be kind enough to remind Mr Hardcastle about the photographs? If he calls my office when he has located them, then I will send someone to collect them – it is very important.'

'Yes, of course.'

'Just one more thing, could the names of the students be printed on the back of the photograph, just to avoid me having to ask who's who?'

'Yes, of course.'

Miss Gordon waved as Jane drove off. The college was very impressive, she had to admit: wonderful facilities and successful, happy students with rich, grateful parents. But somehow it all seemed too good to be true.

For all his helpfulness, there was something Mr Hardcastle was not telling her, and she was determined to find out what it was.

CHAPTER EIGHT

As Jane sat at home having a takeaway curry, she thought about who the best person would be to interview next, deciding that she really needed to have a talk with the retired detective who had led the initial enquiry.

She also made a mental note to take her clothes to the dry cleaner's. Her new suit was filthy from making her office more habitable, and as she emptied her pockets, she found Peter's business card.

She called Pam at home, hoping to speak to Tony, so she was relieved when he answered.

'Hi, Tony, sorry it's a bit late . . . I'm thinking about taking a look at your health club.'

'When were you thinking?'

'Well, I could do it really early in the morning or after I finish work tomorrow evening.'

'I can meet you there at seven a.m. tomorrow, if you like. I can't do the evening, I'm taking the boys to football – unless you want to go later in the week?'

'No, I'm always up early, so seven is good for me. So, if it's all right with you, I'll meet you there?'

'OK, see you at the club tomorrow. Do you want to talk to Pam?'

'No, it's late, don't bother her, but give her my love.'

Jane hung up quickly, afraid that Tony was going to get Pam on the line for a lengthy conversation about her salon or their parents.

It was after 11 p.m. when her phone rang.

'It's Tony . . . Listen, I forgot that I had to take Pam to pick up new supplies for the salon first thing in the morning. I called Peter and he said he would be at the club then anyway, and he'd be happy to show you around. Is that OK with you?'

'Yes, that's fine, thanks for arranging it.'

Jane hung up, pleased that she'd done the right thing by asking Tony first, but that it would be Peter showing her round the club.

* * *

The Chelsea Sports Club was situated in a small side street near a new build area around Chelsea Bridge, with exclusive apartments that had riverside views. It was a new building on two floors with parking bays beside the main entrance. There was a large glass double-doored entrance with the club's logo written in thick gold letters, and there was also a small underground car park to the rear of the building.

Jane walked into the spacious reception area and a young girl wearing a pale blue overall with the club's logo on her breast pocket looked up and smiled pleasantly. Jane approached the desk as the main door opened behind her.

'Good morning, Corinna, this is my guest. I'm here to show her all the amenities, and hopefully she will be impressed enough to become a member.'

'Good morning, Peter. That's fine. You have a squash court booked for eight a.m., do you want it confirmed?'

'No, I'll need to cancel that, Corinna. My partner can't make it. Unless you fancy a game, Jane?'

Jane smiled. 'Unfortunately I don't have any sports kit in my car.'

Corinna asked Jane to sign the visitors' book. 'I hope you find the club to your liking. I have lots of leaflets that I can give you about the various classes we offer, and the club's rules if you decide to become a member.'

'I think we'll get everything from you when she leaves,' Peter said. 'I just need to stash my gear before I show her around.'

Peter was dressed in a light grey tracksuit with a white T-shirt and trainers. He took Jane by the shoulder and guided her out to the club's entrance.

She saw the ladies' shower room and lockers, and then they headed down to the basement to the two squash courts, which were both occupied. As they passed the viewing area Peter received waves of acknowledgement from other members, and then they continued to the indoor sauna and steam rooms.

As they headed back to the main floor, Peter explained that plans were also in progress to build a full-length swimming pool.

'Do you fancy a coffee?' he asked. 'The café's now open for breakfast.'

'Great,' Jane replied. 'I expect it'll be better than the station canteen.'

They sat side by side at the bar and ordered two coffees and two bacon sandwiches.

'So, what do you think?'

'I'm keen to join. I really need to start exercising again. I used to belong to a club where I was last stationed . . . Actually, it was even before that, when I belonged to a club in Fulham.'

'I hope you don't mind me not introducing you with your rank. I just thought that as you would be here in your personal time you might not want people knowing you're a police officer?'

'Thank you. Some people can get a little defensive, or else I end up getting the usual jokes.'

'Are you going to start playing squash again?'

'It's a long time since I've played. I'm not sure how good I'll be.'

'I could give you a game to ease you back gently,' Peter offered.

'Then I guess we'll find out how rusty I am!'

'It's a deal. So you've just started working at a new station? That must be stressful.'

Jane made a face. 'A little bit.'

She was enjoying his company and didn't want to spoil the mood by explaining how much she felt discriminated against.

'So tell me about you. Tony's told me you have been very generous, offering him a lot of work.'

'He's very good, and hard-working. I always need a lot of carpentry work done as my property business buys and renovates not just houses, but offices and warehouses. You can see how much building is going on in this area, which means I need a reliable and experienced team. Making Tony a part of it has been very productive. And I also enjoy our squash games – allows me to let off steam and vent my frustrations!'

'Is it your own company?'

She noticed a slight hesitation.

'No . . . well, not as yet. I built the company up with a partner over the past fifteen years or more, but I now have a situation that is making it all very difficult.' He paused, obviously not wanting to elaborate. 'Would you like another coffee?'

'No, I should be getting to the station.'

They were just about to leave when a young man in a white tracksuit approached and asked Peter if he was up for a game, as there had been a cancellation on court one.

'Perfect timing, I can be with you in five minutes,' Peter said. He walked with Jane to the reception, then leaned forwards and gave her a light kiss on the cheek.

'It was nice seeing you again, and if you do decide to join, please call me.'

After he'd gone, Corinna showed Jane the various membership packages. The options were all more expensive than Jane had anticipated, even with the 'Friend of a Member' discount, but she realised now how much she wanted to join.

'Give me the form to sign and I'll write you a cheque,' she said with a smile.

Maureen was at her desk when Jane breezed into the station.

'Can you ring DI Morgan? I want to meet him as soon as possible. And can you check with Mr Hardcastle about the photographs? I'd like them asap, too.'

'Do you want me to go to Ascot?' Maureen asked. 'It's just that I don't drive, so I'll have to get public transport.'

'No, we should be able to arrange a courier – I do need them as soon as possible. I'd like to interview the boys, too, but you said none of them were local. The one who works on a rig, though: could you contact his mother and see when he's next due home? Then if you could start checking the evidence boxes and start listing the contents.'

'Yes, ma'am.' Maureen quickly got to work and Jane decided to ring DI Morgan herself. He eventually agreed to meet at 10.15, but was not very accommodating, saying he doubted he could give her any information that was not already in the files. As she drove to his house in Wandsworth, her buoyant spirits were beginning to decline.

Arriving at a semi-detached house in a row of Victorian properties, Jane rang the bell and waited. Eventually it was opened by a woman in a wraparound apron with rollers in her hair. A gruff voice called from behind her.

'I said I'd get it, go on – get back into the kitchen.'

The woman grimaced and turned back into the hall as an overweight, thick-set man with grey hair appeared in the doorway. Jane held up her ID and he opened the door wider, standing to one side as she squeezed past him.

'First door on your right.'

The room was gloomy, with a dark green fitted carpet, and the curtains were partly closed. The walls were lined with bookcases and there was a mahogany sideboard filled with framed photographs and china ornaments. Morgan sat down heavily on a worn-looking settee and indicated an easy chair.

Jane sat. 'Thank you for agreeing to speak with me.'

'You didn't give me much option, did you? I spent a long time – years – looking for that missing girl. I had good men working alongside me, too, but with no result. Don't for a second think that was easy to deal with – it was one of the few unsolved cases I ever worked on in a thirty-year career.'

'I want to ask you about some information I received that wasn't in your case file.'

'Enlighten me,' he replied tersely, looking dubious.

'I spoke with Sandra Hall.' Jane then recounted how the young collège girl had approached Sandra and told her about the boys' conversation behind the shed. She looked at her notes.

'She heard one of them saying, "This is bad, real bad, John, what if they find her?" Then someone else said to shut up and stick to the story before they all walked off.'

Morgan sighed, then shook his head. 'Well, she never told me that. If she had, I would have followed it up.'

'In fairness, Mrs Hall did say she didn't speak to you personally about it, but definitely informed one of your detectives who came to her home address.'

Morgan said nothing for a few moments, scratching his head while clearly deep in thought, trying to cast his memory back five years.

'Hang on, I remember now . . . There was a detective who told me about it. He thought Mrs Hall was making it up.'

Jane was surprised. 'Why on earth would he think that?'

'Because she'd been to the school time and time again trying to confront the boys. She'd become obsessed with proving they were involved in her daughter's disappearance. It was also thought to be questionable because the girl apparently never said her name and Mrs Hall's description of her was very vague.'

'That doesn't mean it wasn't true.'

'That's why I told the detective it didn't matter what he thought, and to make enquiries at the college to see if there was a girl who matched the description Mrs Hall had given him.'

'And the result was . . . ?'

'Another dead end. Personally, I couldn't understand, if the girl really existed, why she hadn't come forward and told us herself.'

'But none of this was in your report.'

'I know, but only because I thought it would reflect badly on Mrs Hall if she had made it up. I knew the boys were lying because

their version of events was identical. I went over all the information and statements we'd gathered time and time again to find a
crack in their stories. I can't even remember now how many times
I interviewed them, but it was all to no avail.'

'If you were to make a guess, which one of the three boys do you
think was the ringleader?'

'Without a doubt, John Kilroy.'

'And what do you think happened to Brittany?'

Morgan sighed, then raised his hands. 'I don't know, but I believe
she's dead and those boys were involved. When Brittany was first
reported missing, uniform dealt with the investigation and mistakes
were made. Mrs Hall had told them about Brittany being bullied
and she was considering leaving the college. This made them think
from the start she was a runaway. If they had bothered to search
her room, they'd have realised none of her personal belongings were
missing and called in CID a lot earlier. The boys were the last people
to see her, so their account of events should have been thoroughly
scrutinised, and, I would argue, their clothing seized for forensics,
but it never happened.'

'I read in your report there was some CCTV, but I haven't been
able to view it yet.'

'It was very poor quality. I recall there were a few shots of Brittany
on it, and I think a car, but it was impossible to identify the make
or occupants. Personally, I think that's another thing the boys lied
about. After extensive enquiries we were never able to trace a red
sports car, and nobody at the pub had seen one in the car park. But
it's all water under the bridge now, and sadly I don't think Brittany's
body will ever be found. That's all I can tell you.'

Jane could tell he was still genuinely upset he hadn't been able to
find Brittany or prove she'd been murdered, and there was no point
in pressing him for more information.

'Thanks for your time, DI Morgan. I'll let you know if we make
any progress.'

Jane returned to her car and drove off. It had not been an entire waste of time, as it was still possible the girl who spoke to Mrs Hall did exist and what she said was true. She stopped at a phone box to call Maureen, asking if she had started on the evidence boxes and whether they contained any copies of the CCTV footage. Maureen told her she had put two old cassettes to one side that were labelled CCTV, along with poor-quality still photographs taken from the tapes.

'You'll need a video cassette player. I think there's one in the incident room . . . or I could see if there's one in the property store.'

'Don't bother, I'll get a small TV with a video cassette player for the bedroom in my new flat and use that to view the CCTV. Did you hear from Mr Hardcastle?'

'Yes, his secretary told me he has found three photographs. I tried to order a police courier bike, but got a lot of flak from DCI Shefford as they were in use – so I told his secretary to put them in a taxi.'

'Christ, that's going to cost.'

'You said it was urgent – maybe the college will pay?'

Jane ended the call with Maureen, then drove to the nearest electrical goods store close to her flat and bought a sixteen-inch television with an integral video cassette player. But frustratingly, when she got it home she found only one TV aerial outlet in her flat, which was in the lounge. It was early evening by the time Jane returned to the station.

The taxi had delivered the photographs from the college, and Maureen had paid twelve pounds from her own pocket, but at least had got a receipt. Jane told her to clip the receipt to all the other items she had paid for and submit them to the admin clerk for reimbursement. Maureen was embarrassed to say that she was cash broke, and so Jane gave her ten pounds out of her own wallet.

'Thank you,' Maureen said, blushing.

'That's all right, Maureen. Why don't you go home and we'll go through everything tomorrow morning.'

Jane was eager to see the photographs and cleared her desk so she could lay them out properly. The largest image was of the class sitting together rather formally. The group comprised twelve students – Brittany, four other girls and seven boys. The second image was of a small group standing beside a piano, three different female students with Brittany sitting at the piano. The last photograph was of four students standing on the steps of the main house: Brittany with the same three girls, looking as if they were wearing some kind of Greek costume.

Turning the photographs over, Jane was pleased to see that the names of each of the students had been written in neat felt-tip pen.

Jane checked her watch, then put the photographs into an envelope and then into her briefcase, along with the video cassettes. It was almost 7.30 p.m. by the time she arrived at Mrs Hall's. She knew she should have warned her that she was intending to visit, but she hadn't wanted to risk her saying no.

On seeing Jane at her front door, Mrs Hall looked worried, but relaxed when Jane explained what it was about. They sat side by side on the sofa as Jane eased out one photograph after another from the envelope. She had chosen the sofa as it had a lamp positioned behind it and she wanted as much light as possible.

'Now, I want you to take your time, Mrs Hall. Please look very carefully at all of these photographs and see if you can identify the girl that spoke to you at the college.'

'Oh, it was such a long time ago . . . so I doubt I will be able to recognise her.'

'Don't worry. If it helps, close your eyes for a moment and think back to that time the girl approached you. You were very nervous, very worried, and then she suddenly appeared from behind the pillar in the courtyard'

Mrs Hall was shaking, sitting with her hands tightly clenched together. But she did as Jane had instructed, taking a long time studying first the large photograph, then the second. Then she picked up the third one, holding it closer before placing it back down.

Her voice was hardly audible, and then she pointed.

'I am certain it is this girl . . . She's not in the second photograph, but she's in the first and third – it's the girl with the short dark curly hair.'

Jane took out a pencil and carefully made a ring around the girl's face. Mrs Hall became more confident.

'It's her hair, you know, it's a sort of 1920s style – yes, I'm certain that this is the girl who spoke to me. They were doing a Greek play or something, and I remember Brittany telling me how worried she was because of her stammer. They made the costumes, I think.'

'Did you recognise any of the other girls?'

'No.'

'Did you ever receive any letters or postcards from Brittany when she was at the college?'

'No, we just spoke on the phone.'

Jane's heart was thumping. She turned one of the photographs over to see who the girl was.

'We have made some headway, Mrs Hall – thank you so much. I will be in contact as soon as I have anything further to tell you.'

Driving home, Jane's heart rate quietened down, but she was still excited. This was a huge development, the first major step forward since she had taken over the case. She now knew the girl was called Edwina Summers, and that she had been seventeen at the time. The following morning she would contact the college and get her full contact details so she could interview her.

She made a tuna salad sandwich when she got home, but any thought of having an early night was out of the question. She sat in the lounge with her sandwich and a glass of wine, using the remote to switch on the television. She then jumped up as she remembered the video cassettes in her briefcase.

It was a while before she worked out how to switch the viewing over to the video player and, as promised, the black and white footage was very poor quality.

The film was very grainy and white lines crossed the screen, but then the picture cleared slightly before the relevant footage appeared on the screen. Brittany could be seen standing outside a double-doored bar exit, then turning to her right. It looked as if she was crying, as she was rubbing at her face. She then turned left and walked out of frame. The second video cassette had an even darker and grainier version of the same footage.

Jane leaned back. She had seen many photographs of Brittany by now, but somehow she was still shocked to see how young she was, wearing woollen tights and ankle boots, and a short puffer jacket. She was also very pretty.

CHAPTER NINE

Jane arrived at the station just before 8 a.m. the following morning. She was heading down the corridor when the door to the ladies' opened and a burly man with an unruly haircut stepped out.

'Excuse me, but there is a sign on the door saying this is a ladies' toilet.'

'Excuse me for living! Are you DCI Tennison?'

'Yes, and you are?'

'DCI Brian Hickock. Can I have a quick word? It's about a personal situation.'

Jane led Hickock into her office and offered him a coffee, which he declined on the basis he was pushed for time and had a train to catch to Huddersfield.

'A golfing friend of mine, Martin Jenkins, returned home from work a couple of days ago to find that his wife, Serina, had committed suicide by hanging herself. As you can imagine, he's in a terrible state and his head is all over the place.'

'That's terrible, I'm sorry for his loss,' Jane replied, wondering why Hickock was telling her about it.

'Kernan let me have some time off to visit him. Anyway, Martin called me because he doesn't really understand what is going on. There's been a big development in my fraud case and I've got to go back to Huddersfield. Kernan suggested you could maybe help me out.'

'Exactly what do you want me to do? I'm right in the middle of an investigation myself.'

'Martin was told there would be a postmortem, but he's heard nothing more from the uniform officers who attended, and the Fulham coroner's officer has gone off sick. Obviously, he wants to know what's happening and when her body will be released for burial. I was able to speak with a mortician. He said there was a backlog of bodies in the fridges and the PM hasn't been done yet, though it might be today or tomorrow. I'm just trying to help a grieving friend out, but I have to get back to Huddersfield and can't do much more at the moment.'

Jane was irritated, but didn't want to seem uncaring. 'OK. I'll go to Fulham mortuary and see what's happening, then update your friend. I'll need his and his wife's details, though.'

'Thanks, I really appreciate your help, and so will Martin. I left an envelope with Kernan – everything you should need is in it.'

Hickock walked out as Maureen was coming into the office.

'Morning, sir!' she said brightly, but he passed her without saying a word. She unbuttoned her coat, placing it over her chair. 'What did he want?'

Jane didn't want to discuss it. 'I have made some progress on our misper case. Mrs Hall was able to identify the girl who warned her about the three boys – Edwina Summers. So, I need you to get on to the college and get her contact details as soon as possible. I want to talk to her before I get on to the three boys.'

The desk phone rang, and Maureen answered, then covered the mouthpiece. 'It's Kernan for you.'

'Good morning, sir, I was just on my way down to see you. DCI Hickock just mentioned that . . .' She listened for a moment before replacing the handset.

As Jane passed their toilet, she saw their sign had been tossed on the floor. Someone had drawn a leaking penis over the word 'LADIES'. She kicked it to one side.

As Jane approached Kernan's office, two officers were walking down the corridor, and she gave them both a bright smile. 'Good morning!'

Neither man responded as they walked past her. She knocked on Kernan's door and waited for his gruff 'Come in' before entering.

He was sitting at his desk, working on his HOLMES computer as she walked in and closed the door behind her.

'You have been busy, DCI Tennison. I hear you've asked for the kitchen extractor fans to be replaced. The station has a tight budget, you know, and besides, they were examined not that long ago and were in perfect working order.'

'I disagree, sir. There is an overpowering smell of cooking on the fourth floor. Whether they require replacing or repair, I feel it should be a priority.'

Kernan swivelled round in his chair to face her.

'I have also received numerous invoices – I really have more pressing work to be getting on with than authorising payment for a new toilet seat.'

'Yes, sir.'

'Now, I haven't yet received an update on the cold case review.'

'I have made some progress, sir. I had a breakthrough last night and intend following it up today and will make out a report as soon as I have more information.'

'Is that connected to the three boys that were questioned at the time?'

'No, it's concerning the girl that spoke to the missing girl's mother. That girl was never traced or questioned, and . . .'

Kernan shook his head.

'So the reality is that you've made very little progress.'

Jane bit her lip and decided the wisest thing to do would be to change the subject.

'DCI Hickock mentioned he'd spoken with you about his friend Martin Jenkins' wife committing suicide and—'

'Yes, it's not something we would normally get involved in but I didn't feel it would be right to ignore the situation. Bloody uniform and coroner's officer need a kick up the backside. It's a disgrace, leaving the poor man in the dark after his wife just hanged herself.'

'I believe he left some paperwork and contact details for Jenkins with you?'

Without even a thank you, Kernan passed Jane an envelope, then eased his chair back to indicate the meeting was over. She walked out, tight-lipped, and headed back to her office.

Maureen had used some air freshener to mask the smell of fried food, but it was still permeating the office unpleasantly.

'I have to go to Fulham mortuary but hopefully I won't be too long,' Jane said. 'I've booked an appointment at my new gym for a yoga class at seven and I'm really looking forward to it – might even have a sauna as well.'

Maureen smiled ruefully, thinking that it was all right for some. Jane opened the envelope Kernan had given her and noted Martin Jenkins' details, as well as the details of the incident: Jenkins had discovered his wife's body at 6.30 p.m. on returning home, and the times the ambulance and police had been called had also been recorded. Serina Jenkins had used electric cord, which she tied to the bannister rail. She then placed it round her neck and jumped from the first floor.

Meanwhile, Maureen had already contacted the college and had been transferred from one department to another while they tried unsuccessfully to find a forwarding address for Edwina Summers.

'I got the feeling there might have been some kind of problem,' she told Jane. 'I mean, surely, they retain records of previous students?'

'Tell you what, Maureen, why don't you get on to the matron? She might recall if Brittany or Edwina had any medical issues. Somebody has to know how we track her down.'

Jane drove to Fulham mortuary and was told that Felix Markham, the pathologist, had just completed the Serina Jenkins PM and was still in the swill room. Jane was pleased with her good timing, but it was still half an hour before he appeared, wearing an odd combination of baggy clothes and sandals.

'Right, young lady. We need to be quick as I've got an important meeting to attend.'

'Do you need me to gown up?'

'No, let's not waste any more time.'

Felix pushed open the double doors to the swill room. On a trolley lay a body covered by a green tarpaulin. A mortuary attendant handed Felix a clipboard as he approached the trolley. Jane took out her notebook and dropped her bag at her feet.

'Cause of death was cardiac arrest brought on by asphyxiation from the electric cable around her neck. The bruising on her neck is consistent with hanging herself.'

'She didn't die at the scene?'

'No, resuscitation attempts were unsuccessful, and she died in the ambulance en route to the hospital. The electric cable is bagged and tagged, along with her clothing. She was fully dressed in a cashmere sweater and pleated skirt, but with no footwear. Her underwear and tights were intact.'

Jane glanced over to a side table at the cardboard boxes containing the items he had just described.

'I'm sorry, Felix, can I just ask who removed the cable?'

'I was told her husband said he tried to remove it when he found her, but it was too tight. Then he called the ambulance . . . so I can only assume they removed it. Now, let's have a look at her. I hope you are not going to faint on me.'

'This isn't my first postmortem,' Jane said with a frown.

'Jolly good, now here we go . . .'

Felix slowly pulled down the green cover from Serina Jenkins' head and shoulders. The deep indentations around her neck were disturbing, along with the Y-shaped closure stitches from the PM, but Jane could still see that she had been a good-looking young woman.

Felix looked at his clipboard, then put it down on the victim's chest as he eased out her right hand.

'Now, you can see she has two broken nails, which by the way are false. I found no visible blood residue or fibres beneath any of her fingernails. If we walk round to the other side . . .'

Felix then withdrew the left hand.

'Again, we have one broken false nail. You will find the false nails boxed and listed.'

Jane made notes as she accompanied Felix back to the other side.

'Would you say that she might have tried to loosen the wire from her neck? Could that be why the nails were broken?'

'There are no visible signs on her neck, but it is possible.'

Felix picked up his clipboard again and glanced down at his notes before passing it back to his assistant. He now pulled back the green cloth completely and held it up to be taken from him.

'Right, she was in good physical shape, with good muscle tone. Her septum is perforated and there's congealed blood in her nostrils. Also, there are signs of ante-mortem bruising on the back of her head and chest.'

'Do you think she was assaulted before her death?'

'I can't rule it out, but I have seen suicide by hanging cases where there's an injury to the back of the head. Sometimes when a person jumps from a balcony, or in this case a stairwell, they fall backwards and hit their head hard on the bannister or protruding edge of the platform. In addition to causing potential brain damage, the whiplash effect can cause blood vessels in the nose to burst, which could account for the blood in her nasal passage.'

'Would the damage to the back of her head render her unconscious?'

'Yes, her skull was fractured, and her brain showed signs of a subdural haematoma, bleeding between the brain and the skull. I would say she was probably in a coma while hanging from the bannister.'

'So, she wouldn't have felt any pain as she suffocated?'

'Correct, it could also slow down the time it would take to die. The centralised bruising on her chest was almost certainly caused by the ambulance crew attempting CPR chest compressions. Moving down the torso, note the bruising on both kneecaps ... This most likely occurred when she fell to the floor, her legs buckled, and her knees took the impact.'

Jane looked quizzical. 'How would her feet hit the floor if she hanged herself from the bannister?'

Felix shrugged. 'She probably misjudged the length, and or the wire stretched when she jumped. The wire used will take about seventy to eight pounds before stretching or breaking. And in answer to your next question, your victim is a petite ninety-four pounds.'

'What about stomach contents?' Jane asked.

'The remnants of a cheese sandwich and some biscuits. Chocolate digestives, by the looks of it.'

Felix held out his hand for the green sheet and rather theatrically shook it out before draping it over the body again.

'That's it, my dear. My report will be forthcoming and will obviously contain more detail. I can always be contacted if required.'

'One last thing,' Jane said.

'Make it quick, please.'

'Do you think her death is suspicious in any way, or a definite suicide?'

'As I said, cause of death was cardiac arrest brought on by asphyxiation.' He gave her a sickly smile. 'But whether she jumped or was pushed, I can't say.'

CHAPTER TEN

It was 1.30 p.m. and Maureen was about to go to the canteen when the matron from MEC college returned her call, explaining that she didn't recall Brittany having any medical issues, but Edwina Summers had suffered from a food allergy while at the college. Before she could see a specialist, however, she had been discovered smoking marijuana and came close to being expelled.

'I was informed that she would not be returning for the following term, but I was not given any further details. I only retained her records because of the food allergy tests and the specialist's contact details, in case I needed them for any other student suffering from similar allergies,' she added.

'Do you have contact details for her family?' Maureen asked.

'Yes, we always have to inform parents if we have medical issues that require an outside specialist.'

Maureen took down an address in Kent. She was about to end the call when the matron added that she had tried to contact them but had not received a reply.

'She was here on a music scholarship, very talented. But I was concerned about her – she was such a nervous young woman. I do hope she's all right.'

Jane had been waiting to speak with PC Eric Thompson for twenty minutes at Fulham Road station. So far, all she had been able to discover was that there had been no CID investigation of Serina Jenkins' death, but they were waiting for the coroner's report. She was beginning to feel her visit was a waste of her time when PC Thompson finally appeared, and she was led to a small interview room at the station, where she asked him if he could go through the events of the evening of Serina Jenkins' death.

He thought for a moment. 'That's not one I'll easily forget, ma'am. Myself and PC Myers responded to a 999 call as we were in close proximity, just off the Fulham Road. We arrived at the house just before seven p.m. Martin Jenkins was in the hallway in a distraught state. The ambulance was already there, and the medics were attempting to resuscitate his wife, who was on the hallway floor below.'

'What did Mr Jenkins say when you got there?'

'Like I say, he was very distraught and kept repeating he had come home and found his wife hanging. He cut the cable with some pliers, and because she wasn't breathing, he thought she was dead.'

'Did the ambulance crew say anything to you?'

'She was unconscious when they got there, but they found a faint pulse and immediately started CPR. In fact, they were still doing it as they wheeled her out to the ambulance.'

'Then what happened?' Jane asked.

'Jenkins wanted to accompany his wife in the ambulance, but the medics said no as they needed space to work on her. I asked him if he had checked his wife's pulse. He said he had but couldn't feel one. I offered to drive him to the hospital, but he wanted to call his sister who lived nearby and get her to take him. I was uncertain about exactly what I was required to do, as she was still alive. He was phoning his sister when I got a call over the radio from the control room. I went outside so Mr Jenkins couldn't hear and was informed his wife had died in the ambulance before they got to the hospital. I then went and told him.'

'How did he react?'

'He was in a terrible state and kept blaming himself, saying he should have realised she might still be alive, and he could have saved her. I told him he wasn't to blame and even the trained medics had difficulty in finding a pulse.'

'When you first saw the body, was the wire still around her neck?'

'Yes, it was very tight – the ambulance crew were trying to loosen it. I told Mr Jenkins we would need to remove the rest of the electrical cord and take it, but he asked if we could do it in the morning. I felt sorry for him and said yes. I'm not sure if it's correct procedure, but I did take some pictures. I bought a Kodak disposable camera earlier in the day for a party. It was in my pocket, so I thought . . .'

'I'll need all the pictures you took,' Jane said. 'Get them developed asap and sent over to my office at Southampton Row. Did Mr Jenkins say anything else?'

'No. I called in to ask the duty sergeant what we should do. I was told we would need to get a statement from Mr Jenkins for the police report the following morning. I returned to the property, where Mr Jenkins was with his sister. He had been given sedatives to help him calm down and wasn't in a fit state to make a full statement. I then cut down the rest of the electrical wire, placed it in an evidence bag and took it to the mortuary.'

'Did you wear gloves to remove the wire?'

'Yes, I did.'

'Did he mention anything about finding a note?'

'I did ask him that, but he said there was nothing – he was still extremely distressed.'

'Did you see any false fingernails in the hallway or by the bannister?'

'There were none in the hallway. I didn't go upstairs until the next day and didn't see any then.'

'Was there anything Mr Jenkins did or said that would make you question his version of events?'

'To be honest, no. It was my first suicide . . . When I reported it, my sergeant said we'd need to wait for the PM report and coroner's decision before any further investigation.'

'Did you inform Mr Jenkins about this?'

'No, I thought the coroner's officer would do that.'

Jane closed her notebook and stood up.

'Can I ask what this is all about?' he asked nervously.

Jane shrugged. 'I'm just doing what my senior officer instructed. You have my name and contact details if you want to ask any further questions.'

'I'm certain I did everything by the book,' he said.

Jane gave him a smile and thanked him for his time before walking out. She used a phone in the front office and called Maureen.

'I got contact details for Edwina Summers' parents,' Maureen explained, 'but so far nobody's answering the phone.'

'OK, perhaps they're both at work,' Jane said. 'I've got a couple of things still to do, so I won't be coming back to the office. I'll see you in the morning.'

'Hopefully when you do, the smell will be better,' Maureen giggled. 'A couple of workmen came to check the extractors and it caused all sorts of commotion as they had to close the canteen for lunch.'

Jane sighed as she put the phone down. No doubt she'd get the blame for that.

Jane went to the hospital to see if she could speak with the paramedics who had worked on Serina Jenkins. They were not available, but she was able to read their report, which concurred with PC Thompson's account.

It was now 5.30 p.m. and she decided she still had time to call on Martin Jenkins. She stopped off to buy a takeaway coffee and a sandwich before driving to the address in Ovington Square, Chelsea. She parked in a bay at the far end of the square and sat in the car while she finished her coffee. She watched as several women parked Jaguars, BMWs and other fancy cars and led their children, dressed in smart school uniforms, into their luxurious homes. She was just locking her car when she noticed a Lexus parking in a nearby empty bay. A handsome, well-dressed man locked his car and walked into the house, closing the navy blue door behind him. Jane didn't have a description of Martin Jenkins, but she suspected that she had just seen him.

She took her time walking along the pavement towards the front door, then headed up four white stone steps. She rang the doorbell and waited. After a few moments a brisk male voice came over the intercom.

'Who is it?'

'Detective Chief Inspector Jane Tennison, to see Martin Jenkins.'

After a few moments the door was opened. 'I'm Martin Jenkins.' Jenkins had a five o'clock shadow and his eyes were red-rimmed.

Jane showed him her ID. 'I'm a colleague of DCI Hickock.'

'Oh, why hasn't he come himself?'

'He had to go back to Huddersfield. He asked me to make some enquiries regarding your wife.'

Jenkins stepped back and opened the door wider for Jane to come in. The large open-plan hallway had parquet floors, and there was a wide sweeping staircase up to the first floor, where the bannister rail continued along a balcony. There was an expensive-looking Persian rug placed below the balcony level, under an elegant chandelier.

Jenkins gestured up to the balcony. 'This was where it happened . . .' His voice was cracking. Then he seemed to pull himself together. 'Please come through to the kitchen. I was just about to make coffee.'

The kitchen was ultra-modern, with every possible state-of-the-art appliance and a large island surrounded by chrome stools. He gestured for Jane to sit down as he proceeded to fill the cafetière.

She hesitated, unsure exactly how to start the conversation, or how much she should tell him.

'I'm very sorry for your loss, Mr Jenkins. This must be a very distressing time for you.'

'It's terrible, just terrible,' he said, shaking his head. 'I'm still waiting to be told what the next steps are – I've heard nothing from the constables who were here, or the coroner's officer. I have called numerous times to try and find out when Serina's body will be released, so I can arrange the funeral.'

'I apologise for their lack of contact and can assure you I will be having words with them,' Jane said. 'I can tell you that the postmortem has been done and your wife's body should be released once the coroner has read the pathologist's report.'

'How long will that be?'

'A few days. I, or the coroner's officer when he's back, will keep you updated.'

Jenkins pressed the cafetière's plunger down. He poured two mugs and handed one to Jane.

'It might be a bit on the strong side . . . there's milk and sugar.'

Jane could understand why he would want to know what was happening with his wife's body and knew from experience people suffering a tragic loss could act in strange ways, but there was something about his manner that didn't sit right with her. She decided to probe a bit deeper without giving her concerns away regarding the postmortem findings.

'Thank you, Mr Jenkins. I know it is a distressing time for you, but I wonder if you could tell me what happened in your own words.'

'There's not a lot I can tell you. I came home from work and found Serina – it was horrific. I opened the front door and there she was, hanging from the bannister in front of me. I was hysterical . . . I couldn't find a pulse . . . I thought she was dead and called the ambulance. When the ambulance guys said she was still alive I thought she would be OK. I couldn't believe it when PC Thompson said she'd died.'

'Did Serina leave a note?'

'I've looked everywhere. My sister came round and searched as well, but there was nothing. I went to stay with my sister that night as I couldn't stand to be alone in the house. I have no idea why Serina did it . . . We hadn't argued, there was no reason.'

'So when you went to work that morning, did she show any signs of being distressed?'

He shook his head emphatically. 'No. We'd had breakfast as normal and I left for work. We were supposed to be going out to dinner with friends that evening.'

'Can you think of any reason why your wife may have had suicidal thoughts?'

'No, I have racked my brains . . . The only thing I can think of is that she was very keen to have a baby. We had two rounds of IVF treatment and had already discussed having a third one. Serina had two miscarriages which both affected her very badly . . . but we were eager to keep going with the IVF treatment.'

'Did she have any financial worries?'

'Good God, no . . . that goes for both of us. We have only just had all the refurbishing finished on the house, including a nursery. We were both confident she would get pregnant . . . that we'd have a baby.'

'I was told by the pathologist that the cord used by your wife was an electrical cable?'

Martin Jenkins gave her a quizzical look. 'I've been doing a bit of electrical work, installing a security system, but then decided it was better to get a professional in.'

He walked to the utility room and opened the door. There were washing machines and tumble dryers, along with hoovers and cleaning equipment. An industrial-sized coil of electrical wire was leaning against the side of a plastic-lidded dustbin. He stood staring at it, then rubbed his face with his hands.

'Oh God! This doesn't make sense . . .'

He seemed about to break down when the front door was opened. A woman's voice called out his name and Jenkins shouted that he was in the kitchen. A moment later a tall, blonde, well-dressed woman walked in, carrying two large bags of food shopping.

Mr Jenkins turned to Jane.

'I'm very sorry, but I can't remember your name . . . This is my sister, Adele.'

Jane stood up. 'I'm Detective Chief Inspector Jane Tennison.'

Adele looked older than her brother but they had similar features She put the bags down and eased off an elegant camel-hair coat. Walking over to her brother, she wrapped her arms around his shoulders and hugged him tenderly.

'Are you all right, darling? I would have been here earlier but thought I'd better do some food shopping.'

Adele turned to Jane with her hand outstretched. 'How do you do. This is all such a dreadful thing – shocking, just shocking – none of us can believe it.'

'Would you like a coffee?' Martin asked as she sat on the stool next to Jane.

'Yes, please, just black. I tried to get some information but without much success. I was told that there was going to be a postmortem this afternoon.' She looked at Jane. 'Is that why you're here?'

'Jane is an associate of Brian Hickock, the detective I spoke to,' Jenkins explained.

'Yes, DCI Hickock is busy with a case and asked me to assist your brother regarding the release of his wife's body.'

'And when will that be?'

'The pathologist and the police are making reports for the coroner, who will decide if any further investigation is necessary,' Jane replied, wanting to observe Jenkins' reaction.

'What do you mean?' Adele looked at her brother and then back to Jane, which Jane thought odd.

'It's standard procedure.'

Martin was visibly shaken, and Adele went over and put her arm around him.

'I was asked to speak with your brother on compassionate grounds, but I am not involved in any formal—'

'She has been asking me all these questions,' Jenkins interjected.

Adele turned to look at Jane. 'Just wait a minute – I need to know what is going on here. Surely, if you need to interview my brother then he should have someone with him. He found his wife hanging from the bannister rail, for God's sake. He has been deeply traumatised.'

Jane stood up. 'I am very sorry for your loss and the tragic circumstances, Mr Jenkins. I can show myself out. Goodnight.'

As Jane left, she could hear Martin Jenkins sobbing. After seeing Serina Jenkins' body, listening to Felix Markham's comments about the injuries and the unaccounted-for false nails, she had a gut feeling something wasn't right. She wondered if Jenkins' reaction was as genuine as it seemed.

CHAPTER ELEVEN

Jane was thankful that it was only a very small yoga class, as they were all wearing very expensive-looking exercise attire while she was just wearing an old leotard with leggings.

After forty-five minutes of the hour-long class Jane's energy began to wane, but she persisted, and by the time they were lying still at the end for quiet time, she was almost asleep. As she rolled up her mat afterwards, Jane was approached by the instructor, a tall, athletic black woman with her hair in beaded dreadlocks.

'You did really well. You have a lot of tension in your shoulders and your lower back, though. So try to continue doing some of the simple floor exercises in the evenings, and also turning your neck from side to side – but never force any movement. Did you enjoy the class?'

'Very much. I'd like to make it a regular.'

Returning to the changing rooms, Jane felt surprisingly calm and relaxed. After taking a shower she decided to skip the sauna and head home for an early night. As she was paying for her class at reception, Peter was just walking out with his squash rackets and holdall.

'Hi, are you just arriving or leaving?' he asked, smiling.

'I've just finished a yoga class.'

'Do you fancy a glass of wine?'

'That would be really nice.'

Peter suggested that she follow him to a nearby wine bar on the King's Road. As he opened his car door he turned back to her.

'Or how about getting something to eat? There's a favourite curry place of mine, Chutney Mary's, not far from the Lots Road Antique Emporium.'

Jane realised that she had only had a coffee and roll all day, so she readily accepted.

The restaurant was elegant and welcoming. They sat at one of the tables in two comfortable wing chairs, taking their time over the menus.

'Nice to see you again, Mr Rawlins,' the waiter said before taking down their orders.

Jane leaned back in her armchair. 'You know, I've often passed this place, but from the outside you would never know it was so large inside – I really like the atmosphere.'

Peter smiled. 'Wait until you've tasted the food! I try not to spend too many evenings eating TV dinners, so I've been trying out lots of different restaurants – Italian, French, Lebanese and some really good Indian ones. I had no idea just how many restaurants were virtually on my doorstep.'

'I know what you mean about TV dinners – I've had my fair share of those, especially since I started this new job.'

Their drinks were served, and they clinked glasses.

'Where exactly do you live?' Jane asked.

'Well, I don't know for how long, but now I'm in Napier Road, just around the corner from the Hurlingham Club at the end of the Fulham Road. It's an incredible place. Very exclusive.'

'You're not a member?' Jane asked, smiling.

'No, I used to get access as a guest via my ex-business partner. I used to go there for Sunday lunch with my son when he was learning how to swim.'

Peter's mood had shifted, and Jane was grateful when their starters were served.

She quickly changed the subject, telling him what she had done that afternoon.

'The house was amazing. You're in property, aren't you?'

He nodded. 'Property development.'

'This house was in Ovington Square. It looked as if it had been completely modernised quite recently. How much do you think houses in that area are worth?'

Peter thought for a moment. 'They tend to be semi-detached, pretty big, but with little or no grounds. I'd say they're typically worth two to two and a half million. The location is the key factor. For instance, because of its proximity to the Hurlingham Club my house is worth more than you'd think. It's not in the same league as Ovington Square, but it's worth a lot more than I paid for it ten years ago.'

Their starter plates were removed, and Peter ordered another lager and a glass of rosé for Jane.

'Don't tell me you're looking for a property in that area?' Peter said.

'Good heavens, no! I just happened to be there this afternoon. I've only just moved into my flat ... In fact, let me give you my phone number and address.' Jane opened her bag and took out her notebook, jotting down her office and home contact details. She tore out the page and handed it to him.

'I was going to ask Tony for them, but thank you.'

'I only moved in last week – before that I had a small, terraced house in Chislehurst, near Bromley. My ex-boyfriend renovated it. But we broke up so I decided to sell.'

'So that was recently?'

'Yes, a few months ago.'

Peter smiled ruefully. 'We have something in common, then. I broke up with my wife recently. Actually, it was a double-edged sword for me, as it turned out she was having an affair with my business partner. It was devastating. One minute I had a wife I adored and a son we both doted on ... I also had a partner I trusted and had worked alongside for fifteen years, building up a property development company together. Then she walked out, went to live with him and took my son. To make matters even worse, he now wants out of our company to start up on his own. So, it leaves me in a pretty dire financial situation – either I let him take over the bloody company, or I have to sell my house and buy him out.'

As their main courses were brought to the table, Peter got up to go to the gents'. Jane thought he was on the point of tears.

After a few minutes, Peter returned to the table and picked up his napkin, smiling as he shook it out and placed it on his lap.

'Sorry about that, the floodgates opened. I think it's because I've been going to so many restaurants on my own – not used to having such a good listener!'

They both steered clear of the topic of relationships for the rest of the evening, as well as work, and mostly just talked about movies they had both enjoyed and places they liked to go. Peter chatted enthusiastically about his favourite art galleries, and which paintings he would purchase if he had millions to spend. By the time they had finished dinner and ordered coffee it was almost midnight. After paying the bill, he walked her to her car.

'Now that I have your number, I'd love to see you again. Maybe we could take in a movie, or you can start joining me in testing out all the local restaurants?'

He gave her a kiss on her cheek.

'I'd like that,' she said with a smile.

As he headed to his car, Jane felt for the first time that she was finally over Eddie.

*　*　*

Jane had forgotten to set her alarm and woke with a start, unable to believe what time it was. Arriving at the station just after 9 a.m., she hurried up to her office. Maureen had a pot of coffee ready and quickly updated her on tracing Edwina's parents.

'I should warn you,' she added, 'the canteen is closed for today, so there's probably going to be a riot. The outlet was completely blocked and the extractor fans had to be removed before they install new ones.'

Jane grinned. 'Well, that'll teach me not to have breakfast before coming to the office.'

She wrote a brief report on the previous day for DCS Kernan while Maureen dialled the Summers' phone number. This time, however, the line did not even ring. She called through to the operator and was told that the number was no longer in use.

Frowning, Jane checked their address, guessing it would take at least an hour and a half to drive there.

As Jane headed towards her car, a Vauxhall drove in at speed and screeched into a parking bay. She recognised DCI Hickock, slamming his door closed and hurrying into the staff entrance. She wondered if she should try and talk to him, but he looked so stressed, she decided against it. Soon she was heading towards the M25, on her way to Kent.

* * *

Maureen had printed out Jane's report and delivered it to Kernan's clerk, and was walking to the lifts when a breathless DCI Hickock approached her.

'Is Tennison in her office?'

'No, she just left. She's—' She never finished her sentence as Hickock swore and banged through the double doors. He strode down the corridor, knocked on Kernan's door and went straight in.

'Ah, Brian. I was just coming to track you down. I need some explanation about what the hell is going on.'

Kernan went to his desk and picked up a file, handing it to Hickock.

'This is the PM report on Serina Jenkins from Felix Markham. He says Tennison was questioning some injuries which may be ante-mortem. I just spoke with the coroner – he wants AMIT to investigate as a suspicious death. Look, I know the woman's husband is a personal friend, but . . .'

'Well, he's more of an acquaintance, really,' Hickock said. 'My relationship with him isn't based on much more than a few rounds of golf. It was your suggestion that Tennison attend the PM.'

Kernan handed Hickock Tennison's brief report. 'Well, she did a lot more than that. She went to see your "acquaintance" and started asking questions. Her report doesn't go into detail, but it's clear she thinks it may not be a simple suicide.'

'She's just trying to blow things out of proportion in the hope she'll be asked to do an investigation. I'll speak with Martin and find out what she said.'

'I don't think that's a good idea right now. Go and talk with Tennison first and let me think about how we'll deal with the situation.'

'Yes, sir.'

Hickock was shaking, partly with nerves and at the same time trying to contain his anger. As he opened the office door he paused.

'We had a good result in Huddersfield, sir.'

Kernan nodded. 'I know. Now go and talk to that woman – I knew she would be a problem. Apparently the cold case she's working on may require a visit to an oil rig! And anyone getting pissed off about the closure of the canteen should know it's down to her moaning.'

Hickock closed the door and headed into the incident room. It was unusually quiet, as Shefford was out with his team on a murder investigation. DS Otley was working alone at his desk as Hickock threw the file down onto an empty desk beside him.

'I could murder a bloody coffee.'

Otley shook his head. 'You can thank Tennison for that. I've had to order takeaway for some of the lads on a stake-out. The canteen's going to be closed for days.'

'She doesn't know what she's doing, that bloody woman. The super told me she's asked about going to interview someone on an oil rig!'

Otley sniggered. 'Best place to put her – in the middle of the sea without a paddle.'

'Well, she's certainly put me right in the shit.'

Otley's phone rang and he began ordering a variety of hamburgers and chips, meat pies and toasted sandwiches, along with coffee and teas.

'Can you make sure the cheeseburger has sausage, bacon and egg in it as well, no tomato and no gherkin – have you got that?'

As soon as he finished the call he grabbed his coat.

'Better get the order over to the lads.'

After he'd left, Hickock read the postmortem findings carefully, then started looking through Jane's report. When he'd finished, he slapped the file closed.

'Bloody woman,' he muttered again.

* * *

Maureen was still going through the items in the two evidence boxes, many of them apparently tossed in without proper labels. She started looking through the diary found in Brittany's college room, along with a few letters and drawings. She physically jumped when Hickock barged into the office.

'Is she back yet?'

'No, sir, she was driving to Kent. I'm not sure how long she is going to be, but if she calls in shall I give her a message?'

'I need to talk to her, it's very important. I'm going out to get something to eat and then I'll be back – when she calls, get her to contact me.'

'Yes, sir.'

* * *

Jane arrived in Ashurst and used a map to navigate through the village into a country lane. It had taken longer than she had anticipated. The small lane was flanked by fields on one side and led to a row of cottages. At the end of the row was a fenced garden, with a paved path to the front door.

Before she rang the doorbell there was a loud barking from inside, which got even louder after she pressed the doorbell. She could hear someone shouting for 'Bertie' to be quiet, and then the door opened. A small terrier shot out, and ran around barking. A very elderly, white-haired lady peered through the half-open door.

'I am looking for Edwina Summers' mother or father?'

Jane held up her ID, giving her name and rank, as the woman shouted for Bertie to come back inside. Eventually the dog ran back and the door was opened wider for Jane.

'I am her grandmother, Estelle Summers. Do you need to talk to me?'

'If you don't mind.'

'Come through to the kitchen. I've got a fire going in there. I don't use the other rooms.'

The old-fashioned kitchen was very hot, with a black iron grate which had logs burning in it. On either side of the fireplace were more logs stacked from floor to ceiling. There was a worn armchair close to the fire, near a small TV on a shelf.

'Do you want to sit down?'

Jane pulled out one of the pine chairs from the table and placed it near the armchair. The little terrier had got into a dog basket beside the fire. Mrs Summers gripped the side of the armchair, as she eased herself down into it.

'I'm waiting for Mrs Blake to arrive – she looks after everything.'

Jane nodded and smiled. 'I need to contact Edwina and wondered if you have her current address. I did try calling, but there seems to be a fault on your phone line.'

'Are you from the social services?'

'No, I am a detective chief inspector – my name is Jane Tennison. It is quite important that I contact your granddaughter, but there's nothing for you to worry about. It's in connection with an incident that occurred five years ago. I'm hoping she may be able to help with my enquiries.'

Mrs Summers shrugged her narrow shoulders.

'Perhaps she is living with her parents?' Jane suggested.

'No, they died a long time ago. My husband and I raised Edwina. My son – Edwina's father – was a child prodigy. He became a pianist, travelling the world with his wife.'

'I'm sorry . . . Their loss must have been devastating for you.'

'Yes, it was a plane crash in Africa. Fortunately, Edwina was at their house in London with her nanny when it happened. My husband went to live there for many years, but it was a big rambling house and there was a huge mortgage.'

Mrs Summers showed little emotion, as if she had repeated the information many times.

'We moved many times, to smaller and smaller properties, and after my husband died I was left this little place by an aunt.' She let her hand rest on her lap, just as the front door opened and a woman called out that she was there. The little dog got up and ran from the kitchen.

Jane stood up as a stout woman walked in, carrying a box of groceries. She had her hair secured in a bun at the back of her neck and was wearing a big overcoat. Mrs Summers gestured to Jane.

'This lady is here asking about Edwina.'

'Hello – I'm Nora Blake. Would you like me to make a pot of tea?'

'Not for me, thank you, Mrs Blake. I am DCI Jane Tennison.' She held up her ID card and Mrs Blake glanced at it before removing her overcoat. She crossed to the back door and hung it on a hook, taking down a wraparound apron.

'Mrs Summers has been very helpful, Mrs Blake, but I urgently need to speak to her granddaughter. It's nothing to be worried about, just relating to an investigation from the time Edwina was at college.'

'Good heavens, that was a long time ago. We haven't seen her recently – not for years, actually.'

Mrs Blake began to take out farm produce, potatoes, vegetables and a carton of milk. The little terrier returned to curl up in his basket as she held up a wrapped parcel.

'Giblets for you, and I have some nice lamb chops for you, Mrs Summers.'

Jane was beginning to get frustrated, and was about to try and question Mrs Summers again when Mrs Summers gestured to Mrs Blake.

'Go and see if there's anything useful in the bureau for the detective, would you, and then I'd like a cup of tea.'

'Of course, dear – I'm glad I gave the room a good dusting last week! Would you like to come with me, DCI Tennison?'

Jane followed Mrs Blake from the kitchen, who turned back and said she was closing the door to keep the heat in. They went along the dark, narrow hallway, before she opened an oak door, parting a crimson curtain hanging on the other side.

Jane was surprised to see an impressive grand piano dominating the room. The walls were covered with framed concert posters and numerous photographs of a young, dark-haired, handsome man. In some pictures he was standing by the piano, in others he was sitting at the keys playing, wearing an evening suit with a bow tie. On the mantelpiece were more photographs, and Jane recognised Edwina as a young toddler, and then as a teenager, playing a violin and seated at the same piano.

There was a shelf full of old records, beside an old-fashioned gramophone. The top was open with a record placed on the turntable. Mrs Blake nodded towards it. 'Mrs Summers used to play her son's records all the time, and on occasions she still does. She also used to play the piano, but nowadays she mostly watches television.'

Mrs Blake opened a small bureau, resting the lid on the two slide arms she drew out. There were numerous cubbyholes filled with letters, many tied with ribbons, and some stacked with programmes. She removed a bulging envelope, placing it to one side. She then opened the centre section in the bureau, which had a small arched door with a tiny lock. She took out a leather photo frame.

'Are they photographs of Mrs Summers' son?' Jane asked.

'Yes, he was a child prodigy – a genius who travelled the world and played at Carnegie Hall in America when he was sixteen. This was his piano. Mrs Summers' husband was a very well-known violinist, too.'

Mrs Blake hesitated, holding the thick envelope in one hand and the small photo frame in the other.

'Of course, I never knew them, as it was before my time. I do hope that the reason you're here is not going to distress Mrs Summers. I may be speaking out of turn, but I think there is only so much grief one person can deal with. To lose a precious genius of a son, his lovely wife, and then to have your husband die of cancer aged forty . . . You must be able to tell what a very classy lady she is, and I would hate to have to give her more bad news.'

'I don't have any bad news,' Jane assured her quickly. 'I'm just hoping that Mrs Summers might be able to help me get in touch with Edwina.'

Mrs Blake went to the piano, putting the envelope and the picture frame down on top.

'Well, she became bad news. Mrs Summers reckoned she had inherited her father's talent, as she was a very accomplished pianist and got a scholarship to the Royal College of Music. But then she got ill and had to come back home. Anyway, she then recovered and got another scholarship to go to the college in Ascot.'

'Actually, I want to talk to Edwina about something that happened when she was a student there.'

'Well, she left there years ago . . . but I have some addresses that might help you to contact her via someone else who was there. She has had a drug problem, along with so many other dreadful things, then she had to go into a shelter for domestic abuse . . . I believe she had a place in a halfway house for her and the baby, but I'm not sure if she is still there. We have had no contact for over a year.'

Jane was taken aback by the mention of a baby, remaining silent as Mrs Blake found the various papers and then handed them over.

'I don't think you can take them away with you, but if you want to copy down the details, then I can put them back in the bureau in case Mrs Summers needs to see them. She has tried so hard to help Edwina, but the girl really became such a handful and had this awful, violent man she was involved with. At least I think he is now out of the picture. She never married him, so she will still be using her own surname.'

Jane jotted down the various addresses, underlining the most recent, a council-run shelter. Most of the locations were in London suburbs. She handed the originals back to Mrs Blake, who slipped them back in the envelope. She then gestured to the small leather photograph case. Jane picked it up and opened it, revealing a beautiful baby girl with white-blonde hair, wrapped in a delicate lace shawl.

'She brought her here once, needing money. That was the last time we saw her. The baby is called Emily. It was very hard on Mrs Summers, because I think it would be so good for her to see the child regularly. Perhaps if you do get to talk to Edwina you could say how much it would mean to Mrs Summers. She is very frail now and quite dependent on me.'

'Well, I sincerely hope that I will be able to track her down, and I certainly will encourage her to make contact.' Jane made a brief visit back to the kitchen to say goodbye to Mrs Summers, but she was very uncommunicative, seemingly absorbed in reading a newspaper. She gave Jane a polite nod before returning to stare at the paper. Mrs Blake ushered Jane out, closing the front door after her. As Mrs Blake turned around, she was surprised to see Mrs Summers standing at the open kitchen door.

'Did you find out what she wanted?'

'It was something to do with when Edwina was at the college in Ascot.'

'It couldn't be about not paying their fees, surely?'

'I don't think so, she never mentioned anything about that – and I didn't let her take anything away.'

'Good, I thought she wanted money. Anyone connected to my granddaughter only ever wants money.'

* * *

Jane drove back towards the A20, hoping to find a service station to call Maureen. Passing a small café between a row of shops in the village of Ashurst, she parked and headed towards a nearby phone box. The phone box was occupied, so she went into the café and ordered a coffee and a toasted teacake. She sat at a window table, checking through the contacts for Edwina and placing them in date order so Maureen could work on tracking her down. She hoped that as there was a child involved it might prove to be easier, but the addresses were in very disparate locations, the most recent being in Chalk Farm.

After finishing her coffee, she tried the phone box again, finding it empty. Maureen answered as Jane pressed in the coin to connect the call, eager to forward a message to call DCI Hickock.

'Well, he can just wait until I get back to the station. First of all, I need you to track down Edwina Summers. If you've got a pen and paper, I'll list all the contacts in order. Incidentally, she's now got a baby girl called Emily.'

Jane only just managed to give Maureen all the details before using her last coin. She returned to her car and continued the drive back to the station. By the time she arrived it was after three o'clock. As she headed down the corridor to her office, she saw DCI Hickock standing outside the door. He turned angrily towards her.

'I've been waiting for you since this morning. I need you to tell me exactly what went on when you talked to Martin Jenkins.'

'I have been out working on something connected to my investigation – and I gave DCS Kernan my report regarding—'

'I've read it,' he snapped, as she opened her office door.

Jane took off her jacket and hung it over the back of her desk chair. Hickock stood in the doorway with his hands on his hips, as she turned towards him.

'I don't know why you are being so antagonistic. I did exactly what I was asked, not only by you but by Kernan. I presume you've also read the PM report?'

'Of course I have. Kernan showed it to me. He's also spoken with the coroner who, thanks to you, wants AMIT to investigate Serina Jenkins' death.'

'You can't blame me for the coroner's decision. I'm sorry if you think I have placed you in a difficult situation with Martin Jenkins.'

Hickock slammed the door shut behind him and glared at her.

'I want to make one thing clear. Contrary to what you seem to think, there is nothing inappropriate about my relationship with Martin Jenkins.'

She had to take a deep breath before responding.

'I haven't given the matter any thought. I assumed that being a close friend, you simply wanted to support him under such tragic circumstances.'

'I am not a close friend. We just play the odd round of golf together. Anyway, now I need you to come with me to interview him. I've already organised forensics to get started, so you can tell me everything you discussed with him on the way there.'

Jane looked surprised. 'Do you not think it would be better for someone who doesn't know Jenkins socially to interview him? To avoid any conflict of interest.'

'There is no bloody conflict. I know Jenkins, so he's more likely to be at ease with me than you. And Kernan agreed with me.'

Maureen walked in with a stack of printed documents as Hickock bustled past her.

'I've made some headway with finding Edwina Summers, but it was like herding cats, she has so many different services looking out for her.'

'It'll have to wait – the coroner's decided Serina Jenkins' death is suspicious.'

'Goodness, I know you thought something wasn't right. Oh, this envelope was delivered from Fulham, from PC Eric Thompson.'

'That'll be the photographs. I'll take them with me.'

Hickock loomed impatiently in the corridor and Jane hurried to join him, raising her eyes to Maureen as she grabbed her jacket and put the envelope into her briefcase. She struggled to keep up with Hickock as he strode out from the station to a waiting CID car. He climbed into the front passenger seat, and Jane only just managed to climb into the rear before he barked out the address to the driver and they screeched out of the car park.

'Here we go,' Jane said to herself, gripping the grab handle tightly.

CHAPTER TWELVE

Hickock leaned back in his seat as he listened to Jane recounting her interview with Martin Jenkins and his sister Adele. Hickock was still very tense, nodding his head thoughtfully when Jane mentioned that his sister seemed quite dominant, and very protective of her brother, and that he had apparently stayed the night with Adele after his wife's death. She also recounted her conversation with PC Thompson, who had attended the scene that night, and mentioned the ambulance crew's report.

Hickock shook his head. 'Well, rightly or fucking wrongly, we now have to get this sorted. Martin Jenkins has agreed to meet with us and, so far, he's not asked to have any legal representation.'

'What if he needs to be arrested?'

'There's not enough evidence to arrest him. If he's involved in his wife's death, we need to give him enough rope to hang himself, to coin a phrase. So for now, we just get a statement from him on this.' He removed a pocket tape recorder from his jacket.

'I'm always a bit wary about using these things,' Jane said. 'If the tape gets chewed up, damaged or lost, then you've got nothing. I'll take some pocketbook notes at the same time as a back-up, then get Jenkins to sign them. Are forensics attending?'

'Yeah. We'll seize the clothing he was wearing at the time, but he's had plenty of opportunity to clean up or destroy any incriminating evidence.'

'There was no skin or blood beneath her fingernails,' Jane said.

Hickock turned around and glared at her over the back of his seat. 'For Chrissakes, I've read the PM report – so stop telling me things I already know!'

Jane ignored his outburst. 'Were you aware of any friction in their relationship?' she asked.

He sighed. 'I met her maybe two or three times at golf club events – they appeared to be very happy. She was quite glamorous. Did you look around the house?'

'No, just the hallway and the kitchen.'

'It's all been done up recently – worth a lot, I imagine. No idea whether it's mortgaged or not.'

'The property is certainly worth way over a million,' Jane agreed.

'The funds could be from her side of the family, who own the Globe Guild Wallpaper companies. But he's a lawyer, so he's probably earning a packet.'

'I know that company . . . In fact, when I was refurbishing my old house, I went into one of their shops,' Jane said. 'They have outlets in Harrods and John Lewis, and their prices were way over my budget.'

'That's really fascinating,' Hickock said sarcastically.

Jane leaned back in her seat. She wanted to ask more questions about the Jenkinses, but there was no point when he was in such a foul mood. During the remainder of the drive into the West End he made copious notes in his notebook, and then tersely told the driver to take a short cut, directing him down various side streets.

As they pulled up in front of the Jenkins property, Hickock already had his door open and slammed it shut behind him as he hurried up to the front door. Jane sighed as she got out of the car, following behind him. He rang the doorbell, and the front door was immediately opened by a white-suited forensic officer, stepping back to allow them both to enter.

'No need to suit up, before you ask,' he said over his shoulder.

Martin Jenkins appeared in the kitchen doorway.

'Martin, you've met DCI Jane Tennison. We need to sit down and have a talk. You've obviously been informed of the coroner's decision?'

'Yes, I'm in shock actually. We can go into the kitchen or use the dining room?'

'The kitchen will be fine – you two go ahead and I'll be right with you.'

As Jane accompanied Jenkins into the kitchen, Hickock waited a moment before he gestured to the two forensic officers, who were preparing to use a chemical reagent to test for blood on the staircase carpet. Hickock asked where Serina Jenkins' body had been found after she had been cut down. He was told she had been lying directly below the balcony railing from the floor above. Forensics would begin searching the carpet and make their way gradually up the stairs to the bannisters, testing for blood and collecting samples of any positive reactions.

Hickock looked up to the bannisters and then back to the ground. He opened his notebook, flicking through a couple of pages.

'The electric cord is being held at the mortuary, so I will need to get that over to you. Apparently, it was cut from a reel that's in the utility room, so you will need to take that.'

He gave them the nod to continue working, but as he started walking away, he paused to turn back.

'Did you ask Mr Jenkins for the clothes he was wearing on the night his wife's body was found?'

One of the forensic officers nodded. 'Yes, but he stayed with his sister and said his clothes are still there, then the next day he borrowed some from his brother-in-law. He called his sister and she said she'd bring his clothes over this afternoon.'

'Good, OK . . . What's your names, by the way?'

'I'm Malcom Turner and this is Andrew Fielding.'

'Right, I'll leave you both to it. If you need me for anything I'll be in the kitchen.'

Jane was sitting on a stool at the edge of the kitchen island as Martin was putting out coffee cups. Hickock walked in, trying to appear relaxed as he removed his coat.

'I appreciate this is all a bit of a troubling situation for you, Martin, but there are some further questions I need to ask you. I spoke to Malcom Turner, one of the forensics guys out in the hall. I just want to check that your sister is bringing round the clothes you wore on the night Serina died?'

'Yes, she is. And yes, I understand why you need to check them.'

Hickock perched on one of the stools, took the small recorder out of his jacket pocket and switched it on. He looked at Jane, who shrugged her shoulders as if to say, 'be it on your head'.

'I'll be taping our conversation and DCI Tennison will take some notes as well. Are you all right with that?'

'Yes, of course – I understand.'

'I will also need you to come to the station so we can take your fingerprints and a blood sample for elimination purposes. Perhaps first thing in the morning, if that's convenient?'

'Whatever is necessary. Here's your coffee, and there's milk and sugar on the tray.'

After handing out the coffees, Martin then sat opposite Hickock, while Jane took out her notebook and pen.

'OK,' Hickock began, 'just take your time and explain to me exactly what happened on the evening you returned home.'

'I was home at my usual time, which is generally between six thirty and six forty-five p.m. I opened the front door and Serina was directly in front of me, hanging from an electric cable tied to the balcony bannisters.'

Jane leaned forwards, indicating she wanted to say something.

'I am sorry to ask you this, Mr Jenkins, but were your wife's feet off the ground?'

'Er . . . She was sort of face forwards on her knees, but she wasn't moving at all. I ran over to her. The electric cord around her neck was so tight . . . I tried to loosen it but couldn't, so I ran into the kitchen utility room to get a pair of pliers to cut her down. While I was doing this, I called 999 . . . or it might have been just after I cut her down.'

'Did you do anything to try and resuscitate your wife once you cut her down?' Hickock asked.

'I touched her wrist and neck but couldn't feel a pulse. She wasn't moving either, so stupidly I thought she was dead. I did try some chest compressions, but nothing happened, then the ambulance men arrived, and they found a faint pulse and pretty much took her straight to the hospital.' He started to sound quite emotional as he continued. 'I really thought she was going to survive . . . I couldn't believe it when I was told she'd died in the ambulance. I feel really bad now for thinking she was already dead. Do you think she'd have survived if I'd done more at the time, Brian?'

Jane noticed that Jenkins looked only at Hickock as he spoke about that night. It was if he was trying to garner Hickock's sympathy as a friend. She wondered if Jenkins had deliberately made the initial contact with Hickock to try and get inside information about any possible investigation.

'I'm not a doctor, Martin, and neither are you. The pathologist said even if Serina had survived, she would have suffered irreversible brain damage due to the lack of oxygen to her brain. She would no longer have been the woman you knew and loved.'

Jane knew the pathologist had never said anything about irreversible brain damage, and Hickock was lying to console Jenkins. She indicated she wished to say something.

'Mr Jenkins, when you gave your wife chest compressions, was she bleeding from her nose?'

'I don't remember . . . She might have been.'

'Did you have any blood on your clothes?'

'I might have.'

Jane continued, 'After you cut your wife down, why didn't you try and remove the electric cable that was around her neck?'

Again, he looked at Hickock. 'I did, but it was so tight I couldn't even get the pliers in to cut it off. I guess I might have hesitated because I thought she was dead.'

Hickock checked to see if the recorder was still working. 'Did you and Serina have an argument before you left for work?'

'No, we had breakfast together, then I kissed her goodbye.'

'Did Serina work?' Hickock asked, taking another glance at his recorder.

'Her family sold their company five years ago, but she still owned shares and was intending to start a sort of offshoot designer company. She had been looking for suitable offices and my sister Adele was helping her. They had seen a possible place in Chelsea, off the King's Road.'

'What about her family?'

'Her father died before the company was bought out. A year before he died, he and Serina's mother had a very unpleasant divorce. She married again and now lives in France.'

'Are there any other siblings?'

'No, Serina was an only child. She found the divorce very upsetting. She was sent to boarding school, so never really had a good relationship with her mother or her stepfather.'

Again, Jane leaned forwards, indicating she wanted to ask a question. Hickock glared at her.

'You said her father died before the company was sold – can you tell us who the main beneficiary was? I understand that it's a very successful business.'

'I would say that that's one of the reasons Serina and her mother didn't have a good relationship – her father made Serina the main beneficiary, with a sizeable number of shares to be held in trust for her. He had already organised the sale before he died, so his lawyers acted as Serina's guardian. When she came of age, she inherited everything, and has been exceptionally generous to her mother.'

'So now that she is deceased, who will inherit what I would estimate to be a substantial fortune?' Hickock asked.

Jenkins shrugged. 'I'm certain Serina made a will, but I have never seen it. I will no doubt be able to give you the details when her lawyers contact me.'

'What about life insurance?' Jane asked.

'Yes, she did have it, but again, I'll have to ask the solicitors for details.'

'Do you have a joint bank account?'

'We have separate bank accounts, but one joint account that we used for the household bills and refurbishment.'

'We will need access to your bank accounts, Martin,' Hickock said, yet again checking that he was still recording. He then asked if Serina had any enemies, or if there was anyone Martin felt should be questioned.

'There's no one. She was loved by everyone. I never met anyone that held a grudge, or even had a bad word against her.'

It was clear that Martin Jenkins was becoming anxious, so Jane asked her next question softly.

'You said that Serina was about to undergo a third round of treatment – was she anxious about it?'

'Yes, she had been depressed and emotionally drained by the process. But we both had strong hopes and she was very positive about us continuing with the treatment.'

'Would you say she was anxious but didn't want you to know how she was feeling?'

'No, not at all. We discussed everything together. I would have known if it was making her . . . suicidal.'

'Did it upset you that you had not been able to conceive naturally?'

'Of course it did.'

'Did it make you angry, to the point where you became physically abusive towards your wife?'

'No, I did not!' Jenkins said indignantly.

Jane continued in the same quiet tone of voice. 'I am only asking this, Mr Jenkins, because the postmortem found damage to her septum, and there were blood clots inside her nostrils.'

Martin Jenkins was clearly agitated.

'Why are you asking me these questions? I have been as honest as I can be, but I'm beginning to feel as if you are implicating me in some way in Serina's death, as if I was in some way responsible. I've had enough. If you want to question me any further, I want a lawyer present.'

Hickock leaned forwards, making a calming gesture. 'Martin, I am sorry if you feel we are placing you under undue pressure. You have to understand that the coroner has asked us to investigate Serina's death as part of the inquest process. No one's saying you harmed your wife . . . but the postmortem revealed injuries that are inconsistent with suicide, and therefore suspicious.'

'*Suspicious?* What the fuck does that mean?' Jenkins stood up and his stool fell to one side. He was now visibly angry, and his face twisted as he banged the top of the island with the flat of his hand.

'Please sit down, Martin,' Hickock said. 'If you want to get legal representation, by all means do so, and I will end our interview.'

Adele walked into the kitchen, carrying a dry cleaner's suit cover and laundry bag, as Hickock spoke into the recorder, giving the time and date, before pressing stop.

'What is going on?' she demanded.

'The coroner thinks it was a suspicious death – that's what it's about in a bloody nutshell. Am I right? *Is that correct?*' Jenkins shouted.

Adele looked incredulously at Hickock. 'I don't believe it! Surely you can't be serious?'

She dumped the laundry bag onto the island and hurried over to her brother to put her arms around him.

'Why didn't you call me to come over earlier?'

Hickock placed the tape recorder into his jacket pocket, looking embarrassed. 'Er . . . Have you brought Martin's clothes?' he asked awkwardly.

'Yes,' she replied curtly. 'They were dry-cleaned and laundered this morning. But if you think I had any ulterior motive in cleaning them, that's absolute rubbish. Martin had been up all night in tears, and his clothes were creased and sweat-stained.'

Jane eased off her stool. 'I'm sorry, could I use your bathroom?'

Adele gestured impatiently. 'On the opposite side of the hall.'

Jane picked up her briefcase and coat. 'I'll wait for you in the hall,' she told Hickock.

Jane left her briefcase on the side of the marble washbasin while she used the toilet. She then washed her hands before opening her briefcase to take out the envelope that contained the grainy photographs PC Thompson had taken of the hall, the stairs and the bannister rail. Serina's body could be seen on the floor, with the medics administering CPR. She was not lying on the expensive Persian carpet, however, but on the polished parquet floor.

Jane left the bathroom and quietly joined the forensic officers. Pausing at the side of the staircase, she told them to remove the carpet and test beneath it, then went to stand by the front door. Adele walked out with the dry cleaning over her arm.

'I apologise if I was rude, DCI Tennison. The truth is, I am still in shock. Martin is going to be a little while, I'm afraid, giving DCI Hickock all the bank details.'

Adele glanced at the men rolling up the carpet. 'Would you mind showing me Serina's bedroom?' Jane asked quickly.

'Of course. Follow me.' When they got to the first landing and passed the bannisters Serina had been hanging from, Adele averted her eyes.

The master bedroom was dominated by a massive four-poster bed with silk drapes at the corners and a canopy above. Adele put the dry-cleaning bag onto the bed and opened one of the fitted wardrobes that covered two walls. One section was full of elegant evening gowns, and there were rows and rows of designer shoes.

'She was very particular,' Adele said wistfully. 'Everything had to be in the right place, on the right hanger.'

Jane looked into the bathroom, with its sunken bath and mirror-fronted cabinet stretching the entire length of the wall above the basins. Jane glanced back to Adele in the bedroom, then eased open one of the cabinet doors. It contained rows and rows of vitamin tablets, as well as medications for migraines and headaches. There were also packets of sleeping tablets along with other prescription drugs, including zopiclone, methadone, zolpidem, pregabalin, doxepin, temazepam, diphenhydramine and several others. She had to stop herself from whistling.

'Lovely in there, isn't it?' Adele asked, as Jane quickly closed the cabinet and joined her in the bedroom.

Adele led Jane to an adjoining room.

'I think this is the saddest room,' she said with a sigh.

The nursery was a child's dream. Decorated in pale blue, there was a small bassinet, a cradle, a cot and shelves filled with cuddly toys.

'Serina knew the first baby was a boy, but she miscarried at four months. Then there were all the IVF treatments. Each time they were clinging on to the hope that it would go to full term. Serina did get deeply depressed, but then she would always pull herself back together.'

'Martin mentioned you were going to be working with her, and you were looking for office space in Chelsea?'

'Yes, she kept her eye on the old company as she was a major shareholder, but she wanted to carve her own way with her own business. She did such a good job with this property that she was thinking about doing more interior design and some property development.'

'What role would you have played in her company?'

'Gosh, a bit of a general dogsbody really . . . I think she liked my company.'

Adele suddenly stopped, taking deep breaths and blinking rapidly.

'Are you all right?' Jane asked.

'I just need to sit down for a minute.'

Adele sat on a chair by the empty cot.

'Sorry, it's just that I have had to try and be strong for my brother – he has taken this so badly. I suppose in looking out for him, I've not really faced it all myself. Serina was such an important person in my life, in my family's life. It's only really just sinking in that she's gone. And in such a terrible way.' She turned to Jane. 'Dear God, why did she do it?'

They made their way back down the stairs.

'Did Serina ever mention suicide to you?' Jane asked.

'Never – no matter how depressed she used to get. She was a fighter.'

Hickock stood at the front door with a folder in his hand.

'Adele has very kindly shown me around upstairs,' Jane said.

Hickock nodded. 'Right, I think we've got all we need.'

'I'll go and see how my brother is,' Adele said, turning away.

In the car, Jane opened her briefcase, taking out the envelope of photographs.

'You need to see these. They were taken by one of the officers who attended the house on the night.'

Hickock leaned over the front seat and took the photographs, as they drove off. He flicked through them. 'Anything in particular I'm supposed to be looking at?'

'Yes – after Jenkins said he found his wife, he laid her on the floor, before the ambulance crew turned up and performed CPR.'

'I already know that!' he said irritably.

Jane ignored him. 'The first time I entered the house there was a large Persian carpet laid over the exact spot he found her – it was still there just now, but it is not in the photographs. The forensics team were checking it over inch by inch, and I suggested that they roll it back and inspect the parquet floor underneath.'

Hickock sighed. 'Fine. So what's the problem?'

'Maybe there isn't one – but what if the rug was put there because the floor had recently been cleaned by Jenkins or his sister? It's just a thought.'

Hickock shook his head. 'Well, here's a thought for you. If I found my wife dead in the hallway and there was blood on the floor, I'd want it cleaned or covered up, so it wasn't a constant reminder of what happened.' He handed the photographs back and Jane put them in the envelope.

'When Adele showed me round the house, I had a quick look in the master bedroom ensuite cabinet. It was like a pharmacy, filled with loads of different sleeping pills and prescription drugs with Serina Jenkins' name on them.'

'And your point is?'

'If she wanted to commit suicide painlessly, she could easily have mixed herself a lethal concoction of drugs.'

'I get your logic,' Hickock said, 'but you also run the risk of being found and rushed to hospital to have it all pumped out again. Hanging yourself from a bannister rail means you've got less chance of being resuscitated. Who knows, she may even have wanted her husband to find her in that shocking way as soon as he opened the front door.'

'Then why no suicide note? She might have been given some tablets before the hanging to sedate her.'

Hickock sighed. 'Don't get ahead of yourself, Tennison, let's just wait for the toxicology results before we start seizing everything in the bloody medicine cabinet.'

'It might also be worth speaking to her GP and IVF doctor about her state of mind?'

'I got their details from Jenkins while you were doing the grand tour of the house,' he said smugly.

'Well, I think we need to pay very careful attention to the time-line. When exactly Jenkins left for work in the morning, the time he got to work. What did he do during the day? Did he leave the office? What phone calls did he make . . . ?'

Hickock suddenly whipped round to face her. 'That's enough, Tennison! I am running this investigation, and I don't need you to tell me how to run it.'

Jane shrugged, refusing to rise to the bait. She could see from the expression on the driver's face in the mirror that her dressing-down would be all round the station by the morning, and she didn't want to make it any worse. But she really couldn't stay in the car any longer.

'You can drop me off anywhere. I'll pick my car up in the morning.'

The driver got the nod from Hickock. He pulled over and Jane got out, slamming the door behind her. She was grateful that they were not actually that far from her flat as she headed down the King's Road, stopping off at a shop selling mirrors and lamps, where she bought two old fifties bedside lamps.

As soon as she got home she booked a massage and a sauna at the gym for 6.15 a.m. on Monday morning, then ran a bath to calm herself down.

Jane was just going to have a glass of wine and make a toasted cheese sandwich when her phone rang. It was Peter, explaining that he would be busy over the weekend but asking if she was free for dinner on Monday, as he had found a good Lebanese restaurant he wanted to try out. She readily agreed, then, feeling much more relaxed, called her brother-in-law to ask if he could drop by to rewire her new lamps when it was convenient.

Tony turned up an hour later, by which time she was wearing her dressing gown.

'Would you like a glass of wine?' she offered.

'No, I'm fine, thanks. Actually, a cup of tea would be nice. Let me see what needs doing with these lamps, then I'll check if I've got the right stuff in the van.'

When he got back, Tony took a good look round the flat. 'They did a good job on the conversion,' he said, approvingly. 'I really want to get into that side of the business. Peter's company turns around some great properties. But that ex-partner of his is causing him a lot of aggravation. I think he's going to sell his house and pay the ex-wife off. Then he's going to try and buy his ex-partner out of the business so he can run the entire show. That would be good for me, I have to say.'

He started work on the lamps.

Jane made him a cup of tea and poured herself another glass of wine before returning to watch as Tony attached the cables to two new plugs.

He bent down beside the bed and plugged the first one into the socket and switched it on.

'Very nice, and I've not left too much cord so it just tucks behind the bedside cabinet.'

'How much do I owe you?'

'For goodness' sakes,' he said. 'You're family, Jane! Pam would go ballistic if I charged you.'

With both lamps in position, Tony began to coil the section of cable left on the reel as Jane picked up the discarded bits and put them into the waste bin.

'Can I ask you something? If I cut a section of electrical cable from the reel, like you did, but didn't cut away any of the plastic that holds the small wires inside, would it stretch?'

Tony looked quizzical. 'Not sure I follow you.'

'Well, if I tied it to a railing, say, and then tied a weight on the other end and dropped it, would the cable stretch?'

'I can't think why you'd want to do that,' he said, 'but yes, I'm pretty sure it would.'

Jane was eager for Tony to leave. She had already got a bottle of wine from the fridge to thank him for his time. After putting everything back in his toolbag, he offered to hoover the carpet, but she insisted that he get back home to Pam. He picked up the toolbag and then put it down.

'Something I want to tell you – she asked me not because of that situation you had, the miscarriage and how you might feel – but Pam is pregnant, she's not even told your parents yet. Just so you know, but don't let on that you do, is that all right?'

'That's fine, Tony, and I promise I won't say a word.'

'Goodnight then, and thanks for the wine.'

Jane closed the front door with a sigh, knowing that Pam would tell her when the time was right. Her mind turned to the Jenkins case, and she went over to the waste bin and took out a section of the cable that Tony had cut. She was certain that if handled, it would retain a fingerprint. Taking out her notebook, she made a note to check the measurements of the cable that had been used as a noose.

She also made a note to test how much a cable stretched if a weight equivalent to Serina's was attached to it, to see if that would account for the damage to her knees.

She was certain that if Martin Jenkins had planned the murder, he would have measured the length needed, but had not anticipated that the cable would stretch. Jane realised if that was the case, then Serina might have been semi-conscious when she first hit the floor, before her upper-body weight pulled against the noose, causing gradual asphyxiation.

Jane had almost chewed the end of her pencil off as she underlined that the forensics team should keep searching for the missing false nails. She was becoming more and more certain that this was a premediated murder, and that Serina had been fighting for her life as the cable was tied around her neck and she was pushed from the first-floor landing, most likely by her husband, especially when it dawned on Jane that if Serina had intended to kill herself, she would have to have stood on the bannisters, or climbed over them and gripped the rails before jumping. Jane looked through the pictures PC Thompson had taken and was able to confirm from a couple that Serina was barefoot.

Snapping her notebook closed and wrapping an elastic band around it, she tossed it into her briefcase. She was too tired to think it all through properly now. But she would spend the weekend getting all her ducks in a row, and on Monday she would confront DCI Hickock, whether he liked it or not.

CHAPTER THIRTEEN

Jane was walking to her car after her early-morning massage and sauna, when she saw Peter waiting beside it. He was wearing his usual tracksuit and carrying his kit bag. He smiled as she approached.

'I saw you were at the club, and wanted to confirm plans for dinner tonight, if you're still available?'

'I am,' she said, opening the driver's door. 'But on the condition that this time I'm paying.'

He grinned. 'That's impossible, I'm afraid. That Lebanese place is closed on Mondays, so I'm cooking. You have my address on Napier Road, so shall we say eight o'clock?'

'That's fine, I'll look forward to it.'

He leaned forwards and kissed her on the cheek.

'Until this evening.'

She drove to work in good spirits, thinking about what she would wear for dinner with Peter.

'Steady, Jane,' she told herself, smiling. 'The poor man's only just split up from his wife.'

When Jane got to the station, she rang through to Hickock's office, but there was no reply and no message service, so she decided to call him later. Her first priority was to talk to Edwina Summers, if she could track her down. She left a message for Maureen at the station, then drove to the most recent address in Chalk Farm.

The council estate was vast, with balconies running the entire length of the three-storey block, but it looked to be well maintained.

Maureen had ringed the flat number, 45, with a question mark.

Jane headed up the stone staircase to the second floor and found that from the outside, number 45 was rather run-down, with a peeling front door and a worn doormat. One window had been boarded up with a piece of cardboard. But there was a child's pushchair to one side of the door, which gave her hope this was the right place.

Jane rang the doorbell and waited, hearing the sound of a TV from inside. Eventually the door was opened, but with the chain still firmly in place.

'Hi, I'm DCI Jane Tennison. I am hoping to speak to Edwina Summers.'

'What do you want her for?'

'Just to have a chat, it's nothing to worry about. I just need to ask her a few questions about when she was at college in Ascot.'

Jane could see the overweight girl at the door with red and purple dyed hair was not Edwina.

'Does she live here?'

The girl pursed her lips and eased the door almost shut as she shouted something inaudible. After a moment she inched it open further. 'You from social services or something?'

'No, I'm a police detective.'

Again, the door was virtually closed, and another inaudible conversation occurred before the chain was removed and the girl stepped back and opened the door wider.

'She's in the back room, but be quiet as she's just got the kid to sleep – she had us up half the night.'

Jane stepped into the hall as the girl closed the door behind her. The hallway was quite dark, but Jane could see the wall was covered with posters of rock bands, attached with yellowing Sellotape.

The girl pointed to a room at the end of the hall, then walked into the next room, where the sound of the TV was coming from. She shut the door behind her. Jane walked cautiously down the dimly lit hallway and knocked lightly on the door at the end. After a moment it inched open. Edwina was dressed all in black, her face streaked with make-up. Her hair was dyed black with blonde streaks and she was wearing big black Doc Martens.

'Edwina?'

'Yeah – who are you and what do you want?'

'I'm a police detective. I just need to have a chat with you. It's nothing to be worried about, I just need to ask you about an incident that occurred when you were at college.'

'That was years ago, so I can't help yer.'

'Is there somewhere we can talk? I was told your daughter is sleeping.'

Edwina sighed impatiently and looked back into the room.

'Go into the kitchen – I need to heat some milk. She's been up all night with a stinking cold.'

Unsurprisingly, the kitchen was a tip, with dirty mugs and plates stacked in the sink and on the draining board. There was a table with a filthy plastic cloth, laden with rows of sauce bottles and empty takeaway cartons.

Jane pulled out a chair and sat down while Edwina opened the fridge and smelt a bottle of milk before putting it to one side to clean out a small saucepan.

'I want to ask you about a girl called Brittany Hall. She went missing when you were at the college.'

'Why?'

'I'm reopening the case in an attempt to find out what happened to her.'

'Left it a bit late, haven't yer – it's been years. I got kicked out, so I dunno anything. Shit, yer don't have a few quid, do yer? It's gotta be coins – the meter's just run out.'

Jane handed over some coins and Edwina left the kitchen, returning a few minutes later. She lit the gas stove and poured the milk into the not very clean pan.

'I went to see your grandmother when I was trying to trace you. She showed me a lovely photograph of you with your little girl. I know she would dearly love to see the both of you.'

'Like hell she would! She's a mean-spirited old hag. All she can talk about is her genius son, her brilliant husband, and how she was forced to bring me up because they both died. Well, I'd like to know what happened to my granddad's Stradivarius – I know he had one and she used to have it in a display cabinet. Have yer any idea how much a violin like that is worth?'

'No, I don't.'

'Millions, worth bloody millions . . . I know she had it, or else she sold it and never gave me any money.'

'I know you were a very talented pianist.'

'Yeah, she made me practise day in day out, since I was just a toddler. I got scholarships, so she never had to pay for me being at college.'

Jane watched as Edwina tipped a packet of powdered cereal into a bowl, then poured the heated milk over it and stirred it with a spoon.

'Thing is, I was very good, but reality was I never had the motivation to be any better. In fact, I hated it. I suppose deep down I knew I was always only going to be just good, never brilliant.'

'What do you do now?'

'I go down to Camden Lock on Saturdays and help out on the stalls. But mostly I survive on benefits – did she give yer any money for me?'

'No, but at least I found you. I need to ask you something very important.'

Edwina sat down and began to heap sugar into the cereal, stirring it again. She tasted a spoonful and Jane thought she was testing for her daughter, but then she began to eat it herself.

'Brittany Hall, she was the girl who went missing.'

'Yeah, I remember her – poor girl had a terrible stammer.'

'You spoke to her mother when she visited the college enquiring about Brittany.'

'I don't remember – like I said, I got kicked out. They caught me having a joint in the toilets.'

'But Mrs Hall remembers you – you approached her and said something.'

Edwina shrugged, ate more of the congealed cereal, then wiped her mouth with the back of her hand.

'It was a long time ago and I've been through a hell of a time since then. Got involved with a real dirtbag who beat the shit out me – I almost lost my kid.'

Jane carried on with her questioning. 'There were three boys questioned at the time because they were the last people to see Brittany. Do you recall any of them?'

Edwina ate the last spoonful of cereal and licked the spoon clean.

'Oh yeah, the three musketeers – Justin Moore, Phillip Sayer and the big sporty know-all John Kilroy. They were a nasty bunch of bastards, so I kept well away from them.'

'But you overheard them talking, didn't you?'

Edwina gave Jane a hooded look and got up to dump the cereal bowl on the draining board. Jane hesitated, then opened her bag and took out her wallet. She pulled out a ten-pound note and left it on the table.

Edwina immediately reacted. 'I saw them huddled together behind the groundsman's shed, smoking. I knew they was the last people to see Brittany, so crept over to hear what they was talking about. I heard Phillip say, "This is bad, real bad, John." Justin said, "What if they find her?" . . . then John told them to shut up and stick to the story. As they walked off, I heard Justin say, "Did you clean the car out?" but I don't know who he was talking to.'

'How do you know who said what?' Jane asked.

She laughed. 'Yer don't forget the voices of bullies. They were always together, chatting up various students, but I never saw Brittany with them. She was a loner, and I was a music student, so I was never in her class. But we did this awful Greek play together, so that's how I got to know her. I felt sorry for her, she had this stammer and they all made fun of her.'

'Why did you approach Brittany's mother to repeat what you had heard?'

'She kept turning up at the college, desperate to find out what happened to Brittany. I just felt she needed to know what I heard.'

'Why didn't you tell the police?'

'I was frightened the boys would find out.'

'Did John Kilroy have a car?'

This had not been mentioned in any report that Jane had read. Edwina picked up the ten-pound note. 'Maybe, I dunno – that was all I heard.'

'You were never questioned when the police were looking for her?'

'Not by the police, but the headmaster held a school meeting and said if anyone knew anything about Brittany's disappearance to speak to him. I know now I should have come forward, but like I said, I was scared of the boys.'

Jane stood up and watched Edwina pocket the money, as they heard crying coming from her bedroom.

'I got to go and see to her, she's really poorly.'

'Thank you for your time, Edwina, and I really think it would be good for you to take your daughter to visit your grandmother. I'll show myself out.'

By the time Jane got back to the station, it was late morning and the canteen had now been reopened. Thankfully, there was no smell of fried cooking. She asked Maureen to check if John Kilroy had a driving licence and had had access to a car.

She decided to use the afternoon to interview the first of the three boys, Phillip Sayer. He was based in Eastbourne, working at an estate agents called Taylor Sayer, run by his father. She could drive there that afternoon. The second boy, Justin Moore, was living in Yorkshire, which would entail a long drive or train journey, so she would talk to him next. Because John Kilroy was working on an oil rig, she'd keep him until last. She decided not to call ahead, preferring to keep the element of surprise. As she was leaving, she put in another call to Hickock but was told he was still not available.

By the time Jane arrived in Eastbourne it was almost 3 p.m. She parked on the seafront to have a late lunch, having stopped en route to pick up a coffee and a sandwich, then walked to Taylor Sayer, which was close to the main shopping precinct. She had a quick glance at the houses displayed in the windows and was surprised at how much lower property prices were than in London.

Jane entered the reception area, where two young women were working behind desks.

She showed her ID and asked one of them if she could speak to Phillip Sayer.

'Oh dear, it's not more parking fines, is it?'

Jane smiled. 'No.'

The young woman turned to her colleague.

'Did he go out earlier?'

The other woman shook her head. 'He's not here. He had a viewing at eleven and was then going for lunch, so I'd say he's gone home for the day.'

Jane detected a slight undercurrent between them. 'Could I have his home address, please?'

'Do you want me to check he's there? He might have gone to the golf course,' the blonde woman said.

Her colleague smiled. 'I don't think he's playing this afternoon. He has another viewing at five.' She jotted down an address and phone number and handed the sheet of paper to Jane.

Jane thanked them and left.

Saffrons Court was an elegant contemporary apartment block overlooking the Saffrons cricket ground. She took the lift to the top floor and pressed the bell to number 21. She waited before pressing it again, annoyed with herself for not phoning first to make sure Sayer was at home. She was about to turn back to the lifts when the door was opened by a very well-dressed young man with curly blond hair, wearing a pinstriped suit. He looked at Jane questioningly.

'Phillip Sayer?' she said.

'Yes, who are you?'

Jane showed her ID. He glanced at it and then frowned.

'What's this about?'

'We're reopening the investigation into the disappearance of Brittany Hall. I would appreciate it if you could give me a few moments of your time.'

Phillip Sayer blinked for a moment before letting her in.

'Go straight ahead into the sitting room. Would you like tea or coffee?'

'No, thank you.'

The sitting room was attractively furnished with wide windows and sliding French doors opening onto a balcony with stunning views over the park.

'This is very pleasant,' Jane said, sitting down on one of the sofas.

He nodded. 'It's a wonderful location. But it'll be on the market as soon as we have a new bathroom installed. It's actually quite a new development, but it was previously decorated in poor taste. Buyers don't really like carpeted bathrooms anymore.'

Jane felt as if he was trying to sell her the apartment, talking rather quickly and waving his hand around in explanation, while his blond hair and pale blue eyes gave him an insipid quality.

'Do you usually house-sit in new properties?'

He flushed, shaking his head.

'No, not at all – but this is a first for me as it's my project, so I want to be on site to make sure everything is done properly.'

'Well, I'm sure it will be a very successful project.'

'Thank you.' He was trying hard to appear relaxed, but Jane could sense his nervousness.

'Mr Sayer, can you tell me how well you knew Brittany Hall?'

He chewed his bottom lip.

'Look, I was questioned at the time and told the police every-thing I could – in all honesty, I don't have anything else I could add to my original statement.'

'I'll be the judge of that,' Jane said with a smile. 'I'd like you to tell me about your interaction with Brittany on the day she disap-peared.' She opened her notebook, and turned over a blank page, her pen poised.

He raked his hand through his hair. 'Gosh, this is really unnerv-ing. All I can say is that we were all at the Old Garden, a pub not far from Ascot on the way towards Windsor. I was with John Kilroy and Justin Moore. Brittany Hall was at the pub and had had too much to drink. When we decided to leave, she became very loud, shouting and causing a bit of a stir. We were quite concerned about her, but she refused to come with us, so we left her outside the pub and returned to the college.'

Jane knew this was almost word for word from his original statement. She tapped her notebook.

'Who was driving?'

'Pardon?'

'I believe one of you had a car, and I think the pub is quite a dis-tance from the college.'

'No, we didn't have a car. We walked there and back. It was quite a way, but we didn't think too much about it. We'd done it plenty of times before.'

'Did you not turn back to see if Brittany was all right?'

'John felt concerned, so he walked back to check up on her. But he saw her getting into a red car, so he presumed she was being taken back to the college.'

'After you returned, you didn't worry that she had not come back to college? In fact, it wasn't reported that she was missing until the Monday.'

'To be honest, we had an away cricket match on the Sunday, so none of us really thought about her. I have to say that we were very shocked when we found out that she hadn't returned.'

'What if I was to tell you that we have a witness who overheard the three of you discussing the missing girl, saying that you were all determined to get your statements in line so that each of you would say the same thing?'

'That is not true – we all told the truth.'

'Do you drive, Mr Sayer?'

'Yes, I do . . . well, I do now. At that time, I didn't have either a car or a driving licence, nor did the other two.'

'Did any of you have a sexual relationship with Brittany Hall?'

'No! I hadn't really even noticed her before that evening, she just latched on to us. She wasn't very attractive, to be honest.'

'So, Brittany was in the pub when all three of you arrived?'

'Yes, she had been drinking.'

'Her mother claims she did not drink and was rather a nervous young woman. So, it surprises me that she would have been in the pub by herself.'

Phillip shrugged and gave that double blink again. 'We were asked this, all of us, and either she went there with someone, or she arranged to meet someone there and whoever it was had dumped her, and maybe that is the person who John saw pick her up later that night.'

'You are referring to John seeing her get into a red car?'

'Yes, exactly. I'm sorry, this was all rather a long time ago.'

Jane stood up, ready to leave. 'No matter how long ago it was, Mr Sayer, Brittany's mother still wants to know what happened to her daughter. Thank you for your time.'

'Believe you me, it was not easy for any of us.'

Jane glanced at him with irritation as she headed towards the door. 'Well, I must say it looks as if you have done all right for yourself.'

He laughed ruefully. 'I had hopes for a more academic career.'

As she went down in the lift, Jane was sure Sayer was lying. And he was definitely the sort to crack under pressure. She just needed to find his weak spot.

CHAPTER FOURTEEN

Jane made it home in plenty of time to shower, wash and blow-dry her hair and choose what to wear for the dinner with Peter. She took a bottle of white wine from her fridge, checked the address and looked at her *A to Z* before driving to Napier Road. Peter's house was a large semi-detached property in a row of similar-styled houses, and Jane was impressed as she rang the bell.

Peter opened the door with a smile. 'Come in. Did you find a parking space? This time of night it's sometimes a problem.'

'Yes, further up the road, and this is for you.' She handed him the bottle of wine.

He stepped aside, ushering her into the open-plan hallway, then led her into a glass-domed extension with a long refectory table, wide benches and carved chairs at either end. It could easily seat fourteen and was surrounded with bookcases and cabinets. In the centre of the table was a large vase of roses.

Jane handed Peter her shawl. 'You look stunning!' he said. 'Now, come through to the kitchen and let me offer you a glass of champagne.'

She followed him through an archway into an impressive kitchen with a marble island in the centre and an array of copper pans hanging from hooks. Through the French doors she could see a mass of plants illuminated by a plethora of massive, well-positioned floor lights.

'This is so lovely,' Jane said, perching on a stool.

He grinned. 'It took a lot of hard labour, I can tell you. Just getting the planning permission took forever.'

'It's very misleading. From the outside, you'd never know the house was this big.'

Peter opened a bottle of champagne and poured two glasses, handing one to Jane.

'My wife did a lot of the designs, and my company was working on the house for almost two years before we could move in. Cheers.' He lifted his glass and tapped Jane's. 'Now, I have attempted a beef wellington – no starter, I'm afraid: I was going to go to the local deli but ran out of time – but I have a delicious dessert, tiramisu from a brilliant bakery.'

She laughed delightedly. She could not recall anyone ever going to so much trouble for her. He checked on the potatoes, sorted out plates to be warmed, then went into the dining area with mats, napkins and more glasses for wine.

'Right, we're done. We have ten minutes until the beef's ready. Would you like me to show you around the rest of the house?'

'Yes, please, I am very impressed with everything I have seen so far. It's a really lovely house.'

Peter led Jane up the stairs, and she followed him from one room after another, all decorated to perfection. Finally, he ushered her into his son's bedroom. It seemed like a child's wonderland, stacked with toys, a playhouse and a huge train set.

'This is Joey's room. I have to start packing up most of his clothes and toys to go to my wife's, and I'll just keep a few for when he is here.'

She could tell he was upset, but before she could say anything they heard the oven timer ringing from the kitchen.

'Right, I hope you're hungry.'

Jane poured them both another glass of champagne as he opened the oven and took out the beef wellington.

'What do you think?' Peter asked.

'Looks wonderful. Did you always do the cooking?'

'Not always. My wife was a cordon bleu, and everything I've done tonight she taught me.'

The food was as delicious as it looked and the conversation flowed easily. Jane noticed that Peter did consume quite a large amount of wine, while she mostly sipped the iced water as she was driving.

After dessert, Peter suddenly seemed to become rather anxious, and went to get a cigar, after asking if she minded. He returned to the table smoking, and carrying a bottle of port.

'Not for me, thank you,' Jane said.

He poured port into his empty wine glass, then sat with a glum expression.

'I really have to think about my next move, whether to buy out my ex-partner's share in our company, which would have to be from the sale of the house. If I don't buy him out, then I think he intends to make me an offer. We drew up this bloody contract when we first started together, so there is nothing I can really do about it.'

'Is the business doing well?'

'Better than ever, and I have just put in an offer on a proposed site in a good location, but it would mean a lot of hard graft to get it up and rolling, and a few years before I would reap the benefits.'

'Do you think if you bought out your partner you could handle the company without him?'

He frowned, taking a sip of the port before he slowly nodded. 'I'm certain I could, it's just the in-between unsettled costs, and I would obviously have maintenance and child support to pay, too. I'd be strapped for cash for a while.'

'Has the divorce been finalised?'

'Any day. I'm trying to keep it on an amicable basis, but it's very hard. I think if I did get shirty about all the lies and subterfuge, the way the pair of them carried on behind my back, she would take it out on me by refusing part custody.'

'It must be very hard.'

'That's putting it mildly. I have been in sort of shock for months, you know, hardly able to believe it, but it has started to level out. I am so sorry about going on like this, it must be very boring for you. I honestly meant to not even bring it up, and you have been so lovely, in fact, meeting you has been a really uplifting thing for me.'

'Good, I'm glad. And I do understand the turmoil you must be in as I went through a break-up not long ago.'

'I'm sorry, do you want to talk about it?'

She gave a soft laugh, shaking her head. 'No, it's over and I have moved on.'

'That's what I should do, move on and stop wasting time feeling sorry for myself.'

There was a sound of ringing, and Peter got up and went into the kitchen. She picked up the plates and followed him. He was perching on the island, holding a large receiver-type thing to his ear.

'That's good news. Tell them I'll be on site first thing in the morning. We need to double-check their exterior walls and how much planning permission we will need to extend that length. OK, fine, see you then. Thanks for calling.'

He pressed something on the receiver and grinned. 'Sorry, that was good news, we've had a project under construction for over a week, and we had problems with the next-door building, but now they want to sell off a section of their yard that bordered mine. That was my head engineer, he's been there half the night. We use this newfangled mobile for work because I'm so rarely at home.'

'Don't you have to go through a call centre to pass on messages? Only, funnily enough my ex had one, and, even funnier, it was the girl at the call centre he dumped me for.'

Peter laughed. 'No, these are all battery charged. I can use it in my car, take it everywhere.'

'Right, I am going to help you do the washing-up and then I should make a move.'

'I wouldn't hear of it. I'll walk you to your car.'

'If you're sure.'

'I have a lovely lady who comes in and I will leave it to her. Let me get your wrap.'

Peter slipped her wrap around her shoulders as they walked out of the house together. His security lights came on and he gave a small wave to the house opposite.

'That's my neighbour, the Napier Road watchdog. He had security cameras fitted after we had a spate of burglaries, and he can monitor my property – who comes and goes – as well as his own, obviously. Some of the residents don't like it, but it doesn't bother me, even more so if I am putting it on the market so it'll have people coming and going viewing it.'

'Does it record on tape?'

'Yes, then if nothing is amiss, he just rewinds it. He's in the business and doing a roaring trade. Lots of properties in the Boltons use his cameras. He reckons it'll become a regular precaution.'

Jane looked over the road; she could see the small security camera surrounded with growing ivy and hardly detectable. They reached her car, and she bleeped it open. Peter put his arm around her and lifted her chin up with his hand.

'Thank you for tonight, and I am sorry I went on about my ex. I promise next time I will not mention a word.'

He kissed her gently on the lips, and as she got into the driving seat, carefully closed her door. As she drove off, he waved before turning back towards his house.

As she drove home, Jane made a small detour to Martin Jenkins' house, wondering if any of the houses on his road might also have security cameras.

Jane drove slowly down the road, easing to a crawl speed as she passed Jenkins' house. Looking over to the house opposite, she spotted a security camera above the porch. She did another slow drive down the entire road and back, and counted five other properties with the same surveillance devices.

The following morning Jane arrived at the station early and typed out her report on her meeting with Phillip Sayer. Next, she opened her Serina Jenkins file and added a note suggesting

Hickock should request the camera footage from the property opposite Martin Jenkins', to see if his statements about his movements could be confirmed.

Jane filed the Phillip Sayer report and left the Martin Jenkins one on her desk, then looked at the route she would need to take to call in on the next boy. Justin Moore lived in a small village called Helmsley, outside York. Maureen had found it difficult to track him down as he had changed addresses and workplaces frequently but, as far as she could tell, he was now employed at a small solicitor's office. His family lived in the South of France and had not seen their son for some considerable time.

Maureen arrived just as Jane was finalising the route to Helmsley.

'You know it'll be at least six hours on the motorway,' she said. 'Why not take the train to York and hire a car to drive the last leg to Helmsley? I've made a note of a couple of nice hotels, and then you could get the first train back to London.'

Jane thought Maureen was right. The next train was at 11.30, and she calculated that she would get to Helmsley around 5, to meet Justin Moore at his office. If not, she had his home address. Maureen booked a room at the Feathers Hotel and she was all set.

Jane asked Maureen to forward her updated report on the Brittany Hall case to Kernan, adding that she would be travelling that afternoon to interview the second boy involved in the investigation. She added that she would put in her expenses on her return.

After returning home to pack an overnight bag, she caught a taxi to Euston station and was in plenty of time to catch the train.

* * *

Hickock was due to have a meeting with Kernan, who wanted an update on the Serina Jenkins investigation. Annoyed that he couldn't get his tape machine to replay the interview with Martin Jenkins, Hickock went to see Jane in her office to get a copy of her notes. Finding no one there, he had a quick rummage around Jane's desk and was pleased to find her updated Serina Jenkins file.

'Just what I need,' he said with a grin, tucking it under his arm.

Fifteen minutes later, he was in Kernan's office, talking confidently about how he was going to progress the investigation.

'I'm going to do a reconstruction using sandbags the same weight as Serina Jenkins. I'll also use the same make of electric cable . . .'

Kernan raised his hand. 'Just hold on a minute, Brian . . . What's this all in aid of?'

'There's something niggling me about Jenkins' version of events,' Hickock told him. 'His account of how he found his wife and his subsequent actions doesn't quite add up. I want to determine how quickly and how far the cable would stretch.'

'Is it going to be a costly exercise?'

'No. The groundsman at my golf course said he'd fill some sacks with sand for nothing . . . other than a couple of pints. I've got hold of some photos taken when the ambulance crew attended. It's clear Serina Jenkins was barefooted. If she did intentionally jump from the bannister, then I'd expect to find her footprints on it. Even if she climbed over and stood on the staircase ledge, they should be there. If she held on to the rail to steady herself before jumping, then her fingerprints should be on the underside of the rail. If there's none of Serina's footprints or fingerprints on the bannisters, it suggests to me she was pushed over by her husband.'

'He could have wiped them off,' Kernan countered.

'Yes, but a lack of her prints would be a sort of own goal. He'd have a hard time explaining why he cleaned the bannisters so soon after his wife's death.'

Kernan nodded. 'You've obviously spent some considerable time thinking this through, Brian.'

'Thank you, sir. It's been time-consuming dealing with this and the fraud case at the same time, but I'm confident the end results will be worth it.'

'What about verifying Martin Jenkins' movements?'

'Already on it, sir. I have also been checking through their bank statements. It looks like Mr Jenkins was not in a very good financial position. His wife had sizeable amounts in her current and savings accounts, but he seemed to have drained their joint account.'

'So, who gets her money on her death?'

'I have a meeting scheduled with her lawyers to find out.'

'Well, you need to move fast, Brian, and get this case cleared up either way asap. You know I wasn't entirely happy letting you lead the investigation due to Jenkins being a personal friend of yours. People might start thinking you are advising him on what to do and say.'

'I think my ideas and the way I've approached this investigation show that isn't the case. He's an acquaintance, anyway, not a close friend, and I'm the one who got him to open up more, not Tennison. If his actions led to Serina's death, I'll find the evidence to prove it and nullify any conflict-of-interest crap that comes our way.'

'Good. I want it resolved within the next few days . . . so go and get on with it,' said Kernan.

* * *

After five hours, Jane finally arrived in York and hurried to the rental agency to pick up her car. Supplied with maps, she then headed out towards Helmsley, taking a while to get used to the automatic transmission on the Toyota.

It was growing dark as she made her way through the winding country roads. When she came to a narrow stone bridge, she wondered if she'd taken a wrong turn, but then sighed with relief as she saw a sign for Helmsley. Jane drove through the old market square, then turned left down a wider road to eventually find the Feathers.

After booking in, she unpacked and had a wash and redid her make-up, changing her shoes and putting on a clean blouse. It was now 6.30, and she was beginning to feel very hungry as she'd had only had a coffee and a sandwich on the train, but decided to have her meeting with Justin Moore before getting some dinner.

Luckily, the receptionist was very helpful; she did not personally know Mr Moore but was a very good friend of his wife, who ran a riding school. She said that Jane could actually walk to their cottage, which was situated on the square. She wrote down the directions on a piece of notepaper.

'Thank you. Could I also order dinner in my room for eight thirty?'

Presented with the menu, Jane chose steak and chips with salad and a half bottle of Shiraz.

Walking out of the hotel, she wished she'd brought a heavier coat, as it felt a lot colder than London. But the walk was not that long, and as she arrived at the cottage she was relieved to see lights on. She hoped they also had a big blazing fire. She pulled an old bell pull and waited a short time before the door was opened by a young woman wearing jodhpurs with thick woollen socks, but not boots, and a bright orange pullover.

'Hello?'

'Good evening, I'm sorry that I was unable to call but I don't have your home phone number. I am DCI Jane Tennison from the Metropolitan Police.' She showed her ID.

The young woman had bushy red hair coiled into a loose bun, a ruddy complexion and big bright blue eyes.

'Oh, do you want to speak to me or my husband?'

'Well, if you are Mrs Moore, I'd like to speak to Justin.'

'I am, you'd better come in, he was just lighting a fire in the back room. I'm Celia, and I apologise for the outfit but I've just got back from mucking out the stables. We had a girl off sick, so I've had to run around like a demented ferret all day. It always happens when we're fully booked.'

Jane followed her down a small hallway to an open door.

'Justin, someone to see you, have you managed to light it?'

'Eventually, but a lot of the wood was damp, so I had to use firelighters as well as all the newspaper.'

Jane remained in the doorway as Celia went further into a small, rather cluttered room dominated by a big old brick and stone fireplace. There was a small settee, and two easy chairs with shelves piled with books.

Justin Moore was wearing a white shirt, with the cuffs rolled up, and had a very frazzled expression, with coal dust over one cheek.

'I'm sorry, what's this about?'

His wife turned to go. 'I'm going to get on with dinner, Justin, unless you need me in here?'

Jane smiled. 'I just need to ask your husband some questions about an incident that occurred at his college.'

'Is it going to take long? I was going to say if it takes a while, you could eat with us as I'm doing roast chicken.'

'That's very kind of you, but I have ordered dinner at my hotel.'

'Where are you staying?'

'I'm at the Feathers.'

'Oh, that's a lovely place with a super bar. We often go there for dinner.'

'Celia, go away, and shut the door,' Justin said gruffly, crossing to a cupboard and taking out a bottle of whisky and two glasses. He proffered one to Jane but she shook her head. He unscrewed the cap and poured a large measure into his glass, and then went back to the fire. He picked up a poker to have a dig at the logs, then dumped it in a basket.

Jane knew instinctively that Justin had been called by Phillip Sayer, since he showed no surprise at all that she was there. She opened her notebook and watched as he took a gulp of whisky.

'When you were at college, a girl called Brittany Hall went missing, and you, along with Phillip Sayer and John Kilroy, were the last people to see her alive.'

'Yes, I remember it well,' he said.

'We have reopened the investigation and I'm following a new line of enquiry. A witness overheard the three of you discussing getting your stories straight about that evening.'

'Well, I don't know who this so-called witness is, but obviously we discussed it between us, what we'd seen.'

'At that time, did you drive a car?'

'Me? Good heavens no, I didn't get my driving licence until I went to university.'

'Did any of you own or have access to a car?'

'No. We were just teenagers.'

'What about the car John Kilroy maintained he saw Brittany getting into? Could you describe the make and model?'

'No, I actually never saw the car, but I know John described it as red, possibly a sports car.'

Suddenly a loud barking erupted. It went on for a while and Justin got up and opened the door.

'Celia, let the bloody dog in.' He came back and sat down again. 'Sorry about that.'

'What was Phillip Sayer like? You were all close friends, I believe.'

Justin sat back in his chair. 'He was a bit shy . . . well, at first. He was dominated by his father. He was very academic, but he didn't do as well in his mock A levels as had been expected. His father took him out of his boarding school and warned him if he didn't get the right grades he'd have to go and work alongside him in his estate agents.' He rolled his eyes and took another drink.

'Did he?'

'Did he what?'

'Make good grades.'

'I think so, but I didn't see him after I left. I went to Coventry University and we never really kept in touch. That goes for John as well.'

'So, not Oxford or Cambridge?'

He grimaced and shook his head.

'What was he like?'

'I just told you.'

'Sorry, I meant John Kilroy, tell me about him.'

'John? He was the pride of his previous school, brilliant at cricket *and* rugby, which is unusual. He was bigger than both of us, and fit, always working out in the gym. He was hoping for a professional sports career, but he had some kind of accident skiing and injured his leg.'

'Do you keep in touch with him?'

'No, the usual thing, you go off to uni and lose contact, make new friends. I did hear he was working on an oil rig, but I've no idea where or if he's still there.'

'But you are still in contact with Phillip Sayer?'

'Not really, not spoken to him for a long time.'

'When did you get married?'

'Three years ago. We met at university, I got work in York to be near to her. She was brought up here, and when her father died, she took over the stables. We moved in here about eighteen months ago, renting this place until we have enough to buy a property.'

'Did you invite either of your friends to your wedding?'

'No, well, they wouldn't have known anyone there and Celia has never met them.'

Jane could tell the more he drank, the more confident he got in his answers, becoming quite relaxed.

There was a loud scratching at the door, and Justin got up and quickly opened it, unable to stop the enormous sheepdog hurtling into the room.

'Sorry about this. Caleb, quiet, no, get down.'

The dog started pawing at Jane, but Justin dragged him off and he eventually settled in the chair by the fire. He sat with his tongue out, panting, as Justin closed the door.

'I'm sorry, he shouldn't be allowed in here, I don't approve, but he's Celia's really and doesn't pay any attention to me.'

Justin fetched his glass and gave himself a refill, then perched on the end of the sofa.

'How well did you know Brittany Hall?' Jane asked.

Justin's relaxed demeanour quickly changed. He started tapping his foot nervously. 'I didn't really know her at all.'

'You and your friends gave a statement when the incident occurred, after it became known Brittany was reported missing.'

'Yes, that is correct, in fact I was asked repeatedly about the evening, we all were questioned, and it became very disturbing. I mean, it felt as if we were under suspicion, it was very traumatic because all we could tell them was that we had seen her that night.'

'I know you gave a statement at the time, but could you repeat for me exactly what happened that night?'

'We went to the pub together on the Friday evening, walked from college, it was quite a distance, but we had often done it. We were in the bar and Brittany Hall was already there, she had been drinking. I think we did buy her a beer, it was not that crowded for a Friday and we had also got there quite late, and she was being very boisterous, embarrassing, because you know we have to mind our P's and Q's when out drinking because the college disapproved, although we were allowed as we were eighteen. Anyway, we decided to leave and she came out with us and then became even louder and started to be very silly. We told her to be quiet and we even asked if she would walk back with us, but she refused and so we walked off, leaving her there.'

'Were you not concerned about her?'

'Not really, but I think John was, and he returned to see if she was OK, and then he came back and said he had seen her getting into a car, a red one, but he couldn't tell what make it was or who was driving.'

'When were you all informed that she had not returned to college?'

'Oh, days later. On the Sunday John had a big cricket match and me and Phillip went on the coach to give support. We came back quite late and had supper and went to bed. Monday we were obviously doing our studies, and then on Tuesday the alarm went up.'

Jane tapped her notebook, thoughtfully. His recall was virtually identical to Justin's, bar a few extra details.

The door opened and Celia walked in, beaming. 'Chicken is in, veg is almost ready, and I have even made stuffing with sausage left over from lunch.'

She sat perched on the opposite arm of the sofa. Caleb wagged his tail but stayed in the chair.

'So, what's all this about? You're a detective, right? Justin's not in any trouble, is he?'

'Of course not,' he snapped. 'It's about something that happened when I was at college a long time ago.'

Jane nodded. 'We've reopened the case of a student who went missing when your husband was there. He and two of his friends were the last people to see a missing girl alive.'

'So she's still missing?'

'Correct,' Jane said.

'But that's dreadful.' Celia turned to Justin. 'I'm amazed you never told me any of this.'

'For God's sake, Celia, it was five years ago and I didn't even know her.'

He shifted uncomfortably on the end of the sofa.

'Did John have any relationship with Brittany?' Jane asked.

'God, no. She wasn't his type. Girls flocked around him, so he could pick and choose.'

'Are you still in touch with him?'

'No, I already told you.'

'What about Phillip?'

He shook his head firmly. 'No, likewise.'

Celia turned to him, frowning. Jane felt she was about to say something, but Justin gave her a nasty look and she kept quiet. Jane was now sure that Justin had warned him about her impending visit.

'Well, I think that is everything, and thank you both for your time.' She stood up, put her notebook away and picked up her coat from the back of the chair.

* * *

Justin ushered Jane to the hall, then poured himself another whisky and stood drinking it by the fire.

Celia came in from the kitchen. 'Why have you never told me about that girl before?'

'Christ, I knew you would start on me. What does it matter?'

'But you lied – that friend of yours, Justin, has called you several times this week.'

'Because he was bloody questioned by that woman as well, that's all. I've had enough of it. It was bad enough not getting that place at Cambridge because I was virtually having a bloody nervous break-down about it all. I had to take all my exams again and wait another year before I got a bloody place at Coventry, so, please, just don't bring it up again.'

'Fine, I won't, but at least one good thing came out of it.'

He looked at her, confused.

'Well, we would never have met if you'd gone to Cambridge, would we?'

She walked back to the kitchen.

He stood for a few moments. It was true; if it hadn't been for the whole ghastly business with Brittany Hall, he would not have met Celia. And he wouldn't have been living in a tiny village in a cramped cottage that stank of horses, working for a tin-pot company that paid him peanuts, either.

CHAPTER FIFTEEN

It was a long journey back to London, and late afternoon when Jane arrived at the station, hurrying straight to her office.

'How was your trip? How did the interview go?' Maureen asked.

Jane started unpacking her briefcase. 'I'll tell you all about it later, Maureen. Right now I want to know what you've managed to find out about John Kilroy.'

Maureen consulted her notes. 'Well, he seems to move around a lot, and his permanent address still seems to be his mother's house.'

'What about a car?' Jane asked with a note of impatience.

'I've had a bit more luck on that,' Maureen said. 'There's no vehicle registered in his name, but he did apply for a provisional licence six years ago, though he never got a full one. His mother owns a fifteen-year-old Lancia Beta four-door saloon vehicle, that was taxed and insured four years ago but wasn't renewed after that. But it wasn't sold either.'

'OK, that might be something. Something else, Maureen . . . I need you to go through the files and see if you can find the statements from the bar staff at the pub. I've got to see Kernan about visiting the oil rig, so just leave anything you find on my desk.'

'Right,' Maureen said. 'You do know none of the paperwork was in any kind of order. And there's stuff from other cases, too. I think some of the Brittany Hall files were put in the wrong boxes.'

'Just do your best, Maureen,' Jane said, walking out.

Jane knocked on the chief superintendent's door, waited for a gruff 'Enter!' and walked in.

'Good afternoon, sir. I thought I would give you an update on my case, along with my expenses so far.' She put a file down on his desk. 'I think it is now imperative that I interview John Kilroy—'

He put his hand up to stop her as he read slowly through her reports. He then looked over her expenses, pursing his lips.

'Was it really necessary to stay overnight? From what I can gather, you appear to have uncovered no new evidence from all this running around.'

'Justin Moore and Phillip Sayer repeated their original statements virtually word for word. I'm convinced that they did collude with each other, not just recently, but on the night of the girl's disappearance.'

'Well, I can't see any of that from your report. I can't justify the cost of you travelling to this oil rig unless you can find some real evidence to back up your suspicions. I will sign off your expenses this time, but in future please put in a request before you hare off to God knows where.'

Jane returned to her office in a foul mood, but at least Maureen had managed to find two statements; one was from a young student working at the pub on the night Brittany Hall disappeared, and the other from the head barman.

'It was a busy Friday night, so there must have been quite a lot of bar staff,' Jane said.

'I'll keep looking,' Maureen said with a sigh.

Jane skimmed through the interviews. The student said he had been working at the far end of the bar near to the outside garden area. He was mostly serving people drinking there, so had not paid any attention to the main bar area and did not see any of the three boys or Brittany Hall.

The older barman did recall the three boys arriving together, but did not remember if Brittany Hall came in with them or was already there. He could not recall seeing her with anyone else but them. He said that Friday night was always their busiest time, popular with students but also many tourists visiting Windsor. It was also karaoke night, which meant it was even more crowded. He said the car park behind the pub was full, but he did not see a red sports car there, and parking out front was not allowed. He thought it was quite possible he had served one or other of the boys but was unable to give a proper description of them.

Jane pursed her lips thoughtfully. Phillip Sayer hadn't mentioned anything about karaoke, but it was something she remembered from her interview with Justin Moore that got her attention. She thumbed through her notebook to make sure of his exact words, then nodded to herself. He said they had become embarrassed by Brittany's behaviour, as there were not many people in the bar that night.

It was also odd that none of the bar staff mentioned a drunk woman matching Brittany's description.

She turned to Maureen. 'How are you getting on?'

'No luck on finding any more statements, I'm afraid, but I've got John Kilroy's mother's address. I called to double-check and spoke to her carer. She said that Mrs Kilroy was indisposed but she would pass on a message.'

Jane leaned over the back of Maureen's chair.

'Not too far from Ascot. Well, at least Kernan will be pleased it's not in the Outer Hebrides.' She looked at her watch. It was after 4 p.m. 'I'm going to go home and then make an early start in the morning with a visit to Mrs Kilroy.'

'Should I call and say you're coming?' Maureen asked.

'No, the element of surprise seems to have worked so far. By the way, there was a lot of racket coming from Shefford's mob in the incident room as I was coming back from Kernan's office. Are they celebrating another result?'

'No, they have got a murder investigation, a horrendous one by all accounts. It came in yesterday when you were in Yorkshire. Drive-by shooting with multiple fatalities.'

'What about Hickock? Has he made an appearance?'

'I've not seen him,' Maureen said. 'Although I did hear at lunchtime that Kernan put the screws on about the Serina Jenkins case. Hickock's had forensics called out again.'

Jane made a face. 'He'll be lucky to find anything after this length of time. Right, see you tomorrow.'

After taking a bus and tube home, Jane quickly changed into her tracksuit, hoping to catch one of the classes at the gym. She drove to the club and hurried into reception.

'Hi, Corinna, any chance of a yoga class?'

'There's one in ten minutes. And I've got your private locker key for you. Number 29.' Corinna handed it over.

'Great, thanks.' Jane went down to the locker room and was pleased to find her locker already had her name on it. She changed into her leotard and flip-flops and grabbed a towel. She joined the class just as they were just laying out the mats.

Her body had been very stiff after the last session, but this time she really felt the benefit. At the end of the session, they lay down for a couple of minutes, eyes closed and breathing deeply through their noses and exhaling slowly through their mouths. Jane felt more relaxed than she had for a long time.

Jane was just opening her locker, when she saw Corinna removing a name plate from another locker down the aisle. Jane went over and could see it was Serina Jenkins' locker. Corinna turned, sighing. 'So sad. She was a regular from almost when we first opened.'

'I heard what happened,' Jane said. 'Did you know her well?'

'Not really, you know, just chatted at the desk a little bit, but everyone here that knew her a bit better was shocked. It just didn't seem real, awful. I think one of the girls in your class, Natalie, used to be good friends with her. She was devastated.'

Jane had a shower, then slipped into her swimming costume and joined two other women in the whirlpool bath.

'I think we were just in the same class,' she said, immersing herself in the bubbling water.

One of the women, a blonde, smiled at her. 'It was good, wasn't it? I usually have a massage afterwards, but I left it a bit late and they were all booked up.'

'You can have mine if you like,' Jane said. 'It's at seven thirty and I really should be getting home. I have to be up early in the morning.'

'Gosh, that's really nice of you. Thank you. I'm Gina, by the way.'

Gina got out, wrapped a towel around herself and headed to the showers. Jane couldn't help noticing her stunning figure.

'I'm Natalie,' the other woman said, with a smile. 'And I wish I looked like that, too.'

Jane shifted her position so the warm jets were pummelling her back. 'I hope you don't mind me asking you, Natalie, but I was told that you were good friends with Serina Jenkins.'

'Yes, I was, I mean, we only really met up together here, but we often had breakfast together. I don't think I have ever been so shocked when I was told she had committed suicide. I simply couldn't believe it. We were only here together the day before, and she seemed so happy and positive about things. She was working on this new renovation project and she was excited about it.'

'I was told she was planning to open a business with her sister-in-law?'

Natalie made a face. 'I doubt that. Serina always said she was very bossy, very controlling and overprotective of her waster of a husband. Sorry, I'm speaking out of turn. I mean, I never even met the woman, or her husband, but I suppose when you are as wealthy as Serina it must be hard to know who to trust. I think we got on so well because I'm a dental nurse, nothing to do with designs or furnishing. So what do you do?'

'I try to keep it quiet, to be honest. Sometimes people can get the wrong idea. I'd rather people take me for who I am.'

'Sounds intriguing,' Natalie said. 'But don't tell me if you don't want to.'

'It's OK,' Jane said, smiling. 'I'm a detective with the Met.'

Natalie gave a loud guffaw, ducking her head under the water before bobbing up again.

'Now I understand all the questions. Well, I can see why you might want to keep that quiet! But don't worry, your secret's safe with me.'

'Thank you. Do you fancy a coffee after?'

Natalie grinned. 'Sounds good. I think I'm starting to go wrinkly anyway!'

Natalie stepped out of the whirlpool bath. She was tall and slim, with long dark hair almost down to her waist. Jane followed a minute or two later.

In the café, Jane ordered a toasted muffin and coffee. She had almost finished both when Natalie appeared, wearing a velvet tracksuit in pale blue with smart white trainers. She put her sports bag down and perched on a stool.

'Sorry to take so long, I had to wait for one of the hairdryers and it always takes so long. Do you want another coffee?'

Jane got up. 'It's all right, my treat. What are you having?'

'Oh, I think I'll go for a cappuccino and a toasted avocado, egg and tomato sandwich.'

While Jane ordered at the bar, Natalie took her diary out of her sports bag, and thumbed through it.

'I was thinking about it in the shower,' she said when Jane got back. 'It was the day before Serina died, another reason why I was so shocked, because I'd mentioned a terrific antiques place on the King's Road. It's a huge old warehouse full to the brim of amazing stalls. You can find old fireplaces – I even know someone who bought two massive monastery doors. Anyway, we had sort of agreed to meet up there. I said we could have lunch, because I don't have surgery on Friday afternoons. She seemed really keen. She was always complaining she had to have meetings with her lawyers all the time, and said this would make a pleasant change.'

A server brought their coffees to the table, along with Natalie's toasted sandwich.

Jane waited until she was out of earshot. 'Did Serina ever mention anything about miscarriages, IVF treatments, hoping to have a baby?'

'No, she never mentioned anything like that. The only time she did seem a bit down in the dumps was a while ago. She said she had been with her bankers, checking her joint account, and had been angry that her husband was using it without her knowledge.'

Natalie took a bite of her sandwich, then put it back on her plate and wiped her mouth with a napkin.

'So, if you're a police officer, are you asking me about Serina because you're involved in an enquiry about her suicide?'

'No, I just heard about it at work, as you do. Do you want another cappuccino?'

'No, thank you, this was a real treat.'

Natalie finished her sandwich and Jane paid the bill. 'Can I give you a lift anywhere?'

'Thanks, but I've got my bike.'

They walked out to the car park.

'See you again soon, then.' Jane got into her car and drove off as Natalie was unchaining her bike from the railings. She spent the short drive home turning over what Natalie had said in her mind.

CHAPTER SIXTEEN

At the station the following morning, Jane added the notes from her meeting with Natalie to the file. They were already checking Martin Jenkins' alibi, but she added a note to check what Serina had done all day: did she leave the house at any time? Did she make any phone calls?

Maureen arrived and made a fresh pot of coffee.

'Anything new on the Serina Jenkins investigation?' Jane asked.

'No, Hickock's not been very visible. Here's Mrs Kilroy's address, plus her phone number. It's a village just outside Ascot, not that far from the college as the crow flies.'

'Strange isn't it, that John Kilroy was a boarder when I was told lots of them were day students or returned home at weekends. Also, apparently he was very keen on sport, rugby and cricket. But this kind of crammer doesn't usually do sport. Phillip Sayer mentioned a cricket match – can you ring and double-check it actually happened?'

'Will do.' Maureen handed her an enlarged printout from an *A to Z* with detailed instructions to get to Mrs Kilroy's house.

'Thanks. See you later.'

The sun was shining for a change as Jane drove from the station and headed towards the M4. An hour later, she took the turn-off to Ascot, before driving towards the village of Pirbright. After a couple of wrong turns in the narrow country lanes, she found the village and continued on for a couple of miles before eventually finding the house, set well back from the road.

The tarmac drive had seen better days, with open fields on either side. Jane saw rows of dilapidated beehives and an orchard looking in need of attention. The house was a sprawling Victorian red-brick mansion with a grey slate roof and imposing chimneys. At the side

of the house was a large lean-to, its corrugated iron roof danger-
ously bowed, while on the other side was a large double garage,
the gates painted a faded green. Judging by the piles of dried leaves
heaped up against the doors, it had not been used for many months.
Parked beside the garage was a newish-looking white Land Rover,
its sides splattered with mud.

Jane rang the old-fashioned bell pull, but wasn't sure if it was
working, so tried again, then rapped on the door with her knuckles.

'Are you delivering the groceries?'

An elderly man in an apron worn over trousers tucked into big
wellington boots had come from the side of the lean-to, carrying a
garden rake.

'I'm a police officer, here to speak with Mrs Kilroy.'

'She's in the kitchen, I'll walk you round. We're expecting groceries to be delivered.'

'I'm sorry to disappoint you.' Jane followed him round the side
of the lean-to, then along a narrow path and through a garden gate
to a back door. He knocked loudly and waited a moment before
opening it.

'Mrs Kilroy, it's a woman police officer. I'll let her in, shall I?'

He turned to Jane.

'Please go in, but wipe your feet if you would. She's in the snug
past the kitchen.'

Stepping into the house felt like going through a time warp.
The kitchen was enormous, with an old-fashioned Aga and a huge
scrubbed-pine table. All the cupboards were painted brown with
glass fronts, rows of copper pans hung above the massive double
sink and shining pots for boiling jams were lined up ready to be
used.

Jane walked through to a door with a red velvet drape across it.
She pulled the curtain aside and opened the door.

The snug was well named, dominated by a roaring fire in an old
iron grate with stacks of logs either side of it. An antique carved

coffee table had been placed in front of the fire, stacked with books, and two wall-to-floor bookcases were heaving with similar leather-bound volumes.

Jane hesitated, wondering if she should go further into the house, when another heavy curtain was swished aside from the oak door near to the window.

'Good morning, I am Sylvia Kilroy, the curtains keep the draught out. And you are?'

'Detective Chief Inspector Jane Tennison, from the Metropolitan Police.'

Sylvia Kilroy was not quite what Jane had expected. She was very tall, dressed in an expensive-looking tweed suit, with a polo neck sweater and polished brown brogues. Her greying blonde hair was swept up with two combs either side of her head, and a braid was twisted into a loose bun at the nape of her neck. She took out a pair of thick-lensed glasses from her pocket and held them up by the arms to look at Jane's warrant card before handing it back.

'If this is about the right of way yet again, I am not and will not agree to the proposals as it cuts directly across our land. I have offered an alternative for these ramblers or whatever they call themselves.'

'I am not here about that, Mrs Kilroy,' Jane assured her. 'It's connected with an incident that occurred some time ago at your son's college.'

'Well, it has to be some time ago, then. He's not been at college for more than five years, and he's not at home, so I'm afraid you have had a wasted journey.'

'Could we sit down so that I can explain more fully?' Jane asked.

'By all means.'

Jane sat down on a worn but stylish sofa while Sylvia Kilroy sat in an armchair opposite. She had very pale blue eyes, and with her high cheekbones and wide lips, Jane thought she must have been very striking as a young woman.

'We've reopened a case involving a young student who went missing when your son was at the college. Your son, along with two of his friends, were the last people to see her.'

'Well, as I said to you, John is not here, and I am uncertain when he will be returning. I do have a couple of dates in my diary when I am expecting him, but he's not terribly reliable.'

Mrs Kilroy got up and went over to a tallboy with shelves of books in a glass-fronted top and three sets of drawers beneath. There was a large white telephone with a magnifying glass beside it. She opened one drawer, rummaged around, removing bulging envelopes before taking out a leather-bound diary.

'He's on an oil rig, and it's very difficult to make any kind of contact with him, especially since we are not on very good terms, but see for yourself if there is anything I've written that will give you a date he's expected back.'

Mrs Kilroy's writing was almost illegible, but eventually Jane was able to identify an entry in a month's time.

'Thank you very much.' She handed the diary back and Mrs Kilroy put it back in the drawer. 'Do you know the name of the oil rig or the company John works for?'

'I'm afraid not. There are a lot of rigs and he's worked on quite a few.'

Jane nodded. 'The missing girl was called Brittany Hall. Do you recall your son ever mentioning her?'

'No, I'm sorry, but I have absolutely no recall of anything connected to this poor girl. What I do remember is that John gained very poor results in his exams. If his father had been alive, I think he would have confronted the headmaster. He had this awful accident, skiing, broke his leg in three places, and it put his hopes for an athletic scholarship down the tubes, so to speak. So he really needed to get decent A level grades, which is why we sent him to a crammer. He was always very headstrong, difficult to handle, and losing his father when he was just seventeen obviously impacted him emotionally.'

'I'm sorry. How terrible,' Jane said.

'Yes, a brain tumour, totally unexpected. He ran the farm alongside a high-powered job in the city. Now I rent out the fields to local farmers. We used to have four men working here, but now I just have Donald. The place is falling into rack and ruin without anyone caring for it. I should perhaps explain, my husband left no will, and with inheritance taxes and God knows what else, and with probate lasting over eighteen months, it was imperative I salvage what I could for John. My son owns everything now, so for him to go off working on some godforsaken oil rig instead of being here overseeing the property, or for that matter caring for his mother, it's quite dreadful.'

Mrs Kilroy's voice didn't show any emotion, but her disdain for her son was obvious. 'I did try to get some kind of work, but my eyesight is deteriorating. I have cataracts on both eyes, so that limits what I can do, and obviously I can't drive.'

'Does your son drive?'

'He got a provisional licence, but like everything else, he just didn't bother. The car has just been left to rot in the garage.'

'You didn't sell your car when you found you were unable to drive?'

'No, I should have, I suppose.'

'So, Mrs Kilroy, to go back to the reason I'm here, Brittany Hall went missing during John's final term at the college. You're sure you don't remember him mentioning anything?'

'Well, that was the time I was away. After my husband's death, I went to stay with my niece for quite a while as I was very depressed. Look, do you think John is involved in some way?'

Jane stood up, eager to leave now. 'As I said, we're just reviewing the case. I have interviewed your son's two friends as well. It's all very routine. Thank you so much for your time, Mrs Kilroy, you have been very helpful. But if you do recall anything else, this is my contact number at Southampton Row station.'

Jane jotted down her number on an empty page of her notebook and gave it to Mrs Kilroy.

'I can see myself out. Could I help myself to a glass of water on the way, please?'

'Certainly, there's some cups on the side drainer.'

In the hallway, out of sight, Jane stopped and listened. As expected, she heard Mrs Kilroy dial a number on the phone and then ask to speak to James Appleton. She walked through into the kitchen and then out of the back door. She was eager to take a look in the garage and see the car. She now knew that Mrs Kilroy had not been at home when Brittany went missing, so was it possible that John or one of his friends had driven it that night?

She walked round, hoping she'd be able to look through a window, but the only small dirty windows were high above the doors. As she walked back, Donald was standing by her car with a wheelbarrow full of broken plant pots and weeds, with a large wicker hamper on top.

She held her hand out. 'I didn't really introduce myself. I'm Detective Chief Inspector Jane Tennison.'

He removed a thick work glove to shake her hand. 'Is it about the right of way across the main field?' He had a very aristocratic voice, and closer to, he was not as old as she had first presumed, despite his white hair.

'No, that's not my department, I was actually here hoping to speak to Mrs Kilroy's son John.'

'Been in trouble again, has he? I'm Donald Fitzpatrick-Dunn, old friend of Sylvia's and general dogsbody round here. My wife was her sister, so you could say I'm family.'

'Nice to meet you. She's a very charming woman.'

'She most certainly is, and at one time a top model. She was in *Vogue* and *Tatler*, all very glamorous, and her husband Rupert was a great man too. He had this place running like clockwork, made their own honey and the orchard was always very productive, grew three different types of apples, pears and plums, and the old shed by the stables was used to bottle them up, not for financial gain, they gave most of it to charity. And you'd never believe the man, on the dot of six a.m. he'd depart for the city, starched white shirt and tie and pinstripe suit, with his rolled umbrella and briefcase, then he'd be back mucking out in the evening.'

'He sounds amazing. Did you work here for him then?'

'Good God no, I was in the city. Lesser position than Rupert, retired four years ago, only really started looking after Sylvia when my wife died three years ago.'

'She mentioned that she stayed with her niece after her husband died?'

'I have no children, but the poor darling still tells everyone that, not sure why, but she stayed with us. The truth is she had a very serious nervous breakdown. Rupert went very unexpectedly, only forty-two years old, left a dreadful mess, no will, so it was almost two years before she got probate. Poor Sylvia had no experience handling the estate, or with the finances. All the employees left because she couldn't pay them.'

'So, did you take over the estate when she was away?'

'No, that was later. Maybe a couple of years. I came round and was shocked at the state of the place. I don't live that far, so I come in every day, sometimes sleep over at the weekends.'

'Mrs Kilroy mentioned that she has bequeathed everything to John.'

He sighed, shaking his head. 'He's a waster, I can't stand the fact that he allowed this to happen, and isn't taking care of his mother.'

'It was actually John I was hoping to talk to. About an incident back when he was in college.'

'Well, he's on some oil rig, hardly ever puts in an appearance here, and when he does, I make myself absent. I think his father would turn in his grave at how he turned out. You know when you drive in there are rows of beehives? They were Rupert's pride and joy, made some extraordinary mix with herbs and lavender, never tasted honey like it. To see them in a shambles, heartbreaking, that was down to John. After his father died, a couple of the workers tended to them, but they really didn't have the expertise. I know Sylvia also tried to do something about them, but she was in no fit state to oversee anything. Before she left, with none of the workers still here, she asked John to make sure he tended to them, they had all the proper suits and protective helmets, in the hut beside the hives. Apparently, he got stung and kicked them over. I found out some had swarmed but most couldn't get out, millions of them trapped inside their hives.'

'How awful.' Jane nodded towards the garage. 'Mrs Kilroy mentioned that a car was here in the garage.'

'It is. I would have tried to sort something out with it, but it was damaged, wing buckled, so I left a message for John to take care of it, never has.'

'So how long would you say it's been in the garage?'

'Well, I can't be sure, but John never passed his test, and Sylvia obviously can't drive. It was here when I came round, so it could be years.'

'Do you know if John ever used it, even though he hadn't passed his test?'

He nodded. 'I would say he did, with no one here to stop him, and more than likely he had an accident and just dumped it back in the garage.'

'So it could have been in the garage, say, for five years?'

He shrugged. 'Could be, I stopped the insurance on it for Sylvia. I know he has never taken it out when I've been here.'

Jane hesitated, wondering if she should explain her interest, as a large Fortnum & Mason van drove into the drive. Donald turned towards the van as it drew up, then looked back to Jane.

'It's Mrs Kilroy's groceries, they come once a month with a wicker hamper, take away the old one.'

The van was parked behind Jane's Mini, so she would have to wait. The driver opened up the rear doors of the van and carried out a large hamper, with leather straps. Donald put it in his wheel-barrow and exchanged the empty hamper for the new one.

'Sorry, do you need to ask me anything else?' he called over.

'No, I'll be on my way, thank you.'

He wheeled the barrow closer and the van pulled away.

'You didn't actually tell me why you are here. Is it connected to that old wreck in the garage?'

'Actually, it may be. I am investigating the disappearance of a student at John's college five years ago.'

'So, you want to ask John if he was driving the car at the time, is that correct?'

'Yes. And what about Mrs Kilroy – could she have driven it? I know you said she had a breakdown.'

Fitzpatrick-Dunn reddened. 'Now just wait a minute,' he said, raising his voice. 'Sylvia had a terrible time, she worshipped her husband, and did have a complete nervous breakdown after he died. She was under the care of a specialist and spent a long time recuperating in a Swiss nursing home before returning to live here.'

'I am really trying to establish if Mrs Kilroy was at home on the date Brittany Hall went missing. She was reported missing on the sixteenth of June 1986, and conceivably she may have been brought here by John Kilroy. There would have been considerable publicity surrounding the girl's disappearance that you might also remember.'

He had to take a deep breath to control his anger. Jane could see he had strong feelings towards Sylvia Kilroy.

'Do you recall Mrs Kilroy being at home on those specific dates, just so I can eliminate the possibility that she was driving the car?'

'I can assure you she could not possibly have driven the car, either before that time or since, not only due to her near blindness, but also because sadly she had become dependent on alcohol and morphine. I arranged for her to spend time at a rehabilitation centre in Spain, and I personally drove her to the airport, so to answer your question, Mrs Kilroy was not at home.'

Jane nodded. 'Thank you. We'll need to have the car removed for examination. Would you be willing to give me written permission to do so?'

'Certainly. And probably best you don't return it when you've finished with it.'

Jane wrote the appropriate entry in her pocketbook and Fitzpatrick-Dunn signed it.

'Thank you for your time, Mr Fitzpatrick-Dunn, I really appreciate you being so honest with me.'

He picked up the handles of the wheelbarrow and gave her a cool nod, watching as she got into the Mini and drove off.

As soon as she was back on the road, a wide grin broke over Jane's face. All they had to do now was examine the car and see if anything pointed to Brittany Hall having been in it.

'You want evidence, sir,' she said to herself. 'Well, maybe now I've got some for you.'

The drive back to the station took longer than Jane had anticipated due to a hold-up on the M4, where a lorry had overturned and crashed into the barrier. She decided that she would stop at the first petrol station to fill up her tank and phone Maureen. After filling her tank, she bought some pastries and a packet of cigarettes and walked over to the pay phone.

When she answered, Maureen sounded stressed. 'Hickock's been asking for you.'

'Is that all?' Jane asked.

Maureen hesitated. 'Well, no. I gave him the file. But the odd thing is, he just glanced through the last few pages, muttered something about the CCTV stuff being new, made an entry in his notebook and left. I'm sorry if I've done the wrong thing, ma'am.'

'It's not your fault, Maureen. Looks like he'd been snooping around when we weren't here and already read it. The new bit is a reference to a neighbour's CCTV that overlooks the Jenkins house. Don't worry, I'll deal with Hickock,' she said. Instead of making her angry, it almost amused her that Hickock was still floundering around on the Serina Jenkins case. 'We've got more important things to think about right now, namely arranging for forensics to examine Mrs Kilroy's car. I've got permission, but just to be on the safe side I think it's best to get a seizure warrant. Either this afternoon or first thing in the morning I want you to arrange transport for the car to be brought to the lab. If you have time, I also want . . .'

The pips sounded so she quickly inserted more coins. 'You still there, Maureen?'

'Yes, what else did you want me to do?'

'See what we have in the evidence stack from the Brittany Hall bags, specifically if we have a hairbrush or toothbrush. I need any item that belonged to her we can use for a DNA match with anything we find in the car. Not to worry too much if you can't, as I can always get a blood sample from Mrs Hall.'

'I don't recall either a hairbrush or toothbrush,' Maureen said. 'Can you hold on while I check? I listed everything in an exhibit logbook.'

'Listen, I'll hang on, but if the pips go, I'm out of change.'

Jane waited for a while and could hear the rustle of paper as Maureen looked for the exhibits book, then came back on the line.

'Hello, I have neither item listed, but I should probably go through everything again, it was all in such a mess.'

'Never mind, I won't come in this evening. I'll go and see if her mother has got anything. Just get on with organising the car. You know what you have to do?'

'Yes, I'm not quite sure of the correct procedure but I'll call forensics to be ready for delivery, and maybe, as it's coming up to five thirty, it's best if I get in early tomorrow morning and contact the traffic division to give them the address . . .'

Jane could hear the pips, so hung up and returned to her car.

Mrs Hall was fortunately at home, and yet again Jane had the uncomfortable duty of quickly explaining that there was no big development. Mrs Hall led Jane into her daughter's bedroom, the room she had decorated for her in the hope she would be found. She had brought everything that belonged to Brittany from the old house, including her favourite soft toys from when she was a child, and all her clothes.

'I'm really interested in her hairbrush, perhaps from her room at the college, or one she used when she was at home,' Jane explained.

'Yes, there's one on her dressing table. She took it to college.'

'Did you wash it when you brought it back?'

'No, should I have done?'

'No, I'm hoping it might still have some of her hair.'

Jane saw the look of panic on Mrs Hall's face in the dressing table mirror, as if she knew why it was wanted. Jane picked up the brush and could see numerous strands of Brittany's hair caught in the bristles.

'I will need to take this with me, Mrs Hall. And what about a toothbrush?'

'No, I don't have that, I'm afraid. I'm not sure what happened to it.'

'Don't worry, but I'll also need a blood sample from you. I've located a car that I think Brittany may have been in. It's possible that even after five years we may find a trace of her DNA. We can use your blood for a comparison to tell us if there is a DNA relationship to you as her mother. I hope that makes sense.'

Mrs Hall nodded. 'I think I understand what you mean.'

'Good. I'll get Maureen, my assistant, to contact you and make the arrangement for a divisional surgeon to take the blood sample.'

Jane opened her briefcase and took out a plastic bag, carefully placing the brush inside. She looked around the neat, tidy room, ready and waiting for Brittany. It was heartbreaking, but then something else dawned.

'Mrs Hall, I know you were expecting Brittany to come home on the Friday, not here, but to your previous house.'

'Yes, she was upset about something to do with being there, you know, the Greek play she found upsetting because of her stammer.'

'Yes, I remember about that, but on previous occasions when she had come home for the weekend, can you remember if she brought a haversack, a satchel or a weekend case, something like that?'

'Yes, it was a small backpack, she would have her homework or clean underwear, even sometimes a bit of washing for me.'

'I have read all the statements, including yours, as you were obviously asked what was missing from her room at the college. You just mentioned that the hairbrush I am taking was at home, and Brittany would have had another one at the college along with her toothbrush, is that right?'

'I was asked, but you know I really didn't know, I had only been in her college room once, and I was uncertain what was missing, but thinking about it now, they were not there.'

'What about the backpack?'

'Goodness, it was not there. I didn't think, I was never asked about it.'

'Can you describe it?'

'It was not expensive, just a weekend type, black.'

Jane knew that there had been no mention in the file of any weekend backpack being removed from her college room, but she would need to double-check all the evidence bags. To her, it was further evidence that Brittany had every intention of returning home that Friday for the weekend. After thanking Mrs Hall, and promising that she would keep her updated with any further news, she hurried out to her car, only to find she had a ticket as she had parked in a residents' bay.

She ripped it off the windscreen, furious with herself for not placing her ID card on the dashboard, as querying it would just mean more aggravation. But tired as she was from her long day, even stupidly getting a ticket couldn't dampen her positive mood. She could hardly wait to see what tomorrow would bring.

CHAPTER SEVENTEEN

Jane had overslept. Hurrying to get showered and dressed, the phone rang.

It was Peter. 'Sorry to ring so early, but I was hoping to catch you before you went to work. Are you free for dinner tonight?'

'Only if you let me do the cooking this time. But it won't be anything exotic, I'm afraid. Eight o'clock at the flat?'

'Perfect.'

Jane was pleased he'd rung, but now she had to do a quick shop in Tesco for bolognese ingredients before heading to the station and was even more pushed for time. She practically ran down the aisles, pushing her trolley in front of her as she grabbed items from the shelves.

* * *

At the station, DCI Hickock was also in a state of excited anticipation.

He'd spoken with the mortuary manager to ascertain Serina Jenkins' exact weight at the time of her death. He'd then acquired a sandbag of the same weight from the groundsman at his golf club. But before he could conduct the experiment, he had to tell Martin Jenkins what he was planning to do.

Hickock had not had an easy time with Martin Jenkins up to this point. At first, he had been very cooperative but, as time went on, he had become more recalcitrant, accusing Hickock of harassing him, and saying the investigation was totally unwarranted.

Jenkins admitted draining the joint account to pay off his gambling debts, but claimed that his wife had known about it, and, being a multi-millionaire in her own right, didn't have a problem with it. He pointed out that they could see from the accounts they were still planning further costly IVF treatment, which proved their marriage was strong.

Every subsequent interview with Martin Jenkins had resulted in him losing his temper. He now refused to be interviewed without a lawyer present and angrily dismissed all of the so-called 'evidence' that Hickock uncovered. The forensic team had found drops of Serina's blood, on the stairs, the outside side of one of the rails, also on the floor where her body had been lying, and on the wall by the last step of the staircase. Jenkins explained them all away by saying Serina had suffered from nosebleeds, a story confirmed by his sister.

When Hickock told him he was going to do a reconstruction of Serina's suicide, it was the last straw.

'How can you be so thoughtless, Brian? I won't allow it. I will not have my dead wife compared to a bag of sand!'

'Martin, listen to me, I am just doing my job. If the test confirms the forensic results and supports your version of events, then that's a positive result, and we can conclude the investigation.'

Martin broke down in tears, and then, to Hickock's embarrassment, hugged him.

'Look, I'm sorry for sounding off the way I have, but I loved her, and I had nothing whatsoever to do with the way she died. It has broken me, I am in a terrible state.'

'I understand, Martin, and I assure you, it's all going to be over with very shortly, and you will be able to arrange her funeral.'

'Thank you. I always knew you would help me.'

Hickock felt a twinge of guilt. The reality was, the more he spoke to him, the more convinced he was becoming that Jenkins was a skilled liar who, after careful planning, had killed his wife and made it look like suicide. The problem, though, was proving it.

* * *

It was even later than she had anticipated when Jane finally got to the station.

As she approached her office she could hear sobbing. She quickly opened the door.

Maureen was crying, dabbing her eyes with a crumpled wad of paper tissues.

'Are you all right, Maureen, what's happened?'

Maureen gulped, sniffed and blew her nose. 'I am . . . Well, *we* are in trouble, I just had Detective Sergeant Otley in here and he was yelling at me, telling me I had not gone through the correct procedures and could get into real trouble.'

'What are you talking about?'

'I only did what you told me to do, I can't be blamed for it, I just didn't know the exact procedure you had to go through.'

'What procedure, Maureen?'

'I booked a traffic division tow truck to collect Mrs Kilroy's vehicle and bring it to the lab for examination. I also asked the lab for forensic officers to examine the car for any trace evidence first thing this morning. Otley said we were stupid and should have got a warrant to seize the car.'

'I did say we'd need a seizure warrant, Maureen.'

Maureen started crying again. 'I know, I forgot to write that down.'

Jane sighed. 'It's all right, Maureen. We all make mistakes, but we also learn from them. Did Otley say anything else?'

'Apparently DCI Shefford went ballistic, as he's got this big murder investigation and he'd ordered his team to get two vehicles brought in early this morning. Otley said they had first claim as it was already ordered and passed by Chief Superintendent Kernan, and we could have delayed a live murder enquiry.'

'So, where's the Kilroy car now?'

'Still at her house. Otley cancelled the tow truck.'

'My God, I don't believe this. Just dry your eyes, Maureen, while I go and sort it with Kernan. Like you, I didn't know they had a so-called priority case.'

After running a comb through her hair and freshening her lipstick, Jane went to Kernan's office. As she walked down the corridor, she came face to face with Detective Sergeant Otley.

'Sergeant Otley,' she said, glaring angrily at him, 'if you have any complaint against me, there is no need to behave rudely towards WPC Havers. She was understandably upset, and I think you should apologise.'

His thin lips tightened. 'That won't be forthcoming, ma'am. She needs to understand there is a strict protocol here at the station, and it is imperative everyone obeys the rules. DCI Shefford is investigating a live double murder – not a bloody cold case. He urgently needed two vehicles to be forensically examined. He wasn't happy to discover the correct paperwork hadn't been filled out, or a warrant granted for your poxy car to be seized and examined, so I suggest—'

Jane interrupted him. 'OK, you've made your point and I apologise for any misunderstanding, but I was not aware of the correct etiquette until now.'

'*Etiquette!*' he snarled. 'This is not some fucking society tea party. It's a serious murder investigation. The delay in bringing in our vehicles for examination could lead to the loss or degradation of forensic evidence. Besides, anything found in your car would have been worthless.'

Jane looked confused. 'What do you mean by that?'

'You didn't have a warrant, so any seizure and search would have been unlawful.'

'I agree a warrant would generally be preferable, but I had permission to remove the vehicle!' she insisted.

'Well, Maureen failed to submit a signed statement by the owner to that effect, or a copy of a pocketbook entry countersigned by the owner. So, your car wouldn't have been towed in anyway,' he sneered.

'I have apologised, Detective Sergeant Otley, so please, when speaking to a higher-ranking officer, show some respect. I will let it go this time, but in future I will report your attitude.'

He walked off, hands clenched, as she took a deep breath.

Jane realised she'd made a mistake not sorting out the warrant herself and had wrongly assumed Maureen knew what to do. She took a deep breath and knocked on Kernan's door.

He didn't waste any time before laying into her. 'DCI Tennison, when you first arrived at Southampton Row, you were given a folder with a comprehensive list of the rules and regulations, which I expect every officer to abide by. With three teams of DCIs and detectives involved in major crime investigations, it is imperative that live, urgent cases take priority for any forensic examinations. Ordering vehicles to be towed into the lab without a warrant or other legal documentation is not acceptable . . .'

Jane opened her mouth to say something in her defence, but he slapped the desk.

'Hear me out, DCI Tennison. Flouting rules and regulations is one thing, but not following legal guidelines for the seizure of a vehicle is a gross error of judgement.'

'I had permission to seize it, sir, though not from the owner.'

He frowned. 'I will allow it was a genuine error on your part. However, I am giving you fair warning. You are not a one-man team, you need to go through the proper channels – and that means me – in future.'

'I apologise, sir, and please be aware that Maureen should not take any of the blame, as she was acting under my instructions. But I believe I have made significant headway in the Brittany Hall case, and when there is an available slot, I would like the vehicle that I believe may have been connected to her disappearance to be brought in to be forensically examined. I will, of course, obtain the legal owner's signed permission first.'

'I will look at your report when it comes in. I'd also suggest you get a warrant in case the owner refuses permission to seize it.'

'I will, sir. I believe that John Kilroy had access to the vehicle, and it has been in a garage on his mother's property since Brittany Hall went missing.'

Kernan frowned and picked up his pencil. 'How long ago was this?'

'Approximately five years.'

'Five years! Well, you are hoping for a lot of evidence, apart from a vehicle that may or may not have been used in her abduction. And you have no other new evidence?'

'No, sir, but I would like to interview John Kilroy as soon as possible, because—'

Kernan cut her off. 'Not this oil rig thing again! I told you to wait and find out when he is next due to get off the ruddy thing.'

'Not for months.'

'Well, so be it, then. The case has been cold for over five years, so what's a few more months? That's it, DCI Tennison. I suggest you spend some time familiarising yourself with the AMIT rules and regulations. DCI Shefford is a very experienced and effective investigator – I suggest you watch and learn how he does things. He is what I would call a team player.'

He stood up to indicate the meeting was over. She had to clench her fists, she was so angry, but managed to stay in control and thank him for his advice. By the time she stepped out of the lift she was ready to punch the wall with frustration. Taking a deep breath, she returned to her office, pulled out her chair and slumped noisily into it.

'Is everything all right?' Maureen asked nervously.

Jane pulled herself up. 'Yes, and don't worry about getting into any trouble. I also had a word with Sergeant Otley.'

Maureen looked relieved. 'Thank you. You asked me to double-check with the college about a cricket match the weekend Brittany Hall went missing? It took me a while as Mr Greggory, the sports coach at the time, had left the college at the end of the term when Brittany went missing because they had a very poor turnout for sport, and even PT was not obligatory.'

Jane took a deep breath, unable to recall what Maureen was talking about.

'You said John Kilroy had some kind of injury skiing. I asked if he was unable to play cricket, because one of his friends had spoken about them being at the match.'

'Yes, yes, get to the point,' Jane snapped.

'Well, apparently John Kilroy did have a very bad injury to his right leg, which he got while skiing, and Mr Greggory, the sports coach, said that it was not advisable for him to continue to play rugby.'

Jane took another deep breath to stop herself from shouting at Maureen. 'I wanted to know about the cricket match that the three of them went to on the weekend Brittany Hall disappeared, not rugby.'

Maureen started to look flustered. 'Yes, I know that, and I'm getting to it. Mr Greggory also recalled there was a cricket match that weekend. Kilroy was able to take part and proved to be still a more than competent batsman, apparently, though he was unable to bowl, and scored most of the team's runs, although Mr Greggory said the standard was very inferior to other schools he'd worked at.'

Jane picked up her briefcase, pushing her chair back. 'Thank you for that, Maureen, add it to the file and forward my last report to the superintendent.'

Maureen turned as Jane picked up her coat. 'Is everything all right?'

'Not particularly. I'm going home, and I suggest you take off early too and have a pleasant weekend.'

'Should I ask Hickock to return your file?'

'Don't bother. But I'm through giving him helpful suggestions.'

Jane walked out, taking the lift and then walking out into the car park. She felt like screaming and was relieved not to bump into anyone. How could Kernan accuse her of not being a team player? She didn't have a team – only Maureen. And it was clear Kernan had no interest in her solving the cold case she'd been dumped with. Well, if he wanted her to wait until John Kilroy came home before questioning him, then so be it.

* * *

'Count of three and we'll let it go,' Hickock shouted.

The sandbag was balanced on the edge of the bannister rail, as he counted and then gave it a push. The part of the bag with the noose attached tilted backwards and bumped against the stairs jutting out beyond the bannisters. The cable instantly stretched, causing the sandbag to bang against the floor, then bounce up and down a couple of times as the cable stretched a little more, until the bag was resting on the ground. Hickock turned and looked at the forensic expert.

'What do you think?'

'I'll have to do a closer examination of the cable back at the lab, but, from what I've just seen, I'd say this was a fair reconstruction of events. I noticed that the head replica part of the bag hit the edge of the stairs on the way down. Having read the pathologist's report, this could have been the cause of the ante-mortem injury to the back of her head. It's also possible she landed feet first, sprang upwards a bit with a recoil action, her lower legs went backwards, then her knees hit the ground quite hard.'

Hickock nodded. 'Her husband said she was on her knees when he found her. Thing is, if she was on her knees, she could have tried to remove the noose.'

'If her head hit the edge of the stairs, she may have been knocked unconscious. And even on her knees, her upper-body weight would sag forward and tighten the noose.'

Hickock sighed. 'Honest opinion: did Serina Jenkins jump . . . or was she pushed? That's what I really need to know.'

'I'm a scientist. I deal in facts, not guesses. But to answer your question: from what I've seen so far, I honestly don't know. I'd check with the pathologist, but my guess, as her neck wasn't broken and she was still alive when the ambulance arrived, is she went over the balcony shortly before her husband got home.'

'"Shortly" being how long?'

'The main cause of death by hanging is a lack of oxygen getting to your brain. You may break your neck, you may get knocked out from the sheer force, but as long as the noose remains tight enough, it'll take roughly four minutes. When her husband cut her down, he probably reduced the pressure on her neck, which is why she was still alive when the ambulance arrived.'

Hickock realised Tennison was right about the need for an accurate timeline of Martin Jenkins' movements. The problem was, at present they only had his word to go on. She might be on to something with the missing fingernails, too, but so far none had been recovered.

As the scientist and two detectives removed the sandbag and cables, Hickock went to the master bedroom and started looking around. On top of the dressing table was a silver-backed mirror, a matching brush and comb, and a glass tray with a bracelet and two silver rings in it. He noticed that an area of the wood appeared stained, as if something like bleach had been spilt on it. He leaned over and had a quick sniff. It had a sweet, fruity smell, but although it was familiar, he couldn't identify it. Hickock went out to the landing and asked the scientist to come up to the master bedroom.

'There's something been spilt on the dressing table, leaving a white stain. Worth taking a sample for analysis?'

The scientist smelt it and grinned. 'It's acetone.'

'Is that a poisonous liquid?' Hickock asked.

'It could be if you swallowed enough of it, I suppose. Acetone is more commonly known as nail varnish remover. Mrs Jenkins probably knocked over a bottle.'

Hickock nodded. 'That's why it smelt familiar . . . Could it be used to subdue someone, though?'

'It's possible, but I've never known it to be used for that. Small amounts of acetone won't hurt you. Swallowing a high level might cause you to pass out. It can also damage the skin in your mouth. But if Jenkins had used it on his wife, the ambulance crew would have smelt it. I'll take a scraping sample anyway, just to be on the safe side, then head back to the lab.'

'OK, thanks for your help.'

Hickock went into the ensuite bathroom, opening the mirrored cabinet on the wall. One side had an array of make-up, powders and neatly stacked eyebrow pencils and mascaras, with an astonishing selection of lipsticks lined up in a narrow tray. False eyelashes in different lengths were neatly stacked on top of each other. The other side contained deodorants, razors, waxing strips and boxes of tampons. On a lower shelf there was a neat row of bottles of vitamins, sleeping tablets and other prescribed medications. He recalled Tennison mentioning Serina could easily have taken an overdose, rather than undergoing the lengthy and unpleasant business of hanging herself. He decided it was best to take all the medications, and went to get an exhibits bag from his colleague. Walking along the landing, he suddenly stopped and retraced his steps back into the bedroom.

He couldn't think what it was, but something was missing.

If the Jenkinses lived together, why did he find only Serina's items in the ensuite bathroom? He looked through the contents of the bathroom cabinet again, then he did another search of the dressing table, opening the drawers further and, this time, looking under the clothing. There were no men's underwear, socks or other items.

Next he checked the wardrobes. They were filled with expensive women's designer clothes, but again, no men's. Looking along the shelves, he saw a square black leather box. He pulled it out, undid the clasp and lifted the lid. Inside were drawers and partitions, with rows of different-coloured nail varnishes. It looked like a professional manicure set. He pulled out the drawers until he found what he was looking for: an array of false nails, in various shapes and colours, one box matching the ones removed from Serina's fingers. He stood staring at the packet. Was it possible that Serina had given herself a manicure and fitted a set of false nails the day she died?

Hickock closed the box and took it with him to the second bedroom, where he checked the wardrobe and found it was full of men's clothes. In the ensuite bathroom were toothbrushes, men's deodorants and shaving equipment. Of course, it was possible Jenkins had moved all his belongings into the guest suite after his wife's death, but still, it was strange.

Hickock went downstairs and handed the manicure box to his colleague, DS Frank Brent.

'Put this in an evidence bag, will you? Take it up to the lab, have the contents photographed and the box fingerprinted.'

Brent nodded. 'You still want us to check out the street for home security cameras?' he asked.

'Yeah, and I want it done asap. And get a list of calls made from the house phone three days prior and three after Mrs Jenkins' death. I'm off to see Martin Jenkins.'

Hickock felt the sandbag reconstruction had been useful, but sometimes it was the little things, the things you could easily overlook, that proved to be decisive. And in this case, it was the false nails. If Serina Jenkins hadn't put a full set of false nails on her fingers that day, what – or who – had prevented her from doing so?

CHAPTER EIGHTEEN

Jane had a gin and tonic, then prepared everything for dinner with Peter, peeling the onions and chopping the garlic finely, leaving the cans of tomatoes on the side with the tomato purée. She then cut and buttered the French loaf, wrapping it in tin foil. She put one bottle of white in the fridge and opened the red, placing it on the small dining table with the cutlery and napkins. After a quick hoover around, she put fresh flowers in a vase, then, after a quick lavender spray around the house, ran a bath. She had refused to allow herself to think about what had happened at the station, determined not to let it ruin her evening. But it wasn't easy.

Lying submerged in perfumed oils and bubble bath, she did deep breathing to calm herself, closing her eyes and inhaling through her nose for the count of five before slowly releasing her breath through her mouth. She spent half an hour luxuriating until she began to feel calmer, then washed her hair and started to think about what she would wear.

* * *

Hickock had been in Martin Jenkins' office for over half an hour.

A rather nervous junior called Georgina had made him a coffee.

'Is Martin in a meeting?' he asked.

'No, he's gone to see a client.'

'When do you expect him back?'

'Er . . . I'm not sure. Sometimes he leaves early.'

'Did you know his wife?'

'No, it was terrible, but I never met her. She hardly ever came here.'

'Were you here on the night Mrs Jenkins died?'

'No, I found out the next morning.'

'When did Mr Jenkins leave his office that evening?'

'I don't know. I had to take a delivery to the court, so I left early before they closed. He was in his office all morning, though, because I put two calls through for him.'

'Was his secretary, Miss Collins, here?'

'Yes, she gave me the packages.'

'Who else was here that afternoon and evening?'

'I don't know.'

'How many people actually work here on a permanent basis?'

'Just Mr Jenkins and his partner, and they share the secretary, Miss Collins, she's with Vernon, Mr Carrington, in the boardroom.'

'Thank you very much, Georgina.'

She looked relieved that her interrogation was over. 'That's all right. I'll be leaving shortly. Is there anything else I can help you with before I go?'

'No, thank you.'

She hesitated before walking out and closing the door.

Hickock sipped his tepid coffee and checked his wristwatch: almost six o'clock. He patted his pockets and took out his cigarettes. Lighting one, he moved the coffee cup aside so he could use the saucer as an ashtray. A large black diary sat on the desk in front of him. He opened it to the present date and looked at the appointments: 9.15 central heating engineer; 11.30 dental check; 1.00 lunch at Le Caprice, and then a gap until: 4.45 Mrs Daniels' divorce papers.

Hickock was about to turn back to the night of Serina's death when he heard voices. After a moment the door opened, and Hickock quickly rose to his feet as Miss Collins entered the room.

'I am so sorry to keep you waiting, Inspector. I believe I mentioned to you that Martin might not be able to be here. I have tried to contact him, but I was told he had left his meeting, so I am afraid you have had a wasted journey.'

'Actually, Miss Collins, I also wanted to have a few words with you.'

Marion Collins glanced at the desk and raised an eyebrow at seeing the saucer being used as an ashtray. She was, he estimated, in her early thirties, dressed in a smart suit with a lemon blouse and high-heeled patent leather shoes. She oozed confidence.

'Can I get you another coffee?'

Hickock got out his notebook. 'No, thank you. Now, let me see, you gave a statement that on the day of Serina Jenkins' death, her husband was here at the office, arriving at his usual time in the morning and not leaving until six in the evening.'

'That sounds right.'

'On that day, did you work alongside Mr Jenkins?'

'No, I didn't. We had another member of staff, Norman Stevenson, leave the practice unexpectedly, so, as the senior partner, Mr Carrington had to take over his cases, and I was spending a lot of my working hours assisting him.'

'Why did Mr Stevenson leave?'

'Health issues, but to be honest, there had also been some ill feeling between him and Martin.'

'Ill feeling?'

She gave a small, impatient sigh. 'I can't see how this is relevant, but, it was basically down to Mr Jenkins not being very supportive.'

'What do you mean by that?'

She gave another sigh. 'Martin took considerable time off for personal reasons and Mr Stevenson complained about it.'

'When Mr Jenkins arrived for work on the day in question, did he seem upset?'

'No, he seemed fine. Georgina, the receptionist, made him a coffee, and then Mr Carrington arrived at about nine fifteen and I spent the morning working with him.'

'When did you next see Mr Jenkins?'

'Mr Carrington had a twelve thirty lunch appointment, so had a sandwich in our staff kitchen. At about one thirty Martin walked in, carrying something from the sandwich bar across the road.'

'What was his mood like?'

'I remember him being a bit annoyed about too much mustard in his sandwich or something. I finished lunch at my usual time of one thirty and went back into Mr Carrington's office. I finished some transcripts and parcelled them up so that Georgina could deliver them personally later in the day. Mr Carrington returned to the office at around two fifteen.'

'What time did Georgina leave to deliver the transcripts?'

'Exactly three o'clock. By public transport, it would take her at least three quarters of an hour to get to the court, so I said it was not worth her returning to the office.'

Hickock thought for a moment. 'Let me just check the times again: we have you with Mr Carrington from two fifteen that afternoon, and you remain with him until what time?'

'About five thirty. I then went into the kitchen to wash the coffee cups and tidy up.'

'Do you know what Mr Jenkins was doing during the afternoon?'

'As far as I know he was in his office. Martin often has his radio on during the afternoons, listening to the horse racing. It's not really my business, but sometimes I heard him making calls to his bookmakers.'

'Did you know Serina Jenkins?'

'I did meet her on rare occasions, you know, Christmas drinks and that sort of thing, and we were invited to their previous home before they moved. She was very charming, very attractive.'

'And very wealthy,' Hickock said under his breath.

Miss Collins smiled, then plucked a bit of fluff from her skirt, twisted it between her fingers and dropped it on the floor. 'He also has a rather pushy older sister called Adele. She did come here a few times. I probably shouldn't even mention it, but one afternoon I heard her talking about some business transaction with Mrs Jenkins. I believe she was there to collect some money – well, that was what I was told by Mr Carrington, as Martin had been to the bank earlier that day.'

'Were you aware that Mr Jenkins was in financial trouble?'

'Goodness, I'm afraid I can't really answer that, but I wouldn't be surprised, given his gambling habits.'

Hickock smiled. 'You've been very helpful, Miss Collins. Thank you for your time. There's just one more thing I need to ask you. Did you see Martin Jenkins again before you left the office to go home?'

'Yes, at five thirty, when I went to tidy up the kitchen. Martin came and put his coffee mug in the sink. He said it had been a very productive day as he'd got through a ton of paperwork, and just had one last case to finish off before going to dinner with his wife.'

'Did you see him leave the office?'

'No, but he usually leaves just before six. I check all the office lights are out, lock up and set the alarm at six most nights.'

'That afternoon, did you hear Mr Jenkins' radio?'

'No, I was with Mr Carrington.'

Hickock closed his notebook and stood up.

'If that's all, I'll need to lock up, so if you don't mind showing yourself out . . .'

'Not at all, and thanks again for your assistance.'

Hickock took the stairs down to the ground floor, walked out through the main doors and turned right in the direction of his car. He was about to cross the road, then paused and instead walked to the corner end of the office block. Looking up, he saw an old iron fire escape leading down to a narrow alleyway. Hickock looked up to the dark windows and then gingerly began to climb up the fire escape until he was facing what he thought must be Martin Jenkins' office window.

The blinds were drawn, but there was a slight gap at the bottom, so he bent down to see into the room, then froze as the lights inside were switched on. Hickock pressed himself tight to the wall, then looked through the narrow aperture. He saw Marion Collins, wearing a navy blue wool coat, pick up the small silver tray with the coffee cup, and then tip his cigarette butt into a waste bin, before turning off the lights.

Hickock rocked back on his heels. Martin Jenkins could have left his office after 1.45 p.m., returned home to kill his wife, and still been able to get back to his office to create an alibi. That just left the problem of Serina Jenkins being alive when the ambulance crew found her.

Eager to get back to his car, he almost slipped and fell on the last few steps. Dusting himself off, he decided to call it a day and call the station from home, picking up some fish and chips on the way.

The first person he called was DS Brent. 'Any result with the phone calls and security cameras?' Hickock asked with a mouth full of chips.

Brent asked Hickock to repeat himself, as he couldn't understand what he was saying. Hickock swallowed his food and repeated the question.

'OK. There were four outgoing calls from the Jenkins house that day. The first was at nine a.m. to a local locksmith. The second at one fifty p.m. to Jenkins' office, the third was the 999 call, and shortly after that a call to his sister Adele, which was made while the uniforms were present.'

'Right. I'd guess the one fifty p.m. call must be Serina calling him. Did you make contact with the locksmith?'

'Yeah, Serina Jenkins wanted the locks changed on their property right away. He explained to her he was a one-man business and already had three appointments booked. She offered to pay him in cash with an extra fifty-quid bonus if he could do it before five p.m. – which, of course, would be before her husband got home.'

'Did he do the job?'

'No. He got to the Jenkins house at about three thirty, rang the doorbell and knocked repeatedly, but got no answer. He even went to a nearby phone box and rang the house, but again got no answer. He was pissed off, assuming she'd changed her mind and gone out, so he crossed her off the list and didn't bother calling her again since he had plenty of work scheduled. I've arranged to get a statement off him tomorrow.'

Hickock thought for a moment. 'Interesting. If she was planning to commit suicide, why would she call a locksmith? And there can only be two reasons she didn't answer the door . . . one, she wasn't in, or two, she was incapacitated in some way. I discovered there's a fire escape by Martin Jenkins' office window, by the way. He could have used it to leave the office, go home and return without being noticed.'

'What, you mean to kill her?' Brent said.

'That's the theory, but it's somewhat fucked up by the fact that she was still alive when Jenkins got home, and the ambulance crew arrived.'

'Maybe he did go home and incapacitate her, like you said.'

'That would make more sense. He might have gone home, had a big row with her, knocked her about, then, fearing she'd call the police, gagged and tied her up, then returned home at six thirty and strung her up. But this is all just guesswork at the moment. We need some hard evidence. What about the neighbours' household security cameras?'

'We might have struck lucky with the house opposite, which should have a decent view of the property. The house is owned by a well-known actor, Bernard Marshal. He had his car broken into three months ago, so—'

Hickock got up out of his chair. 'I don't care who the bloody hell he is – did you view the bloody footage?'

'Unfortunately, we couldn't, but we spoke to his secretary, a bloke, very camp but quite accommodating. He told us that

Marshal was on tour in a Terence Rattigan play, *The Deep* something or other. Anyway, he's due home this weekend, as they don't perform on Sundays and the play is scheduled to open in the West End after the tour—'

'Did you seize any bloody recordings!' Hickock shouted.

'No, we have to wait until Mr Marshal returns. His secretary said he didn't know how to remove the tapes, and anyway, didn't want to hand over stuff without his employer's permission.'

Hickock closed his eyes and took a deep breath, thinking, 'If you want something done properly, do it yourself.'

'OK, I'll be in first thing tomorrow. Good work, and no weekend leave for anyone on the team.'

CHAPTER NINETEEN

Jane went into the kitchen wearing just an apron over her under-wear to prepare the bolognese sauce, not wanting to get any stains on her dress. She knew she shouldn't have had a second gin and tonic on an empty stomach. Instead of relaxing her, it made her feel angry again. Frying everything up, the onions and minced beef cooking nicely, she opened the can of sliced tomatoes, swearing as the juice splashed over her apron, then tossed in the chopped garlic and squeezed in the tomato purée, before uncorking the red wine and pouring a liberal amount into the big pan. Filling the electric kettle to the brim, ready to put the boiling water into a pan for the spaghetti, she quickly checked the table, then turned the oven on and put the garlic bread in.

The doorbell rang and she went to open the door. Peter held out a huge bunch of roses and a bottle of champagne.

'Sorry, I'm a bit early. We had a doubles match, and we thrashed them.'

'It's fine, I've almost finished preparing dinner, please come in. I'm afraid it's a very small flat, and I'm just renting, so excuse the rather pallid décor.' She took his coat, turning to hang it on one of the pegs in a row by the front door. She then turned, smiling, as he handed her the roses.

'These are so lovely, and just what I needed.'

'I must say you look lovely. That's a very sexy get-up.'

'Oh fuck.' Jane flushed, suddenly realising she was in her underwear.

'Really, you look very nice.' He grinned. 'Shall I put this on ice?' He held up the champagne.

'Please do, go straight into the kitchen, I won't be a moment.'

She hurried into her bedroom, ripped off the apron and put on her pale green soft wool dress, then kicked off her slippers and put on a pair of heels.

Peter was standing by the cooker, stirring the sauce.

'This smells delicious.' He turned and looked at her. 'Wow, you look wonderful, although I have to say the previous outfit was pretty good, too.'

'Well, I have to put that down to the two very large gin and tonics I consumed earlier. I'm also a messy cook and didn't want to get any sauce over this dress.'

'Then you have to allow me to serve. I found these champagne glasses, so let me open the bottle.'

Peter opened the champagne expertly, and poured two glasses while she sat rather self-consciously on one of her kitchen chairs. He handed her a glass, and then tapped the rim with his own.

'Cheers.'

'Cheers. Are we celebrating your squash victory?'

'Good heavens no, something much more exciting. I have three offers on my house, and it's down to me to see which one is going to gazump the others. Plus, one of the buyers is eager to buy practically all the furniture. It's been on the market less than a week – there hasn't even been time to put a board up outside.'

'Well, that's fantastic news, congratulations.' She sipped at the perfectly chilled champagne. 'Now please sit down. I just have to get the pasta ready, and I promise I will be very careful not to throw anything over me.'

Peter sat at the table as she lowered the gas on the sauce and then went to a cupboard to fetch a vase.

'These are so beautiful, Peter, you really spoil me, and they smell divine.'

She unwrapped the roses and put them in the vase. 'Right, have a look around if you like. It'll only take you about a minute, but dinner won't be long.'

Jane drained the pasta, added the sauce and got the garlic bread out of the oven, before grating some parmesan into a bowl.

Jane called out that dinner was ready and poured two glasses of red wine.

Peter walked in, drew out a chair and sat down. 'Wow, this looks and smells amazing.' He picked up the serving spoons and filled both of their plates.

'I hope it's all right. Nothing else I'm doing seems to be. Not at work, anyway.'

He gave her a sympathetic look. 'Do you want to tell me about it?'

Jane shook her head as she wound spaghetti round her fork and for a few minutes they ate in silence, apart from occasional sounds of appreciation from Peter. Eventually he put his fork down. 'That's fine, of course. But I felt a bit embarrassed at the way I have bent your ear about my problems, while you haven't really told me much about your work. I even asked your brother-in-law about you. Well, that was at first, when I knew I fancied you. Tony wasn't exactly evasive but said he wasn't sure, as you never talked about it.'

Jane laughed. To know he had fancied her from early on was very touching. She had eaten most of her spaghetti by now and Peter poured more wine, then mopped his plate with the garlic bread.

'Let me tell you about my current work situation, then. I was transferred from Bromley on promotion to DCI, and requested a posting to AMIT because they are one of the toughest units in the Met and handle serious major crimes. I was even warned that they were not happy about having women on their teams, but I was eager to be attached to such a prestigious station.'

Jane went through her arrival at the station, the way she had been given a smelly, dirty room as an office, the trials she'd had to get it into working order with the canteen situation, and then her disappointment at being given a five-year-old cold case to investigate.

Peter listened attentively without saying anything, and she was about to change the subject and ask him about his intentions in terms of selling his house and whether or not he was going to buy his ex- partner out, when he spoke.

'Tell me about this case.'

Jane went over the details of the investigation to date. He didn't interrupt, listening intently as she recounted all her interviews and explained her suspicions, ending with her frustration at not only discovering that John Kilroy could have driven his mother's car on the night Brittany disappeared, but also her excitement at finding the clearly damaged vehicle on the family's property – and then how her request for it to be forensically examined had been denied.

'I was just dismissed, my investigation made out to be unimportant as they had a more pressing murder that took precedence. It was just a five-year-old cold case, so whatever new leads I had developed would just have to wait.'

Peter poured them both more wine. 'Did they tell you how long that would be?'

'No, my investigation is too unimportant. But I'm certain John Kilroy was involved. And if they let me investigate properly, I'll be able to prove it.'

'Now, he's the only one of the three boys you haven't interviewed, right?'

'Yes, he works on an oil rig. I requested permission to go and interview him, and that was denied. I was told that it would be too costly, and I should just wait for his next leave.'

'When will that be?'

Jane was pleased he was taking an interest in her work, but all his questions were just bringing her anger and frustration to the surface again. 'A month or so. The point is, I don't want him tipped off by the other two boys.'

'Element of surprise, right?'

'Yes, I want to face him out when he's not expecting it.'

Jane gulped the last of her wine and banged the glass down on the table.

'I've had enough, if you must know. I'm ready to throw in the towel. I won't allow myself to be walked all over and treated with total disrespect, as if my entire career means nothing.'

She suddenly burst into tears and, once they'd started, she couldn't stop. Peter pushed his chair back and tried to put his arms round her, but she waved him away. Undeterred, he gently pulled her out of her chair and hugged her tightly.

'It's all right, it's all right,' he said gently.

She wiped at her face with a napkin. 'I'm sorry, sorry, I am so sorry.'

'Shush, you have nothing to be sorry about. All this has obviously been building up inside you, and it's good to let it all out.'

She sniffed, nodding. 'Yes. You're right.'

'Good, now why don't we go and lie down in your bedroom. Let me just hold you for a while.'

Jane allowed herself to be guided out of the kitchen and into the bedroom. Peter laid her gently on the bed, removed her shoes, then came to lie beside her. She put an arm across his chest and snuggled closer. Suddenly all the anger and frustration she had been feeling fell away, and she drifted into sleep.

Jane woke with a start. She was still wearing her green dress, but the duvet had been tucked around her and she had slept through the night. She sat up, then flopped back, her head throbbing. Dragging herself up to sit on the edge of the bed, she tried to stand up, but instantly felt dizzy, her head pounding as if a migraine was going to start. She made herself undress, and wrapped her big towelling dressing gown around her, then splashed some cold water on her face and staggered into the kitchen.

Peter had washed all the pans, put the dirty plates in the dishwasher and then lined the cutlery up neatly the way she liked. He'd even washed the glasses and put them back in the cupboard. It was so thoughtful of him, she suddenly began to feel tearful again, but quickly pulled herself together. She got out the tin of Andrews liver salts and put a heaped tablespoonful in a tumbler, then downed it along with two paracetamol, trying to remember how much she had drunk – the gins, the champagne and then all the red wine. She sighed. Peter must have been appalled by her passing out, and she wondered if she should call him to apologise. It was only then that she saw the note on her kitchen table.

She sat down and started to read. Peter said he was sorry not to stay, but he had an early morning meeting to discuss the sale of his house. Then he was going to spend time with his son before returning him to his mother in the evening. But he would love to take her for lunch on Sunday, and if it was convenient, he could collect her at 12.30. Peter left his mobile number at the bottom – then added that if she was wearing just her apron, all the better.

Jane laughed, her headache already lifting. She would have all day to recover and get an early night, so she'd be at her best on Sunday.

Feeling better, Jane took a shower and washed her hair, before changing her bed linen, ready to take everything to the laundry on Monday. She then made herself a big fry-up, and, fully restored, went out and did a big grocery shop.

She spent the rest of the day cleaning the flat and getting her outfit ready for lunch the next day. She ironed a white frilled shirt, and pressed a grey pencil skirt she knew was flattering, deciding to wear one of her best jackets, one with a tailored waist. Finally, she took half a sleeping tablet and went to bed.

She hadn't thought about Kernan or the Brittany Hall investigation once.

CHAPTER TWENTY

Hickock had been irritated that DS Brent had not arrived at the station until ten, but was relieved, as he had been to the locksmith and taken a statement. Brent had also contacted forensics regarding the manicure case and false nails that Hickock had asked to be checked against Serina's nails removed during the postmortem. They were a match to the unused ones in the container, which further supported Hickock's belief that Serina had been using the manicure set and attaching the false nails when something occurred to stop her finishing. It was yet another underlined query that if she was considering suicide, why was she attaching and varnishing her false nails. He spent the rest of the day going through all his notes with DS Brent and discussing the possibility Jenkins could have left his office via the fire exit and returned unseen. Hickock ordered four detectives to check for any possible CCTV footage from cameras along the possible routes Jenkins might have used to drive to and from his workplace. Hickock phoned the actor's house, but got no reply. He even requested a local patrol car attended, but they also got no reply. It annoyed him that he couldn't get access to the camera tapes, but he had no choice other than to wait until Sunday when the actor returned home.

* * *

Hickock sat in his car outside number 43, the house opposite Martin Jenkins', waiting for DS Brent. It was almost nine when he turned up, carrying a takeaway coffee and a bacon sandwich.

'For Chrissakes, Frank, eat your breakfast, so we can finally go and have a talk to this Bernard Marshal character and get these effing tapes.'

Brent took a big bite of his sandwich and a gulp of coffee. 'Maybe we can find out what this TV show he's in is. There were posters up in the hallway, it looked like some sort of costume drama.'

Hickock shrugged. 'Sounds like *Upstairs, Downstairs*. Anyway, I don't give a damn about that. I just want those tapes.'

Brent wiped his mouth with a napkin, then drained his coffee cup.

'Ready when you are, guv.'

They got out of the car and approached the house. It was as impressive as Martin Jenkins' property, with white stone steps leading to a black painted front door with a gleaming brass letter-box. Directly above the arch over the front door was the discreet security camera, framed by ivy.

Ringing the bell, Hickock straightened his tie. They heard the sound of multiple locks being turned and a chain being removed before a young man opened the door. He was quite short, wearing a T-shirt, with tweed trousers and velvet slippers with no socks. Streaked blond hair enhanced his boyish features.

'Good morning, I'm Detective Chief Inspector Brian Hickock, and this is Detective Sergeant Brent.'

'Yes, I've already met the lovely Frank. I'm Paul Angelo, Mr Marshal's private secretary. This is rather an inconvenient time, I'm afraid. Mr Marshal only returned home late last night.'

'I'm sorry, but I urgently need access to your security footage,' Hickock told him.

Angelo sighed, theatrically. 'I suppose you'd better come in, then.' He led them into the hall.

'Please wait in the drawing room, while I inform Mr Marshal you're here.'

Unlike the swanky interior of the Jenkins house, the furnishings in the drawing room were rather old-fashioned, and the green fitted carpet looked worn. Every surface of the room seemed to be covered in framed photographs of the same man in a variety of costumes and wigs.

On the mantelpiece above a fake coal gas fire was an array of invitations. Hickock was about to take a closer look when a tall, rather handsome man entered, wearing a flowing silk kimono over a vest and trousers. He was carrying a cardboard box. Angelo followed close on his heels and made the introductions.

Marshal sat on the sofa while Hickock and Brent took the easy chairs. With his thick, iron-grey hair, chiselled jaw, bushy eyebrows and very white teeth, Hickock thought Marshal couldn't be anything else but an actor – even though he still didn't recognise him.

'Now, I think I have what you require here,' Marshal began in a fruity baritone, 'but I can't be absolutely sure. We had this nice young engineer set it all up and I did try to take it all in, but to be honest, it was all a bit much, what with the tape reels and all the instructions. As you know, I've been on tour and Angelo hasn't a clue—'

'I do my best, thank you!' Angelo said indignantly.

'Yes, dear, I know,' Marshal said soothingly, 'but, you must admit that in the past you have not been at your best with electrical stuff.'

He opened the cardboard box and removed an instruction manual and several tapes, which he put on the coffee table.

'Now then, the recorder is in the closet under the stairs, he wired it beneath the carpet, then put the camera above the front door. I was very concerned about how much damage would be done to the brickwork, but . . .'

Hickock held a hand up. 'Sorry, can you tell me the exact date the camera was set up?'

Angelo picked up the installation manual. 'Look, I wrote it down, here.' Hickock was pleased to see it was two days prior to Serina's suicide.

Marshal pointed to a VCR tape. 'I should mention, the engineer said if nothing untoward or suspicious happens, just to record over the previous footage.'

Hickock's heart sank. The camera had been working the day Serina Jenkins died, but any footage of the Jenkins house would be gone. They'd waited all this time for nothing.

He was making a move to get up when Angelo spoke.

'Really? I thought you had to put a new tape in every twenty-four hours. That's why I went out and bought a whole load of blank ones.'

Marshal sighed. 'See what I mean by clueless?'

Hickock smiled with relief. 'So you've still got tapes for every day since the camera was installed?'

Angelo nodded. 'I wrote a number on each one and put the date and time I changed them in a little notebook next to the recorder machine.'

'We'd like to take the notebook and tapes, if that's all right?'

'Certainly. I don't wish to appear nosey,' Marshal added, 'but may I ask what you're hoping to see on them?'

'There's been a spate of burglaries in the area,' Hickock said smoothly. 'It's a long shot, but if they've been caught on tape, that might help us identify them.'

Marshal gasped. 'Oh dear. Well, we're happy to help, of course.' He put the tapes back in the box and handed them over.

'Thank you. Now that we've got the tapes, would it be all right if I used your phone to call our technical support unit at Denmark Hill, so I can arrange to view them asap?'

Marshal got up and waved a hand towards the phone. 'Feel free. I'm off to get changed. Paul and I are off to Oxford to visit friends. We won't be back until late, but should you need us, just leave a message on the answerphone.'

Hickock waited until Marshal and Angelo had left the room, then made the call. Brent started to look alarmed as Hickock listened, getting red in the face.

'What do you mean? You do understand this is a murder investigation? So when can I bring them in? Two days! Yes, of course it's urgent. I told you, it's a . . .'

He held the phone to his ear for a few more seconds, then slammed it down into its cradle.

'What's the problem?' Brent asked.

Hickock shook his head angrily. 'They're currently viewing and copying over thirty tapes for a big Anti-Terrorism Squad investigation. Apparently their cases take precedence over any other investigation.'

As they walked back to the car, Brent stopped for a moment.

'Fatty Littleton might be able to help us,' he said.

'Who's that?'

'He used to be on tech support, but he's just started on Shefford's team. I heard Shefford let him set up some video equipment in an interview room on the first floor.'

'Why wasn't I told about this?'

'Littleton said Shefford had decreed it was for use by his team only. I think he got the same knockback as you from tech support because of an anti-terrorism case. He keeps the room locked, and we'll need him to help us view the tapes.'

Hickock grinned. 'I'll kick the bloody door in if necessary.'

* * *

Jane was dressed and ready for her lunch date when the phone rang. She sighed, hoping it was not Peter cancelling, but instead it was her sister Pam.

'Hi there, glad you're home as we are going over to Mum and Dad's to cook lunch. The boys are playing football and going off for a McDonald's, so it'll just be us. I think it's about time you paid them a visit.'

'Pam, I can't, I have a lunch date, I'm just about to leave.'

'Who with?'

Jane sighed, not really wanting to tell her it was Peter, but knowing her sister wouldn't give up until she did.

'It's Peter, and he's booked a restaurant.'

Pam wasn't fazed. 'Fine, get him to cancel it and join us at Mum and Dad's. It's roast lamb, and I've made a cheesecake.'

'That's a lovely idea, but it's really too late to cancel the restaurant. It'll have to be another time.'

'Which restaurant?'

'For heaven's sake, Pam, just tell Mum and Dad I will see them again soon. I have to go now.'

Jane put the receiver down before Pam could say anything more. She felt a little twinge of guilt, knowing she didn't spend as much time as she should with her parents, but then the doorbell rang and she put it out of her mind.

Peter handed her a bunch of tea roses, and Jane kissed him on the cheek and ushered him inside. He stood back admiringly.

'You look stunning. I'm showing you up in these old cords.'

Jane smiled. 'You look just fine.'

'I've booked a table at Fratelli's. I think you'll like it, a real family restaurant with a great atmosphere.'

'Sounds perfect.'

During the drive to the restaurant Peter seemed distracted. When they got there, a waiter led them to a cosy table in the rear of the restaurant and they busied themselves with looking at the menus and ordering wine.

'So, how did it go with seeing your son?'

He sighed, and then shrugged his shoulders. 'It's tough. I miss him so much, and he's such a lovely little guy. We had some quality time together but it's always over so quickly. They've organised a new school for him, but they're still keen to move to the Cotswolds, which will mean he's going to be even further away from me. They asked about the sale of the house, and I told them it's going ahead, but it'll take a while, which they didn't like, as they want my ex-wife's share of the proceeds to buy their own place.'

'Well,' Jane said, 'the Cotswolds are not that far, and your son can always sleep over.'

'I suppose so,' he said gloomily.

Jane was trying her best to be positive, but it didn't seem to elevate Peter's mood. He hardly ate the delicious starter of prawn and lobster salad, and then started talking about the dilemma he was facing in terms of buying out the 'two-faced bastard', his former business partner.

'What do you want for yourself?' Jane asked. 'You said the business was doing well – I think you even have a big new contract in the offing?'

'Yes, that's true, it's a good deal, but I would still need to use all the money from the sale of the house to pay him off.'

'You could always rent a flat while the business is growing. So why not use the money from the house to realise your dreams?'

For the first time that afternoon, Peter laughed. He reached over and squeezed her hand. 'You're right. It's all so simple and I'm just making things complicated.'

'Truth is, Peter, it probably is. You just need to clear the decks and make a new start.'

'God, I am lucky to have found you, Jane Tennison. You've given me just the kind of kick up the arse I needed.'

He leaned over to embrace her.

'I think we might need another bottle of wine to celebrate!'

*　*　*

Arriving at the station, Hickock and Brent went straight to Shefford's incident room. Shefford's team were celebrating a major breakthrough in their investigation, and it took Hickock a while to get Shefford's attention, explaining he needed DC Littleton to assist him with viewing the security footage.

'Fair enough,' Shefford agreed. 'I expect you'll find him in the canteen. You can't miss him.'

'Cheers.'

Brent went to the canteen and quickly identified a balding, over-weight officer, halfway through a sausage roll.

'DC Littleton? DCI Shefford has said you're to assist myself and DCI Hickock with some videotape footage we urgently need to view.'

Littleton frowned, brushing some crumbs from his chin. 'Can't you see I'm eating?'

Brent put his hands on his hips. 'I told you it was urgent, didn't I? Come on, it won't take long.'

Littleton shrugged, then rummaged in a pocket and came up with a key. He handed it to Brent. 'That's for the viewing room. I'll be down after I've had a word with DCI Shefford.'

Hickock was waiting outside the viewing room when he saw Brent approaching.

'Where's Fatty, then?'

'Stuffing his face. He said he's going to talk to Shefford.'

Brent unlocked the door.

The small, cramped room was full of dirty coffee beakers and an ashtray overflowing with cigarette butts, and smelt strongly of sweat.

Hickock made a face. 'Look at the state of the place – it's like a pigsty.'

Littleton walked in. 'It's a bloody liberty, dragging me back in here. I've been watching tapes all fucking night for Shefford and now the rest of them are all going to the pub.'

Hickock decided to try a different tack. 'I really appreciate it. And it shouldn't take long. We've just got some tapes from a security camera that we need to look through and copy.'

Littleton still didn't look happy. 'I've been all night going cross-eyed checking for two vehicles DCI Shefford reckons were used in that robbery he's working on.'

Hickock smiled ingratiatingly. 'Shefford said you were a whizz with the CCTV stuff. There's only one tape we need to look at for now. And it's a murder investigation, so you'll be doing some vital work.'

Littleton shrugged out of his old donkey jacket as Hickock moved from the desk chair so Littleton could sit in front of the monitors, CCTV machines and keyboards.

'Right, let me see what you got. You can have an hour, max, then I'm out of here.'

Hickock handed him the tape and the manual. Littleton opened the manual, flicked through it, and shook his head.

'I can tell you straightaway this isn't a modern system. It's one of the earlier VCR models and pretty much obsolete now. The VHS tape recordings will be black and white, not to mention very poor quality.'

Hickock was confused. 'What's the difference between VHS and VCR?'

'VCR refers to the machine used to play back and record video tapes, while VHS refers to the tape format used by the VCR. Sometimes, the terms VCR and VHS player are used interchangeably, but there is a slight difference between them. A VCR is a device that can both play and record video tapes, while a VHS player can only play them back.'

Hickock was none the wiser. 'But our man only had the system installed recently.'

'Well, I'd say he was had. Salesman probably bought some old stock as a job lot, then knocked it out for a nice profit. I don't have a VHS player amongst my equipment. This gear is the latest technology for viewing digital multiplex CCTV recordings.'

Hickock put his hand to his head. 'You've lost me.'

'Basically, it allows me to view digital recordings from multiple CCTV cameras on one or more monitors at the same time. My old team at tech support will have the equipment you need to view your VHS tapes.'

'They're tucked up with an anti-terrorism case and Mr Marshal, who owns the recorder, is out all day.'

Littleton handed Brent the manual. 'Well, I suggest you contact the guy who installed that crap. If you're lucky he might have a spare VHS player.' He grinned. 'So excuse me, but I'm off for a well-earned few pints and a bit of nosh.'

He pushed back the desk chair, picked up his donkey jacket and walked out of the room.

Brent shook his head angrily. 'Fat bastard. I'll bet any money he could have helped us. He just wanted to get pissed and stuff his face.'

Hickock shrugged. He was already dialling the number on the manual.

'Good morning, is this Raymond Brooks?'

'Yeah.'

'I am just making an enquiry about the security equipment you installed for a Mr Bernard Marshal.'

'Who is this?'

'I'm Detective Chief Inspector Brian Hickock from Southampton Row station. I need your assistance in an investigation.'

The person on the other end cut the connection.

'Hello? Are you still there?' Hickock slammed the phone down. He was about to redial, but then changed his mind. 'Let's do a quick check and see if this number is for a home address. Run the name Raymond Brooks on the PNC and print off the ones with criminal records.'

'Now?'

'Yes, Frank, now. I'll be in my office. I'm not going to let this go and I'm not prepared to wait. Get an address for Mr Brooks and then we are going straight round there.'

CHAPTER TWENTY-ONE

Back at Jane's flat, Peter made some strong coffee in her new percolator, and she poured them both a brandy. They sat on the sofa in her cosy sitting room and he told her more about how his business had started.

'I started training as an architect, but I left university before finishing my studies.'

'Why?' Jane asked.

'I realised I didn't have the flair to be really successful. And by then I'd met my business partner there. We decided to join forces and see if we could make some money. We started flipping houses – buying up dilapidated properties that were on sale for a good price, refurbishing them and selling them on for a profit. I handled the contracts side of things and did all the negotiating, and my partner did the more creative stuff. We began in a small way, but it worked out well.'

He started explaining in more detail about the financial side of the business, then stopped himself with a smile.

'Are you sure I'm not boring you with all this stuff?'

She shook her head. 'No, I'm genuinely fascinated. You know, I did the same sort of thing in a very small way. I bought a property in Bromley at a very good price and then refurbished it. I made quite a decent profit.'

He grinned. 'Ah, so you know what it feels like. The first time you make a profit is a fantastic feeling. You only really learn from your mistakes, though. We made a few early on, but we learned quickly.'

He leaned forwards, cupping his glass between his fingers.

'And then we got really lucky . . .'

* * *

The old garages in the little mews behind Queen's Gate looked run-down, despite the desirable location, close to Hyde Park. The flats above them also looked shabby, though one or two had clearly been refurbished. Hickock pressed the bell for number 14, one of the shabbier ones, the paint peeling, with a dirty milk bottle left on the step, while Brent waited in the car. He waited for a minute but there was no answer. There was no doubt he had the right address: the property was leased to Raymond and Sydney Brooks and the phone number on the manual was registered to it by BT.

Hickock went back to the car. 'We'll bloody wait, then.' They drove out of the mews and sat parked across the road from the entrance. Raymond Brooks had a police record for petty crimes, serving six months for a drug offence at Feltham Young Offenders Institution before starting his home security business. Just the sort of person who might flog an out-of-date security system to a naïve homeowner.

'How much longer are we going to wait?' asked Brent after an uneventful forty minutes.

Hickock looked at his watch. 'OK, another half hour, then we'll call it quits. But tomorrow I'm going to have a few words with DCS effing Kernan about that lazy sod Fatty Littleton. I don't believe he couldn't have run those tapes for us.'

'Hang on, look who's here.'

A dirty white Ford van with 'Brooks Security Installations' just visible on the side drove into the mews. Hickock jumped out of the car, Brent following behind with the tapes.

'That's got to be our boy,' Hickock said.

They watched him getting out of the van, leaving the driver's door open, before he unlocked the garage door, and heaved it up.

Brent nodded. 'He looked a bit younger in the mugshot, and he's dyed his hair and spiked it up a bit, but I reckon that's him all right.'

Brooks was about to get back in the van when Hickock approached. 'Raymond Brooks?' he said in a loud voice.

Brooks turned and Hickock did a double take.

'No, I'm bloody not, I'm his sister. What do you want?'

Hickock quickly recovered himself. 'I'm sorry, I'm Detective Chief Inspector Hickock.' He showed his ID as Brent joined him. 'And this is Detective Sergeant Brent. We'd like to talk to your brother.'

'Well, he's not here. He's on a job. It's 24/7, this business. But he said he got a call from the Old Bill.' She laughed. 'Said someone called Hiccup wanted his help, reckoned it must be a joke. So what's the idiot done now?'

Tall and slim, she spoke in a deep, rather posh voice. As well as the spiked hair, she also had a nose piercing.

'We need to discuss a security installation he did for a man called Bernard Marshal.'

She laughed again. 'Oh, right, that old queen. So what's the complaint?'

'No complaint. But I need to view the footage on a VHS tape and was hoping Raymond could help.'

She sighed, jerking her head in the direction of the interior of the garage. 'We got a job lot of VHS machines and monitor screens. Stupid, really. They were too cheap, so we should have known better. We've still got twenty-five of the bloody things to flog. The more updated ones have digital cassettes instead of the tapes, which frankly are a pain in the arse.'

'I really need to view the footage on a VHS player,' Hickock said, trying to keep the exasperation out of his voice.

She looked at him dubiously. 'Don't you have your own unit to do that kind of thing?'

'They're busy on another case. I'm sorry, I didn't catch your name?'

'Sydney Brooks. I run the business with my brother. Let me park the van and I'll see what I can do for you.'

Hickock watched as she drove slowly into the cramped garage packed full of security equipment. She got out and squeezed past the van to rejoin them.

'Do me a favour and pull the swing door back down. It's a heavy bastard and I've done my shoulder in.'

Hickock reached up and heaved the door down. She was already opening the small front door to the flat above. Brent and Hickock followed her inside and up a narrow staircase. The walls were lined with framed pictures of Jesus and various saints, the type that seem to move with the light.

'OK, come on through. We've converted the main bedroom into our workshop.'

They passed a small, old-fashioned kitchen and another room with a single unmade bed.

'I don't live here, mind. I've got my own place, thank God. Problem with Ray is he's so methodical it takes him three times longer than it should to install the gear, so I have no idea when he'll be back.'

While they all stood for a moment by a closed door, Hickock had a proper look at Sydney. She was wearing black jeans, a black T-shirt and a black leather studded jacket with thick-soled black boots. The dyed spiked hair and her thickly kohl-ringed eyes gave her a tough quality, but on closer inspection she was rather good-looking, with high cheekbones and full lips, the gold stud in her nose the only jewellery.

'OK, word of warning,' she said before going in. 'Please do not touch anything. I'll do the stuff with the tapes. Raymond has OCD when it comes to letting anyone in here. Apart from me, obviously.'

Sydney opened the door, pushing it as wide as it would go, before moving to one side to let them pass. It was like stepping into a set from *Doctor Who*; one wall was lined with reels of different-sized tapes, all neatly labelled on steel shelves. Another had banks of monitor screens, again neatly arranged on floor-to-ceiling shelves. There were also piles of camera equipment, a very fancy-looking colour printer, and boxes of manuals. On a long desk that reached all the way along one side of the room were four television screens and numerous computer keyboards, alongside a telephone, desk diaries and sales ledgers.

'Impressive, isn't it?' she said, smiling. She gestured to the screens on the desk. 'We're working on a computer game, that's where the dosh is. The security installation is just a sideline until we get the game set up.'

Hickock looked around at all the equipment. 'Well, you've obviously done all right with the business. This lot must have cost a fortune.'

'Well, a bit of inheritance helped. And we're rent-free as Mummy owns most of the mews.'

She fiddled with her nose ring.

'You're sure Ray's not in trouble? I mean, he's not been drawn into anything stupid again, has he? Like when he agreed to buy a brick of cannabis from this bloke and it turned out to be camel dung. He still got arrested.'

'I was being perfectly honest with you, Miss Brooks. I know Ray has a record, but all I'm interested in is seeing what's on these tapes.'

'OK, good. I'm happy to help, seeing as Ray's not here, but, you know, we do have a business to run, so I'll have to charge you for our time.'

Hickock was beginning to get pissed off. 'Well, your business might suffer if I seized all the equipment in here and the garage as suspected stolen goods.'

She held her hands up. 'OK, OK. How many hours of footage do you want to watch? Do you have a time frame?'

'Between six a.m. and ten p.m.'

'Does the VHS tape have a time and date marker on it?'

'Yes – all we need is a copy of the tape and a VHS player to view it on.'

'Why do you need a copy?'

Hickock sighed. 'Because the original may need to be kept as evidence, and we can then work from a copy to make stills and do edits. So can you do it or not?'

She shrugged. 'I suppose so. I'll need two VHS machines, one to play and one to record, but I've never done it before. Ray normally does all those sorts of things.'

'Well, Ray's not here and I need it done asap.'

Brent shifted uncomfortably. 'It might be a bit risky, guv. If she doesn't know what she's doing the tape could get damaged, and we might lose anything of evidential value.'

Sydney nodded. 'That's a good point. Personally, I don't want to get in the shit for destroying evidence.'

'Never mind that. How long will it take?' Hickock asked.

'I don't know. Like I said, I've not done it before.'

'Why don't you call your brother, then?' Hickock said.

She folded her arms. 'Actually, I'm the one who's trained to do most of the electronic installation. I spent over a year on a part-time course to get the qualifications.'

Hickock had had enough. 'Jesus, either you can do it or you can't. Look, I'm not doing this for fun – this is a murder enquiry.'

Her eyes widened. 'Wow, a murder enquiry! Why didn't you say? I'll call Ray now and get him to come home. If you don't mind waiting in the kitchen?'

Brent and Hickock looked at each other, then Hickock nodded and they went out. Sydney closed the door behind them.

'I think we should call it a night, guv,' Brent said, sitting down on a kitchen chair. 'I don't think she's right in the head. I mean, did you clock all those religious pictures on the stairs, with their eyes following you around? Creepy, I call it. I also don't think we can risk her or her brother messing around with the tape.'

Hickock looked at his watch. It was almost five o'clock. 'Let's give her ten minutes. Come on, put the kettle on.'

Brent looked around; although the kitchen was old-fashioned, it was clean and tidy, with nice crockery in the cabinets. He filled the electric kettle and plugged it in. 'I can't fathom this place out, are they rich kids? She said her mother owns most of the mews – I mean, what are these places worth?'

'Dunno, thirty, forty thousand? Probably more.'

'Well, all that video and printing equipment must have cost a bomb, never mind the cameras.'

They both turned as Sydney came out. 'He's just finished the job. He's getting a cab.'

Hickock turned to Brent. 'You get off home, then. I'll wait for Ray. I'll call you if we get anything.'

'Thanks, guv, appreciate it.' Brent hurried out.

'Tea or coffee?' she asked, fetching down two mugs.

'I'll have a coffee, thanks.'

She smiled, taking off her jacket. 'Might as well make ourselves comfortable while we wait.'

* * *

Jane listened, fascinated, as Peter regaled her with stories of his business ventures. She began to appreciate just how complex some property deals could be, with so many angles to consider, as well as the self-confidence needed to take such big risks, with so much invested and so much riding on the outcome.

He then explained the current situation regarding the buy-out. Peter had moved from her small sitting room into the kitchen as she had made them both a coffee. They had spent a lot of time, as he had at first begun to explain how his company had been set up, and then in more detail, using one of her notepads to show the financial structure. Jane had asked if by buying out his partner it would mean losing some of the clients contracted, and if he would be liable to give him a percentage. He started listing the financial side, and she was impressed by the amount of money the company had made over the past ten years. He also listed the purchase of his house, and what he would gain from the sale of it.

'Our house has tripled in value. I reckon by agreeing to give my wife fifty per cent of the proceeds from the sale, with what I've got in my current account, I'll still have enough to buy him out of our contract and without him having any lien on the two new projects I've been working on. That'll leave me with about forty-five grand.'

'That sounds like you're in a very good financial position, doesn't it?' Jane said.

He smiled ruefully. 'Not really. At the start of a project, there's a lot that has to be paid up front. There's wages: my staff, the builders, et cetera. But the biggest outlay will be the purchase of the property and the additional land I'm thinking of buying. All that's going to leave me a bit cash-strapped, to say the least.'

'I could lend you some if you needed it,' Jane said.

He turned to her, looking serious. 'One, thank you for the offer; two, I wouldn't even contemplate borrowing a single penny from you. I can always take out a loan from the bank. But thank you again, that's really very sweet of you.'

He cupped her face in his hands and kissed her, at first gently, but then more passionately, until Jane almost toppled from the chair, before he caught her and held her in his arms. Then he lifted her off her feet and together they headed for the bedroom. He helped her out of her dress, and it seemed like the next moment they were lying together naked.

'There is one thing you could do for me, though, Jane,' he said with a grin.

* * *

Raymond Brooks thudded up the stairs and walked into the kitchen. He had a blond crew cut, and was wearing a big tweed overcoat, jeans and Cuban-heeled boots. But despite the different look, it was immediately obvious to Hickock that he and Sydney were twins.

'This is Detective Chief Inspector Hickock,' Sydney said as Ray took off his coat. Ray nodded shyly. 'Did they pay you in cash?' she asked.

He nodded. 'In the pocket.'

Sydney went through the pockets of his coat and retrieved a wedge of banknotes. She was starting to count it when Hickock stood up.

'Can we get on with it, please?' He turned to Ray. 'As I think your sister explained, we're conducting a murder enquiry and we need to look at the tapes from Mr Marshal's security camera. And make a copy.'

Ray looked at his sister. 'Have you agreed a price?'

She shook her head. 'When I suggested it, DCI Hickock expressed an interest in the contents of the garage.'

Raymond stroked his chin. 'Ah, I see ... Best be upstanding citizens and assist him, then.' He had the same posh accent as his sister. He went and washed his hands at the sink, then hung up his coat on a hook in the hall.

Inside their office, Raymond sat at his desk as Hickock explained exactly what footage he wanted to look at.

Raymond examined the VHS tape in his hand, then swivelled round to face Hickock.

'Shouldn't be too difficult to make a copy. I can link a monitor up so you can watch it while the copying is going on.'

'That would be helpful. How long will it take?'

'A while, but I've got some new equipment that can speed the process up.'

'When you say "a while", are we talking an hour or so?'

'I can have it for you later tonight.'

Hickock ran his hands over his face. He was beginning to lose the will. Perhaps he should forget the whole thing and wait for technical support to do what he needed.

Sydney was lounging in the doorway. 'Why don't you and me go out for dinner and then come back later?'

Hickock hesitated for a moment, then laughed. 'What the hell, why not? I could do with something to eat, and if Raymond comes up trumps, dinner's on me.'

She grinned. 'Super! There's a terrific restaurant at the end of Queen's Gate, we can walk there.'

Raymond glanced at his sister, knowing which restaurant she meant and how pricey it was.

As they went down the stairs, Hickock paused by a blinking-eyed Jesus on the cross. 'These are a bit freaky. You religious?'

'Good God, no. Mummy's chauffeur used to live here. He found God when he quit the booze.'

As they left the mews, Hickock turned and looked up at the blacked-out windows of number 14. He realised he'd just left vital evidence in the hands of a young man who'd bought a brick of cannabis that turned out to be camel dung.

CHAPTER TWENTY-TWO

Jane lay back under the duvet, feeling guilty. During the sex, she couldn't stop thinking about Eddie, and his hard, muscular body. Their relationship had gone wrong, but sex between them had always been thrilling. In comparison, Peter was slightly over-weight and just hadn't managed to excite her in the same way. She'd eventually had to fake an orgasm. She closed her eyes, then felt him gently touching her hair. He drew her close, nestling her head against him.

'You know,' he said, 'I still feel bad about commandeering the entire conversation that day. I want you to know that I did pay attention to everything you said about your case. In fact, I've been thinking about it. Can I ask you a few questions?'

'Sure, go ahead.'

'OK, now, three college boys were the last to see the young girl. One was called Justin Moore, right? And he is an estate agent. The second is in Yorkshire and he is called Phillip Sayer?'

'You have a very good memory.'

'The third boy was John Kilroy, and he's the one you haven't questioned yet because he's working on an oil rig, but you think he had the use of a car and the girl might have been in it at some point.'

'Correct, and the reason I got so pissed off was I wanted it towed into the station for forensics to examine it.'

'So, you want to interview John Kilroy because you suspect him more than the other two boys?'

'Right. It's more of a gut feeling than having actual incriminating evidence against him.'

'Why do you feel that?'

'Well, he hardly ever returns home, works about as far away as he possibly can, it's as if he's hiding out. Plus, he inherited the farm where his mother still lives, but, although it's being left to go to rack and ruin, he refuses to sell.'

'You think he could have buried the girl there?'

Jane sighed. 'I don't know, but I suspect he had intentions of running the farm.'

'And out of the three, you reckon he was the ringleader?'

'Yes, none of them reached their potential, which makes me think they were all involved in some way and then felt guilty, but Kilroy forced them to keep silent.'

'*Omerta*,' Peter said with a smile.

Jane laughed, touched that he had shown such an interest in her work. She reached up to kiss him. Soon all thoughts of Eddie fled from her mind as they made love – and this time she didn't have to fake an orgasm.

* * *

Hickock knew he had made a mistake as soon as they walked into the restaurant. Everything about it, from the elegant wood panelling in the reception area to the plush red carpet and the crystal chandeliers, said 'expensive'. The maître d' welcomed Sydney as if she was an old friend and led them downstairs to a dimly lit dining room, and a small table for two with white napkins folded into cones.

There were a few other diners, a couple of middle-aged couples and two men in evening suits. There was no music and it was all rather hushed. The waiter presented them with menus in red velvet covers, asking if they would like a cocktail. Sydney ordered a Shirley Temple with vodka, and Hickock, a little embarrassed, asked for a glass of the house red.

Hickock was even more alarmed to see there were no prices on the menu, which Sydney was scanning eagerly. 'The soufflé's amazing here – you must try it,' she said. 'And then the fillet steak. It comes with truffle oil chips. Yummy!'

The waiter brought their drinks, and Sydney ordered the souf-flé and steak for both of them before Hickock could get a word in. Then she started a long monologue about her school days at some horrible-sounding boarding school, how she had run away numerous times, and finally her father had not bothered sending her back. The soufflé arrived. Hickock tried to look interested, but was actually just wondering what it would be like to screw her, not that she was really his type. But take away the hair dye and the heavy make-up, not to mention the nose stud, she was actually very attractive.

By the time they started tucking into their steaks, Hickock had learned all about her family. She and Raymond were dependent on handouts from an elder brother, who ran the family estate and who she described as a disgusting snob, while her mother had some decrepit Italian aristocrat lover.

'So that's me and my life,' she said finally. 'So tell me more about this murder enquiry.'

She'd been happily talking about herself and her family for so long, Hickock was surprised to finally be asked a question. 'We're in the early stages. I can't give you details, I'm afraid.'

'So what big murder enquiries have you been on?' she asked.

'Well, to be honest, I specialise in fraud investigations. Very time-consuming, can last for months. Last one took over three years. It's all about following the paper trail.'

'God, it sounds boring,' she pouted. 'How did you like your steak?'

Hickock had to admit the steak was perfect, and the French fries the best he had ever tasted. He'd almost forgotten how much all this was going to cost him, and was about to order a third glass of the excellent house red, when she got a signal from the maître d' that there was a phone call for her. She was gone only a few moments before returning to say Ray would be about another ten minutes. Hickock stood up. At least this would save a few quid, as she had been going on about the amazing desserts.

Even so, when Hickock followed the maître d' to reception and was handed the bill, it turned out to be eighty-five pounds, the most expensive meal he had ever eaten. As he proffered his American Express card, he couldn't help calculating that he could have had a perfectly decent nosh-up for the price of the tip alone.

Raymond was in the kitchen when they returned, drinking a glass of water.

'Right, I've got the original tape for you, plus the copy. I must admit I did have a few concerns to start with, because I wasn't sure if I'd put Mr Marshal's camera in the correct position. I think he really wanted it to focus on their entrance, you know, to check who's visiting—'

Hickock cut him off. 'I'm more interested in the property directly opposite. Did the camera cover that as well?'

'Yes, looks like it.'

'Good. Is there any chance I can borrow one of your VHS players to view it?'

'Yeah, no problem. You can take one of the ones I was just using. You can also have the remote control that comes with it, so you won't have to stop and start it using the buttons on the machine.'

Raymond went to his office and returned with a large box containing the VHS player, the original tape and a copy. There was also a note explaining how to link the VHS player to a TV.

Hickock took it from him. 'Thanks.'

'Thank *you* for dinner,' Sydney said with a charming smile.

'My pleasure,' he said. 'I just hope to God it turns out to be worth it,' he added to himself as he hurried down the stairs.

* * *

Hickock ran up the stairs to his flat, fumbling with the keys, he was so eager to get in and watch the tape. He threw off his jacket, fixed himself a half tumbler of whisky with ice and soda, then connected the VHS player to his TV. After drawing the curtains, he drew up an easy chair.

The first image on the screen was a clock with the hands moving backwards. The screen went blank, and he sat with the remote in his hand before 'THREE-TWO-ONE' appeared in capital letters and then the date and time in the bottom right-hand corner. It was the morning of Serina Jenkins' death. The quality wasn't great, but the entrance to the Jenkins house was clearly visible.

Hickock sipped his drink, seeing nothing but vehicles passing the house. He fast-forwarded to 6 a.m., paying close attention to the seconds, then minutes, as they ticked by. A milk delivery van appeared, then more cars as people started driving to work. He fast-forwarded closer to the time Martin Jenkins said he left home.

'Fuck!' Suddenly the screen went fuzzy. He held his breath, fearing he'd somehow damaged the tape, but then, to his relief, it cleared again. The time stamp now showed 7.30. He sat watching intently for another fifteen minutes, then got up to refresh his drink, keeping his eyes on the screen.

After a while, Hickock got up and started pacing his tiny living room. It was well after 11 p.m. He was feeling exhausted and his eyes were beginning to feel itchy. He needed to pee, but was scared of using the remote, so ran to the bathroom and back, hoping he hadn't missed anything. He sat down again and finished his drink. A few cars passed and a couple walked their dog. The timer was now showing 8.15, and he could feel himself falling asleep. Then, suddenly, at 8.30, he sat bolt upright. This was the time Martin Jenkins had said he left the house to go to work. Hickock grabbed his notebook and pen as the front door opened and Jenkins emerged, carrying a briefcase. Serina Jenkins was in the doorway, wearing a dressing gown. It looked as if she was talking to her husband, then at one point she seemed about to close the front door when Jenkins stepped forward, pushing the door to stop her. They were obviously having a heated conversation. He raised his hand in an angry gesture. Again, she attempted to close the door, and this time she kicked out, forcing him to take a step backwards. Jenkins stumbled as the door slammed shut. He was clearly very angry, alternately banging the door and repeatedly pressing the doorbell.

Hickock watched as Martin put down his briefcase and took out a set of keys. He inserted a key and managed to open the front door a fraction, but couldn't open it further. Hickock recalled the front door had a chain and assumed Serina had put it on. Jenkins picked up his briefcase and stomped off out of shot. A few minutes later, the front door opened and Serina looked out towards the left-hand side of the road, then closed the door again.

Hickock scratched his chin. 'Well, well.'

*   *   *

Peter sat at the kitchen table, pouring them both a cup of tea while Jane made them toasted ham and cheese sandwiches. She was wearing her dressing gown, while Peter had wrapped a bath towel around himself after taking a shower.

'You know, I just had a thought,' he said. 'I have a couple of meetings I can't get out of tomorrow, but I can cancel what I have scheduled for Tuesday.'

'What's the thought?' Jane asked.

'We could get a train to Scotland and stay overnight at a nice hotel.'

'You mean before I go to the oil rig?'

'Why not? We could turn it into a nice break. You've been telling me how badly you want to interview . . . Er, now I can't remember his name.'

'John Kilroy.'

'Right. As it stands now, I think you are in a sort of catch-22. To confirm your suspicions, you need to interview him, but your boss won't let you go all that way until you have more evidence. So if the station won't finance the trip, then let me take you, in more ways than one!' He grinned.

Jane set out the toasties on the table and sat down opposite him. 'I don't know, it's very nice of you to think of it. I do need to try and find some solid evidence, though. I could get Maureen to find out if an accident was reported involving the car five years ago.'

He nodded. 'If the car in Kilroy's garage was in an accident, it was probably a hit-and-run, which is why it's never been taken out again. Or it was too badly damaged.'

Jane opened the fridge and took out the tomato ketchup, putting it down in front of him and giving him a kiss. 'Quite the detective, aren't you?'

'So do we go to Scotland?'

'OK, I accept your offer,' she said, smiling. 'Tomorrow I'll stay home and check out the oil rig situation.'

He grinned. 'Deal! Hopefully I can get things moving with the sale of the house in the morning, so a break after that would be perfect.'

'And I have another deal,' Jane said. 'Why don't you move in here with me until you find a new place, and we can sort out the spare room for your son to stay over?'

'My God, are you serious?'

'I am. You still have some of his things at the house, so just bring them over and he can be here at weekends.'

'Don't you think you need more time to think about this?'

'*I* don't. But maybe, you're unsure about it?'

'Thank you, it's a really very special offer and I appreciate it. But it is all quite quick. Maybe we both need to think about it? Let's make a decision after our trip to Scotland. Agreed?'

She smiled. She hadn't really given her offer any real thought before making it. She didn't need to: everything was so clear in her mind. Peter was such a decent, lovable man and, more importantly, so unlike Eddie.

CHAPTER TWENTY-THREE

Hickock had managed to stay awake watching the film for a few hours, but had been constantly nodding off and then jerking awake. At one point he had even placed a mirror by the door so he could still see the TV set from his kitchen while he brewed a pot of strong black coffee. He had developed a little bit of respect for Sam Littleton, knowing that he spent virtually every hour of the day monitoring CCTV footage for Shefford. The screen showed it was now 12.15, and there had been no further action at the Jenkins property. He had nearly ten hours of footage to watch. He settled down with a mug of coffee, determined to get through it, but at four in the morning he realised he'd reached his limit. He couldn't stay awake for any longer.

* * *

Frank Brent was dreaming about a bell ringing until he finally woke up and fumbled the phone to his ear.

'Frank, it's Brian. You've got to get over here.'

'What do you mean? What's happened?'

Brent's wife sat up in bed. 'Who the hell's calling at this time of the morning?'

Brent made a shushing motion. 'What were you saying, guv?'

'You need to get over here straightaway and take over watching the footage. I'm falling asleep.'

'Well, just freeze-frame the tape, get some rest and watch the rest later.'

'No, I can't, the remote's playing up and I'm worried I'll damage the tape if I use the buttons on the machine. I've already seen Jenkins having a heated argument with his wife on the doorstep, which he never mentioned. We need to get as much as we can from the tape now so I can arrest Jenkins in the morning.'

'It *is* the morning, guv . . . but don't worry, I'll be with you as quick as I can.'

* * *

Hickock was dozing in the chair when the doorbell woke him up. Frank came in, carrying two takeaway coffees and a bag of doughnuts.

Hickock pointed to the chair. 'You take over, I'm gonna crash out, but wake me if you see anything. I'll have my coffee later.' He handed Frank his notebook and pen, then staggered to his bedroom.

* * *

Peter had left just before 7 a.m. Sitting up in bed sipping her tea, Jane decided that she would call into the station just before nine to say she was feeling unwell and then begin to check out the logistics of their trip to Scotland.

After showering and dressing, Jane went into the little box room she'd suggested Peter's son could stay in at weekends. It was small, and filled with things she hadn't yet had a chance to unpack. With some brighter curtains and a chest of drawers, it would be perfect. Jane had never been that good an aunt to her sister's boys, and she was certainly not intending to be any kind of substitute mother for Peter's little boy; she just wanted to do the right thing for Peter. The more she had thought of it, the more she wanted him to move in with her.

By the time Jane had cleared the boxes from the little bedroom and changed the sheets in her own, it was almost 9 a.m. She rang the station and Maureen answered.

'Morning, Maureen. Look, I feel awful – think I'm coming down with the flu – so I'm going to stay home.'

'Oh, I am sorry. It's all been happening here. There was quite a shindig going on here, celebrating DCI Shefford closing this big case he's been on, and I was told that DS Otley was found under his desk by the cleaners this morning!'

'Really! Listen, I don't want to stay online too long – I really am feeling very poorly. I want you to check any vehicle accidents reported around the night of the disappearance of Brittany Hall. Get on to the stations close to the college, the pub and also John Kilroy's address – any report of a damaged vehicle.'

'OK, do you want me to tell them the colour and make of Kilroy's car, the one you wanted towed in?'

'Maybe, but first just see if there's a report.'

'I could check for any CCTV footage, too.'

'These are country roads so I don't think you'll have any joy there, but I know they did have a camera in the pub. I'll call in later to see how you're getting on. Don't call me – I'm going to try and sleep this off so I can hopefully be in tomorrow.'

'OK, ma'am. And I'll report you sick.'

'Thank you, Maureen.'

Jane put the receiver down. She doubted Maureen would get a result, but it would keep her busy. She opened her briefcase and took out her notes about the oil rig. She needed to contact whoever was in charge to arrange an interview with Kilroy without him being forewarned. Aberdeen, the 'Oil Capital of Europe', had the nearest heliport, and she was sure it also had some very good hotels.

* * *

Frank Brent had smoked two cigarettes, using his empty coffee cup as an ashtray. A dog-walker, a postman and a laundry collection service had passed across the screen, but there had been no movement at the Jenkins property. Brent yawned, delved into the paper bag for the other doughnut he'd brought for Hickock, then quickly dropped it and picked up the pocketbook and pen. On the screen at 1.27 p.m. was a tall woman in a long coat. She went up the steps to the house, rang the doorbell, and stood back before the door was opened by Serina Jenkins. There was a short conversation, before she entered the house and the door was closed.

Brent kept his eyes on the screen as he backed away, shouting for Hickock. There was no response, so he went back to stand behind the chair. He jotted down the time and a description of the woman, then shouted for Hickock again. This time he heard him moaning.

'There's a woman at the house, get in here.'

Hickock stumbled into the room.

'The picture quality isn't great and I only saw her from behind. I can't say I recognised her. Do you want me to rewind it?'

'No, she's got to come out again, then we'll get a better look at her, so let it play on.'

They waited, watching the timer ticking away. Hickock picked up his cold takeaway coffee, while Brent sat in the chair. Then at 2.15 p.m. the door opened again; no sign of Serina, but the other woman slammed the door shut and ran from the house in an obvious hurry, turning left and out of sight.

'Her face isn't that clear, but from her height and length of hair I reckon that's Martin Jenkins' sister, Adele, who I met at his house. You sure it was Serina opening the front door?'

'Well, it can't be anyone else, can it?' Brent made a note of the time on the screen.

Hickock was about to get dressed when there was another shout from Brent. He ran into the room with a towel round his waist. Frank was standing up, looking excited.

'He's in the house. He ran up the path and let himself in. Definitely Martin Jenkins. He went in at two twenty-six p.m.'

They sat and watched as Martin Jenkins came out of the house at 3.13 p.m., hurried down the path and turned left, out of view.

'Keep your eyes peeled for a dark BMW – that's his car,' Hickock said.

They waited a few minutes, but the camera hadn't caught his car driving past the house. 'He must have parked round the corner and driven off in the opposite direction,' Brent said.

As Brent jotted down the time, Hickock sifted through his file.

'What time was that call from the house to Jenkins' office?'

'One fifty . . . which means it was either Serina or Adele who called him.'

'Correct. You saw Jenkins use a key to get in, which means the chain lock wasn't on. Which seems odd if Serina didn't want him back in the house and had called a locksmith to change the locks.'

Brent sighed. 'This is all so confusing. We know Serina can't have been dead at this point . . .'

'A logical conclusion is that Serina was incapacitated,' Hickock said. 'Something must have happened between her and Adele. Maybe she knocked her out.'

Brent nodded. 'That would account for the bruise on the back of her head, and it would be a reason for Adele to call Jenkins.'

'At least we know for a fact now that Jenkins and his sister are lying.'

'Shall I fast-forward the tape to six thirty, the time he said he got home?' Brent asked.

'No, we need to sit here and watch every second in case Jenkins or Adele come back again.'

The next moment of excitement came at 3.25 p.m., when a white van parked outside the property. They could make out the word 'locksmith' on the side of the van.

Hickock checked his notes. 'The locksmith said he got to the house at about 3.30 p.m. Ten minutes earlier and he would have seen Jenkins leaving the house.'

'I'm starving,' Brent said. 'You got anything to eat?'

'Not a sausage, mate. Plenty of coffee, though.'

'Can we pause the tape and I'll pop out and get some food?'

Hickock reluctantly agreed. 'There's a decent caff round the corner.'

Brent paused at the door. 'Do me a favour and get changed. Seeing you in just a towel will put me off my grub.'

Hickock laughed and went to get dressed.

Brent returned ten minutes later with two bacon, egg and sausage baps and cappuccino coffees. They sat and ate while watching the video.

Suddenly Hickock excitedly pointed to the TV. 'The bastard has lied again! Look, it's Jenkins walking towards his house at five past six. He said he got home between six thirty and six forty-five!' He flicked through Jenkins' statement. 'He said it takes him half an hour to get to work and the same back again. He must have left the office just after his secretary saw him in the kitchen . . . which was five thirty.'

'And he didn't call an ambulance until six thirty-two p.m.,' Brent said.

'Which means his wife was incapacitated but alive, and he had plenty of time to stage her suicide. He and his sister must have planned the whole thing. He must have strung her up just before or after he called the ambulance, thinking by the time they got there she'd be dead.'

Brent looked through the statements. 'The ambulance crew were only a few streets away when the call went out . . . He obviously thought they wouldn't get there so soon.'

Hickock laughed. 'He must have shit himself when they found a pulse. Right, we need to get to the station, speak with Kernan, then arrest Jenkins and his sister.' Hickock stopped the VHS machine, ejected the tape, then kissed it. 'And we don't want to forget this little baby.'

* * *

Jane had been on the phone for over half an hour, being transferred from one person to another as she tried to track down the foreman of the oil rig, Alister McCormack. Eventually she got a contact number for him, but when she rang it, she was told he was not available until later that afternoon as there had been an incident that required his attention.

It was just after ten when Peter called to say that he was going over to his house with the buyer to discuss what furniture and white goods they wished to purchase.

'That was quick!' she said.

'Well, I said that it had to be done now or I had another buyer, which I do have, but at a lower asking price. Anyway, the reason I called is, do you want to come over at lunchtime to see what would be suitable to move into your flat for Joey?'

Jane was slightly taken aback, as he had been the one suggesting they spend more time thinking about her offer.

'OK, I'll take some measurements. We would need a bed, obviously, and a small chest of drawers and maybe a wardrobe. It's been driving me mad trying to get hold of the foreman of the rig. They seem very reluctant to let anyone talk to him, and I had to be a bit cagey about my reasons, but hopefully I'll be able to speak to him later this afternoon.'

'Great. I'm afraid I haven't had time to check hotels, trains or us driving to Aberdeen.'

'I think it'll be easier to go by train,' she said. 'And we can look into hotels this afternoon at your place.'

'OK, shall we say about one o'clock? I have to go to a meeting now, but I'll be on my mobile if you need to contact me.'

'Perfect.'

Jane put the receiver down with a sigh, then started searching in a drawer for a tape measure before going into the box room to see where a single bed and the other furniture would fit. She returned to the kitchen to get her notebook to take down all the measurements. There was a packet of Marlboro Lights in the drawer, what she called her emergency pack, though she hadn't resorted to it for a while. She lit one, then sat at the kitchen table, her thoughts turning to when she had been pregnant by Eddie. It had turned out to be an ectopic pregnancy, and as a result of the emergency operation she had lost one of her fallopian tubes, so getting pregnant again might be difficult. At the time it had been a relief, and what had been driving her at that time was proving a young boy had been murdered. The determination to bring him justice and win promotion had been more important than her feelings about Eddie and the pregnancy, and had given her little time to grieve the break-up of her relationship.

Stubbing out her cigarette, she decided that perhaps asking Peter to live with her had been a mistake: she should be more cautious, and concentrate on her investigation into the disappearance of Brittany Hall. Like a sign, her phone rang. It was Maureen.

'How are you feeling?'

Jane took a moment to remember she was supposed to be ill. 'Lot better, actually, headache gone, just a bit sniffly.'

'Well, I might have some news, about the possible accident. I have been on the phone all morning and a call-back just came in from the first station I contacted in Ascot. They have a report about a vehicle sideswiping a jeep with a horse box attached. They were leaving the polo club at ten thirty on the night Brittany Hall went missing. The driver stopped when he felt the bang and the horse box almost swerved into a ditch. By the time he had got out of the jeep and looked at the damage, the vehicle had driven off. It had to have damage to the driver's side.'

'That's interesting. Any reason they had retained the report?'

'There was a pony in the horse box, and its ribs were damaged when it went off the road. The owner was adamant that the other driver should be traced to pay for the vet's fees, and has continued to complain to the local station.'

'This is all good, and it was definitely the night Brittany went missing?'

'Yes, I checked the insurance for Mrs Kilroy's vehicle, and the colour is listed as dark green. The owner of the horse box was unable to describe the make of the vehicle, but said it must have been dark green, because he found traces of dark green paint on the trailer.'

'Have they retained the paint chips?'

'Not sure about that, they were going to check for me. There's something else I meant to tell you, when I was checking out the details about Kilroy's vehicle: in the filing cabinet, your file of all your notes on the Martin Jenkins case has been replaced. I told you that Hickock had taken it, but he must have brought it back.'

'He's welcome to it,' Jane said dismissively. 'Anyway, good work on the accident report. I'll check out the address and see how far it is from Pirbright village and Windsor, see if the driver would have driven past the polo club on his way home to stash the car.'

'I checked, the club is not on a main road but it's directly en route.'

'Well done, Maureen. Great initiative. Something else, can you just check out the contact details for Kilroy's solicitor? After I left the house, I overheard his mother make a call to a James Appleton. I might want to talk to him. Right, I'm just going out to the chemist to get some cough medicine. I'll call you later.'

* * *

Forty-five minutes later, Jane parked outside Peter's house. She was just getting out of her car when she saw him coming out with three smart-looking people, two men in suits and a well-dressed woman. He was shaking their hands and smiling warmly, and she thought how handsome and confident he looked. By the time she approached, the group were already moving down the street to a parked Jaguar.

Peter turned with a smile and opened his arms to give her a hug.

'Done deal, Jane, they want virtually all the furnishings, and to move in quickly, so it should all be finalised next week. Come on in.'

Peter seemed elated as he gestured to all the kitchen equipment, the dining room table and chairs and kitchen cabinets. 'All I need to put into storage will be Joey's things, bed linen, some cutlery, a dinner service and wine glasses. They even want most of my office stuff. I've got Mandy looking through what I'll need to keep.'

Jane followed behind him up the stairs to Joey's bedroom. She took out her notebook with the measurements, but the more Peter talked, it felt less and less like he was planning to move in with her. She felt confused, having gone from feeling hesitant about it just hours earlier, to disappointment that he must have decided not to accept her offer.

She was taken aback when a young, very attractive girl wearing a stylish tracksuit gave a light tap on the open door before looking in.

'Jane, this is Mandy, my secretary and brilliant PR junior from my office. Mandy, this is Jane Tennison.'

Mandy smiled. 'Hi. I've noted everything we will be able to use in our main office. All his equipment has been removed, so his office is empty.'

She gestured to the furniture. 'You wanted all Joey's furniture to be put into storage along with all the other items you've listed, is that still right?'

Peter rubbed his head and then shrugged. 'Not quite certain at the moment, Mandy, but it'll basically be everything in here. Have you organised a company to do the move?'

'Just comparing prices. You said you wanted a big spring clean, so I have ordered professionals to do a complete room-by-room, wash carpets and polish the wood floors. They also include washing the windows, it's a good company.'

'That's great, thank you for today, and I'd like you here tomorrow, but I will need you in the office on Wednesday to sort out all the paperwork.'

'Yes, and remember you do have two appointments on that afternoon about the Land Registry situation on the proposed new extension at Collingwood Street.'

'Right, well, you get off home, and thank you again for being here at the crack of dawn.'

'My pleasure. Nice to meet you, Jean, hopefully see you again.'

Jane smiled, not bothering to correct her; she was too fascinated by this other side of Peter she hadn't seen before. He seemed so confident and sophisticated, and it made him even more attractive. She was also certain that for men like Peter Rawlins, 'cash-strapped' didn't really mean the same thing as it did for people like her ex, Eddie.

He folded the note with the measurements and put it into his pocket. 'I don't know about you, but I'm starving. There's a lovely pub that serves great food just by Putney Bridge. We can discuss the trip to Scotland.'

'I was just thinking, it feels like there's a lot of work you need to attend to with the sale going through and everything.'

He shrugged. 'We'll talk about it over lunch.'

Jane followed him down the stairs, feeling unsure of herself. Compared with his luxurious home, her G-Plan-furnished flat seemed tawdry, and she couldn't believe he would ever want to move into it. What had she been thinking? And she felt even more embarrassed that she'd offered to lend him money. No wonder he had instantly refused. Perhaps she should step back a bit.

Peter's mobile rang as they were about to leave the house. He went into the kitchen while she waited in the hall. He came out, listening to the caller on his mobile, then saying, 'She's here with me.' He handed her the phone. 'Jane, it's Tony, he rang you at home and the office and was told you were off sick. It's something about your father.'

Jane took the mobile, surprised that Tony had managed to track her down. 'Tony, it's me, what's happened?'

'Oh, hi, I was actually calling Peter about some work, but he mentioned you were there with him. I did try calling you earlier, though. It's nothing to be too worried about, but your dad took a fall. Pam has a busy day at her salon, and she thinks you should go over and see him as your mother is in a bit of a state.'

'Hang on a minute, Tony.' Jane turned to Peter. 'Could we drive over to my parents'? It's my dad, apparently he's had a fall.'

Peter nodded. 'Yes, of course.'

'I'll be over there straightaway. No, I'm fine, bit of a cold, that's all.'

Jane handed the mobile back to Peter. It was typical of her sister, thinking her work at the salon was more important than Jane's, and Jane could just drop everything to go to see her parents – even though Jane wasn't actually at the station.

They drove to Maida Vale in Peter's Range Rover, and Jane examined his mobile.

'I wouldn't mind getting one of these things. Are they very expensive?'

'Quite,' he said, 'but they're worth every penny. And every few months new models come out, not as cumbersome.'

Jane looked out of the window, recalling how she had laughed at Eddie and the enormous brick of a mobile he had been so enamoured of – though it turned out he was even more enamoured of the woman at the call exchange.

Peter told her how to make a call, and Jane pressed the digits of her parents' number. Her mother answered.

'Mum, it's Jane, I'm on my way to see you. Tony said Dad has had a fall.'

'Oh, Jane, that's very nice of you. He's in bed – he fell down the steps outside the back door of the flats. He was in a lot of pain, but I don't think he'll need to go to hospital. He has been to the doctor recently about having a hip replacement for his arthritis . . . He's had some paracetamol and I'm making chicken soup.'

Jane quickly told her she'd be there in fifteen minutes, knowing that Mrs Tennison was about to get into a lengthy conversation about her own arthritis pains.

'Is he all right?' Peter asked.

'I think he's a bit of a drama queen,' Jane said. 'My mum certainly is. But it's really nice of you to drive me over there.'

They parked in the drive behind her parents' block of flats, and went into the building through the back entrance. It was four steps up to the door, and although there was a railing on one side, it could have been quite a nasty fall.

Mrs Tennison remembered meeting Peter from the anniversary party, and straightaway, even before Jane had seen her dad, insisted they stay for some chicken soup. Peter offered to help her set the table as Jane went into her parents' bedroom. Her father was propped up in bed, reading *The Times*, with a mug of tea and some biscuits on the bedside table.

He was obviously pleased to see her, inviting her to sit on the side of the bed.

'How are you feeling, Dad?' she asked. 'That must have been quite a fall.'

'Not really, it was only on the last step, I sort of toppled over, though I must admit I've had a lot of pain in the right hip recently. Your mother wanted to call an ambulance, you know how hysterical she gets, but I don't think I've broken anything, and I'm already feeling better. Now, tell me what's going on with you.'

Jane told him about her new flat, and how she was almost finished getting it ready for them to come over for dinner one evening. She didn't tell him about her work, but then she never went into any detail about it with her family. She listened as he told her how Pam's boys were both turning into very good footballers, and how Pam's salon was busier than ever, employing two stylists now.

A few minutes later Jane's mother came in with a tray of chicken soup. Her father smiled and winked at Jane.

'The best chicken soup in the world, though maybe a small drop of brandy might make it even better.'

Mrs Tennison fussed around with his napkin, tucking it into his shirt.

'Will you be all right if I leave you while we have our soup in the kitchen with Peter?' she asked.

He rolled his eyes. 'Of course. I've only banged my hip.'

As they went out, Jane's mother nudged her.

'He's head and shoulders above that Eddie, if you want my opinion – and the right age. Don't let this one go.'

CHAPTER TWENTY-FOUR

Hickock and Brent were with Kernan, going over the videotape evidence. Kernan listened intently, every now and then nodding admiringly.

'Terrific work, I'm very impressed. Discovering that CCTV was a game-changer. Without it, I doubt we'd have a case against them.'

'Thank you, sir. It was just an idea that came to me on the spur of the moment,' Hickock said without any trace of embarrassment. 'I'd like to arrest Jenkins, and also bring his sister in for informal questioning this afternoon. If she thinks she's still just assisting us with our enquiries, it'll be easier to catch her out.'

'Again, good thinking, Brian,' Kernan said approvingly. 'Right, go get your arrest and interview teams organised.'

'Yes, sir. I wonder if you could authorise DC Littleton, who's on John Shefford's team, to copy the relevant sections of the videotape for use in the interviews.'

'Consider it done. He's the chap who was on tech support. I recently signed an invoice Shefford gave me for a load of video and monitor equipment. I did say at the time it would be for everyone's use and not just his team's.'

'Can you remember if a VHS player was on the list?' Hickock asked.

Kernan looked through his out tray and found the invoice. 'Yes, there was.'

Hickock looked at Brent and raised his eyebrow. 'That's handy.'

As they were leaving the room, Brent whispered to Hickock, 'Wait till I get my hands on that useless heap of shit!'

Hickock put a hand on his arm. 'I'll deal with him. You go and call the team in for a briefing – I need about ten extra officers – and be ready to go in thirty minutes.'

Hickock found Sam Littleton in the canteen.

'So you didn't have a VHS player, then? DCI Kernan tells me you do.'

Littleton started spluttering. 'Look, I—'

Hickock held a hand up. 'Save it. I've had enough of your bollocks. Just edit the tape for us.'

Littleton nodded furiously. 'Sure, no problem. I'll get right on it.'

Hickock nodded and went out. The truth was, he now understood what it was like watching CCTV footage for twenty-four hours straight, and he had every sympathy for Littleton wanting to go and join the celebrations in the pub. He just wasn't going to tell Littleton that.

* * *

As Chief Superintendent Kernan was heading down the corridor to his office, DCI Shefford approached.

'I hear Hickock is playing a blinder with that Jenkins case.'

Kernan nodded. 'Yes, he's confident he'll be able to make a murder charge stick. He's been more innovative than I had given him credit for. I had concerns that he and the suspect had personal connections, but his diligence has been exemplary. Congratulations to you, too, John, on your recent result. Five arrests, I hear.'

'Thank you, guv. I will be having the vehicles I seized cleared tomorrow, so the forensics team will be available if Hickock requires any vehicles examined.'

'Thank you, John, I'll let him know. Again, congratulations to your team. I believe Tennison wanted some car towed in for forensics, actually.'

'I did try to contact her,' Shefford said, 'but she's off sick.' He rolled his eyes. 'Menstrual cycle, no doubt!'

* * *

Frank Brent quickly gathered a team together for the incident room briefing. Hickock pinned up the crime scene and postmortem photographs, along with the photographs from the video of the weighted bag experiment, and some he'd had taken of the fire escape at Jenkins' office building, then gave a detailed account of the investigation into Serina Jenkins' death. They gave a loud cheer as he informed them Martin Jenkins would be arrested on suspicion of murder. Hickock said he and DS Brent, along with two other detectives, would make the arrest, then instructed two other officers to attend Adele Burton's address at the same time. They were not to tell her Martin had been arrested, just ask her to come to the station as DCI Hickock needed to speak with her as a matter of urgency.

One officer raised his hand. 'What if she refuses?'

'I doubt she will,' Hickock said. 'I reckon she'll be eager to know what's going on so she can feed information back to her brother. But if she does, arrest her for attempting to pervert the course of justice on the grounds she was lying to protect him.'

He then instructed a team of four officers to obtain a search warrant for Adele Burton's address and execute it once she was off the premises. Hickock watched as everyone busied themselves with their allotted tasks.

'Right, Martin, you lying bastard. I think I've got you.'

CHAPTER TWENTY-FIVE

Jane and Peter did not leave her parents' flat until almost four o'clock. When he managed to escape Mrs Tennison fluttering around him, Peter spent a long time chatting to Jane's father. Mr Tennison was fascinated by the mobile phone, and with Peter's assistance put a call into the flat. He was like a teenager, annoying his wife by first telling her he had gone for a walk, before explaining he was using Peter's mobile. He eventually took down all the details so he could order one for himself, thinking that if he ever fell again, it would be handy to be able to make an emergency call.

Due to Peter's mobile being with them in the bedroom, Jane had not heard back from Maureen, or as yet made the call to the oil rig foreman. They decided that if they were to make the trip to Aberdeen, she needed to be at home to make the call and to check on trains and hotels.

As soon as they got back to Jane's flat, Peter drove back to his house, having agreed to drive her Mini back after he had finished his business there.

Jane went into the kitchen and made a cup of coffee before calling Maureen.

' 'So, what's been happening?'

'Well, DCI Hickock seems to be on some kind of high, lots of CID and patrol cars screaming in and out, but being stuck up here on the fourth floor I don't get wind of what is actually going on.'

'What about our case?' Jane asked, testily.

'I looked through John Kilroy's statements and his lawyer *was* James Appleton.'

'Good. Anything new on the horse trailer?'

'They don't have the paint chips, or at least they haven't found them. I know the timing's important: the accident was reported as occurring just before eleven o'clock in the evening. I have the name and address of the horse box owner if you want to interview him. Perhaps I could organise a meeting for tomorrow?'

'I doubt I am going to feel well enough to come in, I'll let you know.'

'Oh, one more thing, the garage where they tow in vehicles for forensics to examine will be available either tomorrow or the following day, now that DCI Shefford's team have completed their investigation. DS Otley called to say whatever you wanted towed in needs to be rubber-stamped by DCS Kernan.'

Jane pursed her lips. 'Fine, I'll be in contact,' she said, ending the call abruptly. She fetched another cigarette and sat calming herself down before she placed in the call to the oil rig foreman. It was now 5.30, and it took an inordinate length of time as her call was transferred several times, even though she had been told that it was McCormack's direct line. After hanging on for five minutes, a guttural brisk voice finally spoke.

'This is Alister McCormack speaking.'

'Thank you for taking my call, Mr McCormack. I'm Detective Chief Inspector Jane Tennison from the Metropolitan Police, and I would like to interview one of your employees in connection with an investigation.'

'How do I know you are who you say you are? We get a lot of bloody journalists calling in, you know, trying to get a story.'

'Mr McCormack, if you want to check my credentials, I can give you the name of my superior at the station to confirm my identity.'

McCormack's answer was lost in a rush of static, not helped by his thick accent. Finally Jane heard him ask what the investigation was about.

'It's a cold case, I'm afraid that's all I can tell you. I know the person I want to interview is presently working on a rig, and I would really appreciate you not informing him of my intentions.'

'We have hundreds of employees on different rigs,' McCormack said. 'Do you know which rig he's working on?'

Jane raised her voice as she grew more impatient. 'I have only been told that he is employed by your company.'

'Well, you need to tell me his name before I can tell you which rig he's working on,' McCormack replied, equally tetchily.

'I understand that, Mr McCormack, but as I said earlier, I would like to interview him without prior warning. Are you able to give me that assurance?'

McCormack said something Jane couldn't hear, and she finally decided enough was enough and gave him John Kilroy's name.

McCormack grunted. 'I'll need to check.'

'How long will that take?' Jane asked.

'Gimme a couple of hours, it's a very busy time right now. We have choppers due to land any minute before it gets dark.'

Jane thanked him for his cooperation, even though he hadn't been very helpful. She just hoped that if John Kilroy's friends had tried to warn him about her investigation, they hadn't found tracking him down any easier than she had. She made herself a cup of strong coffee and lit her third cigarette of the day.

* * *

Hickock and Brent were interviewing Adele Burton. At first, she had been a bit tetchy, saying she had already been very patient, assisting the police in every way possible. She also wondered why the interview was being recorded. Hickock explained that it would just help him complete his report for the coroner more quickly, and then he could close the investigation. He just needed to go over her previous statements to check she agreed everything was correct, then that would be the end of the matter and she could go home. This ploy seemed to put her more at ease, and she said she was quite happy to be interviewed without a solicitor if this would speed the process along.

'There are a few things I need to ask you that haven't been covered in your previous statements. Is that OK with you?' Hickock asked.

She nodded. 'As long as it doesn't take long. I've quite a few things to do around the house.'

Hickock smiled. 'I'll keep my questions short and to the point. Apart from when your brother called you on the evening Serina hanged herself, did you have any form of other contact with him that day?'

'Not that I recall.'

'Is that a no?'

'No, I didn't. He was at work all day. I know he doesn't like to be disturbed at the office.'

'Did you have any contact with Serina the day she died?'

'No. I hadn't seen or spoken to her for a few days.'

'Do you think your brother is capable of murder?'

She sat up straighter, clearly surprised at the direction the interview was taking. 'No, of course he's not. My brother and Serina had a loving relationship – he wouldn't harm a hair on her head.'

'Are you capable of murder, Adele?'

For a moment she was too shocked to speak. 'That's it, I've had enough of this. You let me leave now or question me with a solicitor present.'

Hickock cautioned her. 'Adele Burton, you do not have to say anything unless you wish to do so, but what you say may be given in evidence.'

She was enraged. 'If I am being arrested, I demand a solicitor!'

'I'm cautioning you because I know you are lying, Adele. I have evidence that you did go to Serina's house the day she died. It was just before one thirty p.m., and she let you in. Do you deny it?'

Adele stared, open-mouthed, shocked, then started twisting her hands in her lap. Hickock didn't actually mention the security footage as he wanted to keep her guessing about how he'd got this incriminating evidence.

Hickock spoke calmly. 'Would you like a solicitor or are you happy to answer my questions?'

He could almost see the cogs in her brain turning. She chewed her lip, took a deep breath, and asked for some water.

Hickock was surprised she hadn't asked for a solicitor, but thought perhaps it might be because doing so would imply guilt. She took a few sips of her water, then slowly raised her head and looked at Hickock.

'I did visit Serina. I didn't tell you because I didn't want my brother to find out.'

'Why did you visit her, and what was the problem with your brother knowing?'

Adele hesitated, as if trying to think of a plausible answer.

'It was regarding a business proposition. At first, she didn't want to let me in. Anyway, she did, and I followed her upstairs, where she was giving herself a manicure in her bedroom. I wanted to discuss a visit to a possible business location we had been discussing. I was very excited about the prospects of us working together on the project.'

Hickock detected a change in Adele's tone, as if talking about Serina irritated her.

'What was Serina doing during the discussion?'

'Selecting false nails from her manicure set. She said it was no longer a viable proposition. She had changed her mind. I can't tell you how much I was depending on this; it would have been a lifesaver for me as my husband's business was not going very well.'

'That must have been very distressing.'

'It was, and I became quite angry about it, but she was very dismissive and told me to leave.'

'So it was a brief conversation, then?'

'I suppose so. I wasn't there for very long.'

'Really? Because we know you left the house at about two fifteen p.m. – nearly three quarters of an hour later.'

'Obviously someone saw me go into the house, and I don't deny that . . . but there's no way I was in there that long! Whoever saw me leave is clearly mistaken about the time.'

'Why did you hide this meeting from your brother?'

'Because he already had enough on his plate, and I didn't want to upset him. After Serina killed herself, it didn't really matter anyway, so I kept it from him.'

'There was a phone call that afternoon from your brother's house to his office. Did you make that call?'

'No, it must have been Serina after I left.'

'That's odd, because the call was made at one fifty, while you were still there.'

She looked nervous and started twisting her hands again. 'I went to the toilet at one point. Serina might have phoned him then . . . I really don't know.'

Hickock leaned forwards. 'Well, I know you are digging a deeper and deeper hole for yourself, Adele, so I suggest you start telling the truth.'

'I am telling the truth.'

'Your account of the meeting with Serina doesn't make it sound like she was a woman on the verge of suicide.'

Adele drank the rest of her water, put the glass carefully down on the table and ran her hands through her hair.

'You're deliberately twisting my answers to somehow implicate me and my brother in Serina's death. If you must know, I never particularly liked Serina, she was a spoiled, pampered, rich woman and at times she could be mean-spirited, whereas my brother doesn't have a bad bone in his body. But I'm saying nothing further until I speak with a solicitor.'

Hickock removed some still pictures of Adele taken from the videotape and laid them on the table in front of her.

'We don't have an actual witness, but we have these video pictures of you. As you can see, they are date- and time-stamped. After you left the house, the front door chain was never put back on. It could have been an error by Serina, or something might have happened to her while you were there, rendering her incapable of putting the lock back in place. And for your information, we also have some very damning video of your brother.'

Adele looked furious, but she said nothing.

'You have lied constantly throughout our investigation into your sister's death, whether it's because you are involved or just have some misguided desire to protect Martin, I don't know, but rest assured I will find the truth. Adele Burton, I am now arresting you for attempting to pervert the course of justice. You do not—'

Adele suddenly banged her hand on the table and stood up. 'This is outrageous. I demand to speak with Martin and a solicitor.'

'A solicitor will be called as soon as you are booked in by the custody sergeant. You might not get the opportunity to speak to your brother since he's already in the cells under arrest for murder.'

'You bastard!' Adele started screaming at Hickock, demanding to be released and hurling more insults at him. Brent took her arm and led her out.

* * *

Jane called Peter on his mobile, but got no answer. She called his home but got the same result. Alister McCormack was proving just as elusive. It was now almost 7.30 and she had got nowhere in terms of arranging her trip to Scotland. Having nothing else to do, she opened her briefcase and began looking through her notes, rereading the boys' statements to see if she could find any more discrepancies. After twenty minutes she flung her notebook down in frustration. Kernan was right: she had no solid evidence, just

Edwina Summers' story about an overheard conversation and a gut feeling that the boys had been lying.

She got up and poured herself a stiff gin and tonic, lighting another cigarette. Edwina Summers was hardly a credible witness. She had a history of drugs and had been expelled from the school. Could Jane really take what she said about the boys at face value? What if she went all the way to Scotland behind Kernan's back, tracked down John Kilroy to the oil rig, and he then just stuck to his story, like the other two? She'd have got nowhere, while at the same time she'd have given Kernan more reason to marginalise her within the station.

She needed to get the car to forensics. If she could tie it to the accident with the horse box, then that would prove the car was used the night Brittany Hall disappeared. And if there was any evidence that Brittany Hall had been in the car, then she might have enough to make John Kilroy crack under interrogation.

Downing her gin and tonic and stubbing out her cigarette, she put in another call to Alister McCormack. Given that it was now evening, she was surprised when he answered.

'I was just about to call you,' he barked. 'I checked, and John Kilroy is not one of my team.' She sighed in frustration, ready to put the phone down, when he added, 'But there is a trainee engineer attached to another rig called John Kilroy.'

'Is he still there?' Jane asked, hardly able to contain her excitement.

'I'm afraid not. He's gone on leave due to a family situation.'

'When did this happen?'

'Two days ago. Hello, are you still there?'

'Thank you, Mr McCormack. I'm sorry to have put you to so much trouble.'

Jane put the phone down and lit another cigarette. Her hands were shaking. John Kilroy must have been tipped off about her impending visit by Justin Moore or Phillip Sayer. Could one of them also have contacted John Kilroy? It was too much of a coincidence that he'd suddenly gone home now, especially as his mother wasn't expecting him for another month. What now? She got up and started pacing the room. She thought about driving straight to John Kilroy's farm and confronting him. But what if he wasn't there? She poured herself another gin and tonic, then thumbed through her notes to find Sylvia Kilroy's phone number. She picked up the phone, then put it down again. If Kilroy was there, then she didn't want him to know she was coming. She wished she had taken a number for Donald Fitzpatrick-Dunn. Damn! She forced herself to calm down, then rang directory enquiries but the number was ex-directory.

The doorbell rang, and she got up to let Peter in. 'I've been trying to contact you,' she said angrily.

He held his hands up in apology. 'I'm sorry, mobile's battery ran out, and then I had to go to the office. I've had quite a bad time of it, actually.'

She frowned. 'Wait till you hear what I've been through. You won't believe it, John Kilroy isn't on the oil rig. He left two bloody days ago.' She headed back into the kitchen, and Peter followed.

'Well, perhaps that's a good thing. I don't think I'd be able to drive to Scotland with you now . . . Good heavens, smells like a pub in here! Have you been smoking?'

She turned on him, furious. 'Do you blame me? I've been on the phone tracking down Kilroy, only to discover he's back home. I couldn't go and interview him because I didn't have my bloody car.'

She suddenly noticed Peter's right eye was swollen almost shut, the skin dark and bruised.

'What happened to you? Did you have an accident?'

'No, I had to go to the office because my ex fucking partner demanded a meeting. We got into a big argument; it ended up in a fist fight. But you'll be pleased to know I gave as good as I got, flattened his nose.'

She instantly regretted her bad temper. 'Let me get some ice. Do you want a brandy?'

'Yes, a large one, please. The bastard really tried it on with me, you know, pressing for a bigger cut of the projects I've been working on. I told him to piss off, he's had nothing to do with them and there is no way he's going to get a slice. The outcome is, we have to lawyer up tomorrow morning as the hoped-for amicable split is not going to happen.'

Jane was at the fridge, handing him a bag of frozen peas. 'Hold this. You don't want to go into negotiations with a black eye. Maybe he'll cancel if you've broken his nose.'

'It was just bleeding a lot, and I know him, he can't wait to wring every penny out of me. Anyway, I rang my lawyer and he's coming to the office early in the morning for a briefing before the meeting. I'll need to get all my paperwork in order. You know, when each project started, proving it was after he'd left. The bloody nerve of him even trying it on! He's taken my house, my wife, my son, half my business . . . but I have to say that uppercut I gave him was very satisfying.'

Jane handed him a large brandy, topping up her gin and tonic again before sitting down opposite him at the kitchen table. He held his head tilted to one side as he pressed the bag of frozen peas against his eye.

'Time is of the essence—' Jane started to say, but he quickly interrupted.

'Too damned right it is, I've got Mandy working late to get all our ducks in a row, ready for the morning.'

'I was actually talking about my case,' Jane said. 'I'm damned sure John Kilroy was tipped off.'

'Oh sorry, tell me all about it. I wouldn't mind something to eat, too. I haven't had anything apart from chicken soup at your parents' and I'm starving.'

She got up to check the fridge, and bumped her hip against the table, almost losing her balance.

'Have you been drinking as well as smoking like a chimney in here?' he asked.

'Yes,' she said, 'I have as it happens. Right, it's eggs and bacon or ordering in an Indian.'

'Indian sounds good to me, then I'll get a taxi back to my place.'

He had pressed the peas back over his forehead, so missed her annoyed look as she went to the kitchen drawer to find the takeaway leaflet.

'You know, what felt good after that bastard had left was knowing I was coming to see you. If I didn't have you, I'd have gone home and got drunk, then probably been too hungover to get to the meeting. To have you, a place to come back to, made me think about your offer. I was thinking that after the meeting we could move my son's furniture in here, not send it into storage.'

He slowly removed the frozen peas and looked at her.

'What do you think?'

'I'd like the chicken madras with pilau rice . . . What about you?'

She laughed as he momentarily looked taken aback. Then he held out his arms and she went and sat on his knee.

'I'd like something really hot,' he said with a grin. In that moment Jane's bad mood lifted. She was glad that he was there with her. It felt good to have him in her life. For once, she was going to take her mother's advice: she was not going to let this one go.

* * *

Hickock and Brent were in the lift on the way to the ground-floor custody area to interview Martin Jenkins. Brent turned to Hickock.

'Did you take that video machine back to the camera guy?'

'No, I'm keeping it. His bitch of a sister ripped me off for an expensive meal.'

'I should really have brought this up earlier, guv – and no offence meant – but don't you think it's a bit risky, you interviewing Jenkins? You know, what with you and him being friends.'

'For fuck's sake, Frank, he's just a golf acquaintance. And we've got him by the short and curlies. His brief can bring it up as much as he likes, but when he's confronted with all the evidence we've got he'll have no choice but to roll over.'

Brent didn't look convinced. 'Are you just going to hit him with everything from the start?'

'No, I'm going to do what I did with his sister, get him to lie even more and make things worse for himself. Then we'll confront him with the video. If he doesn't cave then, I'll let him know his sister's been arrested.'

'They're obviously very close,' Brent observed.

'Thick as thieves would be a better description. Mark my words, Frank, he'll either try to protect her and take all the blame, or say she did it to try and save him. Either way, they're both screwed.'

As they entered the custody suite the uniform sergeant approached them, saying that Adele Burton had repeatedly asked to speak to them.

'Has her solicitor arrived?' Hickock asked.

'Not yet,' the sergeant said. 'But she doesn't seem bothered. She just wants to speak to you.'

'OK, tell Jenkins' solicitor we've been delayed and offer them drinks and a sandwich to keep them happy.'

A uniform officer opened Adele's cell door. She was sitting on the bench with her hands in her lap. She'd obviously been crying.

'I've only got a few minutes,' Hickock told her.

'Thank you. I've been a fool. I lied to protect my brother, but I want to tell you the truth now.'

Brent opened his notepad and got a pen out of his pocket.

'When I was at Serina's house, I got upset with her when she said she didn't want to work with me. I told her it was a great business opportunity for us both and asked why she wasn't interested. She just carried on doing her nails, and then looked at me like I was a piece of dirt. She said she didn't want to work with me because she was going to get a divorce from my brother, and had already set the wheels in motion. She was fed up with Martin's gambling addiction draining their joint bank account, so she was kicking him out and getting the locks changed.'

Hickock waited as she sipped some water from a plastic cup. 'Did you have any form of physical altercation?'

'Yes. I grabbed her arm with both hands and begged her not to cast me and Martin aside. She said to get off and then deliberately scratched my arm.' Adele pulled up her right sleeve and showed them three parallel scratch marks. 'I don't know what came over me . . . I just lost it and punched her in the nose. It started to bleed, so I grabbed a tissue from the box on the dressing table and gave it to her. She screamed at me to get out and ran into her ensuite bathroom.'

'Did you phone Martin before you left the house?'

'Yes, it was me. I used the downstairs phone in the kitchen. I told him about the conversation I'd just had with Serina. I was very upset.'

'Did you tell Martin that Serina was going to divorce him?'

'Yes, but he told me she'd threatened that before. They were always bickering over money. She used it to keep him on a short leash.'

'Did he say anything else?'

'He just told me to calm down, leave the house, and he would sort it out.'

'What do you think he meant by "sort it out"?'

'Well, she was always making threats, but Martin usually calmed her down. He said it was all the hormones she had to take, trying to get pregnant.'

'Did you know Martin returned home shortly after your phone call?'

'No, I didn't. After I found out Serina hanged herself, I asked him if he had hurt her. He said he hadn't touched her and couldn't understand why she would want to commit suicide. I believe him . . . I've never known Martin to be violent or lose his temper.'

'He stands to inherit an awful lot of money by her death,' Hickock said.

'I don't know all the details, but Serina had got her solicitor to draw up papers that meant he wouldn't be entitled to any of her business or the earnings from them.'

'Had he signed the papers?'

'I don't know.'

'So why didn't you tell us all this before?'

'Because Martin told me not to. He said it could look bad for both of us. The police might think we were involved in Serina's death. I know now I shouldn't have listened to him, but he was only trying to protect me.'

'Did you hit Serina on the head with anything?'

Adele looked surprised. 'No, I only punched her in the nose, and it wasn't that hard.'

'OK, thank you, Adele,' Hickock said. 'If you could just read over my colleague's notes and sign them if they're accurate.' She nodded and Brent handed her his pen.

'What do you reckon?' Brent asked Hickock as they left the custody area.

'Hard to say. Parts of her story are plausible, and I believe her about punching Serina, but there's other bits that just don't add up. On the plus side, it gives us more ammo to fire at Martin Jenkins. Be interesting to see how he reacts when he finds out his sister's dropped him in the shit.'

CHAPTER TWENTY-SIX

Jane and Peter had opened a bottle of wine when their curry arrived. She was already quite tipsy after the gin and tonics, and now, when Peter led her into the bedroom, she was more than willing. The sex was getting better every time as they got more relaxed with each other. Peter went for a shower, after calling a taxi to take him back to his house. He took a look in the bathroom mirror. It was now clear that by morning he would be sporting a very obvious black eye.

'We can get your son's furniture at the weekend,' Jane told him when he emerged from the shower. 'Or an evening before that, if you want to get it all sorted so you can move out.'

'And move in with you?' He grinned as he hugged her.

After he had left, Jane went into the kitchen. It was in a pretty shambolic state, with food cartons and glasses stacked up in the sink. She rolled up the cuffs on her dressing gown and started washing up. By the time she was finished and had emptied the ashtray into the bin, it was after eleven. She knew tomorrow was going to be a big day, but she was so tired, all she could think about was getting to bed.

* * *

Martin Jenkins was dressed in a smart suit with a white polo neck sweater. He sat with his arms folded, while sitting next to him, his solicitor, a short, plump man with half-moon spectacles, rested his hands on a large leather-bound notebook, with a gold pen sitting on the table beside it.

'Are the statements you made to the police concerning the death of your wife Serina Jenkins true?' Hickock asked Jenkins, after identifying all those present for the tape.

Jenkins kept his arms folded. 'No comment.'

Hickock suspected he was going to be hearing that answer a lot today. He nodded to Brent. Prior to the interview, Brent had installed a VCR player and monitor screen in a small cupboard in the room. He opened the cupboard, put the viewing monitor on top and handed Hickock the remote.

'I'm going to play you some footage from a security camera installed by one of your neighbours,' he told Jenkins.

His solicitor immediately interjected. 'We were not made aware of any videotapes prior to this interview.'

Hickock smiled. 'I am under no legal obligation to disclose all our evidence to you. Prior to this interview, I explained to you that Mr Jenkins has been arrested on suspicion of murdering his wife, which, as you know, is all I am required to do.'

The solicitor frowned, but knew Hickock was right. Hickock first played the clip of Jenkins leaving home that morning.

'It seems to me you and Serina were having some sort of argument and she shut you out of the house using the chain lock. You do not mention this in your statement.'

Jenkins nervously licked his lips. Hickock moved on to the next clip. 'I'd like you to pay special attention to the time shown on the video.' He pressed play, revealing Adele knocking on the door and entering the house. It was followed by her leaving the house.

'Your sister never mentioned in her statements that she'd been to your house for nearly forty-five minutes that day.'

The solicitor shook his head. 'What has that got to do with my client? He can't be expected to know what his sister does while he's at work.'

'That's a very debatable statement, sir. Moving on to the next clip.' Hickock pressed play. 'Mr Jenkins has repeatedly stated he was at work all day, yet here he is returning home and going into his house at two twenty-six p.m., then leaving nearly three quarters of an hour later at three thirteen p.m. Have you any explanation for that, Martin?' Hickock paused the tape.

Jenkins rubbed the back of his neck. 'No comment.'

His solicitor let out a sigh.

Hickock leaned towards Jenkins. 'This next clip is very interesting. You have repeatedly stated you arrived home at approximately six thirty p.m. and found your wife hanging in the hallway . . .' He played the clip. 'Yet here you are arriving home at five past six.'

'No comment.'

'Your call to the emergency services was made at six thirty-five, by which time you'd been in the house for thirty minutes. I'd say that was plenty of time to tie a noose round your wife's neck and throw her over the bannisters so it would look as if she'd committed suicide.'

'No comment.'

Hickock shook his head in disbelief. 'Come on, Martin, the evidence is overwhelming. The only mistake you made was calling 999 before you tried to kill her. You'd probably have got away with it if the ambulance hadn't been nearby. Cutting her down actually relieved the pressure on her neck, but you never checked for a pulse because you thought she was dead. But she was actually in a coma. You must have shit yourself when the medics said she was still alive.'

Jenkins said nothing, but was now starting to sweat profusely. Hickock felt he was close to breaking point.

'We interviewed Adele earlier and she, like you, repeatedly lied . . . until we arrested her. She then made another statement, which DS Brent will read to you.'

Brent opened the notepad and read the second interview with Adele word for word. When he'd finished, he showed Jenkins and his solicitor her signature on each page of the notebook. The solicitor was quick to reply.

'This is something I have not been privy to until now. I would like the interview to be stopped so I can have a private consultation with my client.'

Hickock stood up. 'I don't have a problem with that.' He leaned over to turn the tape recorder off, but stopped himself when Jenkins suddenly spoke.

'My sister is lying. If it wasn't for her, none of this would have happened.'

The solicitor put his hand on Jenkins' arm to stop him talking, but he flicked it away. The solicitor was again quick to react.

'I strongly advise you to say nothing, Martin. I really need to speak with you privately before you answer any further questions.'

Jenkins slapped the table. 'I've had enough of you and this "no comment" crap. This is my life on the line, not yours – so do me a favour and piss off!'

The solicitor opened his mouth in shock. 'As your legal representative, I would advise you—'

'I don't need your bloody advice – so just leave me alone and get out of here!'

Hickock and Brent were taken aback. This was the first time in their careers they had seen a suspect sack their solicitor during an interview. His face reddening, the solicitor sheepishly put his paperwork into his briefcase and left the interview room.

Jenkins' head was bowed as he began to talk. 'You're right, I killed my wife . . . but I had no choice.'

Hickock sat down. 'OK, let's start at the beginning.'

'It's true, I did have an argument with Serina in the morning, about my gambling. I went to work, and then in the early afternoon I received a phone call from Adele, who was in a very distressed state.'

He paused and licked his lips again before continuing.

'What Adele told you about the argument with Serina and punching her in the nose is true. But there was more that happened. Serina went for her and Adele pushed her away. Serina fell backwards, hitting her head on the dressing table hard. It knocked her out. Adele tried to wake her, but she wasn't moving and didn't respond. She didn't know what to do, so she called me at the office and told me everything that had happened. Adele thought she'd killed her. I told her to check for a pulse, but she kept saying she was dead and that she was scared to touch her.'

'What did you do then?' Hickock asked.

'I asked Adele if there was a lot of blood, and she said only some around Serina's nose and mouth, but there was none coming from her head. I told her to go home, and I would go back to the house and sort it out. Then I used the fire escape to sneak out of the office.'

'Why did you need to use the fire escape when you could just have walked out of the office?'

'I don't know . . . Part of me thought that if Adele had killed Serina, she could still end up in prison for murder, even though it was an accident. I thought it was best no one saw me leave.'

'So, you had already decided that if Serina was dead you were going to protect Adele.'

Jenkins nodded. 'Yes, but at that point I still didn't really know what I was going to do.'

'So what happened when you got home?'

'Serina was in her bedroom, lying on her back by the dressing table. There was blood around her nose and on her lips and chin. I tried to rouse her, but she just lay there motionless. I felt her wrist but couldn't feel a pulse, and at that point I really thought she was dead. I panicked and couldn't think straight, so I wrapped her in a blanket and dragged her into the ensuite bathroom. My head was all over the place and I kept thinking about what could happen to Adele.'

'So, you left her in the bathroom and went back to work.'

'Yes. I knew by not calling the police from the start I would also be in trouble, but if I was seen at work, I figured I'd have an alibi if I needed it. It also gave me time to think what to do. At first, I thought I'd make it look like a burglary and she'd been attacked.'

'Why change your plan and make it look like Serina committed suicide?'

'Because I thought it would look more believable, and I could say Serina was suffering from depression about not being able to have a baby. It was also something that I knew Adele could back me up on.'

'So you must have told Adele about your plan.'

'I called her from the office and told her Serina was dead. She was an absolute mess and in floods of tears. I honestly thought she was going to have a mental breakdown. She wanted to call the police and tell them what she'd done, but I said no, and I would make it look like a suicide. I told her that if the police got involved she had to stay strong and stick to the story.'

'We know from the video you arrived home just after six p.m. Can you tell me exactly what you did then?'

Jenkins said he tried to tidy up the bedroom. There were some false nails scattered on the dressing table and the floor and a spilt bottle of nail varnish. There were also a few spots of blood on the bedroom carpet, which he cleaned with warm water until the stains were no longer visible. He put the nails back in the manicure box, which he put in the wardrobe, then went to the bathroom and washed the blood off Serina's face.

'What did you do with the nail varnish remover?'

'I tried to wipe it off, but it had left a stain. I threw the empty bottle in the bin.'

'OK, tell me what you then did with Serina.'

'I dragged her out onto the landing by the bannisters, then went and got the electric cable. I tied it in a noose around her neck and around the bannisters. I wanted it to look like Serina had hanged herself just before I got home . . . you know, as if she wanted me to find her. I looked at my watch and it was just after six thirty, so I went to the bedroom and called an ambulance. I put the phone down and was about to check that I'd cleaned up everything when the phone rang. I didn't dare answer it, and then Adele's voice was on the answer machine asking me to call her. I grabbed the phone and berated her for calling me. She asked if I'd done it yet. I told her I was about to, and I would call her later when the police were here to tell her Serina had committed suicide. I hung up and deleted her message.'

Jenkins paused and took a drink of water. Hickock and Brent were struck by how matter-of-fact he had been about everything, which suggested he was not being totally truthful. Almost as if he'd read their minds, Jenkins started to sound genuinely upset and even remorseful.

'I went out onto the landing, picked up Serina in my arms, kissed her on the cheek, then positioned her body so she'd drop feet first to the floor, then I let go of her.' He took another sip of water. 'The cable stretched, and her feet hit the floor, but she bounced back up a little, then landed on her knees. I was crying and wanted to scream at the top of my voice. I ran downstairs and used the pliers to cut her down . . . then shortly after that the ambulance crew arrived, followed by the police.'

'How did you feel when you were told Serina was still alive?'

'In total shock, I couldn't believe it . . . I really thought they were mistaken. I begged to go in the ambulance with her, but they wouldn't let me.'

Hickock leaned forward. 'There's just a couple more questions I need to ask you. Firstly, your wife's will. Had you signed any paperwork forfeiting your rights to her businesses and the earnings from them?'

'No, I was aware her solicitor had prepared the paperwork, but I hadn't signed anything.'

'Why not?'

'Serina told me she'd had it done to stop me throwing away money on gambling. She said she'd give me one last chance, or else I would have to sign the documents.'

Hickock sat back. 'That makes me think that what you've told me is lies. Did you and your sister plan this whole thing because you stood to gain financially by your wife's death?'

'No, everything I have told you is the truth.'

'Really? A cynical person might think that this is your back-up plan – go down for the lesser offences of manslaughter, assault, perverting the course of justice, which means less jail time . . . Then, of course, there's all that money you'll inherit.'

'I don't care about the money. I know what me and Adele have done is wrong, but we are both prepared to suffer the consequences of our actions.'

'Have you ever heard of the forfeiture rule?'

'No.'

'It's an Act of Parliament which states a person who has unlawfully killed another may not benefit from the latter's death.'

'But I didn't kill anyone,' he replied calmly.

'I think we'll let a judge and jury decide that. This interview is now terminated.' Hickock turned off the recorder, stood up and grabbed Jenkins by the arm.

'Out of kindness, I'll put you in the cell next to your sister!' He pulled Jenkins towards the door.

* * *

Jane woke early, eager to get to the station to organise her visit to John Kilroy's farm. Instead of wearing one of her smart suits, she dressed in a thick sweater over a blouse, a tweed skirt and old brown brogues suitable for walking around the farm and searching the garage. She parked up in her usual slot at the station before 7.30, wanting to confirm that the vehicle in Kilroy's garage could be towed in for forensics to examine. She went to the canteen, but it was closed, and she was about to take the lift to her office when she passed Hickock's incident room.

She walked a few paces past, before hesitating and then turning back. The room needed cleaning, with empty mugs and takeaway food cartons littering the desks and ashtrays spilling over with cigarette butts. Ignoring the mess, Jane made for the three-part whiteboard that dominated one side of the room. Pinned up were several photographs from the crime scene and the postmortem, and then the reconstruction with the weighted sandbags. On another board was an array of still photographs from the surveillance video, showing Martin Jenkins and Adele Burton entering and leaving the house. To one side were their mugshots with the words 'Arrested and charged with murder and perverting the course of justice' written below them.

Jane looked over the scrawled notes accompanying the photos. It was obvious that Hickock had taken every single suggestion she had made, both from her file and from their conversations. She also knew for certain that he wasn't planning on giving her any credit. She took a deep breath. It was nothing she shouldn't have expected. But it still rankled.

Jane rang Kernan's office and informed him a magistrate's warrant had been issued to seize the car, and requested the tow truck be sent to the Kilroys' farm and the forensic lab to be on standby. She then explained the horse box story, but he didn't seem to be very interested in any of it, just responding with the occasional grunt. It was only when she said that at least there would be no expensive trip to Scotland, as John Kilroy had left the oil rig, that he became more voluble. 'Well, that's something, I suppose,' he said.

Maureen came in and started to make a brew.

'We'll be leaving for the farm as soon as the tow truck's good to go,' Jane told her. 'I can tell you, I'm looking forward to confronting John Kilroy at last.'

'Do you know if he's at home?' Maureen asked.

'He left the oil rig, so fingers crossed he is,' Jane said.

It was almost ten when Jane got the call informing her the tow truck was on its way to John Kilroy's property. She was about to leave when Kernan's clerk called and informed her all the DCIs were needed in the boardroom in half an hour for a case update meeting.

Jane threw up her hands. 'Why now, for God's sake?'

'It is on the noticeboard, ma'am,' Maureen told her. 'I also put an entry in your desk diary. Oh, I meant to ask if you are feeling better.'

Jane ignored the question. 'I've got the tow truck on its way and I should be there. Right, I am going for this meeting. Hopefully it won't go on too long – I want you ready to leave with me straight after.'

After checking her hair and make-up in the toilet, Jane headed down to the boardroom. One of the canteen staff was wheeling a trolley with flasks of tea and coffee and a plate of biscuits. Jane held the door open and followed her in. The big oval table took up most of the space, the chairs neatly placed around it. Jane chose to sit at the far end. No one else had arrived.

Then she heard loud voices and heavy footsteps approaching. DCI Shefford walked in, accompanied by DS Otley, giving her a brief nod before drawing out a chair. He was followed by DCI Hickock and DS Brent, with two more officers Jane hadn't met. They helped themselves to coffee before sitting down, then Shefford turned and gave Hickock a high five. The men took their seats around the end of the table, leaving empty ones on either side of Jane. At the same time, the superintendent, accompanied by Commander Trayner, arrived. Jane recognised Trayner from the interview board. She caught his eye and gave him a small nod and a smile. He nodded back. Then Kernan tapped the table with his pen.

'Good morning, everybody. I know how busy all my teams are, so I shall keep this brief, but Commander Trayner is here to add his congratulations on the successful conclusion of DCI Shefford's investigation, which will be heading to trial in the next year. This was a very complex investigation, and he has proved yet again that he is an exceptional detective. I also want to express my admiration for DCI Hickock in an extremely difficult situation, as he was an associate of the man accused, but did not allow any personal attachments to interfere with the investigation. DCI Hickock will be at the magistrates' court later today with the suspect arraigned for the murder of his wife in collusion with his sister, who has also been charged. Excellent intuitive work, going to extraordinary lengths to establish his suspect's guilt.'

There was a round of nods and smiles towards Hickock, and a splattering of applause before Kernan continued with a rare smile on his face.

'I have to say I was sceptical about the use of sandbags, but in the end it proved that the victim could not have been found hanging, as the suspect claimed. That's what I mean about thinking intuitively and going the extra mile. Commander Trayner would now like to say a few words.'

Jane sat in stunned silence, not daring to look at Hickock in case her feelings showed on her face. She dug her nails into her palms as she sat through Commander Trayner expressing the Met's thanks to the detectives for all their dedicated work and excellent results. He then talked briefly about the current live investigations, and lastly hoped that DCI Tennison had been welcomed on to the team, noting the difficulty of reinvestigating a cold case. He looked over to her, but this time she wasn't smiling.

As soon as the meeting was over Jane got up to leave, but Kernan signalled for her to remain behind as everyone else left the room.

'I don't know what you're playing at, Tennison. I've been informed there is no vehicle at the address you gave the tow truck officers. It had apparently been removed. You've wasted everyone's valuable time.'

She felt her legs starting to shake. 'I'm sorry, I was not aware the vehicle had been removed.'

'Obviously.'

'Do they know where it was taken?'

'I have no idea.'

She got a grip of herself, determined not to simply take the blame for the situation. 'We should have had that vehicle towed in when I first requested it, sir.'

'I suggest you stop throwing accusations around and go and find out where it is.' He turned and walked off.

Maureen physically jumped when Jane marched into her office, slamming the door behind her. 'You are not going to believe this, the tow truck arrived at the Kilroys' and the car was gone. It's probably been taken to a breakers' yard, and I have just had a ticking-off by the super as if it's my bloody fault.'

'Do you know where it was taken?'

'No! But I am going to bloody well find out. Get your coat, we're going to the Kilroys' now.'

Maureen hurried after Jane into the car park, carrying her flask and sandwiches. She hardly had time to close the passenger door before Jane was careering out, burning rubber. Maureen held on for dear life until Jane finally calmed down and took her foot off the accelerator.

'It proves one thing, Maureen. He knows I'm on to him.'

They drove in silence for a while, Jane heeding the speed limit, before Maureen asked if she would like to know about Martin Jenkins.

'I was talking to DS Brent when I was in the canteen. He said Hickock's interview with Martin Jenkins and his sister was like being in a masterclass on—'

'I'm not interested, Maureen. I don't want to hear any more about Hickock's bloody case.'

'Sorry, I just thought you might be interested, as a lot of the ideas you gave Hickock turned out to be right—'

'Enough, Maureen! Just drop it. Why don't you check we're on the right bloody route?'

Maureen sighed. She hated it when Tennison was grumpy. She opened her map to study the directions. 'I think we're about twenty minutes away. There should be a turn-off for Pirbright village shortly. We just passed the signs for Ascot, so we're close to where that horse box accident happened, that's about another fifteen minutes the other way.'

'No point in knowing about that, if we don't have the bloody car,' Jane said sullenly.

'Well, it's straight on and then left at the next roundabout.'

A few minutes later they arrived at their destination.

'Dear God, it's like a Whitehall farce,' Jane said, turning into the driveway of the Kilroy farm.

Jane stopped halfway to the house and Maureen quickly opened the passenger door. 'I'm sorry, reading in a moving car makes me feel sick. I just need a bit of fresh air.'

Maureen walked up and down for a few moments, and then stood by the hedgerow, looking into the field. She returned to the car, leaning into the open door. 'There are rows of old beehives. Some look as if they've been deliberately smashed.'

'I was told John Kilroy damaged them, got stung or something. His father made special honey using herbs and lavender, apparently. Look, sorry for being in a foul mood. Are you feeling better?'

'Yes, sorry about that.'

Maureen got into the passenger seat. 'You know they found honey in Tutankhamun's tomb; it was only inedible because of it being in clay pots.'

'Fancy that,' Jane said, starting the engine and continuing towards the house.

'I had an aunt that had beehives,' Maureen said. 'Just small ones, but I was scared stiff when she first took me to see them. She had the proper suits, had to pull on big gloves to my elbow as they could get up your sleeves, or down your collar, which was why we had to wear hoods, you know, with gauze to cover our faces.'

Maureen fell silent as Jane was showing no further interest in the subject of bees. She parked beside the garage. The doors were closed, but the leaves Jane had seen piled against them were now in mounds on either side. She also saw deep tyre tracks had been left in the gravel.

Getting out with the search warrant in her hand, Jane hesitated.

'There's no point in ringing the doorbell. We'll go round to the kitchen entrance at the rear of the house. Mrs Kilroy is almost blind and sort of holes up in a room off the kitchen. I was hoping her brother-in-law would be here, but he mentioned that when John was home, he made himself scarce and his car isn't parked up. So, are you ready?'

'Yes, ma'am.'

'Right, here we go.'

CHAPTER TWENTY-SEVEN

Leaning against the wall was an old bicycle with a basket attached to the handlebars. The kitchen door was open. Jane called out a few times, but heard no reply. Maureen followed her through the huge kitchen, remarking on the impressive array of copper pans, then Jane pulled back the heavy curtain in front of the door leading into the next room. The fire was going, but burning low, and the room was stiflingly hot. Jane paused by the desk Mrs Kilroy had used when looking at her diary. She eased open the drawer to find it was stuffed with bills and receipts. She opened the old leather-bound diary and flicked through to the addresses and phone numbers so she could jot down Donald Fitzpatrick-Dunn's. Jane called out again as she eased open the heavy oak door into the next room.

Walking into the long oak-panelled hall, they both found themselves looking up at the wide, sweeping staircase with dozens of oil paintings along the walls. Crossing the hall, they entered through double doors into an equally impressive dining room, with an elegant chandelier hanging over a polished mahogany dining table surrounded by velvet-covered dining chairs.

Next they entered a large drawing room; again the size was unexpected. Four sofas and plush wing chairs surrounded a brick and marble fireplace with logs stacked in baskets beside the grate. There were more oil paintings, and on a grand piano an array of silver-framed photographs. Jane started looking at them and Maureen walked over to join her.

The photographs were predominantly of Mrs Kilroy and her husband. He was tall and well-built, with thick dark hair and a square jaw. He was mostly dressed either in jodhpurs and riding boots or in immaculate dinner suits.

'What a handsome couple,' Maureen said admiringly. 'She looks stunning.'

'Apparently she used to be a model. Look, this is John with his father. You can see, he's got his father's looks.'

They were both so intent on looking at the photographs, they didn't notice when a woman walked in.

'What are you doing in here?'

Startled, Jane turned, as the woman moved further into the room. She was in her forties, with a thick knitted cardigan beneath a wraparound apron.

'I'm so sorry, I did call out earlier, but I got no reply.' Jane took out her ID. 'I am DCI Jane Tennison, and this is Constable Maureen Havers. I was hoping to have a meeting with John Kilroy, as I was informed he had returned home. I do have a warrant to enter and search the property . . . And you are?'

'Sheila Monkford. I'm here Monday to Friday. I had the hoover on so I didn't hear anyone coming into the house. That's the problem with these old buildings, upstairs I can't hear anyone and sometimes Mrs Kilroy gets furious.'

'Could you tell me where Mr Kilroy is this afternoon?'

'He's with his mother. They went to take Mr Donald home from the hospital. He had a hernia operation last week.'

'When do you expect them back?'

'I don't know, I'm afraid. But I have to leave at three.'

'How long have you worked here?'

'Past three years. My mother worked here before me.'

'Could you please show me around upstairs, perhaps John's bedroom?'

'I don't know if I should do that. I mean, nobody told me you were expected.'

'As I said, I do have a warrant.'

Mrs Monkford hesitated for a moment, then gave a nod for them to follow her.

'You wait down here in case they come back,' Jane told Maureen.

As they walked upstairs, Jane asked Mrs Monkford if she knew when the car had been removed from the garage.

'Soon as John came home,' she said. 'Mr Donald sent him a cable asking him to come back and look after his mother.'

She raised an eyebrow.

'Not that he done anything, never has. Bone idle. Not that I have much to do with him. He's been away working most of the time I've been employed here.'

'Can you tell me what happened to the car?' Jane asked.

'They sent a tow truck to take it to some crushers' yard. His mother has been asking for him to do something about it for years after it got damaged in an accident. Right, this is the master bedroom, not that it's ever used.'

Mrs Monkford opened a carved double door, standing back for Jane to walk ahead of her.

The room was dominated by a four-poster bed with a red silk canopy, carved posts and a carved headboard, but what most captured Jane's attention was the clear indentation, as if a body had just been lying on it.

Mrs Monkford paused beside the bed.

'This is where he was brought when it happened. They laid him down on the bed while they waited for the ambulance, but it was too late. As you can see, the imprint of his body is still there. Mrs Kilroy won't have anyone touch it. She worshipped him.'

Jane felt a chill creep up her spine.

Mrs Monkford went and opened the adjoining bedroom door, again standing back to allow Jane to enter first. This room was very different, much more feminine, with mirror-fronted wardrobes and an elegant dressing table covered in expensive-looking perfumes and powders.

'She doesn't use this very much, usually sleeps down in the snug room. She has problems with her eyesight, but she can spot a bit of dust all right. I have to keep everything polished within an inch of its life.'

Lastly, they went into John Kilroy's bedroom. It was plain, with a king-size bed, and modern desk with computer equipment, a typewriter and a phone. Movie posters lined the walls.

'Is he staying here?'

'Yes, well for the past couple of days, but I believe he's had to take his mother for an eye specialist appointment in London. He doesn't drive, which means the journey takes longer than it might.'

'What's John like?'

'Sullen. Very quiet. I was told his father's death affected him very badly. I never met him, he died before I started working here, but everyone in the village that knew him said he was a wonderful man, very generous and hard-working. My mother said that she thought Mrs Kilroy would never recover from his death. She went into a terrible depression. She went away for a long time in Switzerland shortly after his memorial. When she came back, sometimes she was all right, but she wouldn't socialise like the old days, just stayed up in her room.'

'I was told she had to go to a clinic in Spain,' Jane said.

'Oh, that was before my time. My mum was still here, she said it was very sad what was going on. I mean, I don't know all the details, but I think she had to ask Mr Donald for help with her: drinking herself into a stupor, bottles found all over the house, and she could get quite nasty.'

They were heading down the stairs when Mrs Monkford gestured over the bannisters to the one room Jane had not been in, the library. 'She now spends a lot of time in there. She's a very intelligent woman, I think she's reading all she can before she loses her sight. Sad, isn't it? If you want my opinion, this house is the same, sad, but it pays my wages.'

Maureen was still standing by the front door as they came down the stairs. She shook her head to indicate no arrivals. Mrs Monkford went into the kitchen, removing her wraparound apron as she went. 'Time for me to get off home.'

She put on a puffer jacket and woollen hat. 'I'm in a bit of a quandary now: I mean, I suppose I should stay here with you until they get back. Problem is, I don't know who to call, I always get all my orders from Mr Donald. He sort of runs the place now for her, but he's in hospital.'

'It's quite all right, Mrs Monkford,' Jane said breezily, 'I'll just stay on a while and then lock up after you. I do have a warrant, so it's legally all right for me to wait here.'

Mrs Monkford hesitated, pulling on gloves. 'You've not said why you need to talk to him. I mean, has something happened?'

'It's about an incident that happened a long time ago, when he was a student. A female student went missing, and I have reopened the case. I'm just talking to everyone that knew her.'

'I don't know about that, before my time, I suppose, but if you say you have a right to be here, then I'll get off. No need to lock the kitchen door, it's always open.'

'Thank you for your time, Mrs Monkford.'

Jane went into the hall, where Maureen was sitting in one of the chairs. 'I'm going to have another look around upstairs. It's coming up to three, so maybe stay another half hour and come back tomorrow.'

'Did you get any useful information from her?'

'No, she's only worked here for the last three years. It's a bit freaky up there, a touch of the Miss Havisham.'

Jane got down to searching John Kilroy's bedroom properly. It was devoid of personal items like diaries, and the drawers contained nothing more interesting than underwear, shirts and socks, and the wardrobe just had suits and jackets, overcoats and boots. There was a rucksack and two cases beside a set of skis, but, again, no surprises.

About to return downstairs, she couldn't resist one last look at the master bedroom with the spooky four-poster bed. She turned the lights on and was just studying a huge oil painting when she heard a car. She opened one of the wooden shutters and looked out. A top-of-the-range Mercedes with dark windows had pulled up. A uniformed driver was holding the passenger door open as Mrs Kilroy took his other hand to help her out. John Kilroy got out of the other side. He was taller and broader than Jane had expected, his thick dark hair combed back from his angular face, making his resemblance to his late father obvious. He also had a pronounced limp. He gave Mrs Kilroy his arm, thanking the driver, and they turned towards the house. He looked up.

'Damn!' Jane swore at herself, stepping sharply back. With the lights on, he had to have had a clear view of her. She ran down the stairs, calling for Maureen, who took a moment before hurrying out of the library.

'They're here.'

'Shit, I'm sorry.'

They stood in the hallway, hearing muffled voices from the direction of the kitchen. 'It can't be her: her bicycle's gone,' Mrs Kilroy said. Then the door opened.

Sylvia Kilroy, wearing a full-length mink coat, walked into the hall. She stopped abruptly as Jane stepped forwards.

'Mrs Kilroy, it's DCI Jane Tennison, and this is Constable Maureen Havers. Your cleaner, Mrs Monkford, kindly let me in.'

'Well, she had no business doing that. Did she also give you permission to go into my private rooms?'

Jane spoke quickly to alleviate the tension. 'I have a warrant, and I explained to her that I am also here to talk to your son.'

'She had no right to allow you in here without my permission. I would now like you to leave, as I do not want my son to talk to you without representation.'

'In that case, he will have to accompany me to the station, and we can do the interview there, with, if he wants, a solicitor present.'

John Kilroy walked in, smiling. 'It's fine, Mother. I'll talk to them here. You go and sit near the fire. I've made a pot of tea.'

Mrs Kilroy didn't move. 'I don't think so. A warrant sounds very serious. I would like her to explain exactly what's going on.'

'I did explain when I was last here, Mrs Kilroy. I have reopened a cold case regarding the disappearance of a student from your son's college. He was one of the last people to see her alive.'

'And I told you that he was questioned numerous times when this girl went missing. I cannot see what he could possibly add now.'

'His two friends have been very helpful,' Jane said.

Jane looked at Kilroy and caught a flicker of alarm. He quickly composed himself and led his mother, no longer protesting, into the snug.

Kilroy returned and led Jane and Maureen into the drawing room, gesturing for them to sit on one of the sofas, while he sat in an armchair opposite.

'When did you arrive home, Mr Kilroy?' Jane began briskly.

'A few days ago. I received a cable from my uncle, explaining that he would not be able to look after my mother, and suggesting I came home. He was in hospital for a hernia operation.'

'Doesn't your mother have Mrs Monkford to look after her?'

'Weekdays only, never at weekends, and besides, she couldn't run around after Mother the way Uncle Donald does.'

'Did he suggest you get your car towed to a breakers' yard?'

Again, she caught that flicker in his dark eyes. 'Good heavens, no, that was Mother, in fact she insisted on it, saying while I'm at home I should take my test and get a decent car to drive her around. Due to her deteriorating eyesight, she is unable to drive.'

'So, you intend staying for some time?'

Another small flicker. 'Not sure, it'll depend on Donald's recovery. Not sure how long I can face it. As you've had a tour of the house, you can see that it's like a shrine dedicated to my late father.'

'It must have been a very difficult time for you, losing your father at such an early age.'

'It was, he was a remarkable man. He could turn his hand to anything, hunting, horse breeding, cattle.'

'And beekeeping,' Jane added. 'I noticed all the old hives on the drive to the house.'

There was the same brief flicker, almost of annoyance this time. 'Yes, another of his enthusiasms, and he did produce good honey.'

Jane decided to change tack. 'Do you have the name of the company that towed your car? I presume they're also the breakers' yard?'

'Yes, of course, one moment, it's just outside Windsor. They seemed to be very efficient.'

He opened his wallet and produced a card. 'There you are,' he said with a smile.

'I'd also like the logbook and MOT certificate, please.'

'I'm afraid they were given to the tow truck driver.'

Jane opened her briefcase, and took out her thick file of statements, placing it on her knee.

'I have already questioned your two friends also involved in the Brittany Hall case. Have you spoken to them recently?'

'No, we sort of lost touch with each other when they went on to university.'

'I have here your original statement. You stated that you did not know Brittany well, prior to that evening.'

'Yes, that is correct. We just went to the pub, and she happened to be there.'

'Did you drive there?'

'No, none of us had a licence. It was quite a walk, but we had done it numerous times before.'

'Describe how you met up with Brittany.'

'I wouldn't say we met up with her. She was already at the bar, and rather intoxicated. I had no recollection of who she was with.

We had a couple of beers and she sort of latched on to us. It was a bit embarrassing actually.'

'It was a Friday night. Was the bar full?'

'No, not really.'

'How long did you stay there?'

'Not long.'

'Did you take part in the karaoke?'

He frowned, then shook his head. 'No way, that was not our scene, and anyway it didn't start until late. I had a cricket match that weekend so we went back before that.'

'And when did you last see Brittany?'

He shrugged his shoulders. 'We'd walked up the road a bit, when I think it was Justin who said we should maybe go back and check if she was all right. I walked back towards the pub car park and saw her get into a red car.'

'Were you in the car park or the road at this time?'

'I was up the road a bit, but I could see it was Brittany.'

'Did she come out the front of the pub?'

'No, the pool bar exit.'

'Where exactly was this car parked and what make was it?'

'In the car park near that exit. I couldn't tell you what make it was, just that it was red, like a sports car red, and then she disappeared.'

'So, you went back to join your friends?'

'Yes, and we continued walking back to college.'

'What time was it by then?'

He frowned and shifted his weight. 'Some time after nine, I should think.'

'And the next day you had this away cricket match, correct?'

'Yes, my friends came with me on the coach to cheer the team on.'

'Just one more thing: you suffered quite a bad leg injury skiing, I understand?'

He raised his eyebrows as if surprised by her query. 'Yes, a long time ago. It was more painful than it is now, but I still may need a hip replacement.'

'So even though you had this painful injury, you still decided to make the long walk to the pub?'

'We took it nice and easy.'

'But why didn't one of your friends return to the pub to check on Brittany, if walking was painful for you?'

'They were not that interested, to be honest.'

'So you were interested in her?'

'You are twisting my words; I was concerned that she was very intoxicated.'

'If you were so concerned about her welfare, did you check the next day to see if Brittany had returned safely?'

'I suppose we just assumed she'd got a lift back to college.'

'Do you know Edwina Summers?'

He blinked for a moment, then shook his head.

'She was a music student at the college. She said she overheard you and your friends discussing the evening Brittany went missing.'

'That's not surprising, is it? Everyone was talking about it.'

'But specifically the three of you were discussing getting your stories straight.'

'Obviously we talked about it, and I suppose now she was missing, we felt a bit guilty about not taking her back with us.'

'Miss Summers also recalls that you had access to a car, which you never mentioned in any of the statements taken at the time.'

'That's not right. I only had a provisional licence, plus you weren't allowed to keep a vehicle at college.'

Jane nodded, then closed her notebook. She looked up and smiled.

'At this time, was your mother at home?'

Again, he got that look in his eyes, then sighed, turning away. 'She was being treated for a nervous breakdown, plus alcoholism. She had already spent months in Switzerland after my father's death, but she had a relapse. The farm was in turmoil and she'd found it very difficult to cope—'

There was a scream and a crash of breaking china. Kilroy leaped to his feet, but his leg buckled, and he fell back into the chair. He pulled himself up again, then staggered from the room.

In the hallway, Mrs Kilroy was getting to her feet. The remains of a large vase lay around her. John took her arm, but she swiped him away. 'I'm all right, John. I went to take my fur coat upstairs, you left it over the bannisters, you know I have a place for my furs . . . What have I broken now?'

He picked up the shattered pieces of the vase. 'It's just another Ming vase, Mother.' He turned to Jane and Maureen who had followed him into the hall. 'Just my little joke. We've had a lot of breakages – I doubt there's an ornament that hasn't been super-glued back together at least once.'

Mrs Kilroy looked at him sharply. 'My condition isn't funny, John. Now give me my coat, I'm going to my bedroom.'

'I'll carry it for you?'

'No, just put it over my arm.'

She walked slowly up the stairs, firmly gripping the mahogany bannisters.

Jane asked Maureen to get her briefcase, while Kilroy went into the snug and retrieved the tea tray. Jane followed him into the kitchen.

'Perhaps you should think about selling, especially if you're planning to return to the oil rig.'

'I don't think that is any of your business.'

'Your uncle said the farm was being left in rack and ruin.'

'That is not his bloody business either,' Kilroy snapped.

'He told me it would be your decision as your mother has made over the property to you, to avoid inheritance tax.'

He looked very angry now, his jaw twitching.

'Are we finished?'

'I may have to return, or you might want to contact me after thinking over what we have discussed this afternoon.'

'What exactly do you mean by that? I have answered truthfully and have nothing further to add. It's been five bloody years since it happened.'

'I am aware of that, Mr Kilroy, and so is Brittany Hall's mother. However long it takes, I will get to the truth about what happened that night.'

He opened the back door, standing beside it as Maureen went out first and Jane followed.

'Thank you for your time, Mr Kilroy, and I do hope your uncle makes a good recovery.'

He slammed the door behind them as they walked back to Jane's car. Jane did a U-turn and they headed down the drive and back to the road. For ten minutes, neither said a word. Eventually Jane glanced sidelong at Maureen.

'So, what did you think?'

'It's an amazing house, those antiques must be worth a fortune.'

'You should have seen the upstairs. It's really freaky, her dead husband's bed still has the impression of his body lying on it.'

'After all this time?'

'Apparently no one is allowed to touch it. Kilroy didn't really say much when I asked him about losing his father at such an early age.'

'Yes, I thought that. He didn't show any emotion.'

'No, he didn't, not until I asked about him selling the place, then he got quite worked up.'

'Maybe he won't until his mother lets him. He did seem very caring towards her.'

'He hasn't been in the past, according to his uncle. I want to have a talk with him. You know, Mrs Monkford said something about being unable to hear if anyone was in the house, downstairs.'

'That was fortunate for us,' Maureen said.

'It could also have been fortunate for John Kilroy. It's a possibility that he came back to the house the night Brittany Hall went missing, maybe even with his friends. There has to be a reason for them to stick so firmly to the same story.'

'It could be because it's true,' Maureen said quietly.

Jane slapped the steering wheel with her hand. 'They are all lying, I know it! And I wouldn't put it past Mrs Kilroy to be lying, too.'

'I don't know . . .'

'Just think about Martin Jenkins, and the lies he has been spewing out since his wife died.'

'But they now have the proof. As far as I can see there's no evidence John or his friends had anything to do with the disappearance of Brittany Hall.'

'Didn't you see the way he twitched when I asked a question he didn't like? He was lying!'

Maureen sighed, turning to look through her passenger window. There was no point in arguing. She noticed everything was going past in a blur.

'I'd slow down, ma'am. You don't want to get pulled over for speeding.'

When they got back to the station, Jane was quickly out of the car and hurrying into the station with her briefcase under her arm, with Maureen following in her wake. By the time Maureen reached the office, Jane was already calling the breakers' yard.

'I see, thank you very much.' She slammed the receiver down. 'The bloody car was crushed the day it was towed in!'

'Would you like me to go and bring you something from the canteen?' Maureen said tentatively.

Jane took a breath. 'No, I'd like you to go to the breakers' yard and get the logbook and MOT. Tomorrow, I want to visit Mr Fitzpatrick-Dunn. See if you can contact that man from the polo club who made the report about the hit-and-run. Also, the barman from the pub from that night. The CCTV footage of the night Brittany went missing, set that up for me, would you? We'll need to ask DC Littleton to assist us.'

Maureen hesitated. 'I'll do that first thing in the morning, if that's all right, ma'am. I spoke to one of Hickock's team in the lift. They're having drinks in the pub.'

Jane glared at her. 'Just go to the breakers' yard before it shuts.'

Maureen scuttled out of the room.

CHAPTER TWENTY-EIGHT

The phone rang as soon as Jane arrived home. It was Peter, in high spirits. The sale of his house had been completed, and his ex-partner had agreed to let Peter buy his share of the company for half of the proceeds of the house sale plus another £35,000. Jane tried her best to sound as pleased as Peter was.

'The other thing is, I've now got to move all my furniture out by the weekend at the latest. I'm hiring a van, but do you think you could help me?'

Jane had been so excited that Peter was going to be moving in, but after the frustrating day she'd had, she couldn't really focus on it. 'I've got to be in work tomorrow,' she said, 'but maybe Friday – or even better, the weekend.'

'Fine. And we'll have a proper celebration on Sunday.'

The following morning, Jane had intended making an early start, but not only did she oversleep, on the way to the station she noticed that she was almost out of petrol. By the time she got to the station it was after 9.30.

'Any luck at the breakers' yard?' she asked Maureen as she entered her office.

'The car had been crushed . . . with the MOT and logbook inside it.'

Jane sighed. 'Somehow I knew you were going to say that.'

'I've made some coffee, and I have Sam Littleton available at ten, if you want to view the CCTV footage. It took me forever to get it sorted. As I keep on saying, the files are really still not organised. I've still got to call Jolyon Fairweather.'

'Who?'

'The man from the polo club. I've not as yet tracked down the barman, but I'm working on it. I did try to call Mr Fitzpatrick-Dunn but got no answer, so I'll try again later.'

'Good, so we'll go and see DC Littleton first, then go to the polo club.'

There were still many areas of the station that Jane was not familiar with, and she had to ask a young uniform officer where Sam Littleton's CCTV viewing room was. When she found it, her first instinct was to walk back out again just because of the unpleasant smell of stale food mixed with cigarette smoke. Littleton was sitting in a swivel chair with a padded back, surrounded by video equipment and stacks of videotapes.

'Thank you for giving me your time, Detective Constable Littleton. It's actually a very short section, so it hopefully won't take long for me to review it.'

'I hope not,' he said grumpily. 'I've got more CCTV tapes arriving any minute DCI Shefford wants me to view. Then I had hours to go through and edit for DCI Hickock. Worth it, though, since it got Martin Jenkins and his sister to confess. Your nice little Maureen brought this down earlier. Now you do know this is not very good quality?'

'Sit yourself down.' He gestured to a chair piled with old newspapers.

After removing the papers Jane sat down, easing the chair closer to the desk as Littleton tapped away at his keyboards.

'It's coming up on monitor three.'

It took a while before anything appeared on the screen, and then it was just dark grey with zigzags and white flickering dots.

'Told you it was crap. Must have been used over and over. Right, here we go.'

A murky wide shot of the car park appeared on the screen. Almost out of shot was the pub itself, with the pub's rear exit double doors just about visible.

'CCTV quality was pretty poor five years ago,' Littleton said. 'This looks to me as if it was set up just to monitor the car park. Maureen said it's out in the country towards Windsor. Nice part of the world, that.'

Jane wished he would keep quiet as she watched intently, but nothing else came up on the screen until two cars were seen entering and disappearing into the car park, then a van drove in, but no vehicles exited.

'Is there a time code?'

'No, like I said, this was an early CCTV camera, black and white. The other one was inside the bar, not on the punters drinking but on the tills, you know, in case there was a bit of pilfering.'

'How do you know that?'

'On the report your little Maureen brought in with this tape.'

Jane grimaced. That was not in any report she had read, or if she had, she had missed that detail. She suddenly leaned forward in the chair. Driving into the car park was a low, dark-coloured vehicle that almost clipped one of the wooden posts that marked the entrance. At the same time, exiting from the rear exit of the pub was a young girl carrying a small backpack. She walked towards the car. Headlights flashed, then she walked out of shot. The film then went fuzzy again.

Littleton shrugged. 'That's it. I've tried to enhance the car and identify its make and registration, but it's too far away and, as you can see, the quality is crap.'

'Could I see it again, please?' Jane asked.

He pointedly looked at his wristwatch, and then to a clock on the wall.

'Ten minutes, then I have to get busy on Shefford's case.'

*   *   *

Maureen jumped as Jane barged into the office. 'I need you to get old photographs of the pub, especially car park entrances and exits, so I can see exactly how it looked when Brittany went missing. Get on to it straightaway.'

'I can check with the council planning department for that area.'

Jane nodded. 'Just get on with it, please. I have to make some calls.'

Sitting at her desk, Jane checked through her notebook until she found the number of the Thames Valley uniform inspector.

'Good morning, is this Inspector Sumpter? It's DCI Jane Tennison. I just need to run something by you. I have been looking at the CCTV from the pub that Brittany Hall was last seen leaving, but according to your report there was also a CCTV camera inside the bar of the pub?'

'Hold on, can you slow down a bit?' he said, taken aback by her brusque manner.

'I'm sorry. It's just this is quite urgent. I've only just been told about this second camera monitoring the till on the bar. It will have valuable footage of the customers.'

'We didn't find it to be of any value to the enquiry,' he said tetchily.

'Did you not retain a copy?'

'No, I did not, just the footage of Miss Hall leaving the pub.'

'Did you get any information about the red sports car?'

'We did an extensive enquiry, but we did not have the licence plate, and with Windsor being a big tourist attraction, it could have been driven there from anywhere in the country. The only thing we could verify was that the car was an MG.'

'I see. I have the original files from your investigation and there are no photographs of the location. Do you recall if any were taken at the time?'

'No, I cannot recall.'

Jane sighed. 'I believe still photographs were taken from the CCTV footage, but we do not have any in the file. Do you recall if they were shown to Mrs Hall or people at the school?'

'Who do you think you are talking to?' he said, raising his voice. 'Of course we tried to find anyone who had seen her, but the footage was very poor quality, and we did not get access to it for over a week. I don't like your accusatory tone.'

'Well, if you want my opinion,' Jane said, 'I find your initial investigation of this case to be sadly lacking in detail, and the files incomplete, let alone being in any semblance of order.'

He hung up without replying. She stared at the receiver for a moment, then slammed it down. 'Pompous fucking arsehole. Right, next – where are you going?'

Maureen stopped midway to the door. 'The council are sending through some faxes, so I'm going down to the print room.'

'OK.' Jane turned back to her notebook, and found Fitzpatrick-Dunn's phone number. There was no answer, so she called the operator, identified herself as a police officer, and asked for the address linked to the number. She then sat for a moment, drumming her fingers on the desk.

Maureen returned with reams of fax paper, with black and white photographs of the pub, car park area, entrances and exits. She carefully spread them out on the desk, and stood staring at them, before she let rip with a yell.

'Look! There are two entrances or exits – whatever you like to call them. One outside the pub exit doors and one further along the road, which means you could come into that car park from either one. I guarantee that is not in any of that idiot Sumpter's report. One with a chain across and the "car park" notice, and the other just a dirt drive with hedges either side.'

Jane clapped her hands. 'Well done, Maureen! Right, let's go to chat to this polo bloke, and I now have the address for Uncle Donald, so we can pay a visit to him afterwards.'

It took Maureen a while to catch her up as she folded the faxes and grabbed her coat and bag and left a message that they would be out of the office. Jane was already waiting in the car and Maureen hardly had time to close the passenger door before they were off.

'You need to be heading towards Ascot,' she said. 'Do you want me to direct you?'

'Not if it's going to make you sick. Anyway, I should know the way by now.'

'It's Coworth Park, Ascot. As polo clubs go, I don't think it's very big, so I'll direct you when we're almost there.'

In her eagerness to get there, in the end Jane almost missed the turning.

'Slow down or you'll miss it,' Maureen told her. 'There it is!'

They drove in and parked in a small area cordoned off for visitors. The stables and polo fields were visible in the distance. A very dusty and rather dented Volvo followed them in, parking alongside.

Jolyon Fairweather was a ruddy-faced, cheerful-looking man, wearing a crumpled white suit with a colourful tie.

'I am Jolyon Fairweather, and you must be Detective Tennison?' he said, holding out a hand.

'Detective Chief Inspector, actually, and this is Constable Maureen Havers, who I believe you have been in contact with.'

'Absolutely. I have to be off sharpish as I am giving lessons at another club in forty minutes, so I need to get into the clobber. Now, we can stroll over to the clubhouse, or chat here?'

'Here is fine,' Jane said. 'Can you just go over the details of the accident.'

'Absolutely, quite a while ago now, and sadly without the offending driver being caught. Considerable damage to my horse trailer, almost fell into the ditch.'

'Do you recall what time this occurred?'

'I most certainly do, it was about ten forty-five. It's a very poorly lit lane, I concede, but the car was being driven very erratically, and far too fast, headlights on full blast, blinding me, and it swerved into the horse trailer. I mean, it was quite a swipe, so it had veered right across the road.'

'Do you recall the make of the vehicle?'

'Sadly not, it all happened so fast, and by the time I got out it had screeched off, never stopped for a moment.'

'How about colour?'

'You know, I thought about it at the time. I believe it was dark green, but I was in such a state of shock. I even tried to get a paint chip from the damage, sent it in, but the sides were very muddy.'

'But you reckoned the other vehicle had to have been damaged?'

'Absolutely, driver's side must have been smashed up, left a big dent in the trailer. I was very concerned about my pony inside.'

'Yes, I believe the pony was injured?'

'Yes, nasty bruise to his ribs, he needed a lot of veterinary attention, which sadly I was not insured for. Only my polo ponies are covered.'

'Well, I am very sorry that there has been no result for you.'

'I rather hoped you wanted to see me about tracing the driver.'

'Sadly, we have not been able to do that yet. But could you tell me the exact date that the incident occurred? We have a police report made out on the fourteenth of June 1986, but I'm not sure that's correct.'

'Oh, on the night it happened, it would have been around eleven thirty when I called our local station, but they were busy and asked me to report it in the morning. I couldn't call earlier that evening when it happened as the clubhouse was closed. I was lucky because a friend was in the area and he helped get the horse box back on the road. So I rang again first thing the next morning and I have been calling on the off chance ever since. I'm on quite friendly terms with the station sergeant now!' He chortled.

'Could you recall the exact date?'

'Didn't I just say? Night it happened was the thirteenth of June.'

'Thank you. What about the driver, were you able to give any description?'

'Sadly not, he sped off so fast.'

'Would you be able to recall if it was just one person driving?'

'Yes, and tall, I'd say. Well, I think he was.'

'So just one male driver?'

'I would say so, but I really couldn't give any kind of description.'

Jane thanked Mr Fairweather and she and Maureen returned to the car, leaving Fairweather looking somewhat bemused, wondering why the police had been so keen to talk to him again just to repeat what he'd already told them.

Jane drove carefully out of the club's entrance and onto the narrow country road. She could easily see how the accident had happened. Despite the injury to his pony, Fairweather was probably lucky he himself had emerged unscathed.

'You know, we are not that far from the pub, or at least the new establishment. Why don't we go and have a quick lunch there before meeting with Mr Fitzpatrick-Dunn?'

Maureen nodded. 'If you keep on this road and at the junction turn right, and we go straight onto the main road towards Windsor.'

'Thank you, Maureen. It might seem we came a long way for very little as far as Mr Fairweather was concerned, but at least we now know that the accident did take place on the night that Brittany went missing.'

Maureen didn't reply. As far as she could see, they were clocking up a lot of miles without making any progress at all.

They parked in front of the newly refurbished pub and went into the restaurant, but it was not yet midday and food wasn't being served, so they went round to the bar instead, ordering two ploughman's lunches and two halves of shandy. Jane talked to the barman, but he'd only been working there for a few months and had no knowledge of the previous establishment.

They ate their lunch quickly, Jane checking her watch as if Fitzpatrick-Dunn might slip out of their grasp at any moment. 'I'm just going to the ladies', she said, scrunching up her napkin and putting it on her plate. After washing her hands, Jane walked back along the corridor, then stopped to look at two photographs on the wall just outside the gents'. They showed the pool room that had once been part of the restaurant. One photograph showed the table set up with the balls, the other had two young men with their sleeves rolled up standing by the table, holding the cues. She was about to carry on back to the bar when she noticed in the background of one photograph the old pub's main entrance, with the gravel drive leading to the main doors. She looked at the other photograph: clearly visible was a section of the car park, and the sign above the door to the pool room. She stood for a minute, concentrating intently.

By the time she got back to the bar, Maureen had already left, and was standing by Jane's car. Jane got in with a big grin on her face.

'What's happened?' Maureen asked as she pulled on her seatbelt.

'They all lied, Maureen! In every statement they claimed they'd been walking up the road away from the pub, then Kilroy went back to look for Brittany and was still in the road when he saw her come out of the pool bar exit and get into a red car.'

'You've lost me. Why is that a lie?'

'Because the pool bar exit is not visible from the main road. The only way he could have seen her was from the car park. Which means they must have parked up there and were waiting for her.'

Jane slapped the steering wheel. 'I think we're finally getting somewhere, Maureen. Now, let's see if Mr Fitzpatrick-Dunn has anything useful to say.'

Three quarters of an hour later they drove into a private gated estate of newly built two-storey houses. Fitzpatrick-Dunn's was at the end of the semicircle of properties, with a large garden.

'Well, this is very nice,' Jane said as they got out.

They walked up the path and Jane pressed the bell. She could hear the chimes from inside the house, but no one seemed to be coming. After a few moments she pressed it again, then waited for a full minute.

Jane turned away, irritated with herself for not calling first from the pub. Maureen was already heading back towards the car when the door was opened. Fitzpatrick-Dunn didn't look pleased to see them.

'Good afternoon,' Jane said. 'I am sorry to disturb you, but I was nearby and hoped you might be at home.'

He opened the door wider and gestured for them to come in. He was wearing a dressing gown, with tracksuit bottoms and old slippers. He was unshaven, and his thick white hair was in need of a brush.

'You can go into the drawing room, just give me a moment.'

He opened a door leading into a bright, well-furnished room with modern sofas and matching easy chairs. The top of an antique bureau was covered with numerous framed photographs. Jane put her briefcase down and stood looking at the photographs. Many were of Sylvia Kilroy looking very glamorous in elegant evening gowns. There were another couple of Fitzpatrick-Dunn alongside a tall woman similar in looks to Sylvia, but plainer. Two smaller photographs showed Sylvia and her husband, and one was of a toddler who might have been John Kilroy.

Jane turned as Fitzpatrick-Dunn walked in, dressed in cords and a cashmere sweater. He had combed his hair, and now smelt of cologne.

'Please sit down. Would you like a tea or coffee?'

Maureen shook her head. 'We're fine, thank you,' Jane said.

'I have not been very well, I'm afraid,' he said.

'Yes, I was told. I hope you're feeling better,' Jane said.

'Still rather painful. I have been instructed to take it easy for some time, so I am somewhat housebound.'

He stood with his back to the fireplace.

'May I ask why are you here?'

'I just need to confirm a few things with you,' Jane said. 'It shouldn't take long. I presume you contacted John and asked him to return home?'

'Yes. I am obviously unable to look after Sylvia at the present – and, more to the point, look after the farm, as I am not supposed to do any heavy lifting.'

'Did you mention to John that I was interested in talking to him?'

'No, I did not.'

'Is he staying there for some time?'

'I don't know. Hopefully I will be well enough to go back soon.'

'Could you tell me whose decision it was to have the car removed from the garage?'

He shrugged. 'I might have suggested it, but it could have been Sylvia. Apparently John wants a new car, not my business really.'

'But you knew that I wanted to examine the car.'

'I don't recall exactly what you said, frankly. But that car had been rusting away in the garage for over five years or more. It was high time it was dealt with.'

'It could have been very important to my investigation. But that's not the primary reason I am here. I need you to clarify for me when Sylvia went abroad for medical reasons.'

He sighed. 'She was suffering from depression, heading for a nervous breakdown. I am loath to discuss her private life, but Sylvia was an alcoholic. After the death of her husband she found it difficult to face life without him.'

'How long was Mrs Kilroy an alcoholic for?'

His lips tightened. 'I can't give you exact dates, Inspector.'

'All right, when did you step in to look after her?'

'I didn't, as you put it, "step in". My wife was ill with cancer, and I was tending to her needs. Sylvia had been to Switzerland after Rupert died, then returned, to all intents and purposes fully recovered. But I didn't see very much of her, so I was unaware of how she was coping.'

'But eventually you realised she needed help?'

'Yes, it became apparent at my wife's funeral, if you must know. That was when I decided to spend more time with her. John had left home by this time.'

'So, when did you understand that Sylvia needed more than just your help to recover?'

'It was maybe five years ago. I was shocked at the state of the farm and how she was living. It was heartbreaking for me to see her. I knew she needed help, but Sylvia was adamant that she could not go anywhere she might be recognised.'

'So, you arranged for her to go to a clinic abroad?'

'Yes, but even that took a lot of persuasion.'

'You are obviously very fond of her.'

Jane could see his jaw tightening as if he was grinding his teeth, and then he seemed to deflate, collapsing in one of the easy chairs. 'The truth is I adore her, and, if you must know, I bought this place because I had hopes that when she was fully recovered, she would sell that bloody farm and move in here with me.'

'She refused?'

He slapped the arm of the chair. 'Good heavens, you are a persistent woman, aren't you! Sylvia's legal advisors organised the transfer of the farm to John, to avoid inheritance tax. But he refused to even contemplate selling and Sylvia misguidedly listened to him.'

'Was she aware of your feelings towards her?'

He leaned back and closed his eyes, making no reply.

'Mr Fitzpatrick-Dunn, I need to know the exact date that you took Sylvia to the airport.'

He opened his eyes, sighing. 'I don't believe this. You asked me about this before and I told you. I also made it very clear to you that Sylvia was not in the country when the girl went missing and that John was boarding at his college.'

'I am aware of that,' Jane persisted, 'but I still need confirmation of the exact date. I can, if necessary, look into the flights and the location, which would mean asking more questions about a situation you very obviously wish to remain private.'

He got up, winced in pain for a moment, then crossed to the bureau and opened a drawer. He removed four large leather diaries and an envelope of documents. He sifted through these until he found the correct one, replaced the others, and carried the diary back to where he'd been sitting. Jane leaned forwards, waiting patiently as he turned the pages and then looked up.

'Sylvia was booked on the early morning flight to Spain by British Airways, first class, on the fourteenth of June.'

'Did you spend the night of the thirteenth at the farm?'

'No.'

'May I ask why not, if Mrs Kilroy was so ill?'

'My solicitor was coming over to my house with documents I needed to sign, and I wanted to discuss the sale of my house and other personal matters as well. As you can see, there is an entry in my diary to that effect.'

'When did you book Sylvia's flight?'

'Why do you need to know that?'

'In case it was a rushed booking made the day after Brittany went missing.'

He frowned. 'I really don't like what you're insinuating.' He handed Jane a document. 'I have the flight details here, show-ing the exact date it was booked and paid for, which as you can see was the beginning of June. I drove her to Heathrow and saw her get on to the plane – how much more information do you need?'

Jane opened her briefcase to take out her notebook, then jotted down the details.

'Oh, just one more thing. I am aware of Mrs Kilroy's poor eyesight, and that she is now unable to drive. But do you recall if she was still driving before she left for Spain?'

He gave a dismissive shrug of his shoulders as he replaced the diary in the drawer.

'I very much doubt it. Quite apart from her sight, she would have been unsafe to drive.'

'When you returned to assist Mrs Kilroy, was the car damaged?'

'All I know is that it was in the garage, and I recall her lawyer cancelled the insurance.'

'Did you discuss the damage to the car with Mrs Kilroy, or with John?'

'Good heavens! Why are you so interested in the damned car? I don't recall ever mentioning it. As I have made it clear, I am not on good terms with my nephew and never have been.'

'I am simply trying to establish exactly when Mrs Kilroy's vehicle was damaged.'

'I think I have made it patently clear that I am unable to tell you, just that it was in the garage many months after Mrs Kilroy returned from Spain. You must realise there was a lot that required my attention around the farm, which had been left unattended.'

Jane stood up. 'Thank you for your time, Mr Fitzpatrick-Dunn. You have been very accommodating, and I really appreciate it. Especially since you're recovering from recent surgery.'

Maureen followed Jane to the car.

Jane sat for a moment before driving off. Maureen wasn't sure whether the interview had been useful or not.

'What did you make of him?' she said.

Jane tapped her fingers on the steering wheel. 'I think a few pieces of the jigsaw are beginning to slot into place, Maureen.'

CHAPTER TWENTY-NINE

Jane and Maureen returned to the station and immediately started work on putting up a large whiteboard, similar to the CID office's incident board. At the top of the board was a photograph of Brittany Hall. Alongside was the date she was last seen on the 13th of June, then the date she was officially reported missing, the 16th. Beneath Brittany were the names of the boys and one photograph: John Kilroy; then the faxed pictures of the old pub.

Then there were the details of Jolyon Fairweather's accident.

Next was Sylvia Kilroy: the date she departed for the clinic in Spain, and her return seven months later; the legal situation regarding the ownership of the farm; the details of the damaged vehicle and a picture of a Lancia Beta.

Donald Fitzpatrick-Dunn was next: his association with the family; his dislike of his nephew; and his recent return from hospital.

Maureen stood back, surveying their handiwork. With a thick red felt-tip pen, Jane started drawing lines between the various people.

'Right, all of them connected,' she said finally.

Maureen nodded, glancing at her watch. It was already after six.

'Right, Maureen, let me take you through my thoughts. Firstly, I think I have been wrong to focus solely on John Kilroy. I think all three boys aren't just lying about the events of that night: I believe they were all involved in Brittany Hall's murder. And I think we could even be looking for a fourth person: the driver of the car.'

Jane tapped Sylvia Kilroy's name. 'It is possible that the three boys were using the car, with John Kilroy driving, and they took Brittany back to Kilroy's farm. Whatever happened there resulted in something horrific, maybe they tried to gang-rape her, and then they killed her. This meant they needed someone to get them back to college, and I believe Sylvia Kilroy, a woman suffering not only from alcohol addiction, but poor eyesight, was somehow cajoled or even forced into doing it. This would fit the time frame of the hit-and-run. Sylvia was then taken to the airport the next day by Fitzpatrick-Dunn. Then we have the fact that subsequently John Kilroy has refused to sell the farm or even any of the land, suggesting that Brittany's body may have been buried there. Which is why I want to get a full-scale search.'

Maureen just stared at the board, wide-eyed, as if she couldn't quite digest everything Jane had just told her.

'Come on, what do you think?' Jane snapped.

'Well, it is all circumstantial. I mean, we have no solid evidence about what happened.'

Jane sighed. It was almost seven. 'OK, let's call it quits for today, but first thing in the morning I want you to contact the barman who worked in the old pub.'

'Oh, he's been quite difficult to track down.'

'Well, keep going, I just have a hunch he might have more information for us.'

Maureen had her coat on. 'I'll get on to that first thing. Will you be talking to the super about your theory?'

'I think I just need one more piece of the jigsaw. I'm not on duty call for tonight, am I?'

'No, it's DCI Shefford. Between you and me, he got his nose put out of joint a bit by DCI Hickock's fast conclusion of the suicide case, so he wants to make a grab for anything that'll keep him top dog.'

'That's very interesting, Maureen. Where did you get all this from?'

'New girl in admin. Anyway, you have a nice weekend.'

'You too, Maureen.' Jane stood in front of the board. She hated to admit it, but Maureen was right.

* * *

Fitzpatrick-Dunn put in a call to Sylvia, firstly to check if John was looking after her properly, and secondly to discuss the visit from DCI Tennison. Sylvia answered the phone in the snug, with a thick rug around her, as the fire had gone out.

'John's gone to see someone in Eastbourne about a car. I'm expecting him back this evening or first thing in the morning. But don't worry about me: I'm eating all the delicious food you had delivered.'

When he described the visit from Tennison, she hardly seemed to be paying attention.

'You know I have little or no memory of that time. Anyway, I hope you will be well enough to come over very soon. I miss you and I am not sure how long John intends to stay. He's got Monty back home, so I have him for company. John has been taking him out for walks.'

'Well, that's good. I'll come over as soon as I can. Do take care of yourself and keep warm – and be very careful of the stairs.'

Sylvia replaced the receiver. She was still in her nightdress and dressing gown, not having dressed for a few days. She was really feeling the cold without the big fire she was used to having, and went into the kitchen and put the kettle on for a hot water bottle. The kettle seemed to take an age, then with shaking hands she filled the hot water bottle up. She searched around the counter for the stopper. Left unopened were cartons of food she hadn't bothered to even try and eat. She found the stopper eventually, after knocking one of the cartons onto the floor. She screwed it in tightly before feeling her way from the kitchen, down the steps and into the snug. She reached her big comfortable armchair, and from behind a cushion took the half-full bottle of vodka, before slowly making her way into the hall. She checked the front door was locked and turned off the lights, leaving just the landing light on above.

Sylvia carefully climbed the staircase and walked along the landing, pausing by the master bedroom. The door was ajar and she whispered, 'Goodnight, my beloved.' In her bedroom, the bedside lamp had been left on. She put the bottle of vodka down on the bedside table, then slipped the hot water bottle under the duvet and kicked off her slippers.

She leaned back against the stack of pristine white pillows and reached for the bottle. Having eaten nothing that day, or even the previous one, she felt the alcohol instantly, relaxing and soothing her. She closed her eyes, then quickly opened them, remembering the three empty bottles under the bed.

'Don't forget, Sylvia,' she said, wagging a finger. 'Must get rid of them before Mrs Monkford comes.'

* * *

The following morning Jane was at the station later than usual, having done a grocery shop for the weekend, in preparation for Peter moving in. When she walked into the office, Maureen was looking pleased with herself.

'I finally got hold of Michael Sullivan – you know, the barman – took me eight calls.'

'And?' Jane said.

'He doesn't think he'll have anything to add to his original statement, but if you wanted to come to the restaurant he's working in, he's willing to try.'

'Where is it?'

'Camden Lock. And before lunch is best, otherwise he'll be too busy.'

'Right, then. You'd better give me the address.' Jane put her coat back on while Maureen scribbled it down.

The restaurant turned out to be more of a sandwich bar that also served pizzas. Sullivan was behind the counter, dressed in jeans and a T-shirt with a black apron, trying to fix a faulty cappuccino machine while Jane introduced herself, and it wasn't until another young man, also wearing a black apron, came in and took over that Sullivan acknowledged her and gave her his full attention.

They sat down at one of the tables. 'I'll make this as brief as possible,' Jane said as he looked back at the cappuccino machine anxiously. 'I can see you've got your hands full.'

'Yeah, if we don't get that fixed, we'll be in real trouble,' he said, turning back to her.

'Did my colleague mention to you why I am here, specifically the night of the thirteenth of June, 1986?'

'Gosh, yes, long time ago. The girl that went missing, right?'

'That's right. Now I want you to look at these photographs of the car park and the pool room entrance.'

She spread out the faxes and he looked over them. 'Around that time the pool room was out of action. It had been causing a bit of a problem. The problem was sometimes it got a bit rowdy, the kids were bringing in their own beer, and there weren't enough staff to supervise things, so it was not always open to the public.'

'Was it closed on that particular evening?'

'Yes, it'd been shut for quite a while. The table had been sold and that's where the karaoke sessions would be. The main bar had two double doors and we kept them open for when it started, so the staff could check the punters were behaving themselves.'

'The night in question was a Friday. You said it was quite crowded, is that correct?'

'Yes, and that night there was a stag do. I was looking after the end of the main bar, which meant I would be dealing with the people coming in for the karaoke. It was quite a big party.'

'So, if I was told that there were not many people in the bar at around eight to nine o'clock, that wouldn't really be correct?'

'I was asked this before. Like I said, it was a Friday night. I mean, if it was around seven, it could be described as a bit empty, but not for much longer after that.'

'What time did the karaoke start?'

'About eight.'

'And you're sure there was a stag party that evening?'

'Yeah. I remember because it was a friend of the barman, and they had an open bar for two hours, which I was managing, so I got paid extra.'

'OK, Michael. One last thing.' She showed him the photograph of Brittany Hall. 'She was described as being a bit drunk, a bit silly.'

He shook his head. 'No, I don't recall seeing her. The thing is, I was on sort of lookout as the stag party had asked for the old pool room entrance doors to be kept open. Like I said, they did have an open bar for a couple of hours, and we were worried about gatecrashers having free drinks, so I had the list of names to check when they came in, and they put a cordon up later.'

'So that could mean someone from the main bar could have walked out into the car park via the old pool room area?'

'I suppose so, but it was jam-packed, very busy.'

'Thank you, Michael. I'll let you get back to work. I hope your machine behaves itself.'

Jane returned to the station and added the new details about the karaoke stag night party to the board. She and Maureen stood side by side, staring at the board. Jane got her red felt-tip pen out again. 'I think they all colluded about the time they were at the pub. I'm convinced they were there earlier than they claimed. Our barman, Michael Sullivan, is certain that by eight, when they say they arrived there, it would have begun to fill up, plus on this particular Friday there was the stag night.'

Maureen nodded, as Jane sucked at the end of her pen.

'OK, let's say they arrive at the pub with John driving his mother's car. Parked outside the pool room area in the car park, they were pissed off about the fact there was a private party. Anyway, they are in the car, and coming out, as we have seen from the CCTV, is Brittany Hall.'

Jane went to the board and scribbled for a few seconds.

'So, she comes out, but doesn't, as John Kilroy claimed, get into the red car, but gets into theirs, and they drive out.'

'So are you saying she was in the pub with someone else, as they have claimed?'

Jane blinked, suddenly unsure. Maureen pointed to the board.

'I mean, someone had to be the driver of that red car, and no amount of news coverage and requests for the person to come forward brought a single hit.'

'If we could find out who organised the stag night and get a list of who was invited, maybe we'll find out if one of them drove a red car. As the CCTV footage is not in colour, we are dependent on John Kilroy's statement about the colour.'

Maureen took a deep breath. 'You know, it was five years ago. It's going to be a heck of a job finding out who was having this stag party, let alone tracing and questioning all the guests.'

'Call our barman, Michael Sullivan. He said it was a friend of the old barman, and that he had a list of who was expected. The barman's deceased, so we can't ask him. But maybe Michael might remember who organised it. I could kick myself for not asking him when I was there. You know something else? Didn't they all claim that it was a red sports car?'

Maureen was at her desk, ready to call Michael Sullivan.

'No . . . they just repeated what Kilroy said.'

'But he's lying, because we now know it's impossible to see that pool room exit from where he said he was.'

Maureen waited for the call to be answered. 'Is this Michael Sullivan? Sorry to bother you, but could DCI Tennison, whom you spoke to earlier . . . Yes, could she just have a word with you? It's rather urgent.'

Maureen held the phone out and Jane took it. 'Michael, I know you're very busy, and I apologise for interrupting you at work again. But I need to ask one more question. The evening of the thirteenth of June, the stag party: you said it was a friend of the barman who had organised the open bar.'

There was a slight pause; with the phone held in one hand, Jane crossed her fingers with the other.

'Could you give me his name, Michael?'

'Let me think . . . I've not seen him for a few years.'

'His name, Michael?'

'David Greenwood. That's it.'

'Did David Greenwood own a car?'

'I should think so. He was a mechanic. I actually knew him because he was a member of the same karate gym.'

'Thank you so much, Michael, I really appreciate it,' Jane said.

Maureen went off to check with records, as Jane tried to find an address for David Greenwood in the Windsor area. Half an hour later Maureen returned with a records sheet.

'I have a David Greenwood presently residing in Wormwood Scrubs. He has a record for dealing in cannabis, burglary, handling stolen goods. Last known address in Clapham, but his first arrests have him living with his parents in Bracknell Forest, Windsor.'

It was after lunch when Jane finally got permission to visit David Greenwood, and due to the rigmarole involved in organising a visit, it was almost three when Jane was ushered into a small interview room. It was another fifteen minutes before David Greenwood was led into the room.

He did not look anything like his mugshots: he'd worn his hair long and he was now shaven-headed. He was broad-shouldered and obviously worked out at the prison gym, his bulging arms covered in tattoos.

'What's this about?' he asked in a surly manner.

'Just sit down and behave yourself,' the prison officer told him. The officer then nodded to Jane and indicated that he'd be outside the door.

'Firstly, thank you for agreeing to see me, and I'll try not to take up too much of your time.'

He snorted. 'Time's all I've bloody got in here. So what can I do for you?'

'I am Detective Chief Inspector Jane Tennison, and I am heading up an investigation into a case from five years ago.'

'Someone trying to fuckin' pin something on me?' he snarled.

'No, I'm just hoping you will be able to help me. You organised a stag night at the old pub on the main Windsor Road, on Friday the thirteenth of June 1986.'

He frowned, pushing his shoulders back in the chair. 'I remember, and you want to know why? Not just because it cost me a bundle, free bar and all. My fiancée dumped me, went off with one of my best mates three days before the wedding. Mind you, I reckon it was a good thing as she turned out to be a right slag, but it hit me hard. I always say that was the start of me screwing up my life.'

Jane nodded sympathetically. 'My investigation is regarding a young student that went missing on that night.'

He immediately became aggressive, leaning forwards. 'You trying to say I got something to do with that? I'm out of here, it's bloody lies!'

'Mr Greenwood, please, I know you were not involved in the girl's disappearance, but I'm hoping that you may recall something that could assist my enquiry. I want to ask you to take your mind back to that night. What time did you arrive for the stag party?'

He relaxed in the chair again.

'I got there early, be about seven fifteen, I had to give a list of the lads I'd got coming.'

'Which entrance did you use?'

'The old pool room entrance. Doors were open, and they'd cordoned off the main bar.'

'Did you drive into the car park?'

'Yes, I had an old Triumph Herald convertible.'

'What colour was it?'

'Blue, well, what you could see between the dents.' He laughed.

'Was the car park full?'

'No, but it would be filling up.'

'Can you recall any of the other cars parked up?'

'No, never paid any attention.'

Jane had been allowed to take in an envelope, and she now withdrew the Brittany Hall photograph.

'Can you remember seeing this girl?'

He picked it up and, to Jane's surprise, took his time looking at it before he shook his head and passed it back across the table.

'She wouldn't have been there as it was just lads, no birds.'

'She may have got into an MG. You can see part of it in the picture. It was described as being red.'

He shrugged. 'I don't know any of my mates that had an MG.'

'Is there anything that you can think of that might help me?'

'You reckon this girl got into the MG?'

'It's possible, but we haven't been able to trace the owner, even though at the time there was a lot of press coverage and appeals to whoever it was to come forward.'

'Well, I never heard about it, but then I had just been kicked in the teeth by that bitch I was going to marry. Don't you have a reg plate to track him down?'

'Sadly, we don't. It's such a small section of the car, it might not even be an MG.'

'I'd have thought all your clever dick detectives would get that found out, no offence to you.'

She smiled, replacing the photograph in the envelope.

'It could be a Morgan, you know,' he said. 'They're usually racing green, but low like an MG, and sometimes they have the similar wire wheels. The Morgan's a lovely motor, all still hand-made, you know. I worked for a mechanic straight out of school, and I'd see the odd one.' He laughed, and Jane could see he was now beginning to enjoy himself.

He leaned forwards. 'My dream car was a Cobra, knew a bloke who was reconditioning one, beautiful. I'd also nearly got my hands on an E-Type, bit classier than tooling around in a Triumph Herald, but at the time that was all I could afford.'

Jane was standing up, ready to end the meeting, when Greenwood banged the table. 'Hang on! I just remembered, Eddie Foxley, he had a Sunbeam Alpine. It was more maroon than red, but he was in the main bar. He wasn't invited for the stag night, but he saw me and called over to say have a good time. It was about ten minutes after I'd got there.'

Jane sat down again as Greenwood clapped his hands.

'Dunno why I didn't think of it. He was having words with the old bloke who was running the bar. He said some kids had almost clipped his car driving out of the car park, really pissed him off.'

'Did he say how many kids were in the car?'

'No, I only heard that much.'

'So, you were at the far end of the pool room? Not by the doors?'

'Right, by the cordon to the main bar, and I would say it was about half past seven.'

'Did you see Mr Foxley again?'

'No, I think he had a drink and left.'

'Would you have Mr Foxley's contact number or his address?'

'Nah, not seen him for four years or more. He was a carpet fitter. I remember that because he done my mum's hall. Is all that any help?'

'It certainly is, Mr Greenwood, thank you. I'll make sure the governor knows how helpful you've been.'

He laughed. 'I'll look forward to getting out next week, then.'

When Jane got back to the station, she asked Maureen to find pictures of Sunbeam Alpines and then got down to the task of calling carpet companies, asking if they had a carpet fitter called Eddie Foxley. It was after five by the time she got a hit from a company with a senior fitter called Edward Foxley. By this time Maureen had got a company selling Sunbeam Alpines to fax over some photos, and added some pictures of Lancias in case they were needed, too.

Maureen and Jane looked at the pictures of the car. 'I think you might mistake that for an MG,' Maureen said.

Jane shook her head in exasperation. 'You'd think that old bastard Sumpter would have checked this out. I mean, how many press releases went out asking for the owner of a red MG to come forward, when it could have been this?'

Jane almost physically jumped when her desk phone rang. It was Edward Foxley, just returned to the office after fitting a carpet at a property. 'Can I ask if anyone just calls you Fox, instead of Foxley?'

He chuckled. 'Some of the junior staff call me the "Old Fox" or even the "Silver Fox".'

'And did you know a David Greenwood?'

It took him a moment, then he said, 'Oh, yes, haven't seen or heard from him for many years, though.'

'And did you once own a maroon-coloured Sunbeam Alpine?'

'Sold it three years ago,' he said. 'Look, what's this all about? Someone use the car as a getaway vehicle for a bank robbery or something?'

Jane explained about the Brittany Hall case. 'I'd like to come and see you.'

CHAPTER THIRTY

Edward Foxley lived on the outskirts of Windsor, close to the Ascot racecourse. By now Jane felt she knew the area like the back of her hand, so told Maureen there was no need for her to accompany her. Maureen was visibly relieved.

The drive took Jane longer than expected, as rush hour was just getting going, and she was held up on the M4, but eventually found herself on the main road with the racecourse on her right side, before taking two turnings to arrive at Foxley's property, a well-maintained semi-detached house with similar properties on both sides of the road.

Jane found a space halfway down the road and walked back to Foxley's house.

Foxley opened the door, wearing a rather worn-looking blue boiler suit and T-shirt. He had rather a distinguished face, with thick greying hair. 'You must be DCI Tennison. Come in.'

Jane couldn't help noticing the plush carpet in the hall. When he led her into a small sitting room, the carpet looked equally luxurious, though Jane was a bit put off by the bright orange colour.

'Do sit down. Can I offer you a sherry?'

'No thank you. Hopefully I will not take up too much of your time.' Jane opened her briefcase and took out a large manila envelope and her notebook.

'This will be a test of your memory, Mr Foxley, because I want to take you back to the thirteenth of June, five years ago. I believe you visited the Old Garden pub on the Windsor Road?'

He looked slightly taken aback.

'I asked if you recalled a young man called David Greenwood. He says you had a conversation? It was his stag do.'

'Yes, yes, that's right. It took me a moment to remember him, but I have had a few thoughts about him since you called. I fitted a carpet for his parents, and I believe he was sort of living at home at the time. I think I came across him quite a few times. He was working at a garage and I'd chat about cars with him. He was very impressed with my Sunbeam Alpine, and, if I remember correctly, I went out for a spin with him.'

'That's really very helpful, Mr Foxley, thank you. What colour was your Alpine?'

'Two-tone, cream and maroon.'

Jane was eager to press on. 'Can I go back to the evening I mentioned earlier? David Greenwood's stag party night.'

'Yes, I just dropped in on my way home. I'd been doing a big job in Sheep Street, five-storey house with nightmare narrow stairs and they had ordered a checked carpet. You have no idea how difficult it is to fit them: you have to match the squares, so there is always a lot of waste, and the customer was very difficult about it. I remember thinking it had been a real nasty Friday the thirteenth! I think that's why I needed a drink.'

'Can you remember anything else about that night?'

'I'm not sure . . .' Jane opened the envelope and took out the photograph of Brittany Hall. She passed it to him.

'This is Brittany Hall. Do you recognise her?'

He stared at the photograph, then looked up and shook his head. 'No, I've never seen her.'

'OK, take me through the time after you left Sheep Street and arrived at the pub. What car were you driving?'

'Oh, it was the Alpine, because if it's a big job the carpet is delivered by van, and as a fitter, I arrive to cut and measure the ordered carpet in my own vehicle. I'd been working there for two days and that was my last day.'

He was frowning in concentration, sitting forwards with his hands clasped together.

'I think I left around seven fifteen, maybe just after. It's quite a short drive from Sheep Street onto the main Windsor Road, so

I probably arrived there at about seven thirty. Is that what you wanted to know?'

'Yes, exactly, but carry on. You drove into the car park?'

'Yes, there are two entrances. The main one is off the drive to the pub, and through a gate, well, two posts actually, and when the car park is full, they put a chain up. The other is at the far end of the car park, and back then usually most people exited that way, as it's onto the main road.'

Jane had to take a deep breath as she waited a moment before asking which entrance to the car park he used. He pursed his lips.

'The main entrance, and I couldn't believe it, I had to slam on my brakes, or they would have clipped my front right wing. They virtually drove straight at me. I was winding down my window to yell at them, but they just drove out, louts, so I parked up and went into the pub and I complained to the barman about it.'

Jane clenched her hands together. 'Mr Foxley, this is very important; can you recall what make of car it was?'

'They had their headlights on, and I was shocked at how close they had been to my front bumper, but it wasn't a common make as far as I remember. That's all I can tell you.'

'You referred to the passengers in this car as "they", so that would be the driver and who else?'

'Oh, my goodness, I almost forgot, look, I can't be absolutely sure, but I think there were four people in the car altogether.'

Jane felt like punching the air. 'You described them as louts. Why?'

'They were laughing and yelling, like they weren't adults, or at least behaving like ones.'

'Was it possible they were parking to join the stag night party?'

'No, they drove out. I also remember now a bottle was thrown from a window as they went.'

Jane took out the pictures of the various vehicles and laid them out along the coffee table. Almost instantly Foxley clapped his hands and she looked up sharply.

'That's it! Four doors, Lancia Beta. I just couldn't recall it straight-away, but that is definitely the car those boys were driving.'

Jane could hardly believe it. She carefully put everything back in her briefcase, and stood up.

'Thank you so much for your help, Mr Foxley.'

They shook hands and he walked ahead of her to open the door into the hall. Sitting on the stairs were two little girls in pigtails, wearing dressing gowns. She gave them a smile.

'You've been very good, girls. Now, say goodnight to the police officer.'

They giggled and ran back upstairs.

He opened the front door. Jane turned to him. 'You have my contact number at the station. If you think of anything else that might be helpful, please call me.'

'I most certainly will.' He sighed. 'If anything happened to my two little ones . . . I don't know what I would do.'

She gave him a nod, then walked back to her car. Foxley had given her more than he could ever realise. She now knew it was his car caught on the CCTV camera.

Jane drove back along the main street towards the roundabout, then decided she would see how long it took to drive to the Kilroys' farm.

At the main crossroads, Jane took a wrong turning, heading left instead of right, so at the next roundabout she backtracked on herself, but she was now a bit disorientated and it was a while before she got her bearings, finally spotting the sign for Pirbright village. Her original plan to time the route John Kilroy could have taken from the pub to the farm was no longer feasible, as she had come a very indirect way. She thought about turning round and heading back, but something made her carry on to the farm. She hesitated for a moment by the entrance, then drove slowly down the drive.

By now it was dark, and the long driveway had no lights, but she could just make out the wrecked beehives, the hedgerows of dying rhododendrons and broken fences. She stopped in front of the house, parking behind a car she recognised as Fitzpatrick-Dunn's.

Stepping out of the car she could hear raised voices, then screaming and something crashing. Approaching the open front door with caution, she heard Sylvia Kilroy shouting in a high-pitched voice, then another crash. Stepping inside, she saw Fitzpatrick-Dunn standing at the bottom of the staircase. Sylvia Kilroy was at the top of the stairs, wearing a stained nightdress. She had a bottle in her hand and looked as if she was about to hurl it down the stairs to join a heap of broken glass.

'Get out, you hear me, get the hell out, you pitiful, wretched bastard, *leave me alone!*' she screeched.

He looked up to her. 'Please, Sylvia, I'm here to help you, that is all I am trying to do. Let me take you to hospital. You need help.'

'*Get out, I said!*'

She leaned forward, squinting, and seemed to notice Jane's presence for the first time.

She pointed at Fitzpatrick-Dunn. 'Why have you brought her here?'

Fitzpatrick-Dunn turned towards Jane with a helpless gesture, as Sylvia dropped the bottle and it began to roll down the stairs. She slumped to her knees, still clinging to the bannister. Afraid she was about to fall down, Fitzpatrick-Dunn went up the stairs to her. She tried to push him away, but she was too drunk and collapsed into his arms.

'Help me with her,' he said as he tried to lift Sylvia up, and they half carried her between them into Sylvia's bedroom. The room was in disarray, with clothes and empty bottles strewn over the floor. There was a strong smell of urine and vomit.

Sylvia looked terrible, her greasy hair in rat's tails, and her deathly pale features distorted with smudged make-up. There were dark rings around her unfocused eyes.

'You can't put her into the bed,' Jane said, 'it's filthy. Is there another room we can use?'

'Never mind, just get her to lie down,' Fitzpatrick-Dunn replied. 'We have to clean her up.'

'I am so sorry, so sorry,' Sylvia started moaning. She clung on to him as Jane drew back the stained sheets so he could get her into the bed.

She curled up and started crying. Fitzpatrick-Dunn sat beside her, holding her hand.

'It's all right, dearest, I am going to get you help. No one is going to hurt you, I'm here now, just lie back like a good girl, everything is going to be all right now.'

She closed her eyes, and he drew the clean sheet up and gently settled it around her.

Jane was standing at the end of the bed, unsure what to say or how to explain why she was there. It was such a wretched sight.

'I was worried about the dog,' Fitzpatrick-Dunn said after a few moments. 'He's been missing for days. I have been calling and calling, but she never answered. I knew something was wrong, I just knew it.'

'Where is her son?'

'I don't know. He was here earlier. He said he would go and search for the dog. He's been away, said he had only just got back. I am going to call for an ambulance and get her into a rehab facility.'

He felt her pulse, then looked at Jane. 'I don't know if she's just passed out or is in a coma . . . Dear God, I don't know what to do. They can't see her like this, she has to be bathed.'

'I wouldn't worry about what she looks like,' Jane said. 'But I think you do need to call someone.'

'I can't let anyone see her like this.'

'Yes, you can. The only thing that's important is to get her medical attention.'

He bent forwards, holding his stomach and wincing in pain.

'You stay up here with her,' Jane told him. 'Do you have a number or shall I just call an ambulance?'

He gave her the number of a drying-out clinic that had looked after Sylvia before. 'They'll send an ambulance, and they have medical staff.'

Jane dialled the number on the phone beside the bed, and after a brief conversation, handed the phone to Fitzpatrick-Dunn, who quickly became agitated, insisting they send an ambulance immediately. 'You have treated her before. It's very serious, you understand?'

While he was talking, Jane looked through the dressing table drawers, trying to find a clean nightdress and dressing gown. By the time she had them ready, Fitzpatrick-Dunn told her the ambulance was on its way.

'After she came back from Spain, I understood Mrs Kilroy was much better. Is this her first serious relapse?' Jane asked.

He sighed. 'She's had a couple of bad periods, but I really believed she was back on the right path until now.'

'I suppose having her son home hasn't helped,' Jane said.

He stiffened. 'I don't quite know what you mean by that. I had no other option but to contact him when I went into hospital. I couldn't just leave her alone here.' He got up. 'I'm going to try to tidy her up a little. Can't have her looking like this.' He gently lifted the sheet and took Sylvia's hand to take her pulse again, then touched her brow.

'Would you like me to make you a cup of tea?' Jane asked.

'That would be very kind of you. I have tended to her before, so I can get her showered and dressed.'

Jane paused by the door. 'You said John had just come home after being away.'

'Yes, he said he had to go to Eastbourne, something about buying a car. He just came back after I had found her. I was not best pleased with him, as you can imagine.'

'Did he not realise how sick his mother was?'

'He was never able to cope with her when she was drinking. I suppose he had a lot to deal with after his father died. Anyway, I wouldn't want him to see her like this.'

'You said he went out to look for the dog. He's been gone for quite a while,' Jane said.

'Well, there's acres, all the outhouses and the woods. Mrs Monkford usually takes care of the dog, so he might even have found his way to her house.'

'I'll go and make tea, leave you to it.'

Jane headed down the stairs, while he went into the bathroom. She stepped over two broken bottles at the bottom of the stairs and picked up the half-full one that Sylvia had dropped. She went into the snug: the fire was out, every surface covered with dirty crockery. She moved the curtain aside to step into the kitchen. Cartons of food littered the floor and she noticed the dog's water bowl was empty.

Jane filled the kettle and turned on the gas stove. She ignored the dirty crockery piled up in the sink and found some cups and saucers in a cupboard. An unopened bottle of milk in the fridge still seemed fresh.

Jane walked upstairs with the tea, then waited outside the bedroom door. Sylvia looked stupefied as she sat naked on the bed, her arms raised above her head, while Fitzpatrick-Dunn eased a clean nightdress over her head. She lay back down and he drew the nightdress down over her legs, before covering her with a clean sheet. Jane coughed and entered. He turned but looked pale and shocked.

'She seems much better after a wash and brush-up,' he said nervously.

'I can see, well done,' Jane replied, wondering if Sylvia had told him something disturbing while she was in the kitchen.

Sylvia let him comb her hair, but her eyes were blank, as if she was unaware of what was happening. Jane put the tea tray down on the bedside table.

'I have to say the kitchen is in a bit of a mess,' Jane said. 'Isn't Mrs Monkford supposed to be cleaning the house?'

'She called me to tell me the kitchen door was locked and she couldn't get in. She hasn't been for a few days.'

Fitzpatrick-Dunn picked up one of the cups. 'Ah, Earl Grey tea, let me see if Sylvia would like a sip.'

He leaned towards her, holding the cup, asking her gently if she would like some, but she closed her eyes, ignoring him. He put it back in the saucer.

'There does seem to be a very plentiful supply of vodka,' Jane said.

'I used to find bottles hidden all over the house. She was very adept at hiding her addiction back then.'

'Did they say how long the ambulance would be?' she asked.

'If you need to leave, please go ahead. I can look after her until they arrive.'

'Before I go, on the morning when you drove her to Heathrow, the fourteenth of June, I recall you telling me you were not staying here?'

'I drove over early to make sure she had packed and had everything ready. I told you, I had a meeting with my lawyers and had documents to sign, otherwise I would have stayed over. Why are you asking?'

'So who else was here at the house?'

'No one.'

'That was risky, wasn't it, leaving her alone?'

He sighed. 'It had taken some persuasion on my part to get her to agree to go, but she knew it was the best thing. I think she was relieved that she was getting the help she needed. When I left her, she was resting in bed. She was very tired.'

'When you came to pick her up, did you notice if the garage doors were open?'

'I can't remember. If they had been left open, I would have locked them up. Why are you asking me all these questions?'

'When did you notice that the Lancia was damaged?'

'Oh, a long time afterwards. I didn't come to the farm at all, not until she returned. I assumed John had driven it on a weekend home. I can't understand why you are so interested in the car; you mentioned it the last time you were here, and I told you then it was left in there for years.'

Sylvia stirred and tried to sit up. He quickly slipped another pillow behind her head. She opened her eyes and looked at Jane.

'When we first met,' Jane continued, 'I mentioned my interest in the Lancia, that I wanted it examined. It was unfortunate that it was removed before I got the opportunity, because either Mrs Kilroy or her son sent it to a breakers' yard.'

'For heaven's sake! I told you that if you wanted it removed, you could do so. I can't really understand your fixation with it.'

'I'll tell you,' Jane said. 'I believe John Kilroy and his friends were driving the car, and they had Brittany Hall, the student who went missing, with them. Something happened here, something that got terribly out of hand, and those three boys desperately needed to get back to the college, for an alibi, which meant that someone else had to drive them. I am certain that person was Mrs Kilroy.'

'That is ridiculous! There is no possibility she would have driven at night.'

'There was an accident on the same night, a collision with a horse box on the way between here and the college.'

He stood up, his hands clenched. 'I simply do not believe it. Sylvia was not capable of driving. I think you should leave right now.'

Jane was wondering whether she should go or press him further when they heard the clang of the old-fashioned doorbell.

'Could you let them in,' he said, 'while I get Sylvia ready?'

Jane hurried down the stairs and opened the door. A tall young man in a white coat with the clinic's badge on the pocket nodded to her as he walked in, followed by a middle-aged woman in navy overalls, carrying a medical bag.

'She's upstairs,' Jane said.

'Do we need to restrain her?' he asked.

'No, she's quiet now. I'm Detective Chief Inspector Jane Tennison. I was here on another matter.'

'Is she conscious?'

'Yes. She blacked out but she came round. I believe she may have been drinking for a few days. Mr Fitzpatrick-Dunn is with her, but if you need me, I can come up with you.'

'No, I think we can manage. We have been called out before.'

Jane watched them walk upstairs, then turned to look through the open front door. She saw the light of a torch, then a figure slowly came into focus. It was John Kilroy, holding a length of rope tied to a dog's collar.

'I suppose that ambulance is for Mother again,' he said, dragging his wellington boots over a boot scraper by the front door. 'The dog's filthy, as you can see. He'll want a hose down at some point, but I'm just going to put him in the kitchen. Won't be a minute.'

Jane was unsure if she should go upstairs to join the others or remain in the hall. She heard the dog barking, then Kilroy came out with a dustpan and brush and began to sweep up the glass. He then shook out a black bin liner and tipped everything into it.

'You shouldn't have left your mother here alone,' she said. He ignored her, taking the bag outside and dumping it by the doorstep. Fitzpatrick-Dunn appeared at the top of the stairs, carrying a small overnight case.

'We're bringing her down now.'

The young medic and the nurse appeared on either side of Sylvia. The medic had one arm around her waist, while the nurse was holding her arm. She was wearing a mink coat and seemed very unsteady on her feet. Fitzpatrick-Dunn moved in front of them, in case she fell forwards. They progressed slowly down the stairs, one at a time, while Sylvia stared emptily straight ahead.

Kilroy stood watching the procession, and then, with a half-smile said, 'Oh! *Very* Blanche DuBois in *A Streetcar Named Desire*! Although Uncle Donald doesn't make a very convincing Marlon Brando.'

Fitzpatrick-Dunn reddened. 'You think this is amusing? This is your fault. You should have been taking care of her,' he said angrily.

'Oh, don't worry, I have already been reprimanded by that woman.' He jerked his head towards Jane. 'You and I well know that when she starts on a binge there's no stopping her.'

The medic glanced at the nurse with a frown of distaste at the bickering. Sylvia paid no attention, concentrating on putting one foot after the other.

'You should have called me,' Fitzpatrick-Dunn said.

Kilroy shrugged. 'You were in hospital when she started drinking.'

'Gentlemen, please!' the medic implored. 'Don't worry, you're doing very well, Mrs Kilroy, just a few more stairs and then we'll take you outside. I won't let you go, that's good.'

Her head drooped forwards. 'Thank you, Donald,' she muttered without looking at him. 'Please pay the vet's bill, and get Mrs Monkford to look after Monty. I'm so sorry.'

Sylvia was led towards the front door. She looked up once towards her son; he made a move as if to go towards her and she shrank back, grimacing. They took her out and Fitzpatrick-Dunn helped them get her into the ambulance.

'What are you doing here?' John asked Jane abruptly as Donald walked back in.

'She came to ask Sylvia some questions,' Fitzpatrick-Dunn said wearily.

Kilroy laughed. 'I doubt she would have been able to give you any coherent answers. Anyway, it's all over now, so now you can both get out.'

Donald stared at him. 'Don't you dare talk to me like that. DCI Tennison believes you persuaded your mother to drive you back to the college on the night Brittany Hall went missing. I always assumed you had caused the damage to the car, but now I'm not so sure. Now that I think about it, as soon as I mentioned to you about the police wanting to have the car examined, you had it sent to the breakers' yard. Why would you do that?'

John's face drained of colour as he turned to Jane. 'That is bloody ridiculous. You saw the state my mother gets herself in. Do you really think that she could have driven a car?'

'She was sober that night,' Donald snapped angrily. 'I know because I was with her. I think you are lying, and she is protecting you, isn't she?'

John began to rub at his injured leg, and for the first time he had a look of panic on his face.

Fitzpatrick-Dunn raised his voice. 'What was so important that you had to go to Eastbourne when you knew your mother needed you?'

'Mind your own fucking business.'

'That's what I have been doing regarding your behaviour for too many years,' Fitzpatrick-Dunn retorted.

'I think he went to visit Justin Moore, his old college friend, to make sure you were still all sticking to the same story,' Jane said firmly.

Kilroy snorted. 'He has a car I am thinking of buying, actually. Satisfied? Now, like I just said, I want the pair of you to leave.'

Jane shrugged, then turned to Fitzpatrick-Dunn.

'Thank you for being so helpful tonight, Mr Fitzpatrick-Dunn. I hope Mrs Kilroy is better soon.'

Jane walked towards the front door. As she passed Kilroy, she paused. 'I will find Brittany Hall. I will not stop searching, no matter how long it takes.' He didn't react, but she thought she detected a flicker of fear in his eyes.

She was opening the passenger door when she turned. In the doorway, Fitzpatrick-Dunn was clearly upset as he spoke to John and pointed his finger at him. Kilroy walked off into the house and Fitzpatrick-Dunn then hurried out, avoiding her gaze. He got into his car, his head down. She wondered if Sylvia, through drink, had earlier told him what really happened the night Brittany Hall went missing, and he'd now confronted John with what he knew.

CHAPTER THIRTY-ONE

Jane's weekend was a blur. On Saturday morning she and Peter went through everything in his house, dividing them into items the new owners wanted, things to be taken into storage, and stuff to take to Jane's flat. Four men from a removal firm started packing the items for storage, while Jane and Peter worked all morning packing things to go in the van Peter had rented.

They went to a local pub for a quick lunch, then returned to start loading up the hire van. Tony came round later in the afternoon to help and drove the first vanload to Jane's flat, then came back for a second load.

It was after ten when Tony finally left, leaving Peter to hoover and do some cleaning before the move was completed on the Sunday. Jane and Peter were both exhausted, and decided to leave it to the morning. When they got back to Jane's, they ordered a takeaway curry and then crashed out. The alarm went off at seven and they started unpacking everything and deciding where to put it. After breakfast, they returned to his house for the final haul to be done. After loading up the hire van with the last bits and pieces, they spent two hours hoovering and dusting and putting all the garbage into big plastic bags to take to the tip.

Sunday lunch was another quick sandwich and a glass of wine before the final haul was completed. Peter had to take the van back and hand over the house keys while Jane had a long shower and changed out of her grimy work clothes. It was almost eight when Peter eventually arrived in his Range Rover with a huge bunch of roses to thank Jane for all her hard work.

After Peter had showered and changed, it was after nine, but he had made a reservation at Le Caprice, a posh Italian restaurant behind the Ritz. Jane really wanted an early night, but couldn't say no, and by the time they got home it was almost one in the morning. There was still a lot to do, especially when it came to making Peter's son's bedroom ready, but Jane now had other things to focus on, namely what she suspected was going to be a nasty confrontation with her boss. It was probably a good thing she'd been so busy, she reflected, or she would have been worrying about it all weekend.

Peter was still in his dressing gown when she made breakfast. 'You look very smart,' he commented, noting that she was wearing her most expensive suit. 'I'm impressed you manage to look so fresh after such an exhausting weekend. I still feel totally knackered.'

'It's a big day,' she said. 'I've not had time to tell you all about it, which is probably lucky for you!'

'Well, I wish you luck,' he said. 'I might go into the office later, but I'll just do a bit of organising here before I do, get as much done before you come home.'

She kissed him. It felt good having him here.

As she drove into the station, it was clear something big was going down from the number of squad cars coming and going. She parked up in her usual distant space and walked into the station. Numerous uniform officers were hurrying up and down the corridor, and when the lift finally stopped on the ground floor, it disgorged another load. Entering her office, she was taken aback to see Maureen was in tears, and her prized suspect board missing.

'Where have you been?' she asked between sobs. 'I've been calling you all weekend.'

'I was moving furniture. What's going on? Has something happened? Are you all right?'

Maureen took a deep breath. 'John Kilroy came into the station on Friday night. DCI Shefford was called in and he has a search party at the farm. They brought in Justin Moore on Saturday and they have Phillip Sayer on his way in this morning.'

Jane had to sit down. 'Wait a minute, I don't understand. John Kilroy came into the station? But I saw him on Friday evening.'

'He's made a confession.'

'Jesus Christ, are you serious?'

'Yes, I was called in, and they wanted all your details, and they took our suspects board and all your reports. I called and called you.'

'Wait a minute. This is not happening, they can't do this.'

'They've done it. There's twenty officers out searching the Kilroy farm right now. They went out Sunday morning. John Kilroy is here in the cells.'

Jane had to take several deep breaths, as Maureen kept on repeating that she was sorry.

'Right, I am going to confront Shefford,' Jane told her. 'Just dry your eyes and pull yourself together. They can't do this! I am so bloody angry.'

Jane walked out, took the lift down to the second floor and turned into the corridor leading to DCI Shefford's incident room. As she approached his office, the door swung open and Detective Sergeant Otley almost walked into her.

'Where is DCI Shefford?'

'He's not available right now.'

'I asked you where he was.'

'I just told you, ma'am, he is not available. He's at the crime scene.'

'Are you talking about the Kilroys' farm?'

He nodded. 'Unless he's on his way back to the station.'

'This is my cold case, Detective Sergeant Otley, and I demand to know exactly what DCI Shefford is doing, taking over my investigation.'

He smirked. 'You said it, ma'am. It was a cold case, but now it's a hot one, and as he was the DCI on duty this weekend, he is now handling the investigation.'

She turned away to avoid punching him in the mouth, and went straight to Kernan's office. She knocked loudly, ready to barge in, when the door was opened by his secretary.

'I want to speak to Superintendent Kernan now,' Jane told her.

'I'm afraid he is not available. He's on his way to join DCI Shefford.'

Jane stood there, her mouth opening and closing like a fish. It didn't just feel as if the carpet had been pulled from under her feet; it felt as if the ground was opening to swallow her up.

After taking a deep breath, she turned on her heels. She was heading back down the corridor when DS Otley, accompanied by two of Shefford's team, hurried out from the CID incident room. She stood back, pressing herself against the wall.

'Get a forensic team ready and tell the mortuary to send a van to the scene,' Otley told them.

'Have they found her?' Jane asked.

Otley turned. 'They got Kilroy in a Black Maria taking them to where he buried her. Fast work, eh?'

Otley banged through the double doors and out of sight. Jane felt physically sick as she took the lift back to her office. Maureen looked away uncomfortably, not knowing what to say. Jane took off her jacket and tossed it onto the floor. She put fresh paper into her typewriter and began to type. Maureen poured a mug of coffee and passed it along the desk.

'Thank you,' Jane said, continuing to type, making out a report of her meetings on Friday, and then the events at the Kilroys', pausing only briefly to sip her coffee. Half an hour later she snatched the last sheet, stacked it with two other pages, clipped them together, and turned to Maureen.

'Hand this in to Shefford's office. You can ask if there is any-thing else they want from my investigation, plus give them a memo regarding the items we have in the evidence lockup, in particular the hairbrush from Brittany Hall's mother.'

'Yes, ma'am. Shall I make a copy first?'

'Yes, do that. Then you can stick the original up that bastard's arse if you see him.'

Maureen scuttled out, leaving Jane to finish her coffee and sit wondering just how she was going to deal with the situation. She would have liked to put her jacket back on and walk out, but she forced herself to assess the situation calmly and think rationally what her next move should be. She heard sirens and stepped into the corridor and peered through the window overlooking the car park. The patrol car was not one of theirs. Two uniform officers got out, followed by Justin Moore. He was not handcuffed, but looked terrified as he was led into the station and out of sight.

Moving away from the window, she almost bumped into Maureen, hurrying towards her with the copy of the report. 'I handed it in to one of Shefford's team, and I told them about the evidence we have in the lockup. He didn't even thank me.'

'Do you know what's happening?'

'It's very busy down there, I can tell you that. Shefford has pulled in every possible officer and even some from other districts. I heard he took John Kilroy out in a squad car earlier. His lawyer was here first thing as well.'

'I just saw his friend Justin Moore brought in. Do you know if they still have Justin Moore in the cells?'

'I'm not sure, just that he was brought in from Yorkshire yesterday. Do you want me to go and check who's down there?'

'Yes, but don't make it too obvious.'

Jane had to admit that Shefford had moved fast. Whatever time John Kilroy had arrived at the station on Friday night, Shefford had then organised the arrest of the other two boys, got a warrant and organised a search of the farm. She heard a commotion in the yard and looked out of the window. White-suited forensic officers were hurrying towards their SOCO vans, loaded with equipment in large tin boxes. The rear doors hardly had time to slam shut before it left the yard, siren blaring. She couldn't tell if they had been at the location and were returning for more equipment, or a second team had been called out.

Maureen walked past the duty sergeant, who was standing with two officers as they booked in Justin Moore in the custody room. They took no notice of her as she made her way down the steps leading to the cells, but she quickly backtracked when she saw another duty officer positioned by the entry door, as she knew she would have to give a reason for being down there.

Going into the canteen to see if she could gain any further information, she found it was full of uniforms ordering breakfast. Maureen hovered by the service entrance, behind two officers with their trays. The breakfast supplies were running low and two extra canteen staff were frying up eggs and bacon. All she was able to gather was that the search had started early Sunday, but it now appeared that Kilroy had agreed to point out where the body had been hidden. His lawyer had been with him and Shefford on Saturday evening. One of the uniforms referred to Kilroy's lawyer as a 'posh twat'.

Maureen returned to the office and handed Jane a bacon sandwich. Jane was already on her second mug of strong coffee. 'I didn't get to go down into the cells as there was a duty officer monitoring everyone,' Maureen explained, 'but I did hear that Kilroy had a lawyer at the station for hours. I think they said he was called Appleby or Appleton, something like that.'

Jane flicked through her notebook.

'I knew it, Appleton. I overheard Mrs Kilroy making a phone call to him when I first went to the farm. I thought at the time she was quite fast on the uptake. I think she knows a lot more than she has ever admitted.'

Maureen was relieved that Jane seemed calmer, but then was shocked when she hurled her notebook against the wall. 'Screw them! I'm going down to the cells, and no one had better try and stop me.'

She stormed out of the office, leaving her half-eaten bacon sandwich.

Jane approached the duty sergeant who was updating some custody sheets.

'Good morning, I'm DCI Tennison. I'm involved in the Brittany Hall missing persons case, and I'm aware there have been some arrests. I know John Kilroy has a solicitor – have the others requested legal representation?'

Sergeant Steve Miller, coming up for retirement, shrugged his shoulders.

'Been like a bloody pressure cooker here, they've not had any refreshments yet, but both have requested a duty solicitor, so they'll be here at some point. I expect DCI Shefford will interview them when he returns from the site.'

Jane smiled, nodding her head in sympathy as she turned down the corridor towards the steps that led to the six cells via an iron door. Sitting by the door was a uniform officer reading a copy of the Sun. He got to his feet as Jane approached.

'DCI Tennison, just wanting a quick look at the two boys, to see how they're coping.'

'Checking on them every ten minutes, ma'am. DCI Shefford said for them to be taken care of. I ordered some tea half an hour ago, but it's not appeared.'

'I'll hurry that up for you, but the canteen is inundated at the moment. This won't take long.'

He stepped back, and then pulled open the iron door for her. Common to the cells of every station she'd worked at, the smell of Dettol was very strong. There were three cells on each side of the walkway, and she peered at the cardboard plaques on each door. The boys had been placed in cells at either end, so it would make any contact impossible, and if they shouted to each other, they could easily be heard.

Jane walked silently to cell one, Justin Moore's, and slid the viewing slot back to see what sort of state he was in. Justin was sitting on the bed. He had no shoes and no tie or belt. He looked very pale and shaken, looking up as Jane watched him. He raised a hand as if he wanted to ask something, but she quickly slid the viewing slot shut. Phillip Sayer was at the far end, looking red-eyed, as if he had been crying. When he heard the slot drawn back, he looked up pathetically and made a move towards the door before she slammed it shut.

Jane returned to the duty sergeant, who was drinking a mug of tea. 'Everything all right down there?'

'Appears so, thank you.'

Jane returned to her office. 'Any update, Maureen?'

'No, all quiet on the Western Front, ma'am.'

'Can you try and see if Kernan has come back?'

Maureen put a call through to the super's office but was told that he was unavailable. Jane raised her hands in a frustrated gesture. 'What the fuck am I supposed to do? Just wait and take this shit? It's as if all the work I have done is being deliberately rubbed in my face.'

'I suppose you could go into Shefford's incident room,' Maureen said. 'The team there must be getting updates, and you have every right to be kept abreast of developments.'

Jane rolled her eyes. 'Terrific! Go in there with my tail between my legs: "Please can you tell me what is going on with my fucking case" – the cold case that has languished here for five years until I was transferred. Do you know what that weasel-faced Sergeant Otley said to me . . . ? I confronted him, I said this is my cold case, and he had the audacity to smirk at me and say that it was now hotter than hell.'

Maureen was getting nervous as Jane started pacing up and down.

'What do you think made John Kilroy come in and admit what he had done?' Maureen asked. 'I mean, did you think he was going to fall apart when you last saw him?'

'I saw he was scared, even more so when I told him I would never give up.'

'Maybe that was enough.'

Jane didn't seem to hear her. 'You know why they're doing this?'

Maureen chewed her lip, afraid to even try and think of an answer. Jane looked as if she was going to pick up her desk chair and hurl it at the wall.

'It's because I'm a woman. And that's why they didn't want me here from day one. But if they think I'm going to go quietly, which is what they want, they have another think coming.'

Jane picked up her jacket and shrugged it on, buttoning it up with a vengeance.

'Right, if Kernan is not in, I will stand outside his office and wait until he has the guts to face me out on this. He needs to know the amount of work that I have done, and that I refuse to allow DCI Shefford to ride roughshod over me.'

She snatched up her shoulder bag and marched to the door. Maureen closed her eyes as Jane slammed it shut behind her.

After going to the ladies' to check her hair and make-up, Jane took a deep breath and headed to the lifts.

Exiting on Kernan's floor, Jane had to stand aside as the corridor was jammed with plain clothes and uniform officers passing backwards and forwards. Gritting her teeth, Jane approached Kernan's office and knocked on the door. His secretary opened it almost immediately.

'I need to speak to Superintendent Kernan.'

'I'm afraid he has gone straight to Scotland Yard for a meeting with the Commander about the Brittany Hall case.'

'What's he going to say?' Jane demanded.

'I'm not privy to all the recent developments, only that a body has been recovered and they are waiting for a formal identification.'

'Is it Brittany Hall?'

'I am sorry, DCI Tennison, I have no more information. Perhaps you should speak to someone on DCI Shefford's team?'

'When do you expect the chief back?'

'I really don't know.'

She closed the door firmly, leaving Jane feeling even more frustrated. As she headed towards the lifts, she saw the duty sergeant, Steve Miller, coming towards her.

'Taking an early lunch break before the madness kicks in,' he said. 'I've got duty solicitors waiting to speak with the boys. They're pissed off because I won't tell them what the case against them is. I told them they'll have to wait for DCI Shefford's return to the station, as he's the last person I want to get on the wrong side of.'

Jane hesitated, then took a deep breath, turned on her heel and headed for the lion's den. Opening one of the double doors to Shefford's incident room, she saw it was full of plain clothes detectives, most of them in their shirtsleeves and half of them chain-smoking. The room did not exactly fall silent, but became very quiet as she looked around the faces, hoping to see one she recognised. Her suspects whiteboard had been replaced by an enormous three-section incident board with photographs of the Kilroy estate alongside the information she and Maureen had gathered.

The last person she wanted to speak to was DS Bill Otley, who walked in right behind her.

'Right, lads,' he announced. 'I've cleared it with the canteen, you're on first shift for lunch, so get moving before the search teams get here, and make it just forty-five minutes.'

Jane stood to one side as Otley started calling out names and giving assignments to different officers, who then grabbed jackets and coats and passed her with a cool nod, Otley ushering them out like a traffic warden. He was also pointedly ignoring her presence.

'I would like to be given access to the confession made by John Kilroy, Detective Sergeant Otley.'

'I'm afraid I can't do that. It'll be down to DCI Shefford, and he's not available right now.'

'Has the victim been formally identified as Brittany Hall?'

'Again, can't help you. No ID from the mortuary as yet.'

'Where was she found?'

'The lad took DCI Shefford to where it was.'

It was painfully obvious that Otley was not going to give her any information. Nevertheless, she had one last try, keeping her voice calm.

'I have got to know Brittany Hall's mother very well over the past few weeks, and I would very much like to be the one to see her, when the body you have is identified, obviously. She has waited a long time. It would be better than being told by someone she has not had any relationship with.'

Otley sucked in his breath and his thin lips tightened. 'You will need to run that by DCI Shefford. He's very experienced in these situations.' He turned away, the conversation over.

She took a few paces towards the incident board, focusing on the photographs of the broken-down beehives she had seen on her first visit to the Kilroys. There were also photographs of outhouses and ramshackle stables, as well as drainage pipes and an oil drum. She moved closer.

'I'm afraid I have to ask you to leave, DCI Tennison.'

Otley came and stood between her and the board.

'Detective Sergeant Otley, your attitude is offensive. I have every right to view the entire incident board as I have been investigating Brittany Hall's disappearance.'

'I'm afraid I am simply acting on specific orders that, until we have identified the body discovered at the Kilroys', only DCI Shefford's team are allowed access to the new evidence acquired this weekend.'

She stared at him, but he didn't flinch.

She walked out.

CHAPTER THIRTY-TWO

While these events were going on, Jane sent Maureen on sleuthing trips all afternoon for updates on what was happening, and learned that Shefford had questioned both boys in the company of their solicitors, but things seemed to quieten around six o'clock, even though Shefford's booming voice could still occasionally be heard barking out orders.

Calling the chief's office for the third time that afternoon, she was yet again informed he was not available, and slammed the phone down in frustration. Maureen reported that Brittany Hall's dental records had been requested, and an officer had been sent to collect them earlier in the afternoon, infuriating Jane still further, as they would have to inform Brittany's mother, who would naturally be in a terrible state. She was in half a mind to call Mrs Hall herself when the desk phone rang.

It was Peter, and she first felt bad to be disappointed, then concerned why he was calling.

'Sorry to call you at the station on your big day,' he said, 'but I've got to go away on business. A contractor I'm hoping to do a deal with has asked for a meeting in his Manchester offices. I was about to suggest waiting until he was in London, but we should probably start the negotiations as soon as possible, as he has another company interested.'

'Well, you do what you have to do,' Jane said, 'and I hope it turns out well.'

'Thanks. Anyway, maybe the timing is good as I know you have a lot to deal with today. How is everything going?'

'I'll wait until you get home to give you all the details. Have a safe journey.'

'I love you, take care.'

'I love you too, bye now,' she said, putting the phone down.

Maureen glanced over. She didn't know anything about Jane's private life, but she could tell Jane had not really wanted to talk to whoever was on the other end of the phone.

'I should contact Mrs Hall,' Jane said. 'By now they must have identified the body.'

'I could go and find out,' Maureen offered. 'Unless you want to?'

'No, I'm keeping my distance. But see what you get from Sergeant Miller, he might still be on duty and he's quite chatty. I'll stay put in case the chief calls me back.'

No sooner had Maureen left than the desk phone rang. It was Kernan's secretary, asking if Jane could be down in his office at seven o'clock. That gave her just over an hour to get all her ducks in a row about how she had been forced aside by DCI Shefford.

She started making copious notes, then looked up as Maureen came in, gasping for breath as if she'd just run down the corridor.

'They had a formal identification early this afternoon. The body has been confirmed as Brittany Hall, through her dental records. It was very busy down there, so I didn't get to speak to the duty sergeant. Shefford is charging the boys, all three of them.'

'Take deep breaths, Maureen.'

'I'm sorry, but I ran all the way back up the stairs as the lifts were held up. I wanted to tell you as soon as possible. There'd been a meeting with forensic officers in the boardroom, and they were coming out, but one of them was still sitting at the table so I was a bit cheeky, and went in to speak to him.'

'Get to the point, Maureen, don't blabber on. So what did he tell you? That it was Brittany Hall?'

'Yes, and when I said I was working for DCI Tennison he said he was an old friend, and if you wanted an update he would be there for a while, finishing up a report. His name's Paul Lawrence.'

Jane jumped up from her desk, grabbing her jacket. 'In the boardroom, right? And you can get off home. I'll be here until after seven as I finally have a meeting with Kernan.'

Jane very nearly ran down the corridor herself. The lift was still engaged so she raced down the stairs, then had to sidestep officers until she got to the boardroom. She walked straight in without knocking, closing the door behind her.

Paul Lawrence immediately stood up, smiling. 'Jane, I heard you'd been transferred here, and I was hoping to meet up. Sadly I don't have that long, I have to go back to the lab.'

Paul drew out a chair for her to sit beside him. Laid out on the table were diagrams and photographs with numerous notebooks, and pages of A3 covered in his scrawled handwriting.

'Right,' Jane said, 'I'll get straight to the point, then. Since I've been here, I have been working on a five-year-old cold case, a missing student called Brittany Hall, whose body I think you've just identified. After a lot of hard work, I believed I had at last discovered what had happened to her.'

It was Jane's turn to take a deep breath, but before she could continue, Paul held a hand up.

'Well, we haven't been able to confirm that definitively yet,' he said.

Jane shook her head. 'The point is, I meant that my investigation has been taken over by another DCI, just as I was certain I had found enough evidence to prove my theory. I have been literally shoved aside and not allowed access to the investigation.'

'Listen, Jane, I don't know how all that works. I'm just on the forensic side. But I'm sorry, that does sound tough for you.'

'I know there's nothing you can do,' Jane said. 'But you can tell me what's been happening. Where was she found?'

Paul began to sift through some photographs, passing one to Jane.

'Inside this oil drum by the old stables. The lid had been hammered down, so it was airtight, and then it had been put inside a large drainage pipe.'

He took the photograph back and clipped it to the various other shots of the drainage pipes and oil drums.

'I was told that the farm has not been in any kind of working order for many years. The stables were virtually collapsing.'

'So if the oil drum was airtight, had the body decomposed?'

'Yes. You have to remember it had been there for four or five years. However, partly due to the drum being airtight, there is another reason why we have been brought in.'

Paul selected another photograph, this time of the victim in the oil drum.

'As soon as I saw this, I had the body moved, in the oil drum, straight to the mortuary, where it would be easier to remove and retrieve any evidence in a controlled environment.'

Jane stared at the photograph, unsure what she was seeing due to the staining. Paul leaned towards her, tapping the photograph with a pencil. 'She's wearing a beekeeper's suit, with the helmet over her head. Normally you would also use thick gloves up to the elbow so the bees couldn't get inside the sleeves. Without them the insects were able to get inside.'

'Did she die of bee stings?'

'I couldn't say, it looks as though she might have fallen and knocked over a hive, but the reality is that a human can have over a thousand stings and still survive. Or it's possible that she suffered an anaphylactic shock. The pathologist will certainly have their work cut out to determine that.'

'Was she fully clothed under the suit?'

'We won't know until we remove the suit at the mortuary.'

'But if she was wearing a suit, even without gloves, wouldn't she have been protected?'

'Ah, that is something we are looking in to, because it is possible the suit was put on her after death. I am hoping later tonight, when I get over to the lab, the pathologist will have more information. Do you know that when a honeybee stings you, it dies the most gruesome death. The bee's stinger is structured in such a way that once it punctures the human skin, they can't pull it out without self-amputating. It's like a screwdriver, the coils go in, but can't be drawn out. So, when the honeybee tries to withdraw the stinger it ruptures its own lower abdomen, leaving the stinger embedded, and a gaping hole at the end of its abdomen.'

Paul glanced at his wristwatch, quickly gathered what remained of his papers, and then lifted his briefcase onto the table.

'Paul, could I call you later or tomorrow to see how things have progressed?' Jane asked.

'You can. But I doubt we will have very much more to tell you. This is going to be a lengthy progress. I have an entomologist coming in to help, so I don't want to be late for her. Be a late night, I know that much.'

He stood up, closing his briefcase. 'We should have dinner some time soon.'

She got up and shook his hand. 'That would be nice. And thanks for giving me your time.'

She sat back down again with a sigh. How many times had she passed those broken-down beehives, wondering why they had been left unattended all those years ago? She recalled Fitzpatrick-Dunn telling her that John Kilroy had destroyed them after he'd been stung. It was deeply frustrating that without access to John Kilroy's confession, she didn't know how he explained Brittany's death.

Jane suddenly jumped up, checking her watch. It was ten past seven and she was late for her meeting with Kernan. She grabbed her shoulder bag and hurried to his office.

When she walked in, he was sitting at his desk, a mound of files either side of him. He indicated a chair, frowning.

'You are late. I have very little time at the moment, DCI Tennison, so before you start, I think I can guess why you wanted to see me. Firstly, you were not on duty on Friday night and every attempt to contact you was unsuccessful. DCI Shefford was on call and immediately came to the station to interview John Kilroy, then acted to move the case forwards at impressive speed and with excellent results. That is not a comment on your previous investigation, and DCI Shefford has commended you on your diligent work. DCI Shefford is now heading up the case, having, as I say, done an impressive job since taking over.'

He leaned back with a half-smile, and Jane knew there was nothing she could say to make him change his mind. She took a deep breath. 'If there is anything I can do to assist DCI Shefford, sir, then I am more than willing. I also think it would be useful if I could read John Kilroy's confession.'

He waved a hand dismissively. 'Feel free to ask DCI Shefford. In the meantime, you will have other cases I would like you to look into.'

He stood up to indicate the meeting was over, and all she could do was thank him for his time and walk out. Heading out to the car park, she wanted to scream, but managed to control herself. She sat for a minute, seething with impotent fury, then found the barrier was down to keep out the gaggle of reporters and photographers waiting outside. She waited for the barrier to be lifted, then drove out. No one bothered to take her picture or shout out a question.

Jane spent a sleepless night, glad that Peter was away so he wouldn't see her sobbing.

Getting up early, she had breakfast and wrote out a to-do list. First was a visit to Mrs Hall, or if that wasn't possible, a catch-up with Paul Lawrence. She also wanted to contact the lab for an update on the postmortem, though she knew a personal visit would be against protocol. In the meantime, the thought of going into the station and seeing Shefford and his team busy on the case made her reluctant to go in. She decided to go and have another talk with Fitzpatrick-Dunn instead, setting off without calling ahead, feeling that even if it was a wasted journey, at least she was doing something positive.

By the time she got there it was nine thirty, and she was relieved to see his Land Rover parked outside the garage. The first time she had seen it, it had been covered in mud from the work he had been doing around the farm, but now it looked spotless.

Jane rang the bell, and had to wait only a few moments before Fitzpatrick-Dunn opened it. He looked taken aback, but before he could say anything, she smiled, assuring him that she was not there in a professional capacity and would just like to have an off-the-record chat with him. He hesitated a moment before inviting her in.

'I've just made a fresh pot of coffee.'

She followed him into the kitchen and sat on a stool at the marble-topped island. He was wearing a cashmere polo neck sweater with brown cords, and leather slippers. His hair needed a comb, and he was unshaven, and she could see his hands were shaking as he produced two china mugs, along with milk and sugar.

'Would you like a biscuit?'

'No, thank you, this is just fine.'

He sat opposite and poured the fresh coffee, passing the mug towards her.

'So, this has been quite a weekend for you,' she said.

'Yes, one could say that, probably one of the worst in my entire life. I spent last night with Sylvia, who is obviously very distressed, though I doubt she is privy to all the awful details. Nor am I. All I can do is visit as regularly as possible and hope she doesn't see any newspapers or see the news on television.'

Jane nodded. 'Of course.'

'This has all been such a shock to me, too. I am not yet recovered from my surgery. I've got an appointment with my doctor and I'm hoping he can give me something to calm my anxiety.'

'I understand it must be very distressing, and I will hopefully not make things worse . . . May I call you Donald?'

'Please do. You know, my real name is Donald Dunn. It was good old Rupert, Sylvia's husband, who, years ago, when we were teenagers, said I couldn't go through life with the initials DD, or Donald Duck would quickly become my nickname. He suggested I add my mother's surname with a hyphen. He was like that, you know, always looking out for everyone. On another occasion, again many years ago, when I told him I was marrying Sylvia's sister, I think I said something derogatory about her, that he had the beauty and I had the ugly sister – sounds dreadful but I was just joking around – and he told me I was the lucky one, that marrying beauty with brains would test him for the rest of his life.'

His eyes filled with tears, and he took out a handkerchief.

'I don't know why I brought that up, silly of me, because Sylvia worshipped the ground he walked on, often I think to her detriment, because it left little room for John. He could never live up to his father, you see. At first it looked as if he might, but then everything went wrong when he had that awful skiing accident, made him a cripple, not only physically, but I believe mentally.'

He blew his nose, then stuffed the handkerchief back into his pocket.

'I must sound as if I am making excuses for him, and I suppose I am, but I don't have all the facts, and to be honest I don't think I could cope with them.'

'Believe it or not, I'm not privy to them either,' Jane said. 'Which is why I wanted to ask you if there was something said on that Friday night, something that made John want to confess.'

He sipped his coffee, licking his lips thoughtfully.

'Yes, I think Sylvia may have said something, though I didn't realise the implication at the time. I had given her a cold shower . . . I have done it before on a couple of occasions and it always brought her round. Anyway, while you were in the kitchen making us some tea, she said, "I didn't know there was a pony inside the horse trailer, or anything about paying the vet's fees, Donald."'

He shrugged and took another sip of his coffee.

'She could have still been too drunk to know what she was saying, and I didn't really take it in immediately, with getting her ready to take her down to the ambulance. I pieced it together, because you described the accident with the horse box, and that someone had to have driven the boys back to the college.'

'So, I was right,' Jane said. 'Do you think she knew what had happened, or was she just protecting John?'

'I don't think she knew what he had done, although she may have had her suspicions. When she returned from Switzerland there were times when she started drinking again, as I have told you, and once even tried to commit suicide.'

'From what you have said, I find it hard to believe that it would force John to confess, when he'd lied about it for years.'

He nodded. 'It was what she said in the ambulance . . .'

Jane leaned forwards as he took out his handkerchief again, and this time wiped his eyes.

'I was by the ambulance door, she was sitting up, hugging her fur coat. She said, "I won't take this to my grave, John."'

Jane frowned, repeating the phrase to herself.

'At the front door, when you were leaving, I said to John that Sylvia had every intention of admitting her involvement in the accident, and he should tell the police the truth.'

'This may seem irrelevant, Donald, especially after what you have just told me, but do you recall the morning you drove Sylvia to the airport, did you notice if the beehives were damaged?'

'No, I can't say I did. I stayed away while Sylvia was in Spain, and only noticed them months later, when the housekeeper told me there had been problems with swarms. I think she said that John had been stung and he had damaged them.'

'Would that be Mrs Monkford?'

'No, this was before she took over from her mother.'

'Is she still alive?'

'I believe so, she lives with her daughter. She's very elderly now.'

Jane stayed for another fifteen minutes, but having got Mrs Monkford's address, she was keen to go and talk to her to see if she could find the last clue to explain John Kilroy's confession.

CHAPTER THIRTY-THREE

Jane found Mrs Monkford's cottage, which was only a few miles from the Kilroys' farm. She was careful to keep to the country lanes to avoid coming across the still-active search teams at the farm, but was passed by a couple of squad cars before she drew up outside a row of what looked like old farmworkers' cottages.

The whitewashed cottage was at the end of the row, with a well-tended garden and neatly clipped hedges. Mrs Monkford opened the door, wearing a coat and carrying a large wicker basket. She stared at Jane for a few moments before recognising her, then looked nervous.

'I am sorry to disturb you, Mrs Monkford,' Jane said, trying to put her at her ease. 'I just need to ask a few questions.'

'I was just going to the grocers, and then I have this little job at the corner shop. I don't have anything to say, really, I don't. I've been scared rigid about everything going on at the farm. Mr Fitzpatrick-Dunn just called me, told me not to go into work there until he tells me to, as it's all over the papers.'

She was clutching the wicker basket tightly.

'Please don't be alarmed,' Jane soothed. 'Donald gave me your address, and I thought he might have mentioned that I might stop by. I actually wanted a quick chat with your mother, is that all right with you?'

'Dear God, why do you want to talk to her? She hasn't worked there for years. She's got terrible arthritis and doesn't go out very much.'

'It's just a very simple enquiry, and you can go ahead if you need to be at work.'

Mrs Monkford looked doubtful. 'Oh, I don't know if I should leave her with you. Let me go and see what she thinks. Mr Fitzpatrick-Dunn said we are not to speak to anyone from the press or anyone like that.'

Jane made an effort to remain pleasant. 'You know I'm not the press, don't you? I'm DCI Jane Tennison, and we talked before, and anyway, I really won't stay very long.'

Mrs Monkford half-closed the front door and scurried back into the cottage. Jane waited, and after a minute or two she came back.

'She said for you to go in. Would you like a cup of tea?'

'No, please don't bother, I won't stay very long, and anyway you said you were on your way to work.'

'In that case, just close the door after you.'

'I will. I'm sorry, I don't know your mother's name.'

'It's Mrs Hughes, Edna.'

'Thank you.' Jane walked down the hall as Mrs Monkford left, shutting the front door behind her.

The small sitting room was stiflingly hot, with the fire blazing. Mrs Hughes was sitting in a wing chair with a small table in front of her, and her legs propped up on a stool. There were framed photographs in a corner cabinet while on another table were several more photo albums.

'Thank you so much for agreeing to see me, Mrs Hughes. I am Jane Tennison. I think Mr Fitzpatrick-Dunn called to say I might come by to see you.'

Mrs Hughes spoke in a high, trembling voice. 'Yes, he rang and told me that I had to get these ready for him and he will come by and take them, but he said that if anyone wanted any photographs I was to refuse. My daughter got them out of my room, so I am ready for him, and I've got to take the others out of their frames.'

Mrs Hughes gestured to the framed photographs with her swollen hands. She was white-haired, rather overweight and dressed in a long tweed dress, with an apron.

Jane sat down on the sofa and removed her jacket. It was good that Fitzpatrick-Dunn was being so protective with the vultures of the press circling.

'That's very wise.'

'I'm sorry, what did you say your name was?'

'Jane, Jane Tennison. I just want to ask you a few questions about the time you worked for Mrs Kilroy.'

'I'm seventy-nine. I worked there for most of my life, but my arthritis got ever so bad, and I had to let my daughter take over. By that time there was only Mrs Kilroy and her son. In the old days I got a lot of help – they had a cook and a housekeeper. They used to entertain a lot and sometimes I'd stay over in the evening to help. But eventually it all got too much for me, and I couldn't ride my bike over there. It's my knees as well as everything else, terrible pain, not a lot they can do for it, you know, but I have painkillers and a hot bath with Epsom salts helps. I'm sorry, what did you say your name was again?'

'Jane Tennison. I really wanted to ask you about the time when Mrs Kilroy lived at the farm alone with her son John.'

'You mean after her husband died?'

'Yes, were you working there then?'

She shook her head sadly. 'Dear God, what a terrible day that was, he was such a fit man, had this incredible energy, and never afraid of hard work. He was over at the stables when he collapsed and they had to carry him into the house. It took three men to lift him up the stairs. Six foot five, he was, but he was already gone when they laid him down. She was screaming the place down, didn't want them to take him, clung on to him, she did.'

Jane leaned forwards. 'After Mr Kilroy died, did you continue working there? I want you to remember the time Mrs Kilroy went to Spain to be cared for.'

'Oh, she went to Switzerland first, some specialist. She had a nervous breakdown, you know, she was grief-stricken, didn't come out of her bedroom for weeks, and it was all very sad as he had died without making a will. I mean, I don't know all the facts, but the cook left, then the housekeeper. I was the only one left. Then there was that terrible accident when her son was skiing, broke his leg. He was in a cast from his hip down, but more than that was his problem up here.' She tapped her head.

Jane didn't know any of the details of the skiing accident. 'Did John Kilroy also have a head injury?'

She nodded. 'Yes, he was concussed. When he was brought home, he had this sort of helmet on, and couldn't walk, spent a lot of time in a wheelchair, couldn't go back to school, and it was sad for him because he was doing so well. They had a male nurse come in and look after him for a long time, nice young man, but he left after about six months. That poor boy tried from when he was very young to emulate his father. He adored him, followed him around and copied him. After his father died, then with him suffering his injuries, he was a wretchedly sad boy, like a different personality, bad headaches and a ferocious quick temper. He'd punch walls in frustration, because he couldn't walk properly, never mind excel at sport. Before the accident he was quite a sporting hero at his old school.'

'How did Mrs Kilroy act towards him?'

For the first time, Mrs Hughes looked uncomfortable, so Jane pressed her.

'It must have been very difficult for her.'

'Oh, I would say more than that. She and her husband were such a perfect couple, she couldn't cope without him. It was her grief that made her unable to deal with her son.'

'In what way?'

Mrs Hughes shrugged. 'She could be very cruel.'

'How do you mean?'

'Well, I'll tell you one thing, in the master bedroom, where Mr Kilroy was brought, there was a red satin canopy that was drawn over the duvet. After they took him away, there was this deep impression of where his body had been lying, and God forbid if anyone dared straighten it.'

Thinking of it obviously distressed her, as she patted her pocket, then took out a tissue to wipe her eyes.

'She found John lying there once, as if trying to fit into his father's mould. She got a riding crop and beat him, screaming at him, saying terrible things. Afterwards, when he'd gone to his bedroom, I went in there and she was pressing down the canopy, trying to make the same shape. It took a lot of courage, I can tell you, but I said to her that she had done wrong and that her son needed some comfort from her. She started crying and said to me that she was unable to love him.'

'That's very sad,' Jane said. 'He must have wanted her love very much.'

'She couldn't give it, and I think afterwards, I'm not sure about the dates or anything, but she made a will leaving the boy everything, maybe out of guilt, I don't know.'

'During this time, was Mrs Kilroy driving?'

'Yes, she gave me a lift once to the local library, but after that I wouldn't get in a car with her. She was like a lunatic, almost knocked the postman off his bike. Mr Fitzpatrick-Dunn started to come round about this time to look after her. I mean, I don't want to speak badly of her, but she was drinking herself to death, all that time in Switzerland was undone, she never got out of bed.'

'Would this be around the time Mr Fitzpatrick-Dunn arranged for her to go to a facility in Spain?'

'Yes, and I have to say I was glad of it because I didn't know what to do, and I was not well myself, but she was a very nasty drunk. It was very obvious she needed help.'

'On the day she left to go to Spain, were you at the house?'

'No, as I said, I'd been told I wasn't needed. He had been looking after her and she did seem better. He just asked me to come in and check the house a few times when she was away. I tell you, when she got back . . . My goodness me. She was tanned, and her hair and make-up were like the old days and she was wearing a beautiful white linen dress. I was waiting for her, and you know, she had never been a very warm person, well, not to me, but she put her arms around me. She said she was back, and she would look after John.'

'Can you remember when the damage to the beehives occurred?'

She shrugged and shook her head. 'That was done while she was away. I never went near them, scared the life out of me, they did, and John, he hated them, but Mrs Kilroy was as keen on making the honey as her husband. Nothing scared her. But after he died, she didn't bother with them.'

'I'm sorry if I'm asking you to remember small things from such a long time ago, Mrs Hughes, but when you checked the house while Mrs Kilroy was in Spain, do you know if her son was there? Did he ever come back from college?'

'I think he did. I mean, I only went a few times, but there were always dirty dishes left and I think he might have had a few parties. I cleaned up and was a bit concerned when I found empty spirit bottles, but I never mentioned that to her. It was not my business, and besides, she would hide them all over the house when she was drinking.'

'Do you know if John used his mother's car, the Lancia?'

'He was having driving lessons, one of the workers that used to be at the farm took him out a few times. I don't know if he ever passed his test, but he did drive the car.'

'How was his relationship with his mother after her return from Spain?'

'They had good days, and she tried, I think, but after a year or so, she started drinking again. It was very difficult, as the farm was left unattended and a few times she went away again. I shouldn't say bad things about her, but, like I said before, she was a nasty drunk.'

'You have been very helpful,' Jane said. 'You have an excellent memory.'

Mrs Hughes smiled. 'The brain's still active, dear, it's just the body letting me down. You know, Mrs Kilroy could do *The Times* crossword in such a short time, but my daughter told me about her affliction, that she's going blind and doesn't go out at all. She said that John tries his best with her, but she's mostly looked after by Mr Fitzpatrick-Dunn. Now there's a strange relationship. He married her sister, you know, nice woman. I'd say there's a bit more to his attachment, but that's not for me to say.'

'Do you know what has happened recently at their farm?' Jane asked.

'To be honest, I don't really know what the whole story is, just that they found a body there, poor Mrs Kilroy has been taken bad again, and it's something to do with John.'

There was really nothing more Jane wanted to know. She stood up to thank Mrs Hughes.

'Before you go, dear, could you bring those photographs and help me take them out of the frames? He'll be collecting them soon.'

Jane picked up one frame after another and took them to her table. Mrs Hughes removed one large black and white photograph of people in evening dress seated round an elegant dining table. Prominent at the head of the table was Rupert Kilroy, raising a glass of champagne, next to Sylvia. She was dressed in an off-the-shoulder black velvet gown, with a diamond necklace and drop earrings. She was the only person at the table not looking at the camera, but gazing at her husband with an adoring smile.

Mrs Hughes sighed. 'All their guests were very posh, you wouldn't believe all the Rollses parked up in the drive.' She pointed a swollen finger. 'That's her sister, next to Mr Fitzpatrick-Dunn.'

Jane leaned forwards to look at the photograph. Sylvia's rather square-jawed sister was wearing an unflattering evening gown with some kind of floral spray attached to one shoulder.

'She looks nothing like Sylvia,' Jane said. 'I would never have taken them to be sisters.'

'No, they were very different. Her sister never had the aristocratic manner Sylvia did. Maybe I shouldn't be saying this, but that's how she tried to cover up her past. When she was drunk it would come out.'

'What do you mean?'

Mrs Hughes laughed. 'Her family were from the East End and ran a fish and chip shop – not that Sylvia ever let that slip unless she was drinking, and then she could swear like a fishwife. Beneath the glamour she was tough as nails. Her sister was scared to death of her, you know, in case she said the wrong thing or put her foot in it.'

The other photographs Mrs Hughes removed one by one from the frames were of various events at the farm, but all featured the handsome couple. The last photograph showed John, wearing a smart suit.

Mrs Hughes smiled. 'It was his sixteenth birthday, and they went to a posh restaurant for dinner.'

'He does look like his father,' Jane said, and Mrs Hughes nodded.

'Maybe that's why she finds it so difficult. Similar, but without his father's personality, a shadow of his father really, always was, always will be. It must hurt every time she looks at him.'

Jane thanked her and said she would make sure the front door was closed when she left. Mrs Hughes was so busy looking through the photographs she hardly looked up, just waved a hand.

Returning to her car, Jane reflected on what she'd learned. She was certain now that Mrs Kilroy had driven the boys back to the college on the night Brittany Hall went missing, and it was quite possible that all three returned to the farm with Brittany and she died that same night. She still didn't know when the beehives were damaged.

But perhaps the most interesting discovery was that John Kilroy had suffered a head injury, something that changed his personality, made him angry with a violent temper. Jane didn't want to find excuses for him, but it could explain a scenario where he lost control and attacked Brittany after bringing her and his friends back to the farm.

It was after lunch when Jane finally made an appearance at the station. She checked her desk for any memos or urgent calls.

'Anyone ask for me?' she asked Maureen.

'No, but I was wondering where you were,' Maureen said, looking concerned. 'These old case files were brought down by DS Otley.' She pointed to a pile of files in a cardboard box on the floor. 'Apparently you are supposed to go through them all.'

'What for?'

'To decide if any need to be retained for further lines of enquiry or can be sent for storage at the Mandela Way warehouse.'

Jane just managed to stop herself from banging her fist on the desk. 'I'm not having Otley tell me what to do!'

'I said he might want to speak to you personally – but he said it was a direct order from Kernan.'

'Are they old cases worked from here?'

'Yes, some of the files are years old.'

Jane nodded to herself. 'This is Kernan deliberately lumbering me, so I'm stuck behind a desk and out of everyone's way!' She took a couple of deep breaths. 'All right, Maureen, you go through the files, arrange them in date order, and put to one side any you think should be retained, then I'll double-check them later.'

Maureen sighed and started taking files out of the box, while Jane put a call into Peter's office. Mandy, his secretary, answered and said she had received a message from Mr Rawlins to say he would be staying another night in Manchester and would try to contact her sometime today. Jane then called the pathology department, first giving her name and rank, then asking if the postmortem on Brittany Hall was still in progress, and if Felix Markham was leading the autopsy team. She was informed that Markham was still working in the PM room, but there was no information as to when he would be finished.

Maureen listened as she read through one of the files. Jane next called the forensic science lab, again, giving her name and rank as if she was connected to the investigation, before asking if it was possible to be put through to Paul Lawrence. She was told there was a lengthy meeting in progress and Detective Sergeant Lawrence couldn't be disturbed. She asked if the forensic teams had completed the tests on Brittany Hall and was informed they were still ongoing.

Checking her watch, Jane told Maureen that, from now on, she was to make sure her name was on the rota of DCIs on overnight call-out. Maureen mentioned that it was on a turnaround, but Jane told her that she wanted to be on call permanently.

'That's how Shefford got to John Kilroy, so I want to make sure, any future high-risk crimes that come into the station, I get first call. Now, I will be out of the office until the morning, dental appointment, root canal, and I'll have to have novocaine, so if I am still unwell in the morning, I'll let you know.'

'Yes, ma'am.'

Jane walked out, leaving Maureen in no doubt that she did not have a dental appointment.

Driving home, and then cooking herself a very late lunch, she left near to five, heading for the mortuary. She reckoned that by now Felix would have completed the postmortem. Having worked alongside him in the suicide investigation, his routine was well known to her. Felix would leave the mortuary and go to a pub a short walk away, and have a malt whisky before going home. He was known not to like working all hours into the night unless specifically needed, and would usually leave to complete his work the following morning if he could.

After finding a parking space, Jane walked into the elegant little drinking hole frequented by the people attached to the pathology department just before six. It had one long bar, with high stools and booths surrounding it, the wood-panelled walls giving the pub more of a club atmosphere. Jane ordered a gin and tonic before looking around the booths. There was no sign of Felix, but then she was relieved to see him saunter in with a copy of the *Evening Standard* tucked under his arm. The barman had a large malt whisky ready for him. Jane watched him settle himself down in a booth at the far end of the bar, then walked over.

'Mr Markham, Felix, it's DCI Jane Tennison. I met you recently when you did the PM on Serina Jenkins.'

'Who did you say?'

'Serina Jenkins. She came in as a suicide.'

'No, you. It's age, you know, I remember the corpses and their names, but I'm sorry, I didn't catch yours?'

'DCI Jane Tennison, sir. May I join you?' She slid into the booth, not really giving him the opportunity to say no.

He put his newspaper aside. 'So, DCI Tennison, what do you want?'

'First, I am sorry to intrude, but I don't really have a choice. I was handling the cold case that had been on the files for five years, a missing teenager called Brittany Hall.'

Felix nodded, sipping his whisky.

'To cut a long story short, the case has been taken over by DCI Shefford, and I am therefore no longer involved, but I would like some sense of closure.'

He put his glass down carefully and nodded.

'Shefford is rather like a bull in a china shop. I find his presence quite disturbing when I'm working, even if he is a formidable detective.'

'Have you completed the postmortem?'

'Yes, and frankly, it is a bit unethical of you to be asking me about it . . . The report has been delivered to DCI Shefford, so you will need to ask him for the details of my findings.'

'I thought you may say that, but if there is anything you can tell me about the cause of death, I would really appreciate it . . . off the record, of course.'

'As yet I've not given an exact cause of death . . . Further forensic tests need to be carried out before I'm prepared to do so.'

'What state was her body in?'

'Very decomposed. The fact she was inside a beekeeper's suit made it difficult to remove the remains.'

'Had she been assaulted?'

'It's impossible to tell if she was sexually assaulted due to the level of decomposition. There were no signs of knife wounds or blunt force trauma to her bones. That said, there was a dislocation of her right jaw . . .'

'So, she was assaulted,' Jane said quickly.

He shook his head. 'Don't jump to conclusions, DCI Tennison. The dislocation may have occurred after death, possibly during transportation of the oil drum to the mortuary . . . or when the morticians removed the body from the oil drum. These things can and do happen with skeletal remains.'

'Was she clothed?'

'Yes, a red top, white shorts and panties. Bagged and tagged for forensics.'

Felix took a leisurely sip of his drink.

'You know, dear, I have probably said more than I should have. Paul Lawrence is carrying out forensic tests on her remains and the other contents of the oil drum. He's requested the assistance of Deirdre Wilson, an entomologist, and an anthropologist whose name escapes me.'

Jane wasn't going to give up. 'Can I ask, again off the record, how you think she died?'

He sighed, clearly becoming annoyed by Jane's persistence. 'Possibly from anaphylactic shock, though, as I say, it's hard to be sure due to the decomposition. Now, I think I've told you enough "off the record"!' He stood up to leave.

'Please let me buy you another whisky,' Jane offered.

'Thank you, but no, time for me to go and catch my train.' He folded the newspaper and put it under his arm, then waved to the barman and walked out.

Jane sipped at her gin and tonic. Not having access to Kilroy's interview was increasingly annoying, ensuring her theories could only be based on supposition. She was adamant that tomorrow she would do whatever was necessary to get it. But first she needed to go to the forensic labs.

CHAPTER THIRTY-FOUR

The car park was virtually empty, and the building in semi-darkness. Jane drove in and passed reception, but there were no lights on or anyone sitting at the small desk. She was doing a U-turn to head back towards the exit when she saw a woman walking out of the side door. Jane stopped and got out her ID as she approached the woman.

'Sorry to bother you. I'm DCI Tennison. Do you know if Paul Lawrence is still in the lab? I've got an appointment with him but I'm running a bit late.'

The woman looked at her ID. 'Oh, DCI Tennison. You were going to see me a while ago about a case. Paul recommended me. I'm Deirdre Wilson.'

'Yes, of course, it was the severed head buried under the tarmac.'

'That's it. I've been working with Paul – he's able to go round the clock but I'm getting too old for that. He's up on the third floor. You'll need me to put the code in, as the reception is closed.'

Jane smiled. 'Great. Thank you.'

'No problem. Just go straight down the corridor, then use the lift or go up the stairs to the third floor. The last time I saw him he was in the small office directly opposite the lab.'

Deirdre put in the code and Jane opened the door. 'Thanks again,' she said, as Deirdre gave her a wave before heading to her car. It took Jane a while to find the light switch, and even then the building was eerily silent. She continued past the laboratory and stopped outside an office whose door was ajar. She could hear Paul's voice from inside.

'Thank you, I really appreciate your help. If I need to check anything else I'll contact you again, if it's not too inconvenient. Bye now.'

Jane tapped on the door and walked in.

'Good heavens, how did you get in?'

'Deirdre Wilson. I bumped into her just as she was leaving. She said you've been very busy, and I'm sorry if I'm intruding.'

'I was about to take off home myself, actually, but I can guess what you want from me.'

'It's off the record and just for my own peace of mind,' Jane said. 'I had a drink earlier this evening with Felix, and he said you were looking into some queries he had about Brittany Hall's PM.'

'That is putting it mildly. It's probably been one of the most difficult forensic examinations I've ever had to deal with.'

'He said he was considering anaphylactic shock as the cause of death . . .'

'Did he now?' Paul puffed out his cheeks and began to gather up a stack of papers littering the desk.

'He also mentioned a dislocated jaw, which he believes may have occurred after death. I just wondered if you were of the same opinion?'

'Forensic pathology is not my forte. However, I've asked an anthropologist to examine the skeletal remains for any signs of ante-mortem injuries.'

'Can you elaborate for me? I just need to know how you think she died.'

Paul sighed, shaking his head, as he put the papers into his briefcase and snapped it closed.

'You know it's against the rules, Jane, and whether or not it's off the record, I'm frankly uneasy about it.'

'I know I am no longer on the investigation, but I give you my word, I will never repeat anything you tell me.'

He looked at his watch, hesitated a moment, then gestured for her to leave the office with him. He crossed the corridor and opened the double doors to a lab. This was not the main laboratory, but one of the smaller ones that he had obviously taken over for his team.

He switched on the overhead strip lights to reveal the entire room in a brilliant white glare.

Jane stood in stunned amazement at a large four-panelled whiteboard covered with photographs and diagrams. It contained pictures of the oil drum taken from every angle, including a shot from above showing the beekeeper's hat, which had been squashed flat at the top by the pressure of the lid. The next series of photographs showed the body on the mortuary table in the heavily stained and frayed beekeeper's overalls, with pictures of a similar suit for comparison, to show how much the body fluids had discoloured the fabric. Jane noticed there were no protective gloves or footwear amongst the pictures.

She moved closer to the board. Some pictures showed the now-dried clothes worn by Brittany. Although heavily stained by decomposition, they had been clearly identified as a red stretch fabric top, white shorts and cotton panties.

'Any traces of semen on her clothing?' Jane asked.

'Not as yet, but we'll do further tests . . . Again, the amount of decomposition hasn't helped.'

Paul watched Jane as she moved from one section of the whiteboard to another, the awful sight of the corpse exposed when the beekeeper's suit was cut open, revealing what little was left of Brittany's skin, much of it attached to parts of the suit.

'The airtight drum probably slowed the decomposition down, but Felix estimated her body had been there for about five years. We had to be careful cutting away the suit to remove the body for the PM, as it was very fragile.'

Jane moved on to photographs of the damaged beehives, again taken from various angles. She was about to say something when Paul pointed to a table on top of which were at least twenty 500-milligramme sealed glass jars, containing a dark, liquid substance.

'What's in the jars?' Jane asked.

'Decomposition fluid for the anthropologist to examine. It will help to determine how long the body was in the oil drum, and we can also test it for any drugs or poisons. Felix found something more interesting in the eye and nose sockets.' Paul led Jane over to an optical microscope, turned its light on and invited her to examine what was on the slide.

Jane saw what appeared to be curved insect wings with a silvery, transparent sheen, like glass.

'Are they bees' wings?'

He smiled and put a different slide under the microscope. 'This might help you determine the species.'

Jane looked at the measuring scale on the slide. The object was about 2.5 to 3 millimetres in length.

'It's pointed with serrated edges. I've seen something like this before,' she said, studying the object further.

'It's called an ovipositor,' he informed her.

Jane's mind flashed back to biology classes at school. 'It's a wasp or bee sting!'

'The latter is correct. It's also part of a female bee's reproductive system. The queen bee lays eggs through her ovipositor and can also sting with it. Female worker bees do not lay eggs, so they can only use their ovipositor to sting – males don't sting.'

'How do you know so much about bees?'

'I keep bees and make my own honey.'

'But you live in a flat.'

He grinned. 'Only joking. Deirdre the entomologist examined them. She thinks there may be the remains of a few thousand bees in the beekeeper suit, the decomposition fluid, and nose and eye sockets.'

'Oh my God.'

'I have been working on comparing the forensic evidence against John Kilroy's version of events, and so far I've been unable to find anything to contradict it.'

Jane turned towards him, looking shocked. 'You have access to his interview?'

'He made a prepared statement to Shefford through his solicitor.'

'Do you have a copy?'

Paul hesitated, then nodded. He looked at his watch again. 'Jane, I really need to get going. I have an early start in the morning.'

'Please, I really need to read it. You know I have been working on the investigation for weeks and I've gathered a lot of information that might help you.'

'I can't . . . DCI Shefford was quite insistent that no one should get access to it.'

'Paul, you know you can trust me. I would never tell Shefford I'd read it, but if I can add something beneficial . . .'

He hesitated for a moment, sighed, and then opened his briefcase. 'I was going to make some calls when I got home, but I can do them here in the office. Fifteen minutes, Jane. Sit down in here, and I'll come and get you.'

Paul withdrew a thin folder from his briefcase and handed it to her. She forced herself not to grab it, she was so excited. 'Thank you, Paul. Thank you.'

Jane sat by the Anglepoise lamp at the end of the trestle table and removed Kilroy's statement. There was the day, time and date at the top, and then a list of who was present. DCI Shefford had certainly covered all the bases.

I, John Kilroy, make this statement of my own free will. I am aware I am under caution and not obliged to say anything and this statement may be used as evidence against me.

This statement is true, and I wish to confess my involvement regarding Brittany Hall, the student who went missing from my college on the evening of Friday the thirteenth of June, 1986. On that day I took a taxi early in the afternoon to collect my mother's car from my home address. I parked the car a short distance from the college as I was only a learner driver and didn't want any teachers to see me. I had planned with my friends Phillip Sayer and Justin Moore to go to the Old Garden pub on the Windsor Road to have a karaoke session. I had two large hip flasks of vodka in the car, that we were going to drink in the pub instead of paying at the bar. Just before 7 p.m. Brittany Hall walked past. I asked her where she was going, and she said home for the weekend. We invited her to join us, and I promised I would take her to the train station after our karaoke. She said she would like to hear us sing and to see which of us was best. We drank some of the vodka in the car, including Brittany, and she was laughing and joking when we got to the pub car park. We were pissed off as we were told there was a private stag party and no karaoke. Brittany wanted to go to the ladies' as she had been drinking a lot and the rest of us went back to my car and waited for her.

She came out of the pool bar exit. I drove towards her and she got into the back seat with Justin. She wanted to be taken to the train station, but when I told her we were going back to my place for a party she agreed to join us. We got back to my house around 8 and went to the snug room behind the kitchen where I opened a bottle of champagne and some gin. We also ate some cheese on toast that I made in the kitchen. By this time, we were all very drunk and fooling around. We didn't go into the main hall, or any of the other rooms as I didn't want my mother to know we were having a party or wake her up. It's such a big house you can't really hear much from upstairs. I went up to check on my mother and she was in bed sound asleep wearing a sleeping mask. On seeing her packed suitcase by the bed I remembered my uncle would be taking her to the airport early the following morning for the flight to Spain. I then went back downstairs and joined the others.

Jane frowned. So far Kilroy hadn't confessed to any crime, and she was pretty sure John Kilroy's solicitor had advised him on how to word the statement.

We were all fooling around. Brittany was very drunk and started flirting with Justin. She was wearing this skimpy elasticated top with no bra, and she kept on pulling it down, kissing him, and me and Phillip were egging them on. Then Phillip started to touch her up and she slapped him, but not hard. It was just messing with him really, but we were all very drunk and I suppose it was getting a bit out of hand. From the way Brittany was behaving, I thought she was up for having sex with Justin, but after Phillip touched her she got a bit upset and wanted to be taken to the station. There was no way I could drive as I was drunk. Brittany was angry and shouted that she wanted to leave. I told her to shut up as she'd wake my mother, but she wouldn't stop so I gave her a slap. It wasn't a hard slap. I just thought it would stop her shouting, but it made her worse.

She grabbed her rucksack and swung it at me. I grabbed it and she started trying to pull it away. I let it go and she fell backwards onto the floor. She jumped up and really went for me, kicking and screaming. Justin and Phillip were laughing. She had this stammer, and they were mimicking her. She said we were all perverts and called me a stupid cripple. It annoyed me because I was the only one that hadn't tried to fondle her. I told her to fuck off and find her own way to the station.

She started to cry and ran out the back door. We were worried she might hurt herself, so went after her, but we were falling all over the place because we were so drunk. Phillip hurt his knee when he fell and stayed in the kitchen. When we got outside, we couldn't see Brittany, so me and Justin split up and searched the old barns and garage in case she was hiding in there. Suddenly I heard a woman screaming and shouting 'get off me' repeatedly. I knew it had to be Brittany and at first I thought Justin had found her. I ran towards the sound and found her lying on the ground by the beehives, waving her arms around and still screaming. The moon was bright, and I could see some of the beehives had toppled over and the bees were swarming all over her. It was like a black cloud covering her body. I was scared to go too close in case the bees attacked me.

Justin appeared beside me and was going to help Brittany, but I grabbed his arm to hold him back and said the bees would attack him as well. I told him I needed a beekeeper's suit, so we ran back to the hut and he helped me get into a suit, hood and gloves. Justin then went to get Phillip and I went back to help Brittany but she wasn't moving and the bees were crawling all over her, thousands and thousands of them. As I dragged her away the bees started swarming around me. I turned her over and could see they were covering her face, in her mouth and eyes. I looked up at Justin and Phillip who were standing a good distance away and told them Brittany was dead.

Jane had to take a deep breath; the description of what Brittany had endured was horrific. It was clear John Kilroy was attempting to make her death look like a tragic accident, and she wondered if he and the other boys had actually been chasing Brittany with the intention of raping her. She continued reading the statement.

We were scared because we knew we would get the blame for what had happened. I told Justin to get the other beekeeper's suit from the hut. I put it on Brittany, as well as the face covering and hood, so it would look like she'd been messing around with the hives, but there were still hundreds of bees on her body. We got a wheelbarrow and intended to bury her in the woods behind the stables. As I wheeled her past the house, I saw my mother's bedroom light come on. I panicked, and worried my mother might come out, said we should put Brittany's body in one of the old oil drums by the barn, which we did, and then hammered the lid down with an old lump of wood. I then saw my mother's bedroom light go out and thought she'd probably just been to the toilet and gone back to bed. We then rolled the drum over to some old farmland drainage pipes and pushed it inside.

We agreed I would come back from college when the house was empty and bury Brittany in the woods. I went back to the hives, retrieved her rucksack, and went back to the house. Phillip was crying uncontrollably, and Justin was shaking because he had been stung on his neck. We cut the rucksack into small pieces, then burnt them and her exercise books in the snug fireplace.

We knew Brittany would eventually be reported missing and the students at the college would probably be asked questions about her. We were also worried we might have been seen in the car at the pub with her and agreed on a story about us walking back to college, her being drunk and me seeing her get in a red sports car.

By this time, it was about ten p.m. I was going to call a taxi to take us back to college, but decided it was too risky as there would be a record of us being picked up. We thought about walking back but that would have taken us hours, so we decided I would wake my mother and ask her to drive us back to the college. She was angry and asked what I was doing home. I told her we'd been to the pub, and I'd invited the boys back to the house for a drink. She asked how we'd got there, and I told her in a cab, but there were none available to take us back to college. At first, she refused and said we could walk back. I told her my bad knee was playing up and I'd have difficulty walking that far and I had a cricket match the next day. Mother eventually agreed but wasn't happy about it. I noticed as she got out of bed there was a nearly empty bottle of vodka under the sheets. I suspected she had been drinking, but she seemed OK to drive to me.

A couple of days later we became aware Brittany had been reported missing as the police were at the college asking questions about her. Justin and Phillip said I needed to bury Brittany's body as someone might find her in the oil drum. I got a cab home with the intention of burying her, but the house-keeper, Mrs Monkford, was there so I couldn't until she left. While I was waiting for her to leave I went to the garage to see if there was a tyre iron I could use to open the oil drum lid. It was then I noticed the damage to the Lancia and suspected Mother must have been involved in an accident after dropping us off at college. When she did return from Spain, I asked her if she'd been in an accident that night, but she had no recollection of us even being at the house and blamed me for the damage. I didn't argue with her and was in some ways glad she couldn't remember anything.

When Mrs Monkford left, I went to the drainage pipe. It was then I realised there was no way I could push or pull the oil drum out on my own. There was also a disgusting stench coming from it, so I decided to just leave it there and tell Justin and Phillip I had buried Brittany's body. Although we were questioned about her disappearance many times, we all stuck to our pre-arranged story. We are guilty of hiding Brittany Hall's remains and lying about what happened that night, but we were scared and never meant any harm to come to her. I have flashbacks of her horrible death every time I pass the rotting beehives. I am deeply sorry for not telling the truth, but now I have I hope her mother can understand it was a terrible accident and forgive me for hiding her daughter's body.

This statement is true. Signed: John Kilroy.

Jane was putting the statement back in the folder as Paul walked into the lab.

'What do you think?' he asked.

'His lawyer obviously advised him on how to word the statement, so it looks like an accidental death. The fact they lied to police from the outset means they can at least be charged with conspiracy to pervert the course of justice.'

Paul nodded. 'Yes, and there's also disposal of a corpse with intent to prevent a coroner's inquest and prevention of the lawful and decent burial of a dead body.' He picked up the folder and put it back in his briefcase.

'Maybe gross negligence manslaughter as well,' Jane added. 'Brittany wasn't known to suffer from anaphylaxis, so she could have been in a coma due to the bee stings, and not dead, as Kilroy claims. If they had called an ambulance her life could have been saved.'

Paul thought for a moment. 'Possible, but hard to prove. With honeybees the toxic dose of their venom is estimated to be 8.6 stings per pound of human body weight. We know Brittany was about a hundred and twenty-three pounds which, rounded up, would amount to one thousand and fifty-eight stings ... Then again, it has been known for a human to withstand over a thousand stings.'

'Can you count the stingers to get a rough estimate of how many she received?'

'In theory, but the decomposition would make it very hard. According to Deirdre Wilson, in the height of summer there is an average of thirty-five to forty thousand honeybees in a hive: a single queen; thousands of female worker bees and hundreds of male drones. The drone bees do no work and in the early autumn they are evicted by the workers and die.'

Jane grinned. 'A world where the female of the species is dominant ... I like the sound of that.'

Paul laughed. 'A bee only stings under two conditions: to protect the colony or when frightened. If Brittany did knock over a hive, it could have caused the bees to attack her.'

'But there's also the possibility she was unconscious already and then Kilroy, with his knowledge of bees, and assisted by the other two boys, put her by a hive and deliberately knocked it over so the bees would attack her.'

'It's possible, Jane, but it's all supposition at the moment. No doubt DCI Shefford's report will be very thorough, and the CPS will consider a variety of charges against Kilroy and his friends.'

Jane nodded. 'I'd love to know what Moore and Sayer said in their interviews. It would be interesting if their versions of events differed from Kilroy's, which would imply they are all lying. Then maybe the CPS will charge them with murder and let a jury decide if they are guilty.'

Jane picked up her bag, as Paul was obviously keen to leave.

'There is another possible scenario . . .'

'It's late, Jane, and I really need to get home,' Paul said, turning off the overhead lights.

'The dislocated jaw may be pre-death, correct?'

Paul sighed. 'Yes, but Felix thinks it could also be post-mortem. As I said, the anthropologist is the best person to determine when and how it might have occurred.'

'From what I've been told, John Kilroy has quite a nasty temper,' Jane continued. 'Brittany called him a cripple, which upset him . . . He even admits that he slapped and pushed her before she ran off. In a fit of anger, he could have chased her . . . She ran close to the hives, he punched her, dislocating her jaw, and she fell backwards onto a hive – or he may have deliberately thrown her onto the hive.'

Paul was becoming impatient. 'It's all possible, Jane, but there's no evidence to support it.'

'Then we need to find it,' she said fiercely.

'I get that you're upset Shefford railroaded your investigation,' Paul said, 'but he's the one calling the shots now. If you have any thoughts about the case, you need to speak to him.'

'I suppose so. Thank you again, Paul, and rest assured I won't tell Shefford you showed me Kilroy's statement.'

'Good. You take care. If I find anything that contradicts Kilroy's version of events, I'll let you know.'

Jane got into her car, then sat for a while, thinking about the whole situation.

She had never felt so demoralised. She suspected that John Kilroy and his two friends would not get anywhere near the sentences they deserved, but even then, DCI Shefford would get all the plaudits.

So where did that leave her?

CHAPTER THIRTY-FIVE

Seeing the lights on in her flat was a welcome feeling, as it meant Peter was back home. Before Jane had turned the key in the front door, Peter opened it, drawing her into a big hug. 'I have missed you so much,' he said. 'I was even getting concerned you weren't here, worried something was wrong, it's so late.'

'I'm so sorry, I was over at Lambeth,' Jane explained. 'The meeting went on longer than I had anticipated. What time did you get here?'

'Just before seven. I got two fillet steaks with salad and chips with it, OK?'

'Thanks, sounds delicious. And I can't wait to hear your news.'

Jane hung up her jacket in the hall and followed him into the kitchen. He had set the table and opened a bottle of Merlot, from which he poured her a glass.

'Oh, I needed this, cheers,' she said gratefully.

They clinked glasses and she sat at the table. He stood smiling at her.

'Are you going to cook, or should I?' she asked.

'Leave it to me, because you've not as yet used this beauty . . . I unpacked it as soon as I got in.' He pointed to a deep-fat fryer on the kitchen work surface.

'I only bought this recently. It makes proper chips, nice and crispy. How do you like your steak?'

'Medium rare, please.'

'I'm a rare person myself.'

'You are indeed,' she agreed.

Jane sipped her wine. He just made her feel so at ease as she watched him cook, loving the way he moved confidently around her little kitchen. He served up the steaks while she poured both of them another glass of wine. He watched closely as she took a mouthful.

'This is divine,' she said. 'My compliments to the chef. So, tell me about Manchester.'

'It was hard going,' he said. 'He's a very tough negotiator, but his story's quite impressive: brought up by a single parent on a tough council estate. He started out learning the building trade and worked his way up . . . then, aged eighteen, he bought his first property, did it up and made a huge profit.'

'That is impressive,' Jane said, taking another bite of her steak.

'Yeah, but there was a downside, too. His ambition led to two divorces. He seems to have fingers in a lot of different pies: timeshare flats in Spain, lot of property in Manchester, but the development plan I was there to discuss is a new venture for him in London.'

'Where is it?'

'Canary Wharf: he's got four warehouses to convert into exclusive flats.'

'That's funny – this evening I was with an old friend, a crime scene investigator, who lives in a new-build penthouse in Canary Wharf. It's very modern, huge glass windows overlooking the Thames.'

Peter nodded. 'There's a ton of development going on in that area.'

'So what part would your company play in the development?' Jane asked.

'Well, it will be a change for me. My ex-partner usually did the architectural proposals, and it was down to me to work alongside him, costing it all. I explained to him that I needed to have a good relationship with the architect he chooses.'

Jane poured him another glass of wine and topped up her own. She had finished her steak, and took the plate over to the sink while he was still eating.

'So, do you have to give him your estimate of the costs before he actually gives you the contract?'

'Yes, so it's not a done deal, which, to be honest, he had sort of led me to believe it was. Then it got so late, and as I'd had a few brandies, I thought it best to stay another night. As we left his office a woman pulled up in a Rolls. I don't know if it was his wife or a girlfriend, as he didn't introduce us, but she was very glamorous – looked young enough to be his daughter, in fact.'

'What was your hotel like?'

'Bloody awful for a Hilton. Room service was slow beyond belief . . . Took ages for someone to answer the phone and an hour for the food to turn up.'

Jane laughed, taking his plate to the sink and rinsing them both before putting them into the dishwasher.

'So what's the outcome?'

'Well, after showing him some of the projects I'd worked on and looking over the various plans he was considering, I estimated at least two million for building the properties.'

'Good heavens, that seems like a lot.'

'He didn't bat an eyelid, just said he would be looking into ploughing in a lot of cash so negotiations could move quickly. It made me hesitant, but at the same time I didn't want to blow a good deal. We left it that he would contact me within a week.'

Jane looked concerned.

'Do you think he's trustworthy?'

'To be honest, I'm not sure. On the surface he appears to be very successful, but at times he comes over as a bit of a wide boy. Maybe it is all too good to be true, but I don't want to miss out on what could be a big opportunity. I want my business ventures to be successful . . . not just for me, but for both of us.'

'You should definitely do some research about him at Companies House before signing anything. You should be able to find out how many businesses he actually owns and if any went into liquidation.'

'Could you help me?'

'I don't see how. I know nothing about the world of property development.'

'But you must know about fraudsters and how they operate.'

'Only a bit. I've never dealt with any major fraud cases. They are very time-consuming and pretty boring.'

'Is there anyone at work you could ask about him? His name's Peter Palmer.'

'DCI Hickock's speciality is fraud, but let's just say he and I don't get on. I'd be worried he'd deliberately give me false information.'

'Could you at least do a criminal record check on Palmer, or speak with Manchester CID?'

Jane shook her head emphatically. 'Making personal enquiries on police databases could get me into serious trouble, and that's the last thing I need right now.'

'Who would know?'

'When you access information on criminal records, you have to give your name and rank and it's all date and time recorded.'

'Couldn't you use a different name?'

Jane was becoming annoyed with Peter's persistence. 'I did it once before for Eddie and it nearly got me into serious trouble.'

'Who the hell's Eddie?'

'My ex-boyfriend, but he didn't actually ask me to do the check. I didn't trust his so-called business associate and discovered he was an ex-con with a long criminal record. Eddie accused me of being underhand and interfering – he also threatened to report me. Thankfully he didn't, but that was pretty much the end of our relationship.'

'You really think I would ask you to do me a favour and then use it against you if Palmer has a record?' Peter asked.

'Of course not. If I was still at Bromley, it would have been easier, but now I'm at AMIT I've got to watch every step I make. Kernan is looking for any excuse to get rid of me, and I'm not going to let that happen. You must have plenty of contacts in the business world. Make some enquiries and see if any of them know Palmer.'

Peter shrugged. 'Sure. No problem. Look, I'm pretty bushed, I'm going to bed.' He tipped the empty wine bottle into the pedal bin.

'I'll come up soon,' Jane said. 'I just have some thinking to do.'

He kissed her on the cheek and walked out.

Jane opened another bottle and sat in the kitchen, thinking about her future. She had seriously thought about asking for a transfer, and even considered quitting the Met.

When Peter said that he wanted to make a success of his company, not just for himself but for her, his determination had lifted her spirits. He had been in a dark place, with his ex-partner breaking up his marriage and threatening to destroy their business, but he'd refused to give up his dreams. Now she was full of anger and resentment at the way Kernan, Shefford and the rest were threatening to destroy her career, but she decided that she wasn't going to let them do it. Instead, she would show them just how good a detective she was.

When Jane woke the following morning Peter was already out of bed. Going downstairs, she could smell the bacon and eggs frying, and on entering the kitchen, Peter was standing by the cooker in his dressing gown, making breakfast.

'I'm cooking a full English. A hearty breakfast is what we both need for the day ahead.'

Jane smiled. 'Sounds good, thanks.'

Peter went over to her and put his arms round her.

'I'm sorry for having a go at you last night. Let's just imagine it never happened.'

'I'm sorry as well. I know you're under a lot of pressure right now . . .'

'I think we're both feeling the pressure of work, but I was out of order asking you to do something that could jeopardise your career. You've got quite enough on your plate as it is.'

'I will in a minute,' she said, laughing, 'but it might be burnt if you don't turn the gas off.'

'Oh shit!' He hurriedly lifted the frying pan off the cooker.

'I was thinking about going to the gym a bit more regularly,' she said. 'I want to get fitter and set myself some goals. I'm going to buy a squash racket as well, and teach you how to play properly!'

He laughed. 'You haven't played in years, so I think it might be the other way round.'

'I'll have you know I'm very competitive.'

'I don't doubt that for one moment . . . Right, breakfast is ready.'

They sat down to their breakfast.

'You haven't mentioned your investigation. What's the latest?' he asked as he poured coffee into her mug.

'I think I have probably had the worst few days of my career,' Jane told him. 'Well, there was one time that was worse. It was early on, not long after I left training school, when I was stationed at Hackney. We were trying to stop a bank robbery and there was an explosion. My DCI and a wonderful WPC called Kathy both died.'

Peter nodded. 'Things like that put it all into perspective, I imagine: the risks, the loss, what you face daily as a police officer. I suppose you have to create a sort of protective shell around your emotions to be able to cope.'

Jane nodded. 'Sometimes, as a police officer, you have to suppress your emotions. It's a way of coping with the trauma and grief that go with the job. So, in answer to your question, yes, I'm guilty of that, but I'm not afraid to speak my mind or show emotion when necessary.'

'So, what's been so bad about the past few days?'

Jane hesitated, frowning. 'The total dismissiveness of my male colleagues towards everything I have worked hard to accomplish. It is not just discrimination, but a blatant disregard of my ability and achievements as a detective.'

He reached out to draw her close. 'You OK?'

'I need to be stronger. I've had enough of the way I'm being treated and I'm not going to stand for it anymore.'

He squeezed her tightly. 'Good for you.'

She bent down and kissed him before going to the bathroom to shower and change for work. After a scalding shower, she dried her hair, then chose one of her nicest grey suits, a white blouse and high heels. As she walked into the kitchen, Peter whistled.

'That's a killer outfit. You look like a detective who really means business. Oh, I have something I meant to give you last night.'

Peter opened his briefcase and took out a large bottle of Chanel Nº 5. 'I got this while I was in Manchester . . . I wasn't sure if you'd like it or not.'

'What woman doesn't like Chanel?' Jane replied happily.

She rarely wore perfume at work, but she was so delighted with his gift that she sprayed a little on her wrists and neck, hoping it was not too much.

After arranging to meet at the gym early in the evening, Jane left while Peter was taking his shower. Driving to the station, she maintained a steady calm, refusing to allow any misgivings to derail her. Arriving just after eight thirty, she parked in her usual space, placing a silk headscarf around her freshly washed and blow-dried hair to avoid the wind tunnel that she always had to deal with.

She paused by the noticeboard, with the usual football and rugby fixtures, lists of duty officers, and details of forthcoming social events. As she turned towards the lifts, DCI Hickock was heading in the opposite direction. He glanced at her and smirked.

'Princess Margaret has arrived, then.'

Jane slipped off the headscarf and faced him. 'I'm sorry, what did you say?'

He shrugged. 'Nothing.'

'I think a thank you would be more appropriate. Let's be honest, my work on the Jenkins investigation solved the case. You'd never have thought about the neighbours' CCTV if it wasn't for me.'

'Well, my report will say I did,' he said with a wink.

'That could be a bit awkward for you.'

'What do you mean?'

'Commander Trayner called me yesterday to see how I was getting on. I told him about my involvement in the Jenkins investigation and the suggestions I made. He was quite impressed and asked me to send him a copy of my report . . . which, of course, I did. The sad part is that you couldn't see Jenkins was using you from the start – he wanted inside information about the investigation and thought you'd be a soft touch.'

A stunned Hickock was lost for words. The lift doors opened, and Jane stepped in. As they closed she smiled to herself, pleased with her quick thinking.

Entering her office, she saw Maureen was brewing up fresh coffee and gave her a beaming smile.

'Good morning, Maureen, how are you today?'

'I'm fine, thank you, ma'am.'

Jane eased off her jacket, placing it carefully on the back of her chair. 'Right, let me take a look at all the files we've had dumped on us to review.'

'Yes, ma'am. I've put stickers on the ones I think you might want to read first . . . apart from that one.' Maureen pointed to a brown envelope on Jane's desk, with Kernan's name on it and marked confidential.

'Thank you, Maureen. Why is this one separate from the others?'

'I don't think it should have been included. It's still sealed . . . I wasn't sure what to do with it. Would you like me to return it to him?'

'I'll do it later. Would you mind getting me some toast and marmalade from the canteen, please? I'll pour my own coffee.'

When Maureen had left the office Jane opened the envelope. Inside were photocopies of a Met Police Complaints Investigation Bureau file, along with handwritten notes written by Kernan. Curious, she started reading. To her amazement, the file contained details about an ongoing investigation of a number of AMIT officers. The file should obviously not have been copied, and Jane wondered if

Kernan had been given it illegally as a heads-up, allowing him to prepare a story before CIB interviewed him. She knew the file wasn't supposed to have been in the box and someone must have picked it up accidently. Seeing Maureen return, Jane locked the CIB file in her desk drawer.

'Let's get started on the files you've marked up, Maureen, then I can report my findings to Kernan later today.'

They worked side by side the entire morning, breaking only for a late lunch. Jane invited Maureen to join her in the canteen, but she'd brought in her own sandwiches and was happy to have a working lunch in the office. Jane put on her jacket, then went to the ladies' and checked her hair and make-up before going down to the canteen on the floor below.

The canteen was full of plain clothes and uniform officers. It didn't quite fall silent when Jane walked in, but there was a definite reaction to her presence as she collected her tray and stood behind two uniform officers being served.

Jane took her tray with a tuna salad to an empty table and sat facing the room. She nodded and smiled to any officers familiar to her.

After leaving the canteen, Jane noticed DS Otley hurrying along the corridor in her direction. She was about to step aside, but then decided to stand her ground, so he had to slow down to avoid bumping into her. 'Good afternoon, Sergeant Otley. How's the Brittany Hall investigation going?' she said.

'I don't think that's any of your business,' he said with a frown.

'Please tell DCI Shefford I've developed some useful lines of enquiry, which might assist his investigation. I'll be in my office all afternoon if he wants to have a chat.'

Otley pursed his thin lips. 'I doubt he'll have time for a "chat". He's busy.'

Jane shrugged. 'His loss, not mine – and it's "ma'am" or "guvnor" when addressing me, Sergeant Otley.' She walked off without waiting for a reply.

CHAPTER THIRTY-SIX

It was four o'clock when Jane decided she'd had enough of looking through the old case files.

'Right, Maureen, that's it for today. I'll take the files we've finished to Kernan's office.'

'I'll get a trolley for you, ma'am.'

'No need – the box will be fine,' Jane replied.

Jane removed the confidential CIB file from her desk drawer. Leaving her office, she went straight to the ladies' toilets, where she read more of the CIB file, and Kernan's notes, before heading down to see Kernan. When she got to his office he was just walking out, wearing a raincoat and carrying his briefcase.

'Excuse me, sir, sorry to bother you, but I've reviewed several of the old case files. Some require your personal attention, others I think could be sent to Mandela Way for storage.'

'I've got somewhere to be, so leave them with my clerk,' he said dismissively.

'There's a delicate matter concerning one of the files that I really need to discuss with you, sir.'

Kernan sighed. 'You've been very diligent, Tennison, but can't it wait until tomorrow?'

'It's regarding copies of a CIB file that somehow got mixed up with the others.'

He quickly opened his door and ushered her in. Jane placed the cardboard box on a chair, removed the CIB file from the envelope and handed it to Kernan.

He seemed at a loss for what to say as he sat at his desk and looked at the file.

He glared at her. 'Have you read this, Tennison?'

'Well, by accident really. It was in amongst the other files you sent me. I thought it was one you wanted me to review. I must say it's a bit revealing . . . Lots of personal details about your officers, disciplinary records and accusations of AMIT being a misogynistic organisation . . . not to mention the sexual misconduct of some high-ranking officers. Specifically—'

He held his hand up to stop her. 'The envelope is clearly marked confidential, with my name on it. You had no right to read it and should have returned it to me immediately!'

'It looks like a copy of a CIB file to me,' she said evenly.

'They sent me a copy to inform me of the allegations against my officers so I could identify those who should face disciplinary action. What you've read goes no further. If you divulge its contents to anyone, you could find yourself facing disciplinary charges for interfering with an ongoing internal investigation.'

She suspected Kernan was lying about how the file came to be in his possession. She also thought it best not to mention that it was Otley who'd brought them to her office. If Kernan didn't already know, he'd be pulling his hair out to find out who was responsible.

'I'm guessing one of your staff mistakenly sent it to me. But you can rest assured I won't say a word to anyone, sir. The last thing I want is for CIB or Commander Trayner to discover a confidential file was mishandled. I mean, it could cause a lot of problems—'

'I'm not a fool, Tennison. What are you angling for?'

Jane took the box off the chair and sat down. 'You asked me to reinvestigate the Brittany Hall case. I did a lot of digging and uncovered new evidence that was beneficial to DCI Shefford and his team. Granted, John Kilroy handed himself in and made a written confession, but I believe he did so because he knew I had enough evidence to arrest him. At the same time, I also assisted DCI Hickock's investigation . . .'

'I'm aware of that, Tennison,' he snapped. 'If you want the Hall case back, then—'

'All I want is recognition of my abilities from you and the other AMIT DCIs. You know I'm a good detective and capable of leading a live investigation. To that end, I'd like to be allocated the next murder or major investigation that comes our way.'

'I'm sure that can be arranged,' he replied grudgingly.

'Thank you, sir. I am also available to be placed on the rota for emergency call-outs. I'll return the rest of the case files to your clerk to be reallocated.' Jane put out her hand. He had no option but to shake it.

As she walked out, he smelt the perfume on his hand. He hoped he could wash the smell off before his wife started asking awkward questions. He knew Tennison had him over a barrel and was not going to be as easy to get rid of as he had initially thought. He got up and tripped over the cardboard box Jane had left on the floor. He swore to himself as he kicked the box and left the office.

DCI Shefford was walking out of his incident room when Kernan confronted him.

'I want a word with you. I've just had DCI Tennison in my office with those old case files.'

Shefford looked surprised. 'She's been through the lot already?'

'No. They're coming your way now.'

'What? Why me? I've got enough on my plate; besides, I thought the whole point was to overload her with crap work so she'd quit.'

'Did you take the old case files out of my filing cabinet?' Kernan asked.

'You gave me the key and told me to make sure they were delivered to Tennison's office.'

Kernan took hold of Shefford's arm and led him further down the corridor.

'You didn't check through the bloody files, did you?'

'No . . . Why, should I have?'

Kernan took a deep breath, and prodded Shefford in the chest. 'That confidential CIB case file was in amongst them, which she's now read.'

'Fucking hell, I didn't know that. Why did you put it with the old case files?' Shefford asked with a worried look.

'I locked it in there to keep it away from prying eyes and forgot to tell you. As you know, it's full of disciplinary allegations against AMIT officers. The smug bitch was coming at me with feminist jargon about misogyny.'

Shefford looked aghast. 'Shit! My name's mentioned in that report.'

'We go back a long way, John . . . that's why I told you about it. I can afford to lose some of the junior officers on discipline charges, but not you.'

'Don't worry, I know what to say if CIB interview me.'

'I don't doubt that. But you've put me in a difficult situation. If it gets out that file was leaked to me, then we are all in the shit! Stay clear of Tennison and let me handle the situation. There's more than one way to skin a cat. One other thing. What did you say to Tennison when you gave her the files?'

'I didn't. Bill Otley did. I unlocked the cabinet, then he scooped the files into a box. He said he gave them to that dope WPC who's assisting Tennison, as she was out of the office.'

'Does Otley know about the CIB file?'

'No.'

'Well, he's named in it as well.'

Shefford shrugged. 'Even if he did know, Bill's old school. He hates CIB and knows to keep schtum about things like that.'

'Tell Otley I want to see him in my office first thing in the morning. Now I'm going home for a stiff drink.'

'We're in court tomorrow with the three boys charged in the Brittany Hall case,' Shefford reminded him. 'It's going to be a media frenzy. I was hoping you could front up a press conference at Scotland Yard. It'd be kudos for AMIT and two fingers to CIB.'

Kernan sighed before giving Shefford a brief nod and walking off.

Shefford took a few deep breaths, still fuming from his dressing-down from Kernan. He was respected as being the top DCI at the station, with more successful convictions than anyone else. He didn't need anyone talking to him like that. He went to the incident room, approached DS Otley and said he wanted to speak to him in his office.

'I'm a bit busy getting the paperwork ready for the court appearance,' Otley said.

'It'll have to wait. This is more important,' he said, stern-faced.

Otley followed him and Shefford closed his office door behind him. 'We're in a bit of trouble, Bill. That confidential CIB file I told you about was in amongst the ones you gave Tennison. Now she's read it, and I suspect she's using it as leverage against Kernan, who's really pissed off. He only fucking prodded me in the chest . . . He's never done that before, we're mates, for God's sake, so this is serious.'

'What the fuck was it doing with the old case files?' Otley asked.

'That was Kernan's fault. He hid it in the filing cabinet but forgot to tell me. You should have checked through the files first, Bill.'

'It's not my fault, John. I just did what you asked.'

Shefford sighed. 'I know. Kernan wants to see you in the morning. Just tell him it was a genuine mistake, like I did.'

'Did you say you told me about the CIB file?'

'No, though I'm pretty sure he'll tell you now, especially if he wants to keep a lid on it. In the meantime, don't go upsetting Tennison, just give her a wide berth – show her a little respect to keep her sweet.'

'I can manage a wide berth,' Otley said, shaking his head, 'but respecting the bitch is asking a bit much.'

'Don't worry,' Shefford reassured him. 'Kernan is still determined to get rid of her, but for now, do us all a favour and don't rock the boat.'

* * *

Maureen swivelled round in her chair as Jane breezed into her office.

'How did it go?'

'Better than I could have expected.'

'Was the confidential file supposed to be with the others?'

'No, it definitely wasn't. You did the right thing bringing it to my attention, though. DCS Kernan was relieved to get it back. You can head off home now. In fact, if you want a lift . . .'

'Thanks very much, but I've arranged to meet one of my flatmates for a drink. We need to sort out the other flatmate, who isn't really pulling her weight, and never chips in for the groceries.'

Jane grabbed her bag, checked her desk was clear and picked up her car keys. 'Well, have a pleasant evening. I'll see you in the morning, and thanks for your hard work today.'

Jane got into the car, tossing her bag onto the passenger seat. Driving out of the main gates, she passed a few photographers hovering around, but they paid her no attention. She only had one regret now, and that was not speaking to Brittany's mother, but she knew it would be unwise to pay an unscheduled visit. Her plan was to remain above reproach until Kernan gave her a new investigation.

Peter met Jane at the gym and told her he'd booked a squash court, so she'd better hurry up and get changed.

'I haven't even bought a squash racket yet!' she protested.

Peter reached into his kitbag. 'Just as well I bought one for you, then.' He grinned.

Jane ended up thoroughly enjoying their game, even though he was a much better player and deliberately let her win some vital points. He was a good teacher, explaining what she should have done when her shots went awry, without making her feel small. Even so, she decided to get some private lessons as well so she could eventually win legitimately.

After showering, they decided on dinner at Fratelli's, which was becoming a firm favourite.

At the restaurant Peter couldn't help but remark on her buoyant mood, so she told him all about her meeting with Kernan.

'His jaw nearly hit the ground when I told him I'd "accidentally" read the CIB file.'

Peter laughed, then looked concerned. 'Could you get in trouble for reading it?'

'I doubt it. I'm almost certain the file was given to Kernan illegally, so he isn't going to want to make waves. His notes were all about how to counter the allegations so no further action could be taken. In the meantime, I am going to be pleasant and accommodating. I smiled so much today that my lips were cracking.'

It was late when they got back to the flat, both driving there in their own cars. Given the hour, he didn't call his son to say goodnight as he normally did, but was hoping to see him over the weekend. Jane noticed that whenever he talked about contacting his ex-wife to discuss these arrangements, he would become anxious for a while.

They were getting into bed when Peter asked if she was back on the Brittany Hall investigation. 'No, Shefford's still leading it, but I'm not too bothered because Kernan's going to give me the next murder investigation.'

Peter smiled. 'Well, your dark cloud's certainly had a silver lining.'

'I'm pleased,' Jane said, 'but if I'm being honest, the Brittany Hall investigation still feels like unfinished business. There are still loose ends and unanswered questions. Whether DCI Shefford will tie them up, I just don't know.'

She turned to him, but he was already fast asleep, and she had to lean across him to turn off his bedside light. After turning off her own, she lay awake for a while, thinking about Kilroy's confession. She was sure Kilroy was lying about how Brittany died, and wished she knew what the other two boys had said.

Easing the covers off and getting out of bed, she crept silently into the kitchen. Pouring herself a brandy and lighting a cigarette, she sat at the kitchen table, thumbing through her notebook. She read what she had jotted down from her last meeting with Fitzpatrick-Dunn, when he surmised, and she had agreed, that his last conversation with John Kilroy had pushed him to confess. She closed her eyes, trying to recall exactly what John Kilroy had said in his confession about his mother's movements on the night Brittany died.

He said he suspected his mother had been drinking because of the vodka bottle under the sheets, but she appeared sober. He was also adamant his mother was unaware of what occurred and didn't even know Brittany had been at the house. Jane closed her notebook, tapping it with her finger, then opened it again to flip back to the last conversation she had with Fitzpatrick-Dunn. When she had asked him why he had not stayed that night, as he was caring for her, he said she was sober. He made no mention that she had been drinking on the Friday night when he collected her on the Saturday morning and drove her to Heathrow. Jane knew that after returning from Spain, Sylvia had fallen off the wagon numerous times, but never as badly as the night Jane last saw her.

She remembered clearly how between herself and Fitzpatrick-Dunn they had probably saved Sylvia's life, by calling for the ambulance. Whilst alone in the bedroom with Sylvia, she had admitted to driving the car. Fitzpatrick-Dunn had then accused John of lying and using his mother.

Jane suspected that after Fitzpatrick-Dunn confronted John about his lies, he realised he had no choice other than to make some form of confession, though it was not the whole truth.

After putting her notebook back into her briefcase and emptying the ashtray, Jane returned to bed. Peter remained asleep as she carefully eased back into the bed beside him, unaware she had even left his side. But it was a long time before she managed to go to sleep.

Friday came with no message from Kernan regarding a new investigation, but Jane felt it best to avoid him for a few days. Maureen had begun to reorganise the office, having acquired two new filing cabinets. They also had a naked light bulb hanging from the ceiling, so Jane asked maintenance to install a new fitting, adding a request for two Anglepoise lamps for their desks. When the engineer arrived, he took some measurements, said he would start work early afternoon and hopefully be finished by the evening.

After he'd left, Jane looked at Maureen and asked if she had heard any gossip in the canteen at breakfast.

'It was almost empty, actually,' she said. 'Probably due to Shefford's court hearing this morning. But I did find out that a typist had seen Kernan and Shefford huddled together in the corridor, having what appeared to be a somewhat heated conversation. Then after that, Shefford took Otley into his office, and when Otley came out he looked in a foul mood, too.'

Jane laughed, knowing exactly what Kernan had been angry about. She was pleased he'd confronted Shefford and would now know it was Otley who'd delivered the files to her office. The sad part about it all was that Kernan couldn't discipline or officially reprimand them, as he shouldn't have had a copy of the CIB file in the first place.

'I could bring in a nice pot plant on Monday,' Maureen said as she filed some paperwork in one of the new cabinets.

'That would be good,' Jane said. 'I suppose it would be gilding the lily if I asked for a new carpet? This one really is disgusting.'

'I could say it needs cleaning. They have these machines that wash and dry the carpets, but I doubt it will remove those coffee stains, not to mention the cigarette burns.'

'Give it a try, Maureen, and with the redecoration going on this afternoon, I think we can both get off early and have a long weekend.'

'Oh, thank you.'

'Just check I am on Kernan's rota for any call-out over the weekend before you go.'

CHAPTER THIRTY-SEVEN

Jane had a massage after a workout at the club, and by the time she returned home it was almost six. She stacked the washing machine, changed the sheets and added them to a pile of clothes ready to go to the dry-cleaners.

Peter arrived home just before eight, soaking wet, having been caught in a downpour without a coat or umbrella. 'Let me just get out of these wet clothes and have a shower,' he said. 'What's for dinner?'

'I thought I'd order in Chinese, or would you prefer Indian?'

'I don't mind, whichever comes quicker. I didn't have any lunch.'

'What about crispy duck, pancakes as a starter, rice and a few selections for mains?'

'Sounds good to me.'

Jane made herself a large gin and tonic while Peter showered and changed, leaving his very damp *Evening Standard* newspaper on the draining board. Jane put it to one side and ordered their takeaway. 'As soon as you can, please,' she told them.

She was opening a bottle of Merlot when Peter came into the kitchen, wearing a pale fawn tracksuit. 'That's nice,' she said approvingly. 'I was at the club earlier for a massage and a workout, took the afternoon off.'

He sat at the table and poured himself a glass of wine. 'I need this after the day I've had. I went to oversee this new build that is taking longer than anticipated. So that meant a long round of discussions with the owners, which meant I was late for an appointment at the office, then had to go back to the site again as the cement mixer didn't turn up.'

'Do you have to work this weekend?'

'I hope not. Tony's at the site and he'll look out for any problems.'

'I'm glad you're able to give Tony so much work. My sister is always complaining about him.'

'He's a good man . . . You have no idea the problems I usually have dealing with builders and getting the right crew for a job. Being a one-man band now means along with the projects under construction, I am dealing with all the paperwork.'

Jane topped up his wine along with her own. His mobile started ringing. 'Sorry, I need to get that. I called Joey earlier, but he was on some play date.'

He went up to the bedroom to take the call and Jane picked up the newspaper. On the front page was a photograph of John Kilroy leaving court. 'Wealthy landowner's son charged,' read the headline. Jane then skimmed through the article. Kilroy and his two friends had been charged with manslaughter and perverting the course of justice. Inside were more photographs of the three men and a more detailed account of the case, with quotes from DCI Shefford.

Jane scrunched the still-damp paper into a ball and stuffed it into the rubbish bin. She thought it was unlikely they would be granted bail at the magistrates' court, but it might happen if they applied to the crown court as none of them had any previous convictions. She also knew it could be at least a year before they stood trial.

Peter came back into the kitchen as the doorbell rang for their takeaway, and together they opened all the different cartons on the table.

'My God, this is a feast,' Peter said, starting to dish out the crispy duck while Jane topped up their wine glasses, emptying the bottle.

'I'll open another one,' she said, going to the wine rack by the fridge. Peter began to shred the duck as she started rummaging in a drawer for the corkscrew, then banged it shut.

He stopped what he was doing. 'Are you OK?'

'I'll be all right in a minute,' she said. 'I just read the stuff in the paper about the Brittany Hall case. I'm worried they're going to get bail. I would also bet they'll get off the manslaughter charge. They might get a few years for the other charges, but the reality is they're getting away with murder.'

She sat down at the table.

'You want to talk about it?'

'No, I'm just angry. They have kept me well away from it all, and that's precisely what I should be doing instead of allowing myself to get all wound up about it.'

Peter filled a pancake with shredded duck, vegetables and plum sauce, and handed it to her. She gave him a gloomy smile, before biting into it.

'Good?'

'Yes, delicious. Sorry, I am being tedious?'

'No, of course not. Shall I open that bottle?'

'Go on,' she said with a shrug. 'Might be good for me to get a bit pissed. It'll also help me sleep. I woke up last night and sat in here going over the case. There's a missing link somewhere, but I don't know what it is . . . I should just let it all go.'

'You're probably right,' he said. 'In fact, if I remember, you advised me to do exactly that about the divorce. Actually, I had a halfway decent conversation with my ex earlier, because Joey was at this play date when I made my usual call. They've signed off on their new property and it's also got a bit of land. She was going on about turning it into a donkey sanctuary. She's always been a complete dope, no conception of what that would entail, like mucking out. She could never even pick up dog poo, never mind shovelling up mounds of shit.' He shook his head and laughed. 'Sorry to bring that up while we're eating.'

She smiled. 'Did you get to talk to Joey in the end?'

'Yes, it was past his bedtime, so he was very tired. Then she came back on to tell me they're going to Legoland this weekend. She apologised, which is unlike her, because she knew it was something that I'd promised to do with him. Anyway, why don't we do something special this weekend?' he said, filling her plate with more food.

Jane raised her hand. 'That's plenty, thanks. OK, let me see, there's the theatre, a movie, a day at a spa . . . What about ice-skating?'

He looked aghast. 'Let's just check out the movies and then book a nice restaurant.'

'That's a deal,' she replied, downing the last of her wine and holding up the empty glass. 'Let's go to bed and clear up in the morning.'

'Another deal!' he said, pushing back his chair, as she got up and sashayed towards him, by now quite drunk, and flung her arms around him.

It was almost eleven o'clock on Saturday morning when Jane woke up. She could not recall ever sleeping in so late, or having such a bad hangover. Not since her sister's wedding, anyway. Wrapping her dressing gown around her, she tottered into the kitchen, going straight for the cupboard with the tin of Andrews liver salts. Pouring herself a glass of water, she heaped a spoonful into the water and gulped it down with a couple of paracetamol. Only then did she realise that the kitchen had been cleared, all the food cartons placed in a plastic bag by the rubbish bin. She heard the flat door opening, went into the hallway and saw Peter, carrying a bundle of newspapers.

'Morning,' he said, smiling. 'I'm afraid all the papers are full of the Brittany Hall case.'

Jane grimaced. 'I have a terrible hangover. I couldn't believe what time it was when I woke up.'

'I'll make some coffee, then we can check out which movie you'd like to see. It could either be brunch before or dinner after.'

'Oh God, I can't even think about food.'

He laughed as he filled the percolator and began making fresh coffee. 'You were certainly well away last night. But the striptease was very professional.'

'You are joking . . . aren't you?' she said.

He shook his head. 'No, I'm serious. I think you'll find your underwear scattered around the bedroom, not to mention the baby oil.'

Jane sat with her head in her hands. 'Now I know you're lying . . . I don't remember doing anything like that.'

He kissed the top of her head. 'It made my night; the best sex I have ever had.'

She looked up. 'Did I really do a striptease?'

He nodded as he went to check the coffee.

'Maybe it was me over-relaxing after all the stress at work I've been through,' she said.

He fetched the newspapers and put them on the kitchen table. 'No need for excuses, it was wonderful, at least until you crashed out.'

She winced. 'I can hardly focus, never mind read the papers. I think I'll go and get dressed.'

Jane went to the bedroom with her mug of coffee. Her bra was hanging from the dressing table, with the rest of her clothes and panties scattered on the floor. Most alarming was the item on her bedside table: a bottle of Johnson's baby oil she often used to put drops into the bath when she felt her skin was dry.

After making the bed and putting her clothes away, she had a quick shower, then changed into slacks and a pale blue cashmere sweater. She dried her hair quickly, finishing her now cold coffee before sitting at her dressing table to put on some make-up. Thankfully her headache had faded and she was not feeling as nauseous, though still embarrassed about her behaviour in the bedroom.

Peter had the papers spread out on the kitchen table. He looked up as Jane sidled in, slipping her arms around his shoulders.

'I found a certain suspicious item on my bedside table, and I suspect you might have put it there as evidence to implicate me.'

He looked up. 'You look very nice, that blue sweater really suits you, but we can always relive the evening and forget about the movie.'

She shook her head, then winced. 'No way. I am going to remain completely sober today.'

He laughed as she went to refill her mug of coffee. The percolator was empty, so she prepared a fresh brew and stood leaning against the counter. 'I remember having a couple of gin and tonics before you came home. I also had a few glasses of wine, well, more than a few, and you made lovely tight crispy duck rolls . . . After that I have to admit it's all a blank!'

'Don't worry,' he grinned. 'I have total recall.'

Jane waited for the coffee to percolate, then poured them both a fresh mug. She looked over his shoulder at the *Sun*'s numerous photographs of Sylvia Kilroy, some in her modelling days, then more of John Kilroy and long shots of their farmhouse.

'You know what all those photographs mean?' she said. 'Someone has to have been paid a lot of money, and I would surmise that it is either the old housekeeper or Donald Fitzpatrick-Dunn.'

'How much do you think they would get?'

'Probably thousands.'

'Do you think the police would have a hand in it?'

'Some officers have been caught selling info to the press and dismissed. Journalists are like scavengers, sniffing out the most vulnerable to dangle money at.'

Jane picked up a paper and turned the pages to the cinema listings.

There's a rerun of *Fatal Attraction* at the Curzon in Shaftesbury Avenue, which I'd like to see. We can make the matinee and then decide where to eat afterwards.'

'What's it about?' Peter asked.

Jane laughed. 'It's about an affair which goes horribly wrong.'

'I don't know if I can take two sexually explicit events within twenty-four hours,' Peter said.

'It's only a movie, Peter, and anyway, I might get some useful tips for the next time I overindulge.'

By the time they'd found a place to park Peter's Range Rover and walked to Shaftesbury Avenue, Jane's headache had lifted. Peter had not, in the end, put up much of an argument about her choice of film, as he had always been a fan of Michael Douglas. Jane was an even bigger fan of Glenn Close.

They enjoyed the movie, although the sexual antics were a bit shocking, not to mention the scene where Michael Douglas' daughter's rabbit came to a nasty end. As they left the cinema, Jane was teasing Peter about making sure she didn't bend down too low while filling the fridge. 'Can you imagine how uncomfortable that position must be?' he said, laughing.

They chose a cosy Italian restaurant for an early dinner and Jane refused to have even one glass of wine. But she felt relaxed, just enjoying Peter's company, neither of them talking about their stressful work situations. In the end, Peter had drunk almost a bottle of wine himself, so Jane drove them home. By now it was after ten and they were both feeling tired, so she made them both a hot chocolate. Taking Peter's up to the bedroom, she found him already fast asleep, so she went back into the kitchen to have a cigarette.

The newspapers were still on the table. Jane gathered them up to put into the bin, then found herself for a moment staring at a photograph of the once glamorous Sylvia Kilroy. What had she done that night?

Jane rolled up the paper with the others and stuffed them all into the bin. She stubbed her cigarette out and lit another. She knew what it was like to black out, but not to such an extent that she had no recall of what she had done the previous evening.

Jane stubbed out her cigarette, finished her chocolate and turned off the kitchen lights. She cleaned her teeth, then got into bed and turned off the bedside light. She closed her eyes, but couldn't stop thinking about Sylvia Kilroy. If she remembered nothing about the night Brittany had died, what could she have said to John in the ambulance that made him confess?

CHAPTER THIRTY-EIGHT

Jane arrived at the station a bit later than usual, parked her car and took the lift to the fourth floor. Walking along the corridor, she could smell fresh coffee, then, opening her office door, she had to stop herself from laughing. The new light fittings and lamps made the office much brighter, and the freshly painted walls made the cramped space appear larger, even with the acquisition of extra filing cabinets. Adding to the effect, the old stained carpet had been replaced by a spotless dark green one, almost matching the colour of the new rubber plant.

'This is really astonishing, Maureen.' Jane was beaming.

'The carpets came from a refit of the commander's office. I got the plant from Barrow Street Market on Saturday.'

Jane nodded. 'Well, it certainly doesn't look like an old storeroom anymore.'

Jane was about to hang her jacket on the back of her desk chair when Maureen indicated a row of hooks, another new acquisition. She then poured Jane a coffee.

'Did you read the weekend papers?' Maureen asked.

'I glanced at them. Someone must have earned a tidy sum from all those photographs.'

'Don't they need permission?'

'In some cases, but suing anyone over publishing private photographs costs a fortune. Then you have journalists searching through rubbish bins. You'd be surprised to know how many criminals have been arrested from evidence picked out of their rubbish.'

Opening one of the drawers in her desk, Jane took out a framed quotation Stanley had presented her with when she left Bromley and handed it to Maureen.

'I want you to hang this up, Maureen, maybe on the wall in front of my desk.'

Maureen read it out loud.

No greater honour will ever be bestowed on an officer, or a more profound duty imposed, than when he, or she, is entrusted with the investigation of the death of a human being. It is their duty to find the facts, regardless of colour or creed, without prejudice. To the living we owe respect, but to the dead we owe only the truth.

'That's so inspiring. Who said it?'

Jane shrugged. 'Stanley thought it was J. Edgar Hoover, who was once head of the FBI.'

'I have brought my little toolbox,' Maureen said, taking out nails, picture hooks and a small hammer.

Maureen used her chair to climb up onto the desk, as Jane indicated the exact position she wanted. Maureen fixed the picture hook and Jane handed her the frame. Jane stood back admiringly as Maureen climbed down and closed her toolbox.

'Perfect! Well, now we're all set for the next major investigation – hopefully it will be a murder.'

Maureen hesitated. 'Um, I think DCI Hickock has been allocated a new case.'

'How do you know that?' Jane asked.

'I overheard him talking to Otley in the canteen – said it was a big case.'

'Is it a murder?'

'He didn't say, but he was quite excited about it.'

'This is bloody ridiculous!' Jane exclaimed, startling Maureen. 'I'm not putting up with Kernan's crap any longer ... Any new investigation is supposed to be mine!' She kicked back her chair.

Maureen cringed as the office door banged so hard it shook her rubber plant.

Taking deep breaths, Jane went down in the lift, heading for Kernan's floor. She waited outside his office for a moment before knocking, making sure she was calm, and was just about to try again when the door was opened by Kernan, clutching a case file.

'If it's not inconvenient, I'd like to speak with you, sir.'

Kernan frowned. 'I need to discuss a new job with DCI Hickock. If you come back in about fifteen minutes, I should be available.'

'On Friday you said I would be allocated the next case . . . so why has it been given to Hickock?'

He pursed his lips and looked at his watch. 'You'd better come in.' He indicated for her to sit down and put the file down on his desk. 'It wasn't a murder, which is what I thought you wanted.'

'Naturally I'd prefer a murder, but you agreed it would be any major investigation,' she said firmly.

'Well, I apologise for any misunderstanding. I'll tell Hickock I've reallocated it to you.' He picked up his desk phone and called Hickock's office. 'Brian, regarding what we spoke about earlier, I'm reallocating it to DCI Tennison.' There was a brief pause as Kernan listened to Hickock's reply. 'It's my mistake, and I understand why you're upset, Brian. I forgot she was in line for the next job.' He put the phone down and looked at Jane. 'I don't think he's very happy, but you've got what you wanted.'

Jane smiled. 'Thank you, sir. Can you tell me about the case?'

'It's not the sort of thing usually allocated to AMIT, but it's come from the Commissioner's office . . . It could lead to some high-profile arrests and a lot of media attention.'

Jane leaned forward, eager to hear more.

'I had a direct order for an AMIT DCI to lead a team of officers assisting security at the Epsom Derby when the Royal Family attend.'

Jane suddenly looked confused. 'I thought Royalty Protection looked after them.'

'Yes, but they are close protection officers. Undercover intelligence has identified an animal rights group who intend to disrupt the Derby while the Queen is present. A team of plain clothes detectives will mingle with the crowd and attempt to identify any likely protesters.'

'It's a deployment – not a major investigation,' Jane protested.

'If arrests are made, then there will be something to investigate,' he said airily.

Jane pressed back in her chair, still not quite believing what she was hearing. But one thing was for sure: she'd been stitched up again.

'You will liaise with the uniform chief superintendent who's in overall command at the event, and the racecourse general manager – their details are in the file. I suggest you make contact to arrange a meeting as soon as possible.' He pushed the file across his desk.

'What happens if a major crime comes in while I'm at Epsom?' she asked.

'DCI Hickock will deal with it.'

'This is beyond belief . . . You promised me a major investigation – and this is not it!'

He shrugged. 'The request came from the Commissioner's office, so I'm afraid it's not up for discussion.'

'Well, I'd like to decline the request and respectfully ask for it to be handed back to DCI Hickock,' she said firmly.

'Refusing to comply with a lawful order could lead to disciplinary proceedings,' he said with a thin smile.

She took a deep breath, knowing exactly what his intention was. If disciplined, she could end up being sent back to Division, or worse, demoted. Shaking her head in disgust, she picked up the file.

'I'd like your permission to speak with Sylvia Kilroy.'

'Why?'

'DCI Shefford won't give me the time of day, let alone speak to me. I believe, through my previous dealings with her, that she knows a lot more about what really happened the night Brittany Hall died.'

Kernan sighed. 'Shefford is a very experienced officer. I've no doubt he will have reached the same conclusion.'

'Maybe so, but I believe Sylvia Kilroy is more likely to open up to me than Shefford.'

'I'll inform him of your thoughts, then he can act accordingly. In the meantime, you are not to approach Sylvia Kilroy . . . and that's an order.'

'Yes, sir. I agreed to keep quiet about the CIB file, which up to now I have . . .'

He straightened in his chair. 'Is that some kind of veiled threat, Tennison?'

'No, sir. I have worked hard and done everything you have asked of me. All I want is your assurance that if a murder comes in after the Epsom deployment, then I'll be the lead investigator.'

He thought for a moment. 'Under the circumstances, I'll agree to that. However, we may not get a murder for some time, so you may have to take some other major investigation in the meantime.'

'Thank you, sir. I'm more than capable of dealing with more than one major investigation at the same time – as Shefford and Hickock have done.'

'Point taken.'

Jane forced out a polite nod, then turned to walk out.

'There is one other thing while you're here, Tennison. Did you or WPC Havers make a copy of that CIB file?'

Jane didn't like his accusatory tone. 'No, I did not. As for Maureen, she doesn't even know what was in the envelope. Why do you ask?'

'I seem to have mislaid mine. I've searched everywhere but can't find it. God forbid it accidently ended up in the shredder.'

Jane bit her tongue. She now bitterly regretted giving the file back to him. By shredding it, he had destroyed the evidence, and any allegations she made against him for illegally possessing the file would be a waste of time.

Walking towards the lift, Jane saw Otley step out with a big smile on his face and suspected he was going to see Kernan. He was about to speak, but Jane didn't give him the opportunity.

'You and Hickock made sure Maureen overheard you in the canteen about being given a new investigation. This whole thing is a fucking set-up,' she said fiercely.

'I'm sure I don't know what you're talking about, ma'am ... but have a good day at the races,' he added with a smirk. As he walked off he started singing: 'Camptown ladies sing dis song, doo-dah! doo-dah! Camptown race-track five miles long, Oh, doo-dah day.'

Feeling herself at breaking point, Jane rushed down the stairs to the basement toilet, where she let out a bellow of frustration and punched the cubicle door. She wanted to scream at the top of her voice that they were all bastards, but knew she had to try and control her emotions. Looking in the mirror, she could see how red with rage her face was. Turning on the cold tap, she splashed some water on her face and, staring at her reflection, repeated to herself, 'Don't let them get you down, Jane. They're not worth it. You're better than all of them.'

She dried her face with some paper towels and took a few deep breaths, knowing the way forward was to take the crap that came her way and make them realise she could not be broken or forced out of AMIT. Having composed herself, she returned to her office.

'Did you get the new case, ma'am?' Maureen asked.

'No ... I got lumbered with a security patrol at Epsom race-course,' she replied calmly.

'But I heard DCI Hickock tell DS Otley it was a big investigation.'

'It was a set-up from the start, Maureen. I should have suspected it when you told me, but my anger got the better of me.'

Maureen, close to tears, shook her head. 'I'm sorry, ma'am. I've let you down. If you want to get another assistant, then ...'

'Don't beat yourself up, Maureen. We both fell for it, and you did the right thing telling me what you overheard. Kernan and his sidekicks are hoping I'll ask for a transfer, but that's not going to happen. He said I would get the next murder investigation that comes in, but I don't trust his word. From now on, you and I will keep a record of every bit of crap that comes our way – including any verbal or physical abuse from that bunch of muppets. If the two of us make a formal complaint with supporting evidence, it can't be easily brushed aside.'

Maureen lowered her voice. 'Between you and me, I believe some of the female staff have made an official complaint to CIB about the sexist behaviour of the detectives here.'

Jane didn't want to let on she already knew. 'Let's hope it leads to some disciplinary hearings and a change of attitude in this place.'

Jane opened the Epsom file and handed Maureen the general manager's details. 'Can you give this chap a ring and arrange a meeting with him for this afternoon, while I speak with the chief superintendent in charge of policing the Derby? Also, I'll need the quickest route to the racecourse.'

Maureen smiled. 'Pity it isn't Ascot. You know the way there like the back of your hand.'

'Good point, Maureen.' Jane had a sudden thought. 'Do you know how far Ascot is from Epsom?'

Maureen went to the new filing cabinet for the AA route map and they perused it together.

'It's about thirty miles, which would be forty-five minutes to an hour travelling time . . . depending on the traffic,' Jane observed.

'You sound like you've got a plan,' Maureen remarked.

'I'm not allowed to contact Sylvia Kilroy, but Kernan never said I can't talk to Donald Fitzpatrick-Dunn.'

* * *

Kernan was about to get into his car when Shefford and Otley walked out of the station. He called them over.

'Bill told me Tennison fell for the Epsom job, hook, line and sinker,' Shefford said.

Kernan smiled. 'You should have seen her face when I said I'd lost the CIB file. Thankfully she didn't have a copy. Good idea to shred it, Bill.'

Otley laughed. 'She really is the epitome of a dumb blonde.'

'She's been tougher to break down than we initially thought,' Shefford remarked.

Kernan nodded. 'I made her believe she'd get the next murder, but I reckon it won't be long before she requests a transfer. In the meantime, I've got a boring fraud case she can get on with. A tobacconist and his accountant have been fiddling the books for years.'

Shefford laughed. 'You're determined to push her over the edge.'

'She was still hankering to get involved with your case, wanted to talk to Sylvia Kilroy.'

'Why?'

'Tennison thinks Sylvia Kilroy's lying and she can get her to roll over.'

Shefford huffed. 'According to all three boys, she was pissed the night Brittany Hall died and didn't see or hear a thing. Any evidence Sylvia Kilroy gives is tainted and worthless. In fact, we're just on our way for a meeting with the CPS about the case.'

'You think they'll run to murder and let a jury decide?'

Shefford shook his head. 'Manslaughter, more likely, but a conviction against all three is doubtful. They'll have to plead guilty to perverting the course of justice, disposing of a body, and preventing a lawful burial, though. Those offences alone should see them go down for a good few years.'

Kernan nodded, getting into the rear of the car. Shefford closed the door, then tapped the roof for the driver to move off.

* * *

Jane spoke with the Epsom chief superintendent, who was pleasant to her, obviously grateful for her involvement. He confirmed the intelligence about the animal rights group planning to disrupt the Derby and said he'd send over surveillance photos of the activists. His aim, with her assistance, was to identify and eject the group before the race. They arranged to meet at the racecourse at 10 a.m. on the morning of the event.

Maureen had arranged the appointment with the general manager of the course for late in the afternoon.

'I'd like you to be part of my team at Epsom, Maureen.'

'That would be fantastic! I love having a flutter on the gee-gees.'

'We're there to look out for activists, not watch the races,' Jane said with a smile.

'There's a horse running in the Derby called Corrupt . . .'

Jane laughed. 'No doubt Kernan and his cronies will be backing it. Right, I'm off to Ascot – see you later.'

Jane stopped at a petrol station to fill up, then headed towards Hammersmith, and then on to the M4. She had not wanted to tip off Fitzpatrick-Dunn that she would be paying a visit, so used Maureen to call him to check he was available to receive a package from Fortnum & Mason. He didn't seem surprised.

Jane turned into the little private estate, parking behind Fitzpatrick-Dunn's car. It was just after two, and he answered the door promptly after just one short ring. He stepped back smartly, as if surprised to see her.

'May I come in? I am eager to have a private chat with you,' she said. 'It shouldn't take long.'

'Yes, by all means, do come in,' he said, recovering himself.

He led her into his drawing room.

'Firstly, I want to make it clear that I am here in a purely personal capacity, not in connection with the ongoing investigation.'

He frowned, as if not quite understanding what she meant.

'I wondered if we could have an off-the-record chat.'

He sat down warily.

'How is Mrs Kilroy? I was worried how she was coping with all the press coverage.'

'We have attempted to keep that from her,' he said. 'She is actually recovering very well. In fact, as soon as she is strong enough, we plan to go to New York. I've found a surgeon who is confident he can replace the corneas in both eyes and significantly improve her sight.'

'That is good news,' Jane said. 'Have you been to see John?'

'Yes, I visited him with the family lawyer. John is insisting the property be sold. We presently have both Sotheby's and Christie's estimating the value of the furniture and paintings at auction.'

'Has Sylvia gifted him the house to avoid inheritance tax?'

'Yes. If she dies within seven years, he'll have to pay the tax, but he'll still be a very wealthy young man.'

He was making as if to stand, thinking the meeting was over, when Jane leaned forward.

'Between us, what do you think made John confess? Surely he and the other boys must have thought they'd got away with it after so many years.'

'I can't speak for the other boys, but John has suffered overwhelming guilt since the day Brittany Hall died. He blames himself for what happened.'

'Why does he blame himself?' Jane asked.

'If he hadn't invited her back to the house, the tragic accident would never have occurred, and she'd still be alive. Confessing has changed him; it's as if a weight has been lifted from his shoulders.'

'Do you think that also applies to his mother?'

'It has been made very clear,' he said firmly. 'Sylvia was never aware of the tragic events.'

'Really?' She cocked her head to one side. 'Do you know what I think?'

'I don't care what you think, DCI Tennison,' he said testily. 'I have given you enough of my time, and now I would like you to leave.' He stood up and waved his hand towards the door.

Jane remained seated. 'I believe Sylvia was sober that night. The boys were partying with Brittany Hall in the snug, the room that Sylvia likes to spend most of her time in. I think she did go down there and unexpectedly saw what was going on. Three drunk boys, one her own son, trying to have sex with a defenceless young girl who was begging them to stop.'

'That's an utterly absurd and defamatory statement ...' he spluttered.

'You've always cared for Sylvia and stayed at the house when she's been drunk . . . so why leave her alone that particular night?'

'I regret more than you could ever know that I was not there that night.'

Jane faced him angrily. 'Donald, be honest, you thought it was OK to leave her because she was sober. I recall you telling me you had an appointment to sign documents relating to the sale of your house. I believe John has lied about there being a vodka bottle under the bed sheets. He's hiding something – whether it's to protect his mother or himself, I don't know – but I will find out one way or another.'

'She appeared sober at the time, but that's not to say she didn't start drinking after I left, which has happened many times before.'

Jane was becoming impatient with his lame excuses. 'I don't think Sylvia would have driven the boys back to college if she was drunk. She's not that irresponsible, and has no history of drink-driving. I believe she fled the scene of the accident in sheer panic, knowing that if the police got involved, she would have to tell them where she had just been.'

Fitzpatrick-Dunn said nothing, and Jane was convinced she was on the right track.

'I also think Sylvia knew how Brittany Hall died and kept it a secret all these years.'

Fitzpatrick-Dunn still didn't reply.

'More proof Sylvia was sober is the fact she put the car away, locked the garage doors and was ready to leave with you the following morning. I cannot believe she has no memory of driving the boys, or more importantly, what she had witnessed that night.'

'Then you do not understand an alcoholic,' Fitzpatrick-Dunn said. 'Sylvia had, and still has, complete lapses of memory. Your insinuations are totally unfounded. I refuse to answer any more of your absurd questions. You came here under false pretences and have no right to question me. If you do not leave now, I will call the police.'

Jane stood up, raising her hands in a gesture of submission. 'I'll go now. It wasn't my intention to cause you any distress . . . just to get to the truth.'

'Will you be arresting her?' he asked.

'That's not up to me. The sad thing is, thanks to his mother's silence, John Kilroy is probably getting away with murder. I wonder if Sylvia ever thought for one second about Brittany Hall's mother, and the pain of not knowing what happened to her daughter. Then to discover she'd been dumped in an oil drum and couldn't even be identified due to decomposition. She'll go to her grave never knowing the truth . . . just like you and me.'

He stood in agitated silence by the doorway, head down, unable to look Jane in the face.

He slammed the front door shut, having to take deep breaths before he hurried up the stairs into the bedroom. He eased up the blinds to make sure she'd driven off, then slowly lowered them. Beside the bed were Gucci suitcases containing Sylvia's clothes. A small vanity case contained her perfumes, make-up, and most of her valuable jewellery.

He went downstairs and poured himself a whisky, then leaned on the marble island, taking small sips. He had visited Sylvia regularly at the hospital since the night of her breakdown. On the first occasion he had been worried that she was suicidal. He was holding her hand when she said quietly that she had more to tell him about the boys and Brittany Hall. Just recalling their conversation made him shake.

Sylvia had spoken quietly as she told him what had happened the night before she left for Spain.

'I was in bed when I suddenly heard a woman scream. At first, I thought it might have been someone messing about in the yard ... until I heard it again and realised it was coming from inside the house. I was scared and crept out to the landing. Then I heard a voice shouting "You bitch" over and over, and realised it was John. I went to the snug. He had that poor girl pinned to the floor and was punching her, over and over, while the other two boys were begging him to stop.'

Fitzpatrick-Dunn had closed his eyes, his breath catching in his throat. He was afraid to ask what had happened next.

He squeezed her hand. 'You mustn't tell anyone what you've just told me. If the police find out ...'

She sat up straighter in the bed, gripping his hand hard.

'But there's more.'

'No, please, you don't have to tell me everything that happened.'

'Yes, I fucking do!' she snapped, snatching her hand from his.

She lay back against the pillows, and spoke with her eyes closed.

'He looked straight at me, Donald, his eyes bulging and froth on his mouth like a rabid animal. I was so terrified I ran back to my bedroom. Although the screaming had stopped, I put earplugs in and my sleeping mask on, trying not to think about what I had seen. I did drink some vodka because I was in such a state. Later that night, John came and asked me to drive them back to college. I asked him who the girl was and if she was all right. He said she was fine and got a taxi home, but he didn't tell me her name. At the time, of course, I had no idea it was that girl, Brittany Hall, so I did what he asked. You have to believe me; I swear before God I didn't know she was dead.'

Hardly able to comprehend what Sylvia had just admitted, all he could do was comfort her by saying that it was all over, that John had confessed and would accept his punishment. He told Sylvia firmly that she must never repeat what she had told him, not to anyone. He said he would protect her and told her John had protected her in his confession. She had looked at him with her beautiful eyes that showed no sign of how little she could see, and she had cupped his face in her hands, touching him gently.

'That is what I have done all these years, protected him. I could never give him the love he craved from me.'

Draining his glass, he poured another. He had spent every visit since then comforting and assuring her it was all over. He knew the responsibility of caring for her was now his alone. It was down to him to prevent the memories of that dreadful night overwhelming her, turning her to drink again for a measure of oblivion.

* * *

Jane had a productive meeting with the general manager at Epsom, though she was shocked when he told her they expected more than a hundred thousand people at the race meeting. Her team of twenty officers would clearly have an almost impossible task, identifying the animal rights activists amongst so many people. However, she was up for the challenge, and knew that if any arrests were made the press would be all over it, which would lead to the recognition that she took her job seriously and got results. They arranged to meet the following day, when the manager would give her a tour of the racecourse, which would help her in deploying her team.

Before she left, the manager gave her a tip. 'There's a horse called Generous which is worth a punt at nine to one.'

'What about Corrupt?' she asked.

He laughed. 'Joint favourite, but between you and me I doubt it'll get in the top three.'

Jane arrived back at the station just as Maureen was tidying up her desk before leaving.

'How'd it go with Fitzpatrick-Dunn?'

'He didn't have anything new to tell me, so it was a bit of a wasted trip. As they say, "Some you win, some you lose."'

'Sorry to hear that. What about Epsom?'

'Much more productive. Tomorrow you can come with me. Bring boots and warm clothes – we're walking the entire grounds.'

Maureen looked excited. 'That'll be interesting.'

'The general manager told me to back a horse called Generous – reckons it will win.'

'What about Corrupt?'

Jane grinned. 'Come on, Maureen . . . corruption never wins.'

Maureen laughed, then opened her desk drawer and removed an A4 envelope.

'I didn't tell you about this at first, as I thought you'd be mad at me for being underhand and nosy . . . but with all that's happened, I think it might come in useful.'

Jane took the envelope and removed the contents. Her eyes opened wide when she realised what she was holding.

'This is a bloody copy of that confidential CIB file.'

'I knew it shouldn't have been amongst the files Otley brought down, and I briefly thought about taking it back to him. But then I thought how I can't stand the man, and it might contain something I could use against him if I needed to.'

'If CIB knew about this, it's not just Otley who would be in trouble,' Jane said. 'Kernan, Shefford, Hickock and a bunch of others would all be in the shit.'

'I steamed the envelope open, photocopied the contents and resealed it. I wasn't sure if you would open and read it, but I suspected you had.'

'How did you know?'

'You looked pleased when you came back from Kernan's office and said he was relieved to get it back. I hope you're not mad at me.'

Jane shook her head. 'Far from it, Maureen. This is useful ammunition to have. I know I've been snappy towards you at times and I'm truly sorry, it's just that—'

'No need to explain, ma'am. I know it's them that upset you. I also get days where I want to scream the house down because of their sexist attitude.'

Jane looked up to the framed quote Stanley had given her. 'In reality, Maureen, there have been times when I felt like quitting, but in a funny way, my job is really a whole life sentence and I am damned well going to serve it, and if I have to fight for the right to do so, then so be it. Plus, from now on we've got each other's backs, Maureen. We make a good team, and together we'll show them what we're made of.'

Grinning from ear to ear, a delighted Maureen picked up her handbag and left the office.

Jane put Maureen's copy of the CIB file in her briefcase. For a moment, she had thought to lock it in the new filing cabinet, but she wouldn't put it past Kernan or one of his cronies to search her office.

Next, she laid out the racecourse maps on her desk and studied them carefully before marking points where she thought it would be best to deploy her officers. She then typed up a report of her meeting with the general manager, and how best to deal with any disruption the animal rights activists might cause. When it was finished, she made a copy for Kernan and put the original in an envelope for internal dispatch to the Epsom chief superintendent. She knew she could turn what appeared to be a dull and thankless job to her advantage by being thoroughly professional.

Jane put some blank paper in the typewriter to do a final report of her conclusions on the Brittany Hall case. Due to Fitzpatrick-Dunn's reactions at their earlier meeting, she knew Sylvia Kilroy must have told him what had really happened the night Brittany Hall died. Which, in turn, meant Sylvia must have lied when interviewed. Whether it was out of some misguided loyalty, or just a mother's love for her son, was questionable. But whatever the reason, Sylvia had undoubtedly helped John and the other two boys avoid a murder charge.

Finishing the first page, Jane stopped typing and leaned back in her chair. 'What's the point?' she mused to herself. 'Kernan won't bother to read it or even pass it on to Shefford.' She pulled it from the typewriter, scrunched it into a ball, and threw it in the bin. She picked up her desk phone and put in a call to Peter.

'I want you to put a bet on for me. The Derby. A hundred pounds on Generous to win.' She heard him gasp.

'A hundred pounds? Are you sure?'

'Yes, very sure, one hundred on the nose. I'll see you back home shortly.'

Jane smiled as she put the phone down. Not just because of the bet, even though that was exciting. But also because she felt as if a weight had been lifted off her shoulders. She was now very confident about the way ahead. Kernan and the rest thought they'd beaten her, but they hadn't. She was going to be treated as an equal, with the same rights, opportunities and responsibilities as her fellow DCIs. She would make sure the next major investigation was allocated to her – and if it wasn't?

She patted her briefcase.

Acknowledgements

I would like to thank Nigel Stoneman and Tory Macdonald, the team I work with at La Plante Global.

The forensic scientists and members of the Met Police who help with my research. I could not write without their valuable input.

Cass Sutherland for his valuable advice on police procedures and forensics.

The entire team at my publisher, Bonnier Books UK, with special thanks to my editor Bill Massey. It has been wonderful working with all of you on the Tennison series, your enthusiasm and support is always very much appreciated.

Allen and Unwin in Australia and Jonathan Ball in South Africa, thank you for doing such fantastic work.

All the reviewers, journalists, bloggers and broadcasters who interview me, write reviews and promote my books. Thank you for your time and work.

My readers, without you I would not be able to do a job I love, sincerest thanks.

ENTER THE WORLD OF

Lynda La Plante

ALL THE LATEST NEWS FROM
THE QUEEN OF CRIME DRAMA

DISCOVER THE THRILLING TRUE
STORIES BEHIND THE BOOKS

ENJOY EXCLUSIVE CONTENT
AND OPPORTUNITIES

JOIN THE READERS' CLUB TODAY AT
WWW.LYNDALAPLANTE.COM

Dear Reader,

Thank you very much for picking up *Whole Life Sentence*, the final book in the Tennison series. I hope you enjoyed reading the book as much as I enjoyed writing it.

The writing process for the Tennison series has taken over ten years of research, particularly through meeting female officers attached to various sections of the Metropolitan police. The idea to take Jane Tennison back to a twenty-year-old probationary constable was due to a fan at a writing event who asked in the Q&A session what DCI Tennison was like as a young officer.

DCI Jackie Malton was not only my inspiration but also a dedicated researcher for the original Jane Tennison character. After working with her, I knew I had to find other women working for the Met back in the late seventies and eighties. I was very fortunate to be assisted in the search by Cass Sutherland whose wife had been at Hackney station in the seventies.

Gradually I was able to write ten novels that that could each be read as a standalone thriller. Each book followed Jane's journey, with both her age and experience upped as the series progressed. All the prequels show the growth of Jane Tennison's character, good and bad. At times, the stories were heartbreaking, but they all showcased her positivity and sense of strength.

After what seems like a very long time, I have now reached the point in Jane Tennison's life when she joins AMIT, the coveted and sought after position with the Met's top murder squad. Believing that her past experiences and successes within the force would stand in her in good stead, nothing prepares her for the misogyny, the discrimination and outright abusive attitude towards her arrival. I had a lot to do to make this last book in the prequels, *Whole Life Sentence*, stand up against the formidable and brilliant performance of Dame Helen Mirren.

I really enjoyed drawing upon many of the characters portrayed in the TV series *Prime Suspect*. I also found pleasure in placing

Jane in a position to always be facing opposition – it meant that she was constantly demonstrating her character's achievements. I think *Whole Life Sentence* will truthfully demonstrate how the original *Prime Suspect* became such an iconic innovation. This book introduces such an extraordinary woman, but also hints that there's a hell of a lot more to come.

If you enjoyed *Whole Life Sentence*, then you can catch up with the first eight novels in the Tennison series – *Tennison, Hidden Killers, Good Friday, Murder Mile, The Dirty Dozen, Blunt Force, Unholy Murder, Dark Rooms* and *Taste of Blood* – which are all available to buy in paperback, ebook and audio.

The first four books in my Jack Warr series – *Buried, Judas Horse, Vanished* and *Pure Evil* – are also available now, with the next in the series, *Crucified*, releasing this year. It's been a pleasure to revisit the Trial and Retribution series after its television success and I am thrilled to return to it in print – the first three books, *Trial and Retribution, Alibi* and *Accused*, can be bought now, and this year also sees the reissue of the fourth book in the series, *Appeal*.

I am also very excited that my memoir, *Getting Away with Murder*, published last year. It has been a very time consuming and astonishing process recalling my past for this book. It seemed I was capable of recalling every title and character from all my novels and television series but had no memory of rather important personal events. However, after a lot of encouragement and family albums, I have slowly and truthfully started to enjoy recalling some sad times, some awful times and some hysterically funny times. I am hoping that sharing my life with you will make for an enjoyable read.

If you would like more information on what I'm working on, about any of my series or my upcoming memoir, you can visit **www.bit.ly/LyndaLaPlanteClub** where you can join my Readers' Club. It only takes a few moments to sign up, there are no catches or costs and new members will automatically receive an exclusive message from me.

Bonnier Books UK will keep your data private and confidential, and it will never be passed on to a third party. We won't spam you with loads of emails, just get in touch now and again with news about my books, and you can unsubscribe any time you want. And if you would like to get involved in a wider conversation about my books, please do review *Whole Life Sentence* on Amazon, on Goodreads, on any other e-store, on your own blog and social media accounts, or talk about it with friends, family or reader groups! Sharing your thoughts helps other readers, and I always enjoy hearing about what people experience from my writing.

I would finally like to thank my loyal Tennison readers, you have all followed Jane Tennison's journey with me, and I hope the last will get your approval.

With my very best wishes,
Lynda

BEFORE PRIME SUSPECT THERE WAS

TENNISON

DIVE INTO THE ICONIC *SUNDAY TIMES* BESTSELLING SERIES.

And coming soon
the final Tennison thriller . . .

WHOLE LIFE SENTENCE

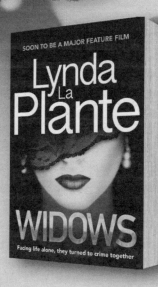